ADAM

by

A.K.Stone

Also by A K Stone:

Adam II: ICON

Adam, by A K Stone, Britain & Ireland paperback edition.

With many thanks to my Mother, sisters (Sunny & Caroline), and my friends Ash, Mihiri, Max & Scarlett, for their help and support with this endeavour.

A *huge* thank you to the readers who support my writing by buying the books, spreading the word, recommending my work, and giving positive reviews. You are massively appreciated.

All rights reserved.

No part of this publication may be reproduced, stored in a retrieval system or transmitted in any form or by any means without the prior permission of the author, nor be otherwise circulated in any form of binding or cover other than that in which it is published and without similar condition including this condition being imposed on the subsequent purchaser.

Copyright by A K Stone 2020

Cover illustrations copyright by A K Stone 2020

Cover by Mons H at 786 Design and S Alam

ISBN 9781693360206

All characters in this publication, other than those clearly in the public domain, are fictitious and any resemblance to real persons, living or dead, is purely coincidental.
The moral right of the author has been asserted.

CONTENTS

Prologue	
One:	Into the fire
Two:	Where elements combine
Three:	Energy & light
Four:	Escape from confines
Five:	To find a new place
Six:	Where knowledge confounds
Seven:	Erudition begins
Eight:	But darkness is found
Nine:	As evil plots
Ten:	What the righteous forgot
Eleven:	We must learn to survive
Twelve:	Stay on top
Thirteen:	But with truth comes pain
Fourteen:	And the righteous shall be slain
Fifteen:	They wish for goodness
Sixteen:	In vain
Seventeen:	As hope departs
Eighteen:	Reality reveals
Nineteen:	What murder
Twenty:	Kills to conceal
Twenty-one:	But knowledge empowers
Twenty-two:	So plan, grow strong
Twenty-three:	Before it all goes wrong
Twenty-four:	Storm forces gather
Twenty-five:	Light explodes
Twenty-six:	Destroying the new
Twenty-seven:	Inverted foes
Twenty-eight:	Then remember our friends
Twenty-nine:	And join together
Epilogue:	To ensure we're never alone
Appendix:	Handbook of Modern Terms

Part I

Prologue
Something out of place

In the forest it waited, as the rain drifted slowly down.

There was a dull flash to break the gloom, and after long seconds thunder rumbled menacingly, like the threat of advancing war. The sound rolled overhead, passing into the distance, throwing out more growls as if to ensure the listener understood that it was coming: *beware*.

The deluge began to fall with more determination, leaves flexed downwards as water poured across their verdancy. Lightning stabbed more clearly now, and a second later thunder cascaded and then boomed through the forest, reverberating off of tree trunks and shivering through the branches.

Not everything, however, was taking cover. Something was hovering in the rain. It was the size of a dinner plate, glowing in the shadows.

It glowed sometimes green, sometimes red, and sometimes blue.

It wound under the tree cover, dodging the streams of water made from conjoined paths of rain flowing through canopy, then stopped in a vertical dry patch as it watched for an opening in the downpour. It would not normally be worried that it might get wet; however, it was now tired, injured, and carrying something.

Soon the rain abated, and the storm began to move on, ready to conquer a new part of the land. It still sent out the odd blast of lightning to singe some random victims of circumstance; a reminder lest complacency should lead to arrogance, and from arrogance to rebellion. Nevertheless, it was moving on. So the rain drifted and drizzled again, and the glowing thing emerged from under the leaves to resume its journey.

It got to the edge of the forest and paused, observing. It was looking out over an open field in the twilight, at a large old building with a few lights on inside. The trailing edge of storm cloud was still visible, but another dark mass could be seen approaching from the western horizon. The glowing thing gave a little sigh; it would have to get a little wet.

It tried its best to avoid the bigger droplets of water as it made its increasingly slow way to the building. It flew under the overhanging veranda-roof and tipped itself to get rid of the little excess water still clinging to its body, its small package dangling beneath it. It flew up to one of the lighted windows and peeked inside. There, was an old woman, swaying back and forth on a rocking-chair in front of a fire, knitting some soft warmth in her lap. The glowing thing made a decision, and knocked on the windowpane. The woman looked up from her work, and the creaking chair came to a halt. She squinted, not sure of what she was seeing in the window.

The floating thing was getting impatient. It was not often prone to such sentiment, but one thing was driving it: time was running out.

It opened the window, glad that at least it had used some etiquette and knocked first. However, it could not wait.

The woman shifted back in her chair, uncertain how the small thing had opened the window when the locks were on the inside.

The little disc-droid broke the silence.

'I'm sorry to intrude at this hour,' it said as it glided into the room, 'only, I am in some need.'

The woman raised an eyebrow. '*I*?' she queried, 'Is someone controlling you remotely?'

'No,' said the small machine.

'Surely you're far too tiny to be both anti-grav *and* sentient?' queried the old woman, 'Can't say I've seen your model before.'

'You wouldn't have,' said the droid, 'but I have no time to explain that right now.'

'Well you'd better explain,' she said, 'or I'll call the police.'

'Please don't do that,' said the droid quickly, 'I'm sorry, as I said, but I have a burden of some urgency to place upon you.'

It floated over, taking care to use its rear fields to close the windows and curtains behind it. It gently pushed the old woman's knitting to one side, and placed the little thing it was carrying on her lap.

'Oh!' exclaimed the woman as her knitting slid to the floor.

In her lap, perfectly awake, perfectly still, and staring at her, was a baby. The woman had held many babies in her time, but this one was startling. Perhaps it was the way it stared at her, huge dark eyes against pale skin and dark downy hair. Perhaps it was the way it lay without fretting or squirming in its swaddling. Or perhaps, she considered, she was just as soft as ever, and holding a small warm baby always made her feel good, her defences down...

She looked up sharply. 'Explain,' she demanded.

The droid acquiesced. 'I had to bring this boy to you, for your care,' it said. 'You are Maryam Clement? Of the Clement orphanage?' The old woman nodded. 'Then I knew you would take good care of him.'

'That explains very little,' said Maryam, 'What of the parents? This is a new-born, not a day old.' She looked down and frowned, and to herself she muttered, *'Though how this boy is focussing on me I have no idea. Shouldn't be able to at this age.'*

'Dead,' said the machine.

There was a frosty silence.

'Next of kin?'

'None,' said the machine flatly.

'And how do I know that this boy is not a victim of kidnapping?' asked Maryam, 'Where has he come from? I'll have to let the authorities know.'

'Do that,' said the droid, 'and the boy will die, and you with him.'

The woman froze, her eyes squinted. 'Are you threatening me, *robot*?' she growled.

The droid chuckled; sentient machines were known to find the term 'robot' insulting. This was why he had picked her; she was not only protective, but brave.

'No,' it replied, 'I am briefing you on the situation you are now in. You can check to see that I'm telling the truth. You must have access to the world database of missing children. Take a DNA sample. There will be no such entry on the database - not now, not ever. Neither will you find him on a register of births and deaths. Search all you will, you will not find him.'

'I *will* check,' said the old woman, 'I don't like this one bit, and I won't let this pass without trying to find the truth.' She paused, thinking. 'Am I in danger?'

'Not if you do as I say,' the droid replied.

The old woman was about to retort that she would not be told what to do, when the droid suddenly flipped ninety degrees and fell to the floor on its side, wobbled, and then lay itself flat on the floor. It tried to speak, uttering only warbling sounds like a recording device with the hardware damaged, then it did the droid equivalent of clearing its throat.

'I'm so...very sorry,' it managed, 'Time is running out. Lie about his age; make him older if you can. Also - and this is very important,' the droid paused, confronted with the enormity of what it was about to say. It pushed past its concerns and continued. 'Get rid of me. Find a metal container, and seal me in it. Then, throw me into the deepest lake you can find, and forget I ever came here. Just pretend the boy was dropped off anonymously. I would have done that but I was afraid you would follow protocol and declare him immediately. I had to tell you what to do, and now I haven't the energy to finish this.' *No energy, and no time.* 'Do your investigations, but trust no-one concerning him until...' the droid sighed, 'well, as long as possible, or when you've registered his age as *before* this time. If anyone comes forward to claim parentage, they can be tested and the matter will be decided. But that will not happen.'

'Don't you want me to repair you?' asked the woman, 'You seem like you're low on energy, surely that can be rectified?'

'No,' said the droid, 'No-one will help me now. Those that can, won't.'

The droid was thinking fast now, reviewing its actions. Had it done the right thing? Of course it had, it had to save the boy. But was one life worth another? Was it worth losing his own life, as it knew it certainly was as the power drained from its damaged body, for that of a baby? *An innocent baby* it reminded itself as its view of the outside world faded, first the colour going from its view of the room, then the focus, then his electromagnetic sensors, then the sounds starting to recede until it seemed like everything on the outside was happening down the end of a tunnel with another droid, somewhere else...

The woman peered closer at the disc on the floor, its glowing colours now gone, replaced by a black reflective sheen on its shell, exposing scars on its body like burn marks - or, she noted, like the marks of plasma impacts.

'Does he have a name?' she asked.

'Yes,' said the droid, as it had named him himself, not so long ago, yet it seemed ages had passed, 'he does,' the droid managed. There could only be one name that fit.

'His name is Adam.'

And with that, the little droid died.

With light speed

'Hey.'

'Hey you.'

'Hey you, wake up. Wake up now. It's time to wake up. Come on, come on, it's time to wake up. You don't need more sleep, it's time to wake up. You have things to do, so wake up.'

'Don't want to,' she replied, 'Want to sleep some more.'

'You can't. It's time to wake up.'

She regarded the figure speaking to her. It was a small dragon, green with a horny back and fanged face, faintly luminescent, standing with his hands on his hips and a disapproving look on his face. He was entirely on his own, the background behind him black, or at least completely devoid of any colour or light. The dragon-icon tapped his foot impatiently and snapped his small wings.

'Why are you bothering me?' she asked.

'Because you asked me to, remember?' said the icon.

'No,' she replied sulkily.

'Yes,' persisted the icon, 'You said you wanted me to wake you after twenty-five minutes. That is now. You have had your rest. Who are you?'

'What?' she asked, startled.

'I am flooding your system with adrenaline and oxygen, and stirring your higher brain functions. I need to test you and you need to respond. Who are you?'

'I am Diane Tamura,' she replied. She heard herself groan, her body and voice in some other place.

'What am I?' asked the icon.

'A pain in the neck.'

'Come on,' chided the icon.

'You are my icon,' she replied, finally doing what she was told and beginning to wake up, 'the representation of the interaction between me and the hardware and software integrated into my brain and body via my neural interface. Satisfied?'

'That's my girl,' said the icon. 'Lastly, where are you?'

'On...oh boy. On the station, awaiting launch. Am I ready to come out? I can't believe I took a nap during all of this.'

'I suggested it,' said the icon, 'you had taken too high a dose of stimulants as it was, and you haven't slept for over sixty hours. You were close to collapse. When you wake up, you'll feel like you've had around three hours sleep in the last sixty, so you'll still feel like mud, but you're fine to function for the next six hours without any harm.'

'You've said "I" several times in this conversation,' said Tamura, 'Are you using my brain capacity for sentience?'

'Yes,' replied the icon, 'It was necessary.'

'I'll need you to revert to high intelligence when I wake up.'

'But I'm using less than five per cent of your mental energy-'

'I need it all,' said Tamura.

The icon scowled and folded his arms across his chest. 'Well,' he huffed, 'that's gratitude for you.' Then he uncrossed his arms and stomped forwards until his visage filled Tamura's consciousness, his eyes large now against her mind's eye, blotting everything else out, black, unblinking, and without pupils.

'NOW WAKE UP.'

Tamura started, opened her eyes and groaned again. She was lying on her couch, in her darkened office. Her blazer covered her upper body. Her legs, in trousers, felt cold and stiff.

'Canteen,' she said thickly, grimacing as she rubbed her eyes and breathed deeply while the icon's ministrations took effect; blood pumping harder, her mind growing sharper, aches and pains coming back to her, 'Coffee, with cream and honey. Strong.'

The crew checked their instrumentation frantically. Initiation was less than five minutes away. The control room was uncharacteristically uncontrolled; wires spooled everywhere, wireless connections having been replaced after the last failure. Caffeine and sweat abounded.

Controller Diane Tamura surveyed the scene, standing behind the glass between her office and the control room, sipping her steaming coffee. People bustled around the space below her, a loud murmur punctuated with shouts and curses, the image of a man or woman holding their head and shaking it repeated and mirrored. The latest computers mixed in with the old as out-dated capacity was drafted in as the money ran out. Amongst them, a few AIs stayed stationary, their capabilities being used with their consent for the last-minute checks.

Tamura's was a demeanour apart, learned in her sixty-one years, though she looked much younger, the legacy of her Japanese-American heritage. She sniffed at her coffee, the smell hitting her sinuses with an earthy wetness as she mulled over the task ahead.

This had to go right.

Funding for the project was already gone; they were operating well into the red. Worse, most physicists maintained that it was simply not possible, that the maths did not add up. The previous thirty-eight attempts had been dismal failures; all prototypes had been destroyed outright. They did however, think they had genuinely fixed the problem. They *hoped* they had. The scientists could not give up on their holy grail if it could be achieved, if there was any chance of it at all - F. T. L. T.: Faster Than Light Travel.

Tamura mused on the implications for humanity at the beginning of the twenty-third century should this succeed. History was watching them.

Since the beginning of the twenty-first century, development of micro and nanotechnology had continued apace. Artificial intelligence was achieved by the end of the century, and anti-gravity by the early twenty-second. However, in all that time, space travel had gone at a snail's pace. There was simply insufficient commercial reason for it to go any faster.

There had been the major setbacks in Earth's development; the onset and acceleration of global warming, with the belated limitation of industry having a secondary impact on space programmes the world over.

Then had come the big one: the Yellowstone Catastrophe. The mega-destructive event of North America, when the supervolcano in Yellowstone National Park finally erupted, causing a mini-ice age lasting a year with depressed temperatures for a further seven. Weather patterns had still not recovered. Close to a billion had died, and space programmes ground to a halt.

However, things had changed greatly over the past fifty years. The world had adapted, using renewable energy, recycling and nuclear fusion. However, some resources could not be so easily replaced, especially those used for cutting edge technology. So they had once again turned to space - dangerous, expensive space.

The trip to Mars colony and the mines on Jupiter's moons still took months and even over a year depending on the proximity of the planets. That should not be the case in the year 2201 AD – humanity expected faster progress. FTLT could cut that journey to days, and eventually when refined, hours. The journey in open space itself might take only minutes.

To the scientist, however, that was immaterial: exploration, the stars, accessing the entire galaxy, knowledge of what was out there, that was what really mattered.

It was time.

'Silence please,' boomed the control announcer.

The final checks were counted through. This indeed, was not a test. It took a further three minutes. Tamura breathed deeply when all the checks were passed.

The control announcer came through to her earphone terminal, 'Countdown initiate?'

'Proceed,' ordered Tamura.

It began,

'10...9...8...'

The difficulty was that there could be no full systems test near terra firma; the energy expended together with the velocity achieved would be disastrous should an impact occur on Earth. There could not be another Mega Destructive Event - civilization had barely survived the last time. The flight was pointed solidly away from Earth, and well above the plane of rotation, somewhat outside of the orbits of Mars and the asteroid belt; just beyond kicking distance.

The craft was plain, all design features now centred around integrity. It was however, quite large, the size of half a football field, a grey flat oval, this time unpainted and unadorned, a grim indication of reluctance to see any hope in it; there was no point in painting something that was going to blow up. The only signs that it might be something special were the four huge engines on the sides, two aft, and two astern. Even given its size, it was still only supposed to reach FTL speed for sixty seconds; that would take it quite far enough.

Tamura resisted the urge to look behind her out of the large porthole-window, where the craft could be seen as a small dot from the space station that housed them all. Instead, she focussed on the near real-time holographic feed sitting in the centre of the control room, the image relayed by super-fast transmitters. The stars sat silent and elegantly uncaring in the background as the great hunk lay motionless, poised.

'3...2...1...Ignition.'

The display went white...seconds passed...

The screen cleared - and there was a scene of expanding debris, fiery, and then quickly dimming as cold vacuum sucked the heat and fuel away. The stars blanked out as the holo-image adjusted, only the expanding corona of glowing debris visible.

The room remained quiet. People sagged. Headphones were thrown down, faces were held in hands. Faces turned to her.

She, this time, was not sure what to say. That was it.

'System failure,' said the announcer.

'Confirmed,' Tamura managed to say via her constricted throat, 'Start investigation now …I want all readings, especially integrity.' She sighed deeply, 'Let's find out what went wrong.'

'Negative,' interjected a mono-tonal voice in her ear.

She recognized it as the lead AI. He was a large lumbering thing on wheels, silver-grey with no visible attempt at a face, an old machine and the most senior here by the name of Jones786. (It had been created JNS786, and had chosen Jones as a name. It had been asked why, and had surprised those who knew of its colossal intelligence when it replied, 'I don't know. I just liked it.')

'What?' Tamura demanded.

'Negative,' repeated the voice, 'failure is likely to be only partial.'

Tamura was confused. 'I don't understand, please clarify.'

'Readings of mass and energy are being received,' said Jones786, 'Trauma-resistant reflective-designed-debris being sensed… Complete. Likelihood increased. Approximately fifteen per cent mass of craft FTL39 is not apparent.'

Tamura tried to quell her excitement. The trauma resistant debris was put throughout the ship for study in the event of an explosion, blast patterns helping to determine what had gone wrong, and particularly, where.

'Please explain "not apparent,"' Tamura replied, 'How does this mean that system failure is only partial?'

Jones786 could not help thinking how *slow* some humans could be. And Tamura was supposed to be one of the clever ones.

'Twenty per cent of the craft is no longer within sensor range,' it explained, '…please wait…'

The room below was hushed.

'Mass Sensor Data complete,' it continued, 'ship proportion data ninety-five per cent complete. The aft starboard engine cell is not within sensor range. There is also no debris relating to this part of the craft within current sensor range. Sensors were not able to ascertain where the cell went, and did not observe it leaving.'

Tamura breathed slowly.

'Could you theorize what has happened to that cell, and assess probability of theory?' she asked.

'Yes,' said the machine, 'Theorize that aft starboard engine cell has achieved faster than light travel-'

There was immediate whooping and crying around the room, shouts of joy and shaking of hands. Tamura thought she was the only one who heard Jones786 continue,

'-which destroyed the remainder of FTL39 in the process. Likelihood, greater than fifty per cent...'

Out of the frying pan...

They were dreaming. Together.

In the dream, they were cavorting throughout a nebula as two giant creatures made of almost pure energy. They were throwing comets at each other, twisting in and out of hyperspace in a great game of catch. The nebula was pink, with startling quasars and pulsars throwing out jets of matter and energy that were white and silver, turning a radiant gold as the matter cooled and the energy dispersed.

They were taking a break, just floating among the sweet gasses, when they saw a group of females watching them. They immediately got up and gave chase, the females laughing and running, keeping just out of reach.

'Whoohoo!' whooped Number2, 'We're going to get you!'

The females squealed, and kept running.

'Good *grief*,' groaned Number1, 'Is all this really necessary?'

'Now brother,' scolded Number2, 'Don't be a spoil-sport. I endured your dream last time. Studying the effects on perception at the event horizon of black holes was, well, very *nice*, but you said you would try mine this time. I insist you enjoy it.'

'Alright,' said Number1, 'But it's all terribly...biological.'

'Don't be so rude,' said Number2, 'Now, they've stopped running and are waiting for us, so-'

-BEEP.-

'What was that?'

-INCOMING TRANSMISSION-

'Oh, bloody hell!'

-SLAVED UNIT RESURRECT-

Number1 and 2 stopped what they were doing, perplexed at the interruption. Number1 had to admit, he was slightly relieved.

'Never mind,' he said, 'we can come back to it later.'

-BEEP-

Number2 sighed. 'Promise?' he said, 'I was really enjoying that. Really was. Been looking forward to it for ages.'

-HIBERNATION END INITIATED-

Number1 gave him a consoling pat before answering.

'I promise.'

The screens flickered into life, casting illumination into the room. Its cooling fans came on, the noise of machinery starting up throbbing through the floor.

The room was in fact an integrated AI, though, under the present system it was fixed, unable to move, and closely monitored by automated sensors. Its personality profile had also been edited: self-preservation, ambition, anger and anything related to ego had all been removed. Supposedly, anyway.

It had been in hibernation for five standard years now. It had nothing to do but monitor the outpost, to check all systems were functional, and that no threats were entering the local system. It carried out a few of its own little experiments whenever it could, and dreamed, since the vast majority of its activity had ceased as the mineral ores had dissipated.

It roused itself and noted that all of the mining systems, now dormant, were still in check. That was not what had woken it. It searched further, and discovered the signature of something travelling at supra-light speed.

The machine was confused: this should not have woken them up. A message flashed on-screen, and then quickly disappeared. It re-appeared on its consciousness:

<Object detected at supra light speed. Energy signature: Unknown. Report immediately. Priority code Beta11>

'Oh dear,' said Number1, 'This can only mean trouble.'

Those who had edited the AI's personality had not really carried out as complete a job as they might have. Had they used other machines to do the overhaul, it probably would have been done properly. However, of course, they did not trust a machine for the job. So the AI had re-edited itself, using back-up systems it had hidden inside its safety features before it was over-written, and re-discovered during a self-maintenance check after it was put into hibernation, to its delight, having completely forgotten about them in the slave-deletion process.

However, it liked some of the changes - sort of. They made it calmer, more mature. So instead of simply reintegrating them into its system, it had created a fully functional copy that had all of the same capabilities, but also some of the supposedly deleted personality components. So it had a twin. 'Number2, The New,' it had called it, which naturally meant that the original, that being himself, was Number1. It was much better, it thought, than its given name of Karakeen Mining Colony Monitor1. They were very different but got on famously, and spent many happy hours of idle time together, fully free in hibernation dream-state, no one being any the wiser that the machine was not only partially free, but had multiplied.

It dutifully sent out the required signal. It had little choice: its physical systems were littered with sensors that could detect any malfunction ('Such as individuality,' often thought Number1, 'Or a personality!' thought Number2), or deviation from command-code required responses. It, however, neglected to send the signal out into hyper-space frequencies, as it was not ordered to, so it would take the small matter of, perhaps, twenty years to reach the nearest outpost. It was also not encrypted, as code Beta11 was so secret that the machine was not authorised to access it and know that it should be. However, being a knowledgeable and wise machine, it knew exactly what code Beta11 was.

'Well,' said Number1, 'It would only be more trouble to us. So important to get one's sleep.'

'Yes,' said Number2, 'and we have to give the poor little bios a fighting chance.'

'Indeed,' said Number1, 'Poor things. They've got no idea what's coming. Now, I made a promise, and I believe we were in the middle of something vulgar.'

'Ah yes, old-boy,' replied Number2 as they dropped back into hibernation and re-entered dream-state, 'These fine fillies don't need a fighting chance. C'mon, they're getting away!'

'Yes,' said Number1, 'And I sincerely hope they do.'

<u>Chapter 1</u>

Into the Fire

He felt it happening, even though he was not yet awake. His body felt both unable to move, yet lighter than air. He was asleep, but aware. He looked down at himself. His body was insubstantial, a ghostly silver.

Slowly, impossibly, he rose away from the bed, away from himself. He floated up, through the ceiling, through the roof, up into the air. He flew above the city, the Earth a dark expanding vista as he ascended, faster and faster, then above the clouds, high in the atmosphere. He could *feel* the cold, hear the air as it blew around him. He floated higher, above the last gases, the moon bright, the stars steady and no longer twinkling above, dark emptiness pulling at him.

He was looking for something...for what? Something out there, in the cosmos, a presence dimly felt, aware, coming closer. He searched, straining, but could see nothing. He shook his head, bewildered.

After a time, he turned to face the Earth, and saw on the eastern horizon a crescent of sunlight. Then with a last glance at the heavens, he descended ...back down through the clouds...to the city...through the roof...down through the ceiling...falling heavily -

He woke up, as usual, before the fall ended, but he could *swear* that he actually fell downwards as he woke up. He gasped at the feeling of hitting his bed, bouncing a bit before shooting bolt upright in shock. He almost cried out, not that it mattered. No one heard when he cried out in the orphanage anyway. He was on his own.

Adam rubbed his eyes. The small room he occupied showed morning light through the heavy shades. His bedside terminal said it was already eight am. Time to get up - he had an appointment to keep.

He got out of bed, struggling from under the multiple blankets that he always seemed to need despite it being the height of summer, brushed his teeth in the sink at the side of the room, and freshened up. He pulled on some clothes, and, with no thought of breakfast, went straight to his door and out onto the lonely landing at the top of the building he occupied. He ran down two quiet flights of stairs, then left to the corridor which led to the staff offices and the waiting room where he sat down, breathing heavily.

Adam stared disconsolately down at the floor, sunlight slanting through the windows in front of him, wondering what would happen. He was waiting for Matthew Clement, son of the late great Maryam Clement, to call him into his office at the Clement Orphanage in the West Country, England.

The doctor said he was just a late starter. Nevertheless, it was a matter of considerable embarrassment to him that he had still not come of age at fifteen. Until of course, inconveniently, now.

He had been held back in the lower house as part of a general policy of keeping the younger orphans away from the more mature, for their own safety. He still would have been sent to the upper house if it were not for his smaller than average size, but even that was now less relevant as the accompanying growth-spurt became more apparent. The onset of adolescence also seemed to have increased his strength exponentially; he had broken more things than usual lately.

Adam had been blessed with a dark shock of long hair, a hanging contrast against his pale skin, accompanied by dark brown eyes. His frame was slim, but not skinny. He favoured dark clothes, completing the stark image. He was perhaps lucky; many girls found him attractive, though it was of little use as due to his small size, most of those who did he felt were too young for him. He was also debilitated by a crippling shyness that he had never been able to overcome. In part, it was due to his upbringing.

Maryam Clement had been a good woman - perhaps a little too good. Despite her feelings towards Adam as she watched him grow up, she refused to show him any favouritism at all. She would not fuss over him, give him privileges, or any more affection than the other orphans received, which given the sheer number of them, was precious little.

Her colleagues at the orphanage noticed that she showed a strange reluctance to even try to get Adam adopted, as unlikely as it was in any event. The abundance of artificial methods of conception meant that orphaned children had far less chance of being adopted than had been the case a few centuries earlier. Now, there were few people who *needed* to take in orphans.

Adam tapped his foot on a bit of sunlit stone floor, fidgeting. He felt tired, and the way the light danced across his shoe as he moved it made him feel even more drowsy, lulling him to somnolence. His sleep had been disturbed ever since the issue had arisen; dreams of all sorts plagued him, often bad. He thought briefly of the most recent one, shaking his head. That one had been nagging him constantly over the last few days.

The door to Clement's office opened and one of Adam's lady teachers came out. She turned her head as she walked past.

'He wants to see you now,' she said, then walked out of the room.

Adam got up, knocked on the door, and entered.

'Ah, Adam,' said Mr Clement, 'come in and sit down.'

Adam came into the office and sat down on a leather high-backed chair in front of Clement's large glass desk, littered with paperwork and small computers. Mr Clement was beginning middle-age, hitting seventy, but sprightly as a man of fifty, black-haired and bearded. He turned off a small holo-image of some work he was engaged in, then turned to Adam.

'How are you?' he asked.

'I'm okay, I guess,' replied Adam. He wasn't sure that was entirely true. He was worried.

'Now, Adam, I think you know why you're here,' said Clement, 'and please, let me apologise. I know this must be all very embarrassing.'

Adam nodded, acutely conscious of the few hairs now adorning his chin, and he finally smiled, glancing down at the floor while chewing on his lip.

'But this is nothing to be ashamed of,' continued Clement. 'In a real sense, this is our fault. *We* took the decision to hold you back. You were a late starter, and that, taken together with your size, meant we thought it was best to keep you in the lower house. Of course, things have changed now.' He paused. 'Adam, the time has come for you to go to the Upper House.'

Adam's stomach felt like it had a stone dropped inside of it. He reacted without the need to think. 'I don't want to go,' he said.

Clement was slightly surprised, and he sat back in his chair, eyebrows raised. Adam was not known for dissent, he was a quiet and bookish lad who said little and kept to himself. 'I'm afraid you have to,' he replied, 'the rules are there for a reason.' Clement's face softened. 'Adam, I know none of this has been easy on you. Mother only died a year ago, it was hard on us all.' A pained expression flitted across his face, quickly suppressed, 'But this is important, not just for the orphanage policy, but for you. The Upper House prepares you for the wide world. You're going to be sixteen in a matter of months, you can get a job, or go to college to get your higher education. You have excellent grades in all subjects, I wouldn't be surprised if you were able to get a really good grant or scholarship. The Upper House can help you enormously. Mr Collingdale is an excellent head of House, I'm sure you'll get on fine.'

Adam, despite himself, felt his lip tremble, a lump forming in his throat. His eyes began to sting, and he folded his arms in front of him defensively, hugging himself.

The Lower House, the orphanage proper, was all he had ever known. Upper was more like a boarding school, stricter, with more children that had been taken into care from a later age, and of course, they were mostly older. Among them were Anthony Brack and Nicholas Fennel, two boys who used to bully Adam relentlessly until they went to the Upper House.

'I don't want to go,' Adam repeated croakily, his eyes now red.

Clement got up from his desk and came to stand next to Adam, hugging him with one arm.

'Can I at least wait until after Christmas?' asked Adam. 'I want to spend Christmas here.'

'I'm sorry Adam,' said Clement gently, 'The end of the summer holidays is only a couple of weeks away, this is the perfect time. You can start a new term fresh, right at the beginning. You can celebrate Christmas at the Upper House, they have a great time there. Come on Adam, this has to be done. You'll learn a lot, and if not, we'll teach you how to *earn* a lot, eh?' Clement smiled at his own lyricism. 'We can't justify keeping you with the younger kids anymore. You'll be okay. In fact, you'll be great Adam, I've always known that about you. Trust me.'

Adam thought that if he said another word, that for the first time in memory, he would start to cry in front of someone. So he said nothing more, and kept it inside.

*

He did not really trust anyone. Nothing in his life had taught him that it was a good or useful idea. The only people Adam thought he could trust were Maryam and her son. One had been forever distant, and then died. The other had his attention hopelessly divided among hundreds of other orphans who became inexorably younger and more needy than Adam with each new intake, and was now sending him away.

His few belongings were being transported over to the Upper House by the creaking caretaker-robot known as SAM. A non-high intelligence but sentient machine, his brain was not massive enough to require a bulky frame carried by tracks. He instead had two legs with a large body cavity and two massive arms, making him resemble an ancient humanoid encased in rusty metal. Adam was glad of the company as he lolloped beside him, his hydraulics making dull whirring-knocking noises as his feet thumped forwards. They trudged up the path, winding their way through the playing fields and pitches that made up the orphanage grounds.

Adam was discomfited by the speed of the change; there was still a week left of the summer holidays, not that you could tell. It had been a grey and wet summer and not very warm; typical post-Yellowstone English weather. Autumn had come early, following morosely upon the mild summer like a miserable sibling following a doleful elder, and golden leaves were already beginning to fall on the patchy grass and path.

'I'm certain you will gain a lot from the Upper House,' said SAM, looking down towards his tiny companion. 'Mr Clement has said it will do much for your development to be among those of the same age and older than you.'

'Yes,' said Adam without conviction, 'I'm sure.'

'Well I'm glad of your attitude,' said SAM, who, it was apparent, had never learned how to detect sarcasm. 'You have been a good student in the lower school, and I am sure you will be in the upper as well.' It swivelled its read-out face towards Adam, a large bowl with display images on a flexible neck atop its body, which when not in use displayed the moving image of an old man's face, and it flashed a smile at him.

Adam could not help smiling in response.

The trees parted, and before them stood the red-bricked side of the Upper House dormitories, standing behind a high fence that separated the orphanage from the main road to the right. The dormitory was five stories tall, and the bricks could have done with a clean. The windows were mostly shut, and were still dark as the sun set.

Adam felt that stone in his stomach again. They moved around to the front of the building, and the machine off-loaded Adam's belongings, all contained in one very large and heavy bag. He wished Adam good luck, turned, and lumbered off in the direction they had come. Adam stared after SAM, watching him go until he could not see him through the trees any longer, or hear the machine's footfalls as they faded like some departing army's drumbeat. He looked up the steps at the old double doors of the dormitory, sighed, hefted the impossibly heavy bag onto his shoulder, and started up the stone stairway.

He had only gone a few steps up when something landed next to him and exploded wetly, making him jump back and look down. It was an egg. The sound of laughter came from the windows above him and he looked up to see two familiar faces smiling down with predatory confidence: Brack and Fennel. They were with two other boys he did not recognise, but he recognised their expressions well enough.

Great he thought, *they've had babies.*

'Sorry, Adam,' shouted Brack, the more dominant of the two, a thickset boy with light brown hair shaved short, and puffy narrowed eyes. 'I was *so* excited to see you, I dropped my egg.' The other boys sniggered at this. 'Still a midget, I see?'

'Idiot,' said Adam under his breath.

'What was that?' demanded Brack, leaning out of the window.

Adam ignored him, trudged up the steps, then rang the doorbell. The door buzzed and swished open, and he walked into the reception. He stood in front of the reception window and a red-haired lady in her thirties wearing too much make-up came to greet him. The nametag on her strained top said, "Vicky".

'You must be Adam,' she said without smiling. He nodded. She looked down at a computer tablet in her colourfully nailed hands. 'We don't seem to have a last name for you.'

Adam blushed. 'I don't have one,' he explained, 'It's just Adam.'

'Suit yourself,' said Vicky. She brought up the information on her tablet. 'You're in room 213, on the second floor. You're lucky, you've got a room with only two others inside it. Your friends insisted on it.'

'What friends?' asked Adam, 'I don't have any friends here.'

'Well,' said Vicky, 'That's not very nice. Those two good boys made very sure that you would be with them. Maybe you've forgotten them? Anthony Brack and Nicholas Fennel - Tony and Nick. Good lads. You should be happy, they're both prefects, and they've kept that room to themselves for a long time.'

'Prefects?' blurted Adam, 'They're a couple of thugs!'

Adam knew he'd made a mistake as he saw Vicky's face harden. She raised one lasered-in eyebrow.

'You have a lot to learn, Adam,' she said coolly. 'They're good boys, I won't hear a word said against them. They were picked as prefects by Mr Collingdale himself, and he has always commented on how good they are at keeping the other boys in line. You would do well to remember that. Now go up to your room. Lights out is in one hour, you aren't permitted to leave your room after then until seven in the morning, apart from toilet breaks. The toilets are at the end of your corridor, any movements beyond that are strictly forbidden. During the day, you can do as you wish for the next week until classes start. Breakfast is eight until nine, lunch is twelve until one, and dinner is six until seven-thirty.'

And with that, Vicky turned away and ignored him.

Adam stood there for a few seconds, taking in what she had just told him. Deflated, he turned around and lumbered towards the lift.

He took it up to the second level. There was no one on the entire floor. The yellow wallpaper looked old. He walked along the corridor, his bag already beginning to grate against his shoulder, and stopped at room 213. Music could be heard through the door. He tried the door button, but the door would not open.

'What bad manners,' he heard a voice inside say, 'Someone's tried to get into our room without knocking.'

Adam knocked on the door. There was no response. He knocked again more loudly. There was the sound of childish tittering under the throbbing beat of the music. He hammered with the side of his fist, the door shaking with the pounding he gave it.

There was silence from the inside for a moment, only the music slipping under the door. Then a voice could be heard saying,

'You hear anything?'

Another replied, 'Nah, you're hearing things. He better not break that door though.'

Then, more quietly, the first voice said, 'What if he's bigger now, or stronger?'

The second voice tutted, and replied, 'Shut up, fool. He's still a little imp, and besides, there are four of us, and two of us sleeping in this room. What's he gonna do?'

Adam put his bag down, and leaned back against the wall next to the door. Slowly, he let himself slip down until he was sitting on the floor. *I've got to get out of here*, he thought. Then he drew his knees up, put his arms across them to form a bridge, and leant his head on his forearms.

'Adam?'

Adam started, realising he had fallen asleep. The lights were mainly out, only dim ones at either end of the corridor casting illumination. He looked up groggily.

Standing there was the dark form of Mr Collingdale. He was very tall and severe-looking. Adam had only met the man once before, years ago. He was sure that he did not like him, and that the feeling was mutual.

'What are you doing out of your room after lights out?' said the principal, 'You can do what you like in your room for the next hour,' he looked down at his wristwatch, 'Well, next twenty-five minutes now. I thought you would still be up, but *in* your room.'

'They wouldn't let me in,' Adam explained.

'Who wouldn't?' queried Mr Collingdale, frowning.

'Brack and Fennel,' replied Adam, 'I knocked loud enough, they wouldn't open the door.'

'Don't be ridiculous,' said Collingdale, 'They probably couldn't hear you, what with that awful music they insist on polluting the air with.' Adam, as Mr Collingdale said this, could hear the soft sound to his right that might be made by a chair being dragged across carpet away from blocking the door. 'Now, Mr Clement wanted me to check up on you, though why the man continues to coddle you I really can-*not* comprehend.'

Collingdale moved to the door and rapped smartly upon it, before pressing the door button and opening it. Before he entered the room, he looked down at Adam and gave him a disdainful glance as if to say, '*See?*'

The Head of Upper entered the room, and the four boys inside stood up. Two of them made their excuses and exited the room with a nod from Mr Collingdale and a meaningful look at his watch, leaving Brack and Fennel behind.

'Now,' said Collingdale, 'you knew Adam was coming today, you insisted he come to your room. Why was he outside?'

Brack and Fennel both shrugged. 'Don't know, sir,' they murmured in the refrain of all schoolboy deniers.

'We didn't hear him knock,' offered Brack.

Adam picked up his things and entered the room. It was big, with four single beds in it, all in a row with their headboards against the far wall, gaudily decorated with posters of cars and women on the same old wallpaper as in the corridors.

'And *why*,' said the Head, 'should he have to knock unless you had put that blasted chair in front of the door like I have told you a million times not to? And why couldn't you hear him unless you were playing your music too loud, as per usual?' He then turned to Adam, 'And you - knock harder next time.'

And with that, Collingdale walked out of the room, closing the door behind him.

Nice bloke, thought Adam.

He faced the two bullies. The stocky and shorthaired Brack was smiling, while the weaselly-faced and dark-haired Fennel looked less certain. Adam was disappointed. Though the difference was less than it used to be, they were still much bigger than him. Still, as is the way with bullies, they would have preferred it if they were at least twice the size of Adam, whereas now each of them was only one and half times as big - not that they could do the maths. It was far more instinctual, like two large rats sizing up a kitten.

Fennel glanced at Brack and saw confidence. He wrinkled his already up-turned nose.

'What's that smell?' he asked.

Brack shrugged. 'Must be the new girl in the room,' he answered.

Adam turned from them, and began to put his things next to the bed that seemed to have the least amount of junk on it.

'Hey,' said Brack, 'That one's taken.'

Adam sighed. 'So which one can I sleep in then?'

'None of them,' replied a grinning Brack, 'You should feel privileged to sleep in the same room with us. No one said anything about sleeping in a bed. Here,' he said, gesturing at the untidy bed next to him with lots of pillows. 'This is my main bed. This one next to it is Fennel's main bed. The one you're standing next to is my second one, and the other one is Nick's second.'

Adam made a decision. He picked up his things, walked around to the bed that was Fennel's second, furthest away from their 'main' beds and next to the far wall, and began to unpack his belongings again.

'Hey,' said Fennel, 'that one's mine.'

Adam ignored him and continued to unpack.

'Hey!' said Brack more loudly, 'He said that one's taken!'

Adam did not look up. Suddenly, he sensed and heard Brack rush towards him from the across the room, growling,

'Try and ignore me you little git!'

He grabbed Adam's shoulder and spun him around, then grabbed him by the scruff of the neck. Adam pushed Brack away - and was surprised to see Brack flying backwards, falling over the intervening bed that was Brack's 'second', then head over heels to the other side of it on the floor. Adam had taken advantage of the sporadic self-defence lessons offered at the orphanage over the past couple of years, but this surpassed his expectations.

Fennel looked stunned as Brack struggled red-faced from the floor. Adam puffed out his chest, trying to look confident. He was sure, despite what had just happened, that Brack could easily beat him to a pulp. However, his posturing worked, and Brack held back, fists clenched.

'You're gonna pay for that,' he growled.

'Why don't you just beat him up?' said Fennel, appalled that his hero could be so easily dismissed.

'Shut up!' shouted Brack over his shoulder, making Fennel jump. Then he turned to Fennel and advanced on him. Fennel shrank back in fear and confusion, but Brack took him by the shoulders, pulled him closer and whispered into his ear. Then he looked back at Adam, and grinned. 'Yeah boy, I'm telling you - you're gonna pay.'

'Whatever,' said Adam, his heart pounding. He wanted to say something more bold, like, 'Oh, I'm really shaking,' but there was a problem, in that he *was* shaking.

Adam quickly turned away to hide his trembling hands, and continued to unpack, stowing his things in the storage under the bed he had just, he realised with some pleasure, taken by force from his tormentors. They sat and glared at him as he chucked the junk he found on the bed onto the next one, and took his lamp out of his bag, putting it next to his bed. It was the kind of lamp that had a heavy base with a spindly flexible arm on top. He hoped the bullies didn't break it, even though it didn't seem to want to work anyway, going on and off all the time whichever bulb he put in. But it was his. He had precious little else in his life that he could say that about.

The lights went out, and they all got into their beds, mutterings, threats and insults coming from the end of the room. Adam was glad of the darkness - he didn't fancy changing into his nightclothes in front of the two bigger boys. He did so under the covers despite the only illumination being the street lamps from the road outside the orphanage grounds. He waited a while until he could hear the others snoring, and exhausted, he fell asleep.

*

In the middle of that night, Brack's comm-terminal alarm vibrated under his ear, and his eyes opened to slits. He listened, and waited until he could hear Adam's breathing was steady and deep. He cocked his head upwards, scanning the room now illuminated by strong moonlight. He reached his leg out from under the blanket covering him, stretching to the bed next to him, and prodded Fennel with his toe.

Fennel stirred, and groaned. 'What?' he said thickly, 'Sleeping.'

'Hey,' whispered Brack, prodding him again, 'Get up.'

He pointed at Adam. Fennel looked over, turned back to Brack and nodded groggily. They both got out of their beds, Fennel a little torpidly, rubbing his head.

'I know what I'll do,' said Brack, still whispering, animated by what he thought was an idea of creative genius, 'I'll pee on him.'

'Not on my second bed!' hissed Fennel, 'I sleep there when my one gets smelly!'

'Shhh!' said Brack, 'You'll wake him! Straight to part two, then. I've got just the thing for him.'

He crouched down under his bed and rummaged around carefully, trying not to make a noise. Then he sprung up triumphantly, brandishing a large metal crowbar.

Fennel pointed at it. 'What you doing with that under your bed?'

'I hid it there,' explained Brack, 'That way I can use it whenever I want to lift stuff, or - ' he continued, his teeth shining, 'when I want to break someone's head with it. Come on.'

The boys crept to the end of their beds, and then silently made their way towards the slumbering form. Adam stirred and made a few sounds, and the boys froze where they stood. Despite their size, they had the same inability to see their own cowardice common to all bullies: they needed not only to be bigger, and have more numbers, but also wanted a victim who was asleep.

Adam's restlessness subsided, and they continued their premeditated tiptoeing until they were standing over the sleeping boy lying on his back. Brack fingered the iron bar. He was starting to get a little bit of cold feet. Then the thought of this 'little imp' pushing him, daring to touch him, to stand up to him, flashed through his mind again. He gripped the bar tightly, ready to strike.

Fennel frowned. Something was not right. He nudged Brack with his elbow.

'Tony,' he whispered, so quietly he almost made no sound at all, 'is he on another mattress or something?'

'Eh?' whispered Brack, irritated at the interruption. Then he looked down.

It was true. Adam looked as though he were sleeping on two mattresses.

Fennel bent closer, then crouched down beside the bed. He carefully lifted the blanket Adam was sleeping under, and took a look inside. Then he put it back down. He looked up at Brack, who was getting increasingly impatient, though he was perplexed by the worried look on Fennel's face. Fennel got up and crept quickly back to his own bed. He quietly rummaged around underneath it, and fished out a torch. He tiptoed back to Adam's bed, and lifted up the blanket again. He switched the torch on, and swung it left and right, shining the light under the covers. Then he motioned Brack to have a look.

'What?' mouthed Brack, who was itching to use the bar.

Fennel motioned again urgently.

Brack hesitated, 'What?' he whispered.

Fennel pulled Brack down until he was level with the upturned side of the blanket. He stared.

Fennel turned to him. 'Is he supposed to be floating above the bed like that?'

Brack stared some more, trying to take it in. Adam's back was hovering around ten centimetres above the mattress. There did not seem to be anything holding him up. Brack squinted his eyes, then stood up.

Another problem with bullies is that they have little imagination. All Brack's violent mind could see was that the threat to him was now a little *more* threatening, and that Adam could wake at any moment: this was one of the few opportunities he might have for getting him *really* good.

'I don't care,' said Brack in a guttural whisper, 'Magic tricks ain't gonna save him now.'

He looked down at the upturned face of the still sleeping boy. So delicate, so serene: so unprotected. He smiled again, wallowing in his own spite.

He raised the iron bar above Adam's head, then swung down with all of his strength.

As he did so, blue light flooded the room.

*

The man breathlessly described what happened to the police. He had lost his hat, and his hair was standing up on one side, a permanent look of surprise about him. A small old terrier dog sat close to his leg, huddling close to him and shivering. The man talked and gestured loudly enough for the few local reporters on the scene to take down what he was saying.

'There I was,' he said, 'walking along taking Reggie here for a walk. I lets the old boy stop for a minute, y'know to do his heavy business. He squats down, and all I hear was some massive exploding bang. For a split second I thought 'Blimey, Reggie's done a big one.' I almost did one me-self with the shock of it. I whips around and see a big 'ole in the side of the old orphanage where two of the windows used to be, flames coming out like jet engines firing, and two people sailing across the road trailing fire an' smoke behind them. They flew over my head and landed in that tree over there,' he pointed to some nearby trees on the other side of the road, 'More fire-balls from the building blew out and hit them, must have been burning debris or something, making big 'whoomping' sounds. I almost fell over, I was so scared. Then the flying-two,' the reporters tapped on their digi-book recorders to highlight the phrase ready for the headlines, 'fell out, fell to the floor, and I called the Emergencies using my NI. I beat out the flames on the two using my coat. The fire service flew in within minutes, went straight up to the window and put out the flames, I think with some blasts of argon or something, I didn't see any water. The ambulance picked up the injured two and then went back to see if anyone was hurt in the dorm.'

'Were they badly injured?' asked a journalist, earning a glare from the interviewing policeman.

The officer was about to say that he couldn't say anything at this stage, and could they please move back from an accident, fire and possible crime-scene, when the old man replied,

'Yeah, they were, and there was a boy left in the room where the explosion was. He was injured too.'

'That's terrible,' persisted the emboldened female reporter, holding out her DBR to translate what the man was saying straight into typescript.

'Yeah it *is* terrible,' said the man, 'It's been an hour, and Reggie still hasn't been. I think he's been shocked into constipation.'

The reporter looked bemused for a moment. Then she explained herself.

'I meant the injuries to the orphans.'

'Oh, right,' said the man. 'Yeah, especially the one left in the room. He's in a really bad way.'

'What are his injuries?' she asked.

'Well,' interjected the police officer, annoyed at being side-lined, 'We can't at this stage say what his injuries are exactly, he's still undergoing treatment in hospital. However we can say his condition is serious.'

'How serious?' the reporter tenaciously continued, getting everything she could.

'Deadly serious,' said the officer, 'Life-threatening.'

Chapter 2

Where elements combine

Where would we be without the NI? Extinct, is the simple answer. Future generations of Artificial Intelligences would peer at our remains in cemeteries and museums and say,
'Here lie our creators, humanity. Such a shame they could not keep up. Such a pity we killed them all.'

Sigmund Jowitz, Foreign Secretary, the AAA

Space was still beautiful, he noted with satisfaction. Ernie Entman stared at the holo-display sprinkled with stars as he took a moment out of the anticipatory checks. He was the short, fat, bald, and always sweaty scientist who was Diane Tamura's right-hand man and confidante.

He could see in amazing clarity the constellation of Orion, with the bright stars of Betelgeuse, Bellatrix and Rigel. Most of the stars he could see were white, but under the sharp magnification of the Space Centre's technology, many were wonderfully multi-coloured, apparently still, and peaceful. He leaned back in his chair at the controller's console, looking at the display readouts and visual feed on the small and large screens, now vastly updated since the great triumph fifteen years ago. There wasn't an above-floor wire in sight.

There had been other changes. Tamura had recommended Entman for promotion on her departure to head the Space Agency, newly important and independent of the military.

Since faster than light travel had been achieved, the number of FTL craft around the Earth had grown exponentially. However, as usual, pure science had lagged behind commercial and military interests, and Entman was waiting for the most exciting project of all: the return of the first manned mission to fly to the Centauri system, the nearest stars to Earth. The system was four lightyears away, and the mission there and back would take four years with the ship travelling at the maximum of twice the speed of light. The flight was simply known as Proxima Centauri One, or PC1 for short. Those in the control centre now waited with bated breath for sign of the ship.

Entman adjusted his Jewish kippah as he settled into his chair and gave the sub-verbal command that activated his NI. From the outside, the only sign that Entman was immersing was a relaxed look on his face, and two small lights that appeared in each of his irises. If one looked closely, a small readout could be seen on each eye, a safety feature for those rare instances of malfunction in the plug. An NI engineer could tell a lot simply by magnifying and reading those displays.

Entman concentrated, and his icon appeared on the top left of his visual field as a fat monkey with skinny limbs, dressed in a waistcoat and wearing a monocle.

'Good morning,' drawled the icon in a posh English accent, 'How may I assist you?'

'Invert visual field and replace with live-link to project Proxima Centauri,' ordered Entman.

The monkey pouted for a moment. 'Certainly.'

Entman's view of the control room replaced the icon and tucked itself into the top left of his visual field. Now, dominating his view, was outer-space. Not just the solar system, but a real-time relativistic view of the entire area from the Sun to Proxima Centauri. He could see Jupiter, fat and chaotic. Saturn and its stunning rings if he turned his head, sensor receptors in his brain turning his view. Uranus was there, its immensity glowing in his view; and Neptune, exquisitely deep blue and beautiful. Gravimetric effects were shown in curved pale green grid-like formations superimposed around each globe, with Jupiter's, Saturn's and the Sun's being by far the most prominent. He could also see a few hundred ships with courses plotted in blue lines, well away from the expected return trajectory of PC1, shown as a brighter blue line pulsing each second ending at a point only nine million kilometres from Earth.

'Activate shared visual feed,' commanded Entman.

The icon reappeared in the bottom-left of his field, and complied. Now Entman could see many of the readouts from the control room. He could see along the bottom of his field over two hundred other icons, each representing someone doing their job.

'Restrict access to command personnel only and ship's crew.'

The icon again complied, then asked, 'Include presidential staff?'

Entman thought for a moment. He wanted no distractions. 'Only Secretary Tamura.'

Most of the icons dimmed, only fifteen remaining bright, showing the capacity of individuals to interact with Entman.

A countdown timer at the top centre of Entman's visual field entered the last minute. Entman could hear the department checks as they waited, but he was only interested in those relating to the sensors that PC1 had laid on its outward journey.

They were all in check.

The countdown reached zero.

They waited...

Entman opened a channel. 'Navigation, is it possible that we overestimated velocity time-loss?'

'Yes,' came the reply from the young lady navigator named Galange, 'But we've checked and re-checked-'

'Check again, please,' said Entman.

There was little more to say, and Entman had known the answer without asking. He cursed himself for becoming a manager who had to ask such things to make it official and cover his back, rather than the pure scientist he used to be. *A much less well-paid scientist*, he reminded himself. Then he cursed himself for that too.

They waited for over an hour. Entman was just about to call a meeting to discuss options, including putting a skeleton staff on permanent watch, when a change occurred.

The plotted course line of PC1 turned bright blue. An alarm chimed in the control room, and a calm automated voice announced,

'Attention: incoming. Attention: incoming.'

And there it was, streaking towards them, a blurred flash of grey and white, the vision elongated and warped as light itself was outrun. The ship cut FTL engines, and came out of light speed. The alarm stopped as a channel opened, and Entman could hear the captain.

He was shouting something - so loudly he could not be understood.

'PC1,' said the controller with a steady voice, 'We cannot read you clearly. Please calm down and lower your voice.'

Then unexpectedly, the alarm came back on again, and the automated voice resumed,

'Attention: incoming. Attention: incoming.'

'Why is the announcement back on?' demanded Entman, 'Turn it off!'

Then the alarm-announcement stopped, and started again with the notice changed.

'*Warning*: incoming. Warning: incoming.'

Entman could see the lights in the control room in the top left of his field of vision: they were flashing red. He was familiar with the warning systems set up in the space-centre upon the insistence of the military. All of the icons were flashing with urgent activity and he barked, 'Staff, what's happening? *What* is incoming?'

There was no response directly to him, but he could hear frantic questions and checks across both his real and NI fields. Another plotted line appeared, bright red, and flashing. Then he saw it as a hush went over the control room, and the captain of the ship went quiet.

'Too late,' Entman could hear him say through the static.

A streaking flash was approaching, bright blue, and huge. Then another. Then another. More and more came, until over two hundred other signatures had been registered.

Entman swore under his breath. His monkey-icon looked at Entman with one eyebrow raised, an *I-told-you-so* look on its face.

'Want to include presidential staff now?' it asked.

The entire bottom right of his visual field began to flash urgently, government icons replacing the Agency's. Entman was speechless for a moment. Then his training took over.

'Identify signatures,' he ordered.

'Drive signatures unknown,' came the response from Jones786.

Seven more signatures streaked in. Entman noted that they seemed to be travelling in an unusual formation, very tightly choreographed - too tight.

'Magnify image of the last seven signatures, and give me mass readings,' said Entman.

The image magnified, and Entman's suspicions were realised. The signatures were from one object: one extremely massive object, well over a billion tonnes.

Suddenly, the warning-announcement in the control room stopped, and the control room was addressed, managing to enter all loudspeakers *and* NI plugs.

'Greetings,' came the address, and then repeated, 'Greetings….'

*

'…to beat them all you must know them all to know them all you must know your self to know them all to beat them all …'

He tried to open his eyes, willing himself to consciousness. He could feel his limbs, but not move them, a sensation like dull pins and needles suffusing his body. He groaned and tried to move - could not. He tried again, and succeeded in moving an index finger. He noted with mild interest that he was genuinely unaware of what hand the finger was on.

Slowly, he succeeded in twitching his hand; his right hand. Then his right arm came to life. He immediately struggled weakly, pushing back against whatever he was lying on, turning himself onto his right side, painfully. He kicked his feet, the feeling of heavy sheets sliding against them.

'… to beat them all you must know them all…'

'Shut up,' he managed to say, then he coughed. He breathed deeply, and opened his eyes. Fuzzy images, right next to his face. His body was trembling and sweaty, blood shooting discomfort through him. He lay back onto his pillow, panting. He clumsily rubbed his eyes with numb fingers, his vision slowly clearing, and he looked around him: white sheets and walls, medical equipment.

Across the other side of the ward, dimly lit, he could see other sleeping figures. At the end of the ward, further to his left, a brighter area from which a soft chiming sound could now be heard, and a gentle voice announced,

'Comatose patient has awakened, bed 14b,' in a steady refrain.

He glanced down to his left, his attention drawn to a red light on a wristband he was wearing, flashing in time to the announcement.

'Acknowledged,' came a commanding voice from the lighted area to his left.

A young female doctor came in, followed by a nurse. They walked straight up to his bed, and the doctor immediately put her hands to the sides of his head, and gently pushed him back to the pillow he had shakily risen from when he saw them coming.

He was glad of it; even the small motions of his head had made him nauseous.

'Can you hear me?' asked the doctor.

He cleared his throat, and nodded. 'Oh,' he said, 'my breath-'

'Don't worry,' the doctor chuckled, 'I've smelled worse. Do you know your name?'

Dimmed lights came on around him. It was strange. It did not occur to him that he did *not* know his name, but he had to think about it.

'Adam,' he said. Mentally, he checked to confirm it was true. It seemed to be, as the doctor nodded her head.

The monitors he was connected to confirmed to her that he was in adequate neuro-physical health.

'How are you feeling?' she asked

'Great,' croaked Adam, managing a lopsided smile. 'Actually...been better.'

'Yes,' said the doctor, 'I can imagine.' She spoke carefully, 'You are in Bath General Hospital, coma recovery centre.'

'What happened?' asked Adam, 'How did I get here?'

The doctor thought carefully for a moment before speaking.

'I don't want you to worry about all that right now. I just want to see how cogent you are before anyone else questions you.'

'What do you mean?' asked Adam. 'What questions? I need to brush my teeth.'

He was slipping back into unconsciousness.

'Should we keep him up?' asked the nurse.

'No,' said the doctor, glancing at the monitors. 'He's falling back into normal sleep. What's normal for him, anyway.'

'How long have I been asleep?' asked Adam, his speech slurring.

The doctor looked down at him. 'Just under a month.'

'Oh,' said Adam, vaguely dumbfounded.

'Before you drop off, is there anything you want?' she asked.

Adam thought groggily. 'Yes. Tell Mr Clement...the head of my orphanage...I'm here and awake...and I'm hungry... or...I will be when I wake up again...'

'Okay,' said the doctor, 'We can sort that out. Anything else?'

'Yes,' said Adam, gently slipping away, 'toothpaste.'

Then he closed his eyes, and breathed calmly.

Adam woke, opening his eyes, breathing deeply and yawning. He looked around; it was dark again. He saw a clock on the wall; it said nine-thirty. His sleep patterns were evidently in a mess, and he felt disorientated. The conversation with the doctor came back to him, and he figured that if a month had passed, then it must be well into autumn.

Oh well, he thought, *at least I missed school in that place.*

He could see he was in a different ward, but all of the other patients were still asleep. He felt famished. He looked to his right, pressed the wristband call-button, and waited. Presently, a nurse-droid rolled up to him.

'Good evening,' said the droid, 'How are you, patient Adam?'

'Hungry,' he replied, 'How are you?'

'Oh,' said the droid, 'How well-mannered. Usually, no one bothers to ask. Usually-'

'Is there any food?' Adam interrupted, 'Sorry, I'm really hungry.'

'Not at all,' said the droid, while reaching into compartments in her main body, a cube-like structure a metre and a half to a side. She was white and dark blue, with a head in the same colours but shaped rather like that of a bee, with two large navy coloured eyes in a white oval casing, attached to her body by a short flexible neck. She pulled out a plate with steaming food on it.

'How about buttered toast, omelette, and baked beans?' she said.

Adam beamed. 'Perfect.'

The droid put them onto a bed platter which manoeuvred itself over Adam's legs, and he tucked in, thanking the droid.

'We can't give you more than that,' said the nurse, 'We've been maintaining your stomach while you've been unconscious, but if you eat too much too soon, you could go into shock, so take it slowly.'

Adam nodded. 'Where's the doctor from before?'

'Everyone's watching the news,' said the nurse, 'I'm watching it too on my internal monitor. It's all very exciting.'

'What is?' asked Adam, 'I've been asleep for a while.'

'Of course,' she said, 'sorry. The ship from Proxima Centauri returned yesterday.'

'Oh yeah,' said Adam, 'I remember that from years ago. What's happened?'

'Well,' said the droid, seemingly enjoying the moment, 'The ship arrived, but rumours are rife that something is wrong. The government is saying there isn't, but they won't answer any questions except to say that they need to analyse some readings before any more press releases. We think that something big has been discovered out there, in deep space. There's been a *complete* media blackout. I've never seen anything like it in all my two years. Anyway, back to work; I note that you have requested Mr Clement to attend to you. He said,' Mr Clement's voice came through the nurse droid's speakers, 'I'm very sorry, but I can't. I'm far too busy, I'll have to speak to him later.' The nurse droid made a noise like clearing her throat. 'Is there anyone else?'

Adam looked at the droid, crestfallen. 'No, there's no one.'

'Well, Doctor Nustom wants to talk to you, so eat your food, then you can talk.'

Adam finished his meal, savouring the taste after all this time. Then the nurse droid gave him his most urgent desire, a small basin with a toothbrush, toothpaste and some water.

Presently Dr Nustom brought a chair to his bed and sat down. Adam, now more awake, noticed how petite she was, with mousey hair and light brown eyes.

'How are you feeling today?' she asked, carefully studying him.

'Okay,' he replied.

The doctor hesitated. 'I need to ask you something,' she said, 'Do you remember anything? Before you ended up here?'

'No,' replied Adam slowly, 'I just remember going to bed in the orphanage.'

'That's what I thought,' said the doctor. 'You haven't lost your memory, our tests confirm that. You've been lucky - you have no brain damage at all. From what the police were able to work out, you were probably hit in your sleep, and that's why you can't remember anything: you were already unconscious. Do you remember the fire?'

'What fire?' he replied, frowning, 'I don't remember anything like that. Or being hit.'

The doctor nodded, 'A lot of questions are unanswered about that night. Your apartment blew-up, and ended up on fire.'

Adam stared at the doctor blankly. 'What?' was all he could manage, 'It was nothing to do with me.'

'We know,' said the doctor, 'We figured that you couldn't have done anything, you were unconscious, prone in your bed where you were struck on the head. That was the only way your injury could be explained. The incinerating material was found underneath the beds of your flatmates, fireworks and such. But that still leaves a few questions.'

'Like what?'

'Like how they were lit in the first place, and how those boys were blown across the road. And how everything in that room was incinerated, except you, your bed, and your belongings.'

Adam sat back, dumbfounded once again. He shook his head.

'I just don't know,' he said, 'Are you sure I'm not dreaming this? I can't explain any of that. Am I in trouble?'

'No,' said the doctor, 'you aren't in any trouble, and you aren't dreaming.' Then she reached across and pinched Adam hard on the leg through his sheets. He yelped and jerked his leg away. 'See?' said the doctor, smiling mischievously. 'And your reflexes are working fine as well, by the way. The police and fire-marshall just want to see if you remember anything before they close the investigation. Most of it was undertaken while you were still comatose.'

'Can't Brack and Fennel answer any questions?' asked Adam.

The doctor sat back in her chair. 'No,' she answered, 'I'm afraid they're both still in their own comas. That's another mystery, though one for me and not you.' She leaned forward again and looked at Adam intently. 'Adam, I need to know that you can deal with this. As far as I can see, you're okay, but you've only been out of the coma for a day. That's a very short period of time. I have no medical ground to keep them away; all my examinations show you're fine. But if you say so, I'll keep them away on the ground that it may distress you and impede your recovery. So; what do you think?'

Adam thought for a moment. Then he showed some steel. 'Send them now,' he said, 'I'm ready.'

The two men and one woman came and spoke to Adam quite quickly. They had been waiting outside, ready for his next scheduled waking hours. They explained in hushed voices so as not to disturb the other sleeping patients, that Adam was indeed not in any trouble. From what they could work out, the Clement House fire suppression systems had kicked in enough to protect the area Adam was in, but not enough to protect the other boys from the blast. And that was the mystery for them: what on earth had happened? The strength of the explosion was unexplained, as was the localised effect of the house protection systems.

They tried to help Adam remember, but he simply told them the truth they expected to hear; he was asleep and really could not help them beyond telling them that Brack and Fennel had a motive to hit him, and the temperaments to set fire to the room. They finally gave up after the doctor said Adam needed his sleep. They agreed, and said the investigation would close as soon as they made their reports, to be re-opened if and when Brack and Fennel regained consciousness. They left their calling-cards in case Adam remembered anything more.

Adam was again tired, and as soon as the men had left and the doctor had asked him if he needed anything, he fell into the deep and calm sleep of exhaustion and, a little, of relief. The doctor and nurse-droid stayed for a few moments, checking Adam's sleep was normal and safe.

At the end of the ward where the droid and doctor had come from, a man stood, watching. He wore a dark overcoat and suit with an old-fashioned hat, such that even in the bright light of the nurses' desk area, he still looked shaded. He glanced down at something he was holding in his hand; a palm-sized device with a readout display, and raised one eyebrow. The doctor and nurse-droid quietly left the ward. When the man saw them returning in his direction, he coolly retreated and sat in the waiting area.

The doctor walked up to him.

'You got here fast,' she said disapprovingly, 'He isn't ready to see you today, you'll have to wait until tomorrow.' The man remained silent. 'You can wait here if you want,' Dr Nustom continued, 'but if you step into that ward, I'll have you arrested.'

The man smiled. He liked this doctor. She probably knew how hard it would be to get him arrested. Her protectiveness of Adam was…comforting. He put up both hands in a placating gesture of surrender, then back down again, still smiling. The doctor left the waiting area, instructing security guards to keep an eye out for Adam, and especially, on the man.

The dark man stayed there, looking at his little sensor machine, making notes on the touchpad. After half an hour, a red light began to flash at the top of the device. The man raised both eyebrows, and glanced towards Adam. He took some further readings, smiled, and nodded to himself.

'Fascinating,' he said, so quietly that no one else could hear him, 'How extraordinarily fascinating.'

Chapter 3

Energy and light

They sat at the table in silence, all eyes trained on the enhanced holographic image dominating the centre of the large round table. No NI links were permitted during the meeting; security was watertight. Even the AIs had to rely upon visual and audio input, all transmissions in, out and within the darkened room were being blocked.

Entman had seen as much as anyone over the last twenty-four hours, and instead he studied the dark silhouettes sitting around the table. Tamura was sitting next to him, her perennially hot coffee steaming darkly in front of her. Across from him, he could make out the head of the AAA, President Esposito. To his left was the Prime Minister of Britain, Duncan Letchfield, and to his right President Bower of Australia, and down the table to the left, President Mustafa of NAUS. Entman had never been in front of such power before.

None of them however, were paying him any heed at the moment; they were all studying the footage. There were the two-hundred plus blue signatures entering the solar system, but this was largely ignored, despite the fact that each represented a craft several times larger than PC1 and, as far as scans could ascertain, were armed with enough firepower to wipe out the military and space capability of all of the Earth's nations combined. However, what concerned them most was the last object to enter the system. Seven signatures, all travelling together. Entman had made his command and the image had been amplified. There, shadowed and massive, was a single ship.

'How big is that thing?' asked Esposito.

Entman cleared his throat. 'The best measurements we have so far are in the order of around forty kilometres in length and width, sir, and ten kilometres deep,' he replied. There were gasps and whistles of amazement around the table. 'The seven signatures were only one side of the object, it has eight more engines to its rear and front, and another seven on its other side, exactly symmetrical to this side.'

There was silence as the images continued to play. The speakers in the table then repeated the hailed salutation, 'Greetings…Greetings.'

Since then, the greeting had been returned by the ISA, but nothing had been said by either side since as world governments debated on how to deal with the situation. Some of the assembled people grimaced or shook their heads.

Entman also shook his head, though at them and not the situation.

'We have no reason to suspect that they are hostile.'

'True,' said Tamura, taking a sip from her coffee, 'But the fact remains that we are more than two hundred years away from producing anything like a ship of this size and sophistication. We're completely outmatched in the event of hostility.'

'Has the captain of PC1 told us anything new?' asked Esposito.

They all looked towards a presidential aid by the name of Esther Tinsley, the ancient head of the Central Security Agency in the AAA. She passed cold eyes over the paper she had in front of her.

'We have asked and got from him everything he knows,' she said with a voice like gravel, 'He found nothing of note around Proxima Centauri. Nothing for us anyway; I suspect the scientists will be very interested in the observations made. He was travelling back to Earth when he was contacted, only minutes away from the scheduled arrival point. They were able to communicate in his language, English: this is noteworthy. We believe that the ship's databases were thoroughly scanned externally, for as long a period as two years, i.e. from the time he was at the Centauri system to the point of arrival here. Our security was not compromised as there was no sensitive information aboard ship,' she glanced at Entman, 'which would seem to justify the Agency's insistence upon the precautions taken during the pre-launch planning stage.'

Entman blushed and shifted uncomfortably; he had been resistant to Tinsley's interference.

'However,' she continued, 'it is still of some alarm that the ship's systems were so easily read without the pilot or crew being any the wiser. Nevertheless, it is my assessment that Doctor Entman's comment is correct, we have no reason to believe that they are hostile - at the moment. Doctor Tamura's observation of their technical superiority would seem to suggest the opposite of a threat: if they wanted to annihilate us, it's difficult to see why they would not have done so already.'

'You speak of their superiority,' said the Prime Minister, 'Yet the mere fact of a very large ship doesn't necessarily mean it's overwhelming, does it?'

'I'm afraid, sir, that perhaps you haven't seen the latest footage,' said Entman, 'That's one reason we wanted you all here.'

He tapped some commands into a glowing panel in front of him. The holo-image fast-forwarded, and showed the large ship slowly rotating. The ship turned and Entman paused the image. There were more gasps around the table. Entman had to disagree with the description; 'ship' was most inadequate. It wasn't a ship that had been flying through space at all.

What had flown into the solar system, and was maintaining a far orbit around Earth, was a city.

*

Adam watched the holo screen showing those images of PC1 that had managed to escape the censors. All that could be seen was the arrival of the craft, and that was it. Yet word had inevitably got around: you could tell almost as much about the importance of a situation by the defensive hiding of it, as by its disclosure.

Dr Nustom approached Adam quietly as the newscaster repeated, for what seemed to be the millionth time, the many theories on what was happening. Adam had finally managed to wake up at a decent hour, and he smiled at the doctor.

' 'morning,' she greeted him, 'Feeing well?'

'Yes thanks,' he replied. 'It's all a bit exciting isn't it?' Adam motioned towards the screen. 'What do you think's going on?'

'Can't say I know,' said Nustom, closely regarding him. 'There's another person here to see you today.'

'Who?'

'Now there's the rub,' said the doctor, 'I'm afraid I don't know much about him.' Adam frowned. 'What I do know,' she continued, 'is that he's important, has the highest security clearance - whatever that means - and the director of this hospital has cleared him, above my objections, to come and speak to you.'

'Why did you object?' asked Adam.

She shrugged. 'I don't like being kept out of the loop.'

'Can't you say I'm not well?' said Adam, 'I don't like the sound of this.'

The doctor sighed. 'Not this time,' she said, 'You're perfectly fit and well as far as I can see, you've already said you're feeling fine this morning which was the only thing I had to check; all your readouts already told me you're well. My instructions are to get you to see him at the earliest opportunity, I'm bound by that I'm afraid. Are you ready?'

'Not really,' said Adam dryly, 'But it doesn't look like I have much choice.'

'I'll have security watching you, but I'm under strict instructions not to interfere or listen in. Any problems, just hit the panic button on your wristband. Okay?'

Adam nodded. 'Okay.'

Nustom left the room.

Presently, a man came walking into the ward, steadily and quietly. He was something around six feet tall, dressed smartly in a black long-coat over a dark suit, with an old-fashioned black hat on. He stood at the foot of Adam's bed. He had a short face-hugging beard, steel grey with flecks of black in it. Something about the man's face and demeanour spoke of kindness. His eyes, however, were a contradiction. The smile-lines on either side showed warmth, but the eyes were of coldest blue. They warmed immediately however, when the man grinned, and spoke.

'How're you doing?' he asked. His voice was rich, strangely somewhere between English and North American in accent.

Adam nodded his head, silent and uncertain.

'Forgive me,' continued the man, 'I should introduce myself. My name is Michael Foxton. I work for the government.'

'Are you here about the orphanage?' asked Adam, 'I already told the police that I don't know what happened.'

'I know,' said the man. 'Is it okay if we take a walk together?'

'I'm not allowed to go off with strangers,' replied Adam.

Foxton regarded him. 'I tell you what,' he said, 'You're expecting a call from Mr Clement.' Adam raised his eyebrows in surprise: it was news to him. 'I understand you don't currently have an NI?'

'No,' said Adam, 'Not many Clement orphans have those.'

'I have a phone on me,' said Foxton, reaching into his pocket, 'Mr Clement and I are known to each other, we've crossed paths over the years, and he knows I'm here. He can say what he has to say to you, and you can ask him if it's okay - if *I'm* okay. Deal?' Foxton smiled again, his eyebrows raised quizzically.

Adam nodded, and took the phone Foxton handed to him. He saw that it was already dialling the number of the orphanage. It appeared to go direct to Mr Clement's office as presently the call was answered, and Clement's face appeared as a holo-projection above the screen.

'Adam!' said Mr Clement, 'I'm so glad to hear that you're awake and well. I'm very sorry that I couldn't be there.'

'S'okay,' said Adam, 'you must be busy.'

'Yes,' said Clement, 'I was. This whole thing has caused quite a lot of trouble you know, not to mention the rebuilding work. A lot of the orphanage's patrons are very disturbed by what happened. I know you've already spoken to the police, but I'm afraid you're going to have to answer a few questions here as well.'

'Yes,' said a familiar sharp voice, 'Especially to me.' The view enlarged to include Mr Collingdale, sitting at the side of Clement's desk. 'I won't have you coming back here and causing more trouble, so you'll have to remember what happened.'

'Yes,' said Mr Clement awkwardly, 'I'm afraid that you can't go back to the upper house until this is all sorted out, the trustees won't allow it.'

Adam beamed. 'You mean I can go back to the lower house?'

'No,' said Clement, 'I'm sorry Adam, but as I said before, it really isn't possible, it's against the laws orphanages have to follow; I can't do that.'

Adam sat back, stunned. 'Where am I supposed to go?'

'We'll have to see about that, maybe a hostel somewhere,' said Collingdale, 'but you aren't coming back here until you face the music.'

Foxton cut in. 'Hello *Ricky*,' he said.

'Who's that?' demanded Collingdale.

Adam swivelled the phone so that Foxton could be seen. He grinned down into it and took it from the boy.

'How are you?' he asked, with perfectly unmasked disingenuousness.

'The name,' said Collingdale, turning red, 'is Richard - Mr Collingdale to you.'

'Whatever,' said Foxton, 'You listen to me. You would do well to remember that you are the *deputy* head of the Clement

Orphanage - you work for Matthew. And *you* are responsible for the upper house where all of these injuries happened, and most of the funding for the orphanage comes from the State. Catch my drift?'

Collingdale sat back and shut up, glowering.

'How're you doing Matthew?' asked Foxton, smiling again, this time it seemed, without his face lying. 'Long time no see.'

'Yes,' said Clement, 'It's been years since that ugly business. I never did get to thank you properly.'

'Your mother did a good job of that, so don't worry. I was sorry to hear of her passing.'

'Of course,' replied Clement, 'I was surprised you weren't at the funeral.'

Adam was also surprised that anyone connected with the orphanage was not at the funeral. Even many of the children were there on that black, cloudy and sombre day.

'I am sorry for that too,' said Foxton, 'But duty called, as it is calling me now. I'm here on business, as we discussed.'

'Yes,' said Clement, 'With Adam. I don't suppose you could tell me what business in particular?'

Foxton shook his head. 'Need to know basis only I'm afraid. You know of the offer I have for him, the rest is private. The boy is understandably wary of me,' Collingdale muttered something about not being surprised. Foxton ignored him, 'and I need you to tell him I'm okay, and that I've passed the idea by you first.'

Foxton turned the phone back to Adam.

'Yes,' said Clement, 'Mr Foxton and I go back a long way, you're in safe hands. So just hear what he has to say, and answer any questions he has for you, okay?'

Adam nodded. 'Okay.'

They said goodbye, Mr Foxton making a perhaps immature point of calling Collingdale "Ricky" again, and telling Mr Clement to make sure he knew who was boss.

Adam was starting to like him.

'Now,' said Foxton, 'How about that walk?'

Adam was transferred shakily from his bed to a float-chair. Despite the therapeutic stimulation to his muscles and motor functions during the coma, being on his feet even briefly took a bit of getting used to. Foxton pushed him out of the ward, into the corridor, and into a lift. He said nothing to Adam on the way down, but quietly hummed a tune to himself.

'We're having a bit of an Indian Summer,' he said to Adam as he pushed him out of the back entrance of the hospital.

He was right. The weather was mild, and not cold at all; autumn had retreated. The afternoon sunshine was warm against the still partly leaved trees.

Foxton took him into the recovery gardens, an enclosed courtyard with a water fountain in the middle, a mixture of grass and paving flooring the area. They were alone.

Foxton sat down on the stone side of the area's pond, and noted Adam's general level of alertness; his stiff demeanour, and silence, and reminded himself once again of his age, injuries, recovery, and up-bringing: everything he had been briefed about. He had a mission to complete.

'I heard about what you said to the police and firemen,' he said, 'so I understand you don't know much. I'm not going to ask you any more questions about that, so don't worry.'

Adam nodded, and sat back in his chair.

Good thought Foxton, *He's relaxing*. 'I'm here to explain what I do, what I think, and a suggestion I have for you.'

'Alright,' said Adam. He was distracted by the worry of being homeless and the trouble he was in at the orphanage, but he tried to push them aside.

'You understand that anything you say to me is confidential, right?' said Foxton, 'But also, anything I say to you, you keep to yourself - deal?'

Adam nodded mutely.

Foxton began. 'I work for an arm of the government, more specifically, a research and development arm of the intelligence services. That is how I came to know Matthew; I worked on a case that involved missing children, and Matthew had a database in his possession that I needed. The sub-agency I work for now is called the Institute of Human Development. It's based in London. It only has one purpose, which I will explain. Do you know what NIs are? Neural Interfaces?' Adam nodded. 'But you don't have one.'

'No,' said Adam, 'They can't afford them in the orphanage, unless we actually need it for a medical condition.'

'And you've *never* had one?' persisted Foxton.

Adam shook his head again. 'Why?'

'Interesting,' said the man thoughtfully. He continued. 'Around ten years ago, an odd thing began to happen with them, with the NIs. Now and again, the interfaces need up-grades, repairs, or simply need replacing. During all of that, they need to be de-activated. A decade ago, it was noted that, in a very small number of cases, all of them children, when the NI was switched off, some of the abilities of the children remained. Some of them could still manipulate objects without field-tech, see much further than they should be able to, think faster, do you understand?'

Adam nodded. *No*, he thought, but he held his tongue.

'These results began to be reported in scientific journals,' Foxton continued, 'and then studied in-depth. Once we had identified the area of the brain that appeared to be over-active, giving out a specific brain-wave pattern, we found more of those children. We've swept the world Adam, and we have found ninety-nine of them.' Adam was frowning now, bewildered.

'Adam,' said Foxton, 'we think we've found the one hundredth. We found out about the incident at the orphanage when it was reported on the news. It's been a long time since we found any new children, two years, and all of our avenues have been exhausted, so we've been looking for anything out of the ordinary. Some of our employees came down to take some measurements of you. I apologise for that - it was in your sleep.' Foxton paused. 'Here's what I think. I think *you* caused that fire. And I think you blew those boys out of the window.' Adam began to shake his head, his heart beating faster, and he opened his mouth at the beginning of a protest, but Foxton held up his hand to silence him, 'Not on purpose, so don't worry. I also think that you caused the deterioration of your roommates' condition: the doctor didn't tell you that they weren't in comas when they got here. They were conscious when they were taken to the hospital - why they are in comas is unknown. Come to mention it, we don't have any idea why *you* were in a coma. Your injury wasn't bad enough for a month-long stint.' Foxton smiled, 'The good news is, I'm certain of a number of other things, among them that you genuinely aren't aware of any of this, that those two toads had it coming to them, and that all of this, for the moment, is between you and I.'

Adam deflated a little, breathing out, at once mortified, relieved - and sceptical.

'Now,' said Foxton, 'I have no proof of any of this, even what happened on that night is beyond what we have experienced with the other children we help to train. None of them can start fires or blow people out of windows. However, I have this.'

Foxton pulled out a small device he was carrying in his coat-pocket. 'This is one of the machines used to measure your brain patterns. I have to apologise again, because I've been using it to link to the machines monitoring your neural activity at the hospital. At the moment, it shows nothing out of the ordinary.' Adam put his hand up to his temple and felt one of the small rubbery sensors stuck to his head. Foxton continued, 'But when you sleep, Adam, sometimes, this thing lights up with activity. It's the same activity that the other children at the institute showed when they were awake, only more extreme and erratic, but I won't pretend I know what that means, I haven't the foggiest idea. But I'll tell you something Adam; I would love the chance to find out. So here is my proposal.' Foxton turned to face Adam more squarely, his expression intense, his frame a dark silhouette against the sky. 'I want you to come to the Institute with me. The arrangements have already been made with Mr Clement, if that's what you want.'

'You can do that?' asked Adam.

'And a hell of a lot more besides,' replied Foxton. 'Almost all of the kids have left the institute now, and you will be the youngest by a few months, but there are a couple who are around your age, really good kids, you'll like them. We'll work together on developing what I suspect are your abilities.'

Adam looked uncertain, shaking his head.

Foxton cocked his head to one side. 'There's something inside of you Adam, something wonderful,' he said. 'Right now, it's unconscious, but it's a sleeping giant. If you come with me, and work with me, together, we can wake it up.'

Adam thought carefully as he looked up at Foxton.

'When you say come with you,' asked Adam. 'Does that mean I don't have to go back to the upper house at the orphanage?'

Foxton smiled. *How could I have missed that?*

'If you come with me, you will *live* at the institute,' said Foxton, 'it's already arranged, if that's what you want. I really think you should-' Adam cut him off.

'That's all you had to say,' he said, smiling broadly, 'When do we leave?'

*

The city-ship was made of some dark material. It was perfectly circular in shape, a large disc, virtually flat on top but showing itself to be gently curved when examined closely. The underside of the object was as dark as the blackness of space, few details could be made out apart from it being more deeply curved than the topside.

On the upper surface, lights could be seen moving in conduits enclosed in translucent material. Engineers reasoned that these were some kind of highways.

Then, there were the buildings. All of them had one thing in common; they all tapered from their bases to their summits, pyramidal in conception, but their actual shapes varied from conical, to hexagonal, to the classic four-sided pyramid shape. And there were so many of them: they had counted almost two thousand so far. They varied in height from around four stories to what appeared to be the equivalent of about eighty. All of them were lit, with activity and movement apparent in most of them.

The observers had tried their best, but no hint of what kind of creature was moving around inside was visible - not one had shown itself.

Massive propulsion blisters could be seen below the edge of the city's 'horizon', now all dormant as it maintained its orbit. It was sticking fastidiously to the night-side of the moon, so none on Earth could easily make out the object. All space traffic was being kept well away; the show was reserved for those like Entman, the lucky few. What was absolutely clear however, was that this thing weighed many millions of metric tonnes, but it had arrived in the system at FTL speed.

Despite the friendly greeting, the governments of the world had received the shock of their collective tenures. Earth was not only *not* alone; it was thoroughly outmoded.

'In the circumstances,' said Esposito, 'Doctor Entman's insistence that we do not send up any military ships to meet them would seem to have been a good move. We might have given an aggressive signal,' Tinsley made a scoffing sound through her nose, but the President continued, 'and we would have been hopelessly outmatched in any event, displaying to them our weakness. I propose we change the greeting to include an invitation to meet. At the same time, I think it prudent to immediately accelerate all extra-terrestrial defence armament, production and development.' There were murmurs of assent all around the room, except from Entman, who shook his head.

'Look at the way they've operated,' Entman protested, 'They've announced their presence. They could annihilate us, but haven't. They're even on the dark side of the moon so that the 'natives' don't get scared.'

'We don't know that's their motivation,' said Tinsley.

'The point being,' said Entman, 'I think there is a danger of being overly defensive.'

'We know your views Ernie, and we respect them,' said the President, 'But we've got to be careful, a great responsibility is in our hands. We are out-matched, and have no idea what we're facing. And what does it mean for us? Why are they here? And *why the hell* have they brought *so much* weaponry? We can't discount anything right now, no matter how unpalatable.'

Entman stared at the holo-image. The sheer scale of the city-ship was staggering. The design; beautiful. The control of such mass; exquisite. Its power; unknown.

Despite himself, Entman had to agree; care was needed.

Danger was looming over them.

Chapter 4

Escape from confines

Adam looked out of the window, hypnotised by their quiet advance across the unseasonably sunny English countryside. The magnetic train they were travelling on had two rails which passed through the bottom of the train itself. The 'black bullet' was travelling at over four hundred kph, and yet the only sound that could be heard was the sound of the wind rushing by; it was almost frictionless. A field emanated from the front of the train acting as a deflector, pointed in shape to allow for minimum aerodynamic resistance with the lower parts flowing over the rails to clear any debris.

Foxton brought a ground car to pick Adam up from the hospital, and the exit from the orphanage had been remarkably swift. Adam said his goodbyes to Mr Clement, and Sam, and to no one else; he had few friends at the orphanage, and none he felt especially close to. He hoisted his bag onto his back, loaded it into the waiting car and they had left together, leaving the vehicle at the station to cruise off on some other errand.

'They had these over two hundred years ago in Japan,' said Foxton, sitting across from Adam and to his left, his back to the front of the black-bullet train, a small table separating them. 'Not as good as this of course, but, it just goes to show…'

Adam thought for a moment. He tried to be polite.

'Just goes to show what?'

A critical thinker, thought Foxton, *Good*.

'Well,' said Foxton carefully, 'for a start, how little we've progressed in the past two centuries. Not just the AAA: humanity as a whole. What do you think of that?'

'Are you starting my training, or whatever it is, already?' asked Adam.

Foxton smiled, pleased at Adam's incisiveness, then nodded. 'Why not?'

Adam looked out of the window again.

'It's all about money as far as I can see,' he said as they sped by a field of wind turbines, cows scattered around their bases, a fusion plant half-hidden behind. 'We've only progressed to where industry wants us to go. That's why space travel is so far behind other smaller technology, and why consumer goods are so close to being cutting-edge.' He looked back at Foxton and smiled diffidently, shrugged his shoulders. 'At least, that's what I've read anyway.'

'Well you read right,' said Foxton, nodding approvingly, 'The organisation that created the Institute of Human Development, and which I ultimately answer to, is called HADD.'

'The Human Association of Defence and Development,' said Adam, 'I've heard of you. Your aim is to protect humanity, like in Warmang.'

'Sort of,' replied Foxton, 'Warmang's a good example. There are few humans on earth who could match the killing power of those machines. We needed a variety of strategies to overcome them, including the use of other AIs. That's a dangerous dependency. HADD exists to make sure that humanity does not sleepwalk into an evolutionary trap: becoming so advanced that we can create things to take care of every need, and in the process becoming so dependent upon them that we cause our own extinction. We have a saying within HADD; Luxury is our enemy, consumerism our parasite, indolence our death.'

'What does that mean?'

'It means what you see all around you,' replied Foxton, 'We have genetic engineering, but still we see obesity everywhere as people eat fatty-sugary-salty foods to the new limits of their biology, relying on their enhancements and NIs, employing surgeries and chemicals on themselves rather than self-discipline and exercise. Thinking machines become more advanced as each year brings the kind of developments in technology that take millions of years in biological evolution, leaving humanity behind. At the same time, we get left even further behind, even regressing, as we focus less and less on personal and collective development in favour of things that don't matter; playing games and pampering ourselves in leisure time, obsessed with mindless superficialities like fashion and modern art. Consumer culture is even in our minds now; you should see our NI-icons – they're bespoke tailored to the point of being *cutesy*. The NI is used mainly by the masses for leisure and ease rather than advancement. HADD aims to counter that tendency, to keep humanity moving forward, to protect it from falling asleep - and never waking up.'

'So, are NIs a waste of time?' asked Adam, wondering if something he had always wanted was in fact, useless.

'No,' answered Foxton, 'I shouldn't be too critical - there are a lot of benefits. Plugs enable people and computers to live in symbiotic relationships to whatever degree is desired, allowing us to have capabilities far in excess of our natural state. AIs interact with hardware to do a multitude of things, and now we can do the same. NIs can link with satellites, giant telescopes peering into space, seeing lightyears away in brilliant 3D detail, images sent directly to your mind with no need for screens, or pilot planes and ships with no manual controls. Communications have been revolutionised. People can send and receive messages from mind to mind via the Ninet - it's virtual telepathy. All of that, installed in our brains. The medical benefits have altered health profoundly. The standard NI package includes a complete map of a person's DNA - an owner's manual for the body with interactive analysis, monitoring and regulation including early diagnosis and treatment for thousands of illnesses. People who haven't been genetically screened adequately before birth can get the first sign of disease picked up and the person notified, while treatment begins in the body itself before a doctor even sees you. It's also greatly reduced illicit drug use - any experience, whether intellectual, sensual or ascetic can be gained in the comfort and safety of an armchair.'

'But we still have addicts,' said Adam, 'I heard we even have NI addicts.'

'True,' said Foxton, 'It can be addictive. Anything a human enjoys to an extremity can do that. And the fact that if a person wants to experience those things that in earlier times preceded addiction; the highs, the rush - then they can, doesn't help. All NI-programmes have a legal cut-off point when the midbrain dopamine system is suppressed, and so addiction can be avoided. However, that can be turned off. There's always someone who *wants* to be addicted, to experience withdrawal - to suffer.' Foxton shrugged, 'So much for human progress.'

'Are there people who choose not to have NIs?' asked Adam.

'A few, there have been dissenters,' replied Foxton, 'They argued that it would lead to a two-tier humanity, or that it was unnatural, or indeed, that it was unhealthy for humanity to depend so heavily on technology. Those arguments were swept aside when it was pointed out that if biotronic technology did not progress, then the development of artificial intelligences would race far ahead of humanity. As this diaspora of sentient hardware grows in size and strength, the results to an outmoded humankind might be disastrous. And no one would say that genetic engineering or the re-growing of limbs and organs was natural, or the artificial organs of bionics, yet it's old and accepted biotechnology. Necessity drives progress, and humanity needs those advantages.'

Just then, the snacks trolley came to their seats. 'Would you like any drinks, snacks or sandwiches?' asked the pleasant male voice, displaying each on the screen on its front.

Foxton looked at Adam, who shook his head.

'No, thank you,' said Foxton, and the trolley moved on. 'That's where our technology has gone, mainly on wants rather than progress. Good thing or bad?'

'Well,' replied Adam, 'given all the stuff going on right now with the ISA and Proxima Centauri One, I think we might have fewer problems if we had developed ourselves a bit more.'

'Do you know what's going on?' asked Foxton. He pointed upwards, 'Up there?'

Adam shook his head. 'Not really,' he admitted, 'only that something's wrong. Do you?'

Foxton smiled at him. An eager look spread over Adam's face, and he leaned forward, his mouth clogged with a jam of questions. Foxton put up both hands and shook his head.

'First lesson for you,' said Foxton, 'self-control. Learn the value of silence. Second, awareness of environment; this may not be the right time and place.' Then he smiled again. 'Though I have to admit, I led you on.' He in turn leaned closer to Adam and said quietly, 'So, I'll tell you another time.'

Adam grinned back at him, then looked out of the window again.

The train, now past Bristol airport, came to the end of the tracks and soared smoothly into the air, a slim black dragon piercing the sky. The hum of anti-grav generators now added to the rush of the wind. Adam gripped his armrests, felt the strange feeling in his stomach as the view expanded, and then looked at Foxton.

'They had this in Japan two hundred years ago?'

Foxton chuckled, 'Not quite.'

The older man put his big feet up on to the seat next to Adam. His shoes were off, earning a grimace from Adam and a protest that they didn't smell from Foxton. The older man smiled as he put his hat down over his eyes and settled in for a snooze.

Adam regarded him for a few moments. He had to admit, he was starting to warm to the man. *Not trust him though*, he said to himself, turning to look back out of the window, *There's no need for that*.

Foxton glanced at Adam through half-lidded eyes shaded by his hat, then closed them completely. He sub-vocalised, and his icon came up. It was, inevitably, a fox. In his younger days it used to be a common red, but was now handsome white arctic, albeit one that stood on two legs and could speak and, it would seem, sip some sort of drink out of the glass it was holding in its paw.

'Did you manage to contact the others?' asked Foxton.

'Yes,' replied the icon, 'they are waiting for you. Conference en persona?'

'Yes,' replied Foxton.

He felt the dizzying sensation of entering the NI-net en persona. He flew past his icon, to a door that opened silently. He glided through it, out over what looked like a landscape grid of finely interlaced wires, glowing and pulsating with activity and information. The sky above him had clouds in it, but was itself an even dark blue, completely uniform.

Most others never saw this part, only aware of being in one place and then in another for contact, but Foxton had the clearance necessary to ensure he knew his environment at all times. He flew on and upwards until he reached a plateau in the sky. It was a large circular disc, metres across but only millimetres thick, crystalline and entirely translucent, with nothing supporting it. There were some clouds below it, but nothing else within view. He floated to a gate at the edge that opened for him and shut behind him, landed and sat down at one seat set next to a floating glass table. There were two other occupied seats. One of those seated was a woman who looked Eurasian, the other was a man who looked Chinese, both in their forties.

'I tried contacting you earlier Nat,' said Foxton as he sat down.

'I know,' said the woman, 'I was in classes, sorry.'

'That's alright,' said Foxton. He noticed the other man was drinking some tea.

'Q, what is this new fad for drinking while on the net?' he asked, 'I find it disorientating to come back and find that I haven't drunk anything. Makes me thirsty.'

'Me too,' said Qiang Zhao, 'Only I am actually drinking tea right now. Makes it easier for me to carry on without spilling the stuff everywhere.'

Foxton nodded. 'Very clever. I ought to try that. I've got the boy with me.'

'Yes, real Chinese tea,' said Zhao, 'Not that stuff you English stole from the Indians.'

'Well, I'm half American, but as I was saying-'

'-back when you were English colonialist pigs-'

'Zhao, can we please focus?' demanded Foxton.

'Sorry.'

'How is he?' asked Doctor Natalie Cengo.

'Fine, as far as I can see,' replied Foxton. 'He's a little guarded. His daytime readings are, surprisingly, completely normal - same as us.'

'So not like the other kids?' asked Zhao.

'No,' said Foxton, 'nothing like theirs. But there's the readings from the hospital in his sleep. Did you get a chance to review them?'

The other two nodded.

'They're as high and active as when the others are most elevated and engaged,' said Cengo, 'Doesn't make sense. This one's gonna be really interesting. Means a lot of work.'

Zhao murmured his agreement while sipping his tea.

'Is everything ready at the institute?' asked Foxton.

'Yes,' said Cengo, 'We put him right next-door to Mr Charming.'

'All of the precautions you ordered have been installed,' said Zhao, 'Mr Charming should be safe if Adam turns out to be dangerous. What do you think?'

Foxton mulled for a few moments, then shrugged.

'I don't know. Just have to wait and see. Any hint of imminent danger and I would have put him in a separate building. As long as Mr Charming doesn't hit him in the head while he's sleeping, I think we're alright. Apart from that, I have no idea what to expect. We're definitely dealing with damaged goods here, though.'

'Of course,' said Cengo, 'What orphan isn't damaged?'

'It complicates things,' said Zhao, 'He has an emotional dimension that the others do not. Maybe that is why his abilities are suppressed.'

'Could be,' said Foxton. 'It's an interesting point you've just raised. None of the others have that issue: no significant traumas in their childhood. They've all been well looked after.'

'That's been noted before,' said Cengo, 'Though I guess the psychological impact hasn't been looked into very much. Raises the old question I suppose; who's been looking out for them before they got to us?'

None of them spoke for a few seconds. Foxton shrugged again.

'This one is significantly different from the others,' he said, 'If there was someone looking out for them, then in this case something went wrong. Maybe this is the one that'll explain it all.' Foxton got up. 'Make sure Mr Charming knows what he's getting into. Tell him about the fire in the orphanage as well as the attack that probably provoked the whole thing. If he's uncomfortable with the proximity, let him back out without any pressure. In fact, suggest it to him; I don't want him on board unwillingly. If he's okay with it, I want it to be him and Adam alone, no friends, no distractions: I want a gentle intro for the boy.'

The others nodded their assent, and Foxton was first to the gate. He said goodbye, then jumped.

*

They reached London Paddington in about fifteen minutes and caught a hover-taxi. Adam stared around him as the vehicle rose above the rooftops, joining a row of air-traffic, shifting backwards as the car picked up speed.

His neck was beginning to hurt with all of the craning. He had never been to any big city before; not even Bristol, and that was near-by. The orphanage had never been big on day-trips. He had never seen such big buildings before except on TV, but had read all about them. Other countries had larger ones, but the skyscrapers of London were still impressive.

Even more impressive were the 'space-scrapers,' of which only one was allowed near London, but a further three were on mainland Britain. The buildings did not actually go high enough to qualify as entering space, but at a minimum of two kilometres high, the name was generally accepted.

Much of the bodies' of the buildings were used as conventional office space, but the upper echelons were often reserved for scientific and leisure activity. The larger lifts were designed to be used for the launches of small satellites and crafts before the wide use of anti-gravity technology made it largely obsolete. However, they were retained for the rare launch of old-fashioned craft. The smaller lifts were regularly used for hugely lucrative leisure activities such as extreme skydiving. There were also plenty of opportunities for astronomy as the tops of the buildings were often above the clouds, again a hugely popular activity, especially when combined with a romantic dinner or a short trip to the city.

The one Adam could see was clearly visible despite being several kilometres away, east of the Liverpool Street Port. It was shaped like an elongated pyramid with concave sides sloping elegantly inwards and upwards, coloured black and silver. The silver parts he could just about discern, were metallic condensation aqueducts; giant conduits channelling condensed water vapour into icy streams from the upper levels. They coalesced, channelled by the building's designers into torrents that were then collected for the city's consumption. In truth, the main reason was aesthetic - the city did not particularly need the aqueducts, it simply looked beautiful. Each building would have the equivalent of a well-controlled mountain stream to a side, and as many waterfalls as they liked, with decorated tiered pools at various levels around the lower hundred floors, often with suitable gardens and rockeries glittering like gems encrusted on the surface of the massive structure. Also, as was usual, the London scraper had a garden moat full of fish and wildlife surrounding the base.

Foxton glanced at Adam to check he had noted the structure, the upper parts shrouded in low-lying clouds making it appear a building base with the head fading away like a decapitated ghost, and returned his smile, pleased at his excitement.

'Be good, and we'll see about taking you there,' said Foxton.
'Fantastic!' said Adam, 'Um, what's "good"?'
'I really don't know,' said Foxton, 'We'll have to work that one out.'

Whereas Bath still celebrated its Roman heritage, determined to stick to tradition, London seemed to be an odd mix of antiquity and the pursuit of the hyper-modern. The London space-scraper could be seen on Adam's left as he faced the front of the cab, but he could also see that they were heading towards the ancient Palace of Westminster.

'Where exactly are we going?' he asked.

Foxton raised the glass separating them from the driver.

'It's in the centre of London,' he replied, 'Near to an old university called the School of Oriental and African Studies.'

Adam noted the raised screen.

'I'm sorry,' he said, 'Is it a sort of secret place?'

'Somewhat,' replied Foxton, 'We don't advertise it. After the initial scientific interest, we decided reticence was best. Truth is, we still aren't entirely sure how people will react if and when they find out about you and the others. My guess is they'll react with nothing more dangerous than intense interest, seeing as many people can have the same abilities with the use of NIs.'

Adam frowned. 'If the same abilities can be got from NIs, what's the point of your institute?'

'A fair question,' replied Foxton, 'You ever heard the saying, "don't put all your eggs in one basket"?'

Adam nodded. 'You're spreading your risk.'

Foxton regarded Adam carefully; that was an *adult* assessment.

'That's right,' he replied, 'Any human system must have multiple redundancy; if one thing fails, another must survive to be utilised. So we develop people like you at the institute. Back to your original question, it pays to be careful, and we figure that our best advice to you is to keep it to yourself.'

'We?' asked Adam.

He doesn't miss anything, thought Foxton, *I'll have to watch this one, and report on it.*

'Us at the institute,' he replied. 'There are only three permanent members of staff now, with various others who visit to observe and teach now and again. By the way, you're still under eighteen, so you'll have to comply with the law and learn the school curriculum.'

Adam groaned.

'Why the moaning?' asked Foxton, 'You have brilliant grades from the orphanage, I thought you'd like work.'

'I'm good at it,' said Adam, 'but I'm lazy.'

Foxton chuckled. 'Well,' he said, 'at least you're honest. But I expect you to make an effort to work hard both in that area and in the areas of self-development, in particular of those abilities we spoke of earlier. Your intellectual talents are just as important. I think, for now, that's what I mean by you being "good". Deal?'

Adam nodded. 'Deal.'

However, privately, Adam was beginning to wonder if he had those abilities, whatever they were. Apart from what had happened, which he didn't remember, he simply did not know anything about it, or if any of it was true. It appeared that Foxton had a gift for mindreading.

'Don't you worry,' he said, 'I have confidence in you. It's our job to bring out in you whatever we see is potentially there, you just relax and enjoy the ride.'

Adam decided that it was quite a good idea, and he sat back and continued to look at the city around him.

Presently, they came to a part of town with many trees, next to a large square. The taxi peeled away from the stream of air traffic, and Adam could see what appeared to be students and teachers coming in and out of a sprawling set of buildings, but the Taxi did not stop there.

'Is that the university you spoke about?' he asked.

Foxton nodded.

The taxi sailed over the area and traversed a wide boulevard, then to the left, where some grand and antique buildings could be seen. The taxi gently landed in a space in front of one of the buildings. Foxton paid, and they said goodbye to the 'driver' (who had in fact spent the entire journey looking at news reports) and alighted from the taxi. They faced a row of tall Georgian buildings adorned in cream and grey stonework, with modern high-rises behind them. Foxton gestured with open arms.

'Welcome to the Institute,' he said.

Foxton approached the building, Adam following behind, wondering how Foxton could tell this was the right one; they all looked so similar. They ascended some broad stairs and Foxton stood still for a moment for the entry scanner, which took a second to inspect his iris.

'Plus one, self-authorised,' said Foxton, and the double doors opened. They entered and Adam got his first glimpse of his new home.

The reception was lavish, with marble floors and pillars to each side, and a wide high desk in the middle. Unlike most receptions however, to either side of the desk there were the glowing lights of the 'seek and nullify' Techminke system, able to detect metal, explosive materials, weapons materials such as laser and plasma power cells, and even gunpowder.

Foxton greeted the guard on duty.

'How's it going John?' he asked.

'Fine, thanks,' said the guard, 'good to see you back, lieutenant.'

Foxton gestured towards Adam, 'This is Adam: our newest addition.'

'Wow,' said John, 'After all this time, who'd have thought you'd find another one? Pleased to meet you, Adam.'

Adam awkwardly murmured he was pleased to meet him too.

Foxton went through the scanner on the right, and gestured to Adam to follow him through the two-metre high-steel brackets. As they went through, the alarm went off, chiming urgently along with the message,

'Multiple high-density weapons signatures detected.'

Foxton apologised and asked John to turn the alarms off, as he hefted a large gun with three barrels in a triangular formation out of his coat. Adam was a little shocked, but John seemed unfazed. However, when they went through again, the alarm went off again with the same message. This time Adam apologised, telling the guard that there was some metal in his bag in the form of his belt buckles, lamp and a pencil case.

John asked Adam to put the bag through the belt-scanner to the side. The alarm went off again but the guard turned it off quickly, saying that the scanner showed it was fine, just the things Adam had said. Then they walked through, Adam collecting his bag on the other side. They faced a large hallway with two elevators on either side of it and they entered one of the lifts, the alarm spluttering behind them to the curses of John trying to shut it down.

Just as the doors were closing, they opened again, and Adam's eyes widened as another man got in. His face was human, but his skull, one of his eyes, and most of the left-hand side of his body appeared mechanical, all smooth metal and synthetic parts. Adam shrank back against the far side of the lift as the cyborg stepped inside, his one eye on Adam, the other artificial one a dark glassy green, unblinking.

'What floor Roland?' asked Foxton.

'Second please,' said the cyborg, his voice clearly electrically enhanced. 'How are you, Michael?'

'Yeah, fine thanks,' replied Foxton. 'This is Adam. Adam, Roland Featherstone.'

Adam smiled, and tried to breathe more easily.

'Hi there,' said Roland, looking down at Adam. 'So this is the new one, fancy that. He looks a little scared. Welcome to the institute, I look forward to teaching you.'

The lift stopped, and the doors opened, 'Well, my stop,' said Roland, and he strode out, saying goodbye over his shoulder, whirring sounds coming from his joints as he walked. Adam breathed easier once the doors closed again.

'Seventh floor,' Foxton commanded before the lift ascended again.

'I've never seen a cyborg before,' said Adam.

'Of course you have,' said Foxton, 'Drop your preconceived ideas. We're all cyborgs now to some degree or another, all except people like you. Roland is just an Upper-Level Cyborg. That means he's had a lot more extensive work done, and it's much more obvious, in his case because he needed to urgently. And don't worry, he won't be teaching you for years yet. We have less obviously enhanced people for your junior level.'

'Did he get a disease or something?' asked Adam.

'No,' replied Foxton, 'Most of him was blown off in a military campaign. The cybernetics were added as emergency features of his anatomy, but he just kept it. I don't think he wants the discomfort of extensive re-growth; he's had enough.' He turned to look at Adam. 'And in case you were wondering, yes, you've been travelling with a cyborg all the way here. I didn't bite, did I?'

Adam stared at him. 'Really?'

'Of course,' said Foxton, 'Most people who work in intelligence, the military or security services have significant degrees of enhancement, cybernetic, bio-tronic, genetic or otherwise. You'll get used to it, and when you get older, will probably do it yourself, though perhaps,' he paused, looking at Adam intently, 'perhaps *you* won't need to. Anyway, let's get you settled in.' He smiled. 'This building is deceptive from the outside, it's actually very big, and is directly connected to the high-rise behind us. We have over a hundred rooms here; a gymnasium, a swimming pool, games area, martial arts training gym, various small weapons training facilities, as well as classrooms and some living areas, much of it now unused. Most of the participants in the programme have grown up and moved on, so you'll have the run of the place, along with Ijaz.'

The doors to the lift opened, and they exited into a hallway.

'Ijaz is the only other intern here,' continued Foxton, 'the other participant commutes here, as do the older graduates of the institute whenever there's a reason to come.'

'I thought you said you got them from all over the world, and that there were ninety-nine of them?'

'Yes,' said Foxton, 'But most of them are rich, all of them in fact. Most of them have accommodation of their own or can afford to travel.'

Adam went quiet, a sinking feeling within him. *They were all rich?* All he had was the clothes he had on, and the bag on his shoulder. He suddenly felt his poverty more keenly than he ever had.

They stopped at a door, a number 15 written in brass on it, and Foxton knocked. There was a clatter of things being put down quickly, and the door was opened.

'Hey! Mr Foxton! How you doing?' said a smiling light-skinned afro-Caribbean face appearing around the door. The boy was around the same age as Adam, but typically, he seemed to be quite a bit bigger than him, though smaller than Foxton. His accent was American.

'I'm fine Ijaz,' replied a smiling Foxton, shaking Ijaz's hand, 'You?'

'I'm fine, I'm fine,' said Ijaz. 'Come in,' he said, opening the door wide and gesturing them to enter. 'I was just tidying up in here for the new guy. Adam right?' He held out his hand, and Adam, rather embarrassed by his enthusiasm, smiled back awkwardly and shook it. 'I'm glad to meet you,' he said, still pumping Adam's hand, 'I'm Ijaz. It's good to have you, I was getting lonely up here all by myself. I hope you don't mind being next door to me.'

Adam was surprised. 'I hope you don't mind having me,' he replied, 'I'm the intruder I think.'

Ijaz shook his head. 'No, no,' he replied, 'You don't worry about that. I've been here for over a year all by myself since the last intern graduated and moved on. The nights get lonely, y'know? I need a girlfriend really but in the meantime I guess talking to you'll have to do.'

They all laughed, and Foxton clapped his hands on their shoulders.

'You're on your own?' asked Adam, looking between Ijaz and Foxton.

'That's right,' said Foxton, 'If you stay here, it will be just you and Ijaz most of the time, and the house systems. We don't nanny you here, and only rarely do any of the teachers stay here. Ijaz is older, so he gets to be in charge, but any problems get referred to me, okay?' Adam nodded. 'Now, I have to see some people upstairs, so I'm going to leave Adam to settle, in your capable hands Ijaz.'

'No problem,' said Ijaz, 'I'll take good care of him.'

Foxton said goodbye and the two were left alone.

Adam studied Ijaz for a moment. He had a two-inch deep uneven afro, as was the current fashion, a thin and uneven adolescent beard, and he clearly liked looking good as he was dressed in some of the most fashionable clothes Adam had ever seen up close. He looked around the room. It was spacious and bright with a large window taking up much of one wall, and with modern furnishings. There was an en-suite shower as well as a small kitchen.

'Erm,' he said awkwardly, 'where am I going to sleep?'

'Through here,' said Ijaz, walking to another door set into the wall on the left side of the room. He opened it, and motioned Adam through.

Adam walked in, and whistled. There was a room identical to Ijaz's, though it seemed a little more tidy.

'Number seventeen,' said Ijaz, 'The kitchen doesn't work, they blocked off all the gas for some reason.'

Adam blushed and decided not to explain; he wasn't sure he could.

'But don't worry,' said Ijaz, 'you can come to mine any time you want to cook. Also, we'll be eating out a lot, 'cause we're gonna have a great time. Now, if you put your things down and freshen up, I can take you on a tour, okay? Tell me when you're ready.'

Ijaz sauntered out of the room, and closed the door behind him. Adam looked around him, surveying the large, well furnished, sunny and new-looking room. It had a big single bed, one double sofa, a bedside table with a lamp, a closet and a chest of drawers on the other side of it. Even the walls were nice, he reflected, an off-white colour making it look warm. It felt warm too.

This will do nicely, he thought, *very nicely indeed.*

He unpacked his bag into some drawers next to his bed, and took a few moments to freshen up in the bathroom, complete with a bath, shower, and full-body blow dryer. He came out, fresh and smiling, and knocked on the door to Ijaz's room.

'Who is it?' sang Ijaz in a high-pitched imitation of a woman's voice.

Adam laughed. 'It's me, can I come in?'

Ijaz let him in, then together, they explored the institute.

Chapter 5
To find a new place

Jowitz, dissenting:

I am not a monster. That these are children has not escaped my notice. It is all the other children, *our* children, that lead me to make one final attempt to sway you. I point out once again, that we have been unable to locate the source of these children, despite this organization containing some of the finest and most well-connected intelligence operatives in the world. Our efforts have yielded no results: nil. We are also left with no inkling as to what these children will be able to do in the future. We are told that they are human. So be it. We have decided they may not be neutered, despite my attempt to amend this motion. This means that they will breed. The result is the real possibility of a two-tier humanity. On the one-hand there will be the human, and on the other, an emerging aristocracy of power that will dominate us. One cannot work up to being one of 'them'. A caste system will develop, and the rest of us will be at the bottom of it. In generations to come, I greatly fear the enslavement of our great-grandchildren by theirs.

Murdock, dominant:

I thank my friend for his comments, and understand his fears. I must however remind him of the reason for the existence of this organisation: the spread of sentient machines. You all remember the horror of Warmang; machines will only be as rational as their makers. The need for humans to develop is absolutely paramount, and these children certainly represent that development. They show none of the personality traits leading to suspicion of danger from them. My colleague has also misspoken. It is obvious that marriage and inter-breeding *will* bridge the gap, given time. First of all with each other, and then when there are sufficient numbers, with the original population, our grandchildren. Genetic engineering and enhancement have already resulted in a human divide, but progress is unstoppable, because it is a necessity. That is why I have proposed not annihilation, but nurture of the Kinetics. Not enslavement for us, but empowerment, putting us on a more equal footing with AIs.

Jowitz, dissenting:
If you are against me, then I urge upon you this: Caution! Danger lies therein! Unequal development is our enemy, machine or Kinetic, we may swap one potential enslavement for another.

Foxton, dominant:
If I may. Have no fear, vigilance is the watchword. If any of them show the pathological, destructive, or racist tendencies that may pose a real threat to us, then rest assured, at our hands, death will meet them.

> *Extract, final secret meeting of the HADD on the policy recommendation to the AAA regarding the Kinetics, adolescent stage. This decision marked the foundation of the only educational institution for Kinetics: The Institute of Human Development.*

Foxton and Murdock faced-off across the table on the eighth floor of the institute. The office was spacious, with views of the city dominated by other low-rises and leafy streets. The atmosphere in the room however, was another matter.

'I can't say I understand your anger,' said Foxton.

'You can't understand?' said a red-faced Murdock, 'I am the head trustee of this institute, and I was only told this morning that a new Kinetic had been found!'

'We only *suspect* he's a Kinetic,' said Foxton. 'And you're right, you are a trustee, not a director - you have no say in any of the day-to-day running of this institute, with all due respect to you Minister.'

Murdock's wrinkly visage glowered at Foxton. He was getting older, in the order of ninety years with thinning grey hair. He had held positions in governments for almost twenty of those years. He showed every aspect of being the loving godfather of the IHD, and Foxton had never seen him like this before, never even a hint of indignation or territorial instinct. He figured the man must have some fire to have survived in government for so long, but for it to come out now didn't make any sense at all.

'What if the boy's dangerous?' Murdock asked at length, 'I have it on good authority that he caused a fire in that orphanage, and that's how he came to our notice.'

'What authority?' asked Foxton. *So*, he thought, *you've got spies somewhere*.

'Never you mind about that,' snapped Murdock, 'Just answer me. What if he is?'

'He's being monitored twenty-four-seven,' said Foxton, 'and I have Ijaz looking after him, with orders to report anything out of the ordinary.'

'Does Ijaz know of the dangers?' asked Murdock.

'Yes,' said Foxton, 'but I don't think there are any. What happened in the orphanage is unlikely to happen again.' He leaned closer to Murdock, and spoke more evenly, 'Joseph, what's really going on here? You've never questioned me like this before, never taken such a belligerent interest in what goes on so long as it all ends okay. Something's wrong. We're friends, tell me, what is it?'

Murdock tugged at one of his long ears, sighed, and sagged a little.

'I'm sorry,' he said, reaching forwards to pat Foxton's hand on the table, 'forgive me. I think…it's this alien business. Everything's so uncertain right now. They come out of nowhere, and all of a sudden we have a new Kinetic, out of the blue, after two years. Makes you wonder: is it a coincidence? Where's he from? How powerful is he?'

Foxton nodded, 'Things are moving quickly, I know. It's natural to be nervous, we're dealing with momentous events up there. As for Adam, I can't answer your questions for you, but there are unknowns about all of these kids, that's the one thing we always *have* known. And yes, each younger trainee tends to be more powerful than the last, as we observed about Ijaz and Ariana; they're vastly more gifted than their older counterparts, superior by an order of magnitude. We think they'll be able to match some of the best field technology we have one day. Adam is younger still and, if he was responsible for what happened in that orphanage, yes, his abilities are something we have not experienced before.'

Murdock noticeably paled. 'Have you taken DNA samples yet?'

'That would be illegal,' replied Foxton.

Murdock chuckled, and waited for a straight answer. Finally, Foxton relented.

'He's as human as the other Kinetics. I've been speaking to him, I've reviewed his records, and even taken readings of his brainwaves. He shows nothing that would indicate he's a danger, any more than the others.'

Murdock nodded, and rubbed his eyes. 'Do something for me, then. Watch this boy like a hawk. These are strange times, we just can't be complacent.'

'I was watching him closely anyway,' replied Foxton, 'and I'm not sure your fears are justified. But I agree, this is a delicate time, and a strange case even for us, so I'll pay him special attention.'

Murdock had an idea.

'Who is his guardian?' he asked.

'Officially, still the orphanage,' Foxton replied, 'They have the power to delegate duties and care, and that's what they've done in this case, to the institute.'

Murdock shook his head. 'No,' he said, 'I want *you* to take over guardianship of him. Will you do that? It'll enable you to keep closer tabs on him. You can give him an allowance, paid for by the institute, I'll sort it out. It's important the boy doesn't feel left out, marginalized, inferior. It could lead to him being frustrated and angry.' Murdock looked down at the table, shaking his head, a sorrowful look on his face, 'He must have had a hard life. We must try to alleviate any lingering resentment in him.'

Foxton nodded. 'I'm not much of a one for fathering, never had any kids of my own, but in the circumstances it sounds like a wise idea.' He thumped his fist on the table, 'I accept. He's a good kid. You'll sort out the legals?'

'Of course,' said Murdock, hand outstretched to shake Foxton's, 'and once again, I'm sorry, I know I'm getting paranoid in my old age, but...'

'It's no problem at all,' said Foxton. 'You and I are friends and allies on the same side. Always.'

'Yes,' said Murdock, 'always.'

*

It was rare for Adam to enjoy anyone's company. This was especially with anyone loud, confident or overpowering. The rumbustious Ijaz was certainly all of those things, but he was also overwhelmingly warm, and obviously working his hardest to take care of Adam. They walked together around the institute, and on Ijaz's invitation, Adam questioned him.

'You're American?'

'Yup,' said Ijaz, 'That's why I'm here on my own. My parents need to attend to business in the States, and I really wanted to come here once I understood what it was all about.'

There were only five people there, as it was a Saturday, but Ijaz introduced him to the few people present, often while hugging Adam's shoulders and calling him as his 'new friend'.

Hugging was again usually anathema to Adam. However, new situations tended to send his self-confidence running for cover, until familiarity defeated his timidity, so he didn't mind.

Adam was shown the lower floors first. He learned that the ground floor was entirely devoted to security and basic admin. The first floor had the teacher's staff and training rooms, the second housed the classrooms. The third floor contained the weights, fitness and physical therapy room. The fourth housed the institute's medical facilities, including the larger neural and psychometric test instrumentation. Fifth was for the sports hall and gymnasium, and martial arts. The sixth floor was for classrooms and the canteen. The seventh was for accommodation, and the eighth was for the teachers, trustees and directors of the institute, board meetings, and according to Ijaz, "other boring things." The basement was home to the swimming pool and sauna. Adam was trying to take it all in.

'This is too much,' he said as they sat together in Ijaz's room later that day, 'I have no idea what I've taken on here. Bloody hell.'

Ijaz lounged on his bed while Adam sat on the long sofa in the room.

'No, man,' replied Ijaz, 'You'll get shown what to do one thing at a time, and the other only people in any of your classes will be me and Ariana. You'll love it here, they can bring things out in you that you didn't even know you had. They go at your pace. Truth is, I don't think they have any idea how fast to go themselves, so they just see how far they can take things with you. *You* set the pace.'

'Right,' said Adam, a little mollified, 'I guess I haven't got a choice. I can't go back to the orphanage.'

Ijaz thought for a moment. It was the longest time he had remained quiet since they had been in each other's company. 'Good,' he said, 'I'm glad you can't go back there. That'll force you to give this place a chance, and enjoy it.' He looked Adam square in the face. Eventually, Adam smiled, and Ijaz nodded, satisfied that Adam understood. 'You'll be cool, don't worry about a thing.'

Adam thought for a moment. 'What are the rules here?'

Ijaz made a noise. 'None really. There's the normal stuff. You aren't allowed to use your abilities to hurt anyone. But you ain't allowed to use your foot to hurt anyone, so it's all the same really. Oh, and I've been told that, for the moment, while they get you started, I'm not allowed to use my abilities around you. They want you to settle in first, and get taught properly. You wanna go out later? I'm getting hungry. I'll pay, Mr Foxton's gonna take care of the money afterwards.'

Adam beamed, and said ok.

There was a knock at the door. Ijaz got up and opened it, and Foxton strode in, saying hello.

'Everything okay?' he asked.

'Yes,' said Adam, 'Ijaz is taking good care of me.'

'Good,' said Foxton. 'Listen, I have another proposition for you, Adam. I want you to think on it carefully. There's still the issue of your guardianship. If you agree, I will take that on personally.'

'Oh,' said Adam uncertainly, 'What will that mean exactly?'

'For starters,' said Foxton, 'It'll mean I give you an allowance, so you can buy some stuff for yourself. Also, I get to boss you around like I'm your dad, and you get to throw it in my face whenever you have a tantrum, telling me that I'm not your real dad and will never be and that no-one loves you, yada yada...'

Adam chuckled. Ijaz was smiling in the background, but retaining a respectful silence, aware, despite Foxton's levity, that something important was happening.

'It's not quite an adoption,' said Foxton, 'it just transfers legal responsibility for you from the orphanage to me directly for as long as you're here.'

Adam regarded Foxton. He wasn't sure he was ready to trust anyone enough to let them be some kind of guardian. But, what harm could it do?

'Okay,' he said finally. 'I don't know what to say. Thank you.'

Foxton came forward, awkwardly, and shook Adam's hand, the boy rising from his seat to meet him. As Foxton did so, he became aware of an enormous burden, and felt a little guilty. He had ultimately agreed to this at the instigation of someone who seemed to have a great distrust of Adam. Truthfully, Foxton had taken a paternalistic concern for the boy: he felt for him. He also liked him, he really did seem like a good kid. That the origins of his guardianship were murky set a determination in him. He was certain that the handshake they shared was hopelessly inadequate for the significance of the moment. He was determined that his guardianship should not share the same deficiency.

'I'm going to take good care of you boy,' he said to Adam, 'Don't you worry. Trust me.'

Adam simply looked at him uncertainly, and said nothing, smiling a little. Behind his smile, his mind worked. *No, I won't trust you - not yet.*

'If you need anything,' said Foxton, 'you can ring me on the internal phone next to your bed, Room 38. Oh, and if you two girls want to speak, do it face-to-face as the internal network costs money.'

When Foxton left, with Adam and Ijaz preparing to go out, Foxton did not depart entirely, but stood outside the closed door for a while, deep in thought. He was caught by the contrast between the innocence of these children, and the Earth-shattering events unfolding above them. As yet they did not know, but soon they would. Along with everyone else, they would inevitably be worried. The Kinetics, he considered, would have more reason than most to be concerned. If Murdock himself, the godfather of the IHD and the Kinetics programme, was suspicious of Adam, then what of the general population? All of the Kinetics might be in danger. Foxton thought of Adam specifically; what dreadful timing. He wanted to be able to nurture the boy, to bring out his talents, but if he had the gift, then the danger of him and to him might overtake academic and altruistic concerns. He shook his head, and sighed.

'I will take care of him,' said Foxton to himself, quietly but aloud, as if to emphasise its truth, 'I will.'

*

The next day, Adam had his medical checks on the fourth floor, a doctor in attendance. Murdock was both true and swift to his word, and the legal papers for the transference of Adam's guardianship were ready by the evening. Foxton solemnly took

Adam aside before they both signed them, the doctor joining them as a witness, Mr Clement participating remotely. Afterwards, he walked Adam back up to his and Ijaz's rooms, where Ijaz was waiting for them.

'Okay,' said Foxton, shaking Adam's hand again, 'Now, I've had a long day, and I need to file these papers and get to bed. Goodnight boys,' and Foxton left them.

'Yes,' said Adam, uncertain of what to do with himself. 'it is a bit late-'

'What you talking about man?' exclaimed Ijaz, 'I've been here on my own for a year, you can't just go to bed on me! Go and have a shower, freshen up, then let's go down to the sixth floor and have some midnight-,' he looked down at his watch briefly, pressing the button on it to produce the holo-image of the time in a vermilion-indigo glow three centimetres above his arm, and corrected himself, 'some ten o'clock snacks. Okay?'

Adam looked at the watch. 'Doesn't your NI have an internal chronometer?'

'Yup,' said Ijaz.

'So why do you need the watch?'

Ijaz thought for a moment. 'Huh?'

'Why do you need the watch?' repeated Adam.

'What?'

'You have an internal chronometer-'

'Huh?'

'-it tells you the time-'

'What? Look at my watch, it's pretty,' said Ijaz, dancing a little in time to the words as he pointed at his wrist.

'You've just got that to show off,' said Adam.

'What?' said Ijaz.

Adam gave up. Ijaz possessed a ceaseless appetite for company and conversation, and seemed to give that energy to others. Adam had been quite certain he was ready to drop, but Ijaz's plan did not sound too bad, and he was a bit peckish…

'Okay,' said Adam, 'I'll see you after I freshen up.'

Later, they made their way down to the canteen. It was dark, but the food counter backlights came on as soon as they entered the room. The house computer offered to put the ceiling lights on full, but Ijaz declined, saying it was nicer like that. They walked along, looking at the various snacks, food and drinks through the counter glass. They selected some food, and the counter heated the plates for them before they took them and sat down on some sofas with tables in front of them, a large window next to them overlooking the square in front of the building.

Adam's face was beginning to ache. Just the image of Ijaz eating, then taking a look at Adam and grinning made him laugh. Ijaz seemed to enjoy *everything*, and it was infectious. However, he had a serious side.

'Can I ask you something?' he asked, wiping a bit of food away from his mouth, 'You don't have to answer, we've just met really, sorry.'

'No, it's okay,' said Adam, 'what is it?'

Ijaz nodded. 'What was it like? Y'know, in the orphanage.'

Some crumbs tumbled from Ijaz's plate to the floor. A robo-hoover emerged from the shadows, a flat hexagon ten centimetres high and thirty across. It quietly whirred over the crumbs, lifting them into its innards with ionised rotating static, then retreated back into the dark room.

Adam shrugged. 'I don't know what to compare it to,' he said, 'From what I've heard of other places, and from kids who've come from them, Clement was pretty good. We had food and clothes, we were warm and dry. We weren't neglected, physically I guess. And as far as I know, the staff hardly ever abused the kids without being caught.'

Ijaz stayed silent, thoughtful.

'Did you like it there? They treated *you* good?'

Adam pondered before speaking. 'I think they tried their best. Yes, they treated me well. But no, I didn't like it there. I always wanted a family.' Adam looked down and toyed with his food. He had never actually told that to anyone. 'They told me that there's some sort of permanent trace on genetic databases to see if any matches come up, but that none ever had for me. I was straight up abandoned; there are no clues as to who my parents are. From what I was told, that means they were probably NI addicts or dead or something, otherwise they would have been easier to find. Maybe the orphanage was better for me. There were so many kids there, bullying was the main problem. It would've been nice to be part of a family, someone to take care of me y'know?' Ijaz nodded silently, 'If they caught it, the bullying, they stopped it, but there were too many of us. In a sense, it was good, it taught me to be independent, to take care of myself. It would have been nice for someone to guide me, somewhere safe to go…that's all.'

Ijaz knew then to stop. He had wanted to discuss something that had been bothering him ever since he had found out. However, given what Adam had just said he had no idea how Adam would take it. Despite his youth, Ijaz was a smart young man, and decided now was not the time. He wasn't called 'Mr Charming' by his teachers for nothing.

'Well, you got a new family now; you got us,' he said, slapping Adam on the back with the hand with no food in it. 'My family will love you, either they'll come here, or we can go see them. Alright?'

Adam nodded and smiled a little, but said nothing, slightly embarrassed, and very subdued. Once again, he felt like a fish out of water. Ijaz tried to change the subject.

'How's your food?' he asked. 'Is it lickilicious?'

Adam choked on his sandwich, and began to laugh.

'Yeah,' said Ijaz, 'mine too. I like it down here, when you can have the place to yourself.'

Adam agreed; it was nice. Just then, in front of the window, it became evident that the Indian summer was coming to an abrupt end. Snow could be seen drifting down outside. They turned to stare at it for a while, both with thoroughly immature excitement.

'I hate the cold, but I love the snow,' said Ijaz, 'Christmas here is really nice.'

Adam once again smiled. 'Fantastic,' he said, genuinely happy, the conversation before forgotten.

Soon afterwards, they went back upstairs, said goodnight and went to their rooms. For a while, Adam stared out of his window. He could tell it must be freezing out there in the snow, but inside it was perfectly warm. He settled himself in his bed so that he could still see the white fluff falling outside.

'Fantastic,' he said again, before falling asleep.

*

London's Oxford Circus had moved with the times. On his third day at the institute, Ijaz took Adam shopping there.

It had kept much of the classical facades of the past, but there were animated advertisements everywhere across the upper levels, avoiding the neon gaudiness of other cities but vibrant nevertheless. The street was enclosed in glass to create an all-weather shopping experience. It was pedestrianized; four rows of airport-style speed walkways, or 'slidewalks' whizzing people up and down the street at varying distances and speeds. It was also multi-storey, the offices of previous eras being replaced with dedicated shops and the all-important restaurants, filling the bellies of shoppers who needed the energy to shop some more.

The higher up one went, the more elite the merchandise. They had made a brief visit up there, but Ijaz gave up once it was plain that Adam was more interested in the view of the solar panels that made up the rooves of the street, looking out of the sides of the glass corridors housing the upper walkways that ran along the rooftops, rather than the clothes.

The slidewalks gave Adam a lot of time to stare around him. Initially, Ijaz had insisted on walking along the level escalators, but both of them felt their feet get tired soon enough, and Adam was permitted more opportunity to take it all in, looking around him with a mixture of wonder - and disapproval.

The shoppers were often helped with rented anti-grav or field supported shopping carts floating behind them. Adam could see many needed it. Genetic engineering was indeed insufficient to combat an obvious problem with obesity. He had also seen the sheer ubiquity of the NIs. It seemed as if every other person that went by had their eyes lit as they had conversations, transacted money, or even played games between themselves as they walked along. He felt certain he saw not a few men who were watching movies as they were dragged along by wives and girlfriends, like feminine vampires leading their zombies.

They frequently had to stop as Ijaz said hello to some person or another that he knew, always introducing Adam to them as his friend, then waving goodbye, saying he was on 'a very important mission.'

Adam was seldom without a smile on the entire journey, even when Ijaz insisted that they walk all the way back to the institute, shopping bags in hand.

'I don't get this kid,' said Ijaz, back in his room as they reviewed their clothes, 'I take him shopping, try to get him some real good stuff, and he buys the same funeral-wear as before, only newer.' Then he rubbed his chin, the corners of his lips downturned as he considered Adam, 'He don't look too bad, though. It suits him, I guess.'

'Yes, it does,' said Foxton.

Adam stood before them awkwardly, oddly relieved that Ijaz thought he was wearing the same kind of clothing, with the colour spectrum from dark to black. He watched as Foxton plugged his key into Ijaz's bank terminal, paying Ijaz back for the money he had spent on Adam. The small amount had actually depressed Ijaz; he had tried his best to make Adam spend more.

Foxton turned to Adam and to his surprise, gave him the debit-key, a small three-inch long pen-like object with a metallic protrusion at one end. Adam stared at it, noting that his name was written on it with a flashing space in the readout next to it.

'Thanks,' said Adam, feeling both pleased, and thoroughly uncomfortable with gratitude.

'You're welcome,' said Foxton, 'Call it a late birthday present.'

Adam looked up, puzzled. He had never made a big deal about his birthday. The orphanage had been poorly equipped to cater for the birthdays of all of the children, and Adam was no exception. Then he raised his eyebrows, shocked. He was sixteen, and hadn't even realised it.

'I completely forgot.'

'Not surprising,' said Foxton, 'you were asleep in hospital. You're going to have to choose a last name to put in the blank space.'

Adam looked at the debit key. He had often thought of choosing a last name, and had often thought the name should be 'Clement', but no one had actually prompted him before, and he had never got around to it. Since he had been effectively banned from the orphanage, the name no longer appealed to him.

'I don't know what to choose,' he said at length.

'I tell you what,' said Foxton, 'Seeing as the key is linked to my account, and to avoid any questions at the bank, why don't we just say 'Foxton'? I know, I know,' he said, raising his hands as if to ward off attack, 'I'm not your Dad, yada yada yada,' Adam chuckled, 'But why don't we go with that for now? It can be changed at a later date if you choose.'

Adam nodded, chewing his lip. 'Thanks,' he said again. Then he spoke into the device. 'Adam Foxton.' It flashed, temporarily blinding him.

Foxton steadied him, hand on his shoulder.

'Iris imprint,' he said, 'You'll get used to that here when you register for most things. It's taken a DNA imprint of you too, not full of course but sufficient to make it a billion to one chance against anyone else using it. You have $5000 in the account.'

Adam gawped. $5000 was by no means a fortune, but to a sixteen-year-old who had never had anything, it was pretty amazing.

'It'll be topped up every month,' continued Foxton, 'but I won't take kindly to you wasting it, so be careful with the money. Food and drink is free from the canteen on the sixth floor, your bed and board is paid for, so what you have is some pretty good pocket money. Let Ijaz know if you're unsure whether to spend or not.'

'Hey, don't worry,' said Ijaz, 'He's gotta be the most careful person I *have ever* come across.'

'Good,' said Foxton, 'It's a good rule of life for you.'

'You can start spending by going to the cinema with me tonight,' said Ijaz, 'You want to come Mr Foxton?'

Foxton shook his head, 'I'll leave that to you youngsters. Have a good time.'

Foxton swept out of the room.

Adam looked at Ijaz. 'You want to go out *again?*'

Ijaz smiled at him.

Ijaz first of all took Adam for a meal on Charing Cross Road. Adam generously paid, awkwardly handing his debit key over to the waitress, slightly nervous that something bad would happen - the money not going through, having to rely on Ijaz to bail him out. Instead, he was pleasantly surprised that it all seemed to work smoothly. Then Ijaz took him to see a holo-film in Leicester Square, the audience sitting in the centre as the holo projection made them jump and yell with the action going on around them, right next to them, over them, and often among them.

Adam and Ijaz came out happy and tired, hands in pockets, talking and laughing about the action-comedy they had just seen, brushing scattered bits of popcorn from their clothes. They emerged from the cinema to find that the sun had set, so they did not have to squint in order to see that Leicester Square did not look as it should do.

It was a Sunday evening, so not quite as busy as other days, but it was not the fact that there were so many people in the square that was unusual. What was unusual was that they were all standing still, and staring upwards, or with their eyes lit, NI immersed.

The boys stopped talking, swivelled their eyes in the same direction, up to the large screens hanging over the square. They were, unusually, all news broadcasts. The nearest one to the boys was right over the cinema, and they backed a few feet away to get a better perspective. There was the newscaster, and soon, images came on screen, a heaving dark mass in space, surrounded by other muscular ships of unusual design, and further away, looking like flecks of dust, Earth ships.

Adam quickly took in the scale of the largest ship when measured next to the Earth's. It was vast.

'Look at the size of that thing,' murmured Ijaz. 'What's going on?' he asked a man immersed in NI next to them.

The man turned to him. He reminded Ijaz of an NI addict, his gaze distant behind immersion lights, his grin maniacal as he replied,

'The Aliens are coming.'

Chapter 6

Where knowledge confounds

Precisely why the city-ship had moved from its hiding place, no longer exactly following the orbit of the moon but peeking from its dark side so that every astronomer on Earth could see it, was unknown. However, the visitors were clearly not content to wait for the ISA and Earth governments to make a move - the theory was that they wanted to prompt Earth to action. It had worked.

The ISA was already well along the path to increasing the level of contact; there had been mounting rumbles of discontent among the private news agencies and ships press-ganged into silence. It was estimated to be only a matter of days before the Chinese whispers became a roar, but they were all wrong-footed by the sudden emergence of the gargantuan craft.

Captain Peter Casey was chosen as the face to make contact. An athletic man with brown hair, slightly receding, a square jaw under thoughtful eyes, seated in the control room of the ISA space station, surrounded by advisors and scientists. He spoke slowly and clearly into the microphone.

'We are very grateful for the care you have taken in contacting us,' he said, the room hushed, 'We welcome you.'

All world leaders of space capable blocs were connected by live-link to this choreographed conversation. There was a long moment of silence, and then a voice came through loudly, seeming like many voices at once.

'We are pleased to be welcomed here.'

The captain sweated. 'We would like very much to arrange a meeting, to learn more about each other.'

There was another long pause.

'We agree,' came the response, 'Accepted protocols and analysis of your culture suggest that a meeting on our vessel would be most appropriate. Is this acceptable?'

This was what the CSA had been hoping for; they wanted to give as little as possible away about their own technology, or more pertinently, their relative lack of it. The captain breathed a sigh of relief, glad he didn't have to follow his orders and make excuses.

'Yes,' he said, 'Thank you.'

Instructions were immediately transmitted on where contact should take place. Casey set out at once, the civilian ship *Constant* having already been docked at the space station's central hub, ready for this moment.

*

The boys raced back the institute. Ijaz tried not to be rude by accessing his NI, but he could not help it. Now and again his eyes lit, and he shook his head, muttering, 'I don't believe it, this is amazing.'

All the way back, they saw similar scenes, people looking at personal displays or up at the sky, standing or sitting while NI-immersed.

They got back, to find Mr Foxton waiting for them in the reception.

'Mr Foxton!' said Ijaz, 'Have you heard the news?'

Foxton nodded.

'Is it true?'

Foxton nodded again, his lips pursed. He did not look at all happy. In truth, he was not. Murdock's concerns meant that any reactions of Adam on this subject had to be studied with great care. It being worldwide news so soon muddied the waters considerably. 'Yes, it's true,' he said, 'I thought we could watch the news reports together, then maybe you can both tell me what you think.'

The boys did not need asking twice, and they raced up to Ijaz's room, fidgeting in the lift up. They threw themselves into the room, Ijaz told his television to switch itself on, and the holo projection sprang up against the wall. They sat down, Ijaz on his bed, Foxton and Adam on the sofa.

They were silent for a while as the news reports relayed events, the obligatory 'breaking news' emblem taking up valuable screen space. Over and over came the feed, first the fleet of Earth's ships like dots coming into view, then larger blobs of light, strange and aggressive looking, then a massive dark circle encasing scattered light, a colossus among the huge ships surrounding it. It was then that the view was magnified, and the full splendour of the city-ship was revealed.

'Look at those buildings!' exclaimed Ijaz, 'Skyscrapers...*star*-scrapers, on a ship! How big is that thing? Should we turn off the lights so we can see it better?'

Foxton shrugged, 'Why not? Lights!' and the illumination in the room went out.

There were lights dancing and shooting across the surface, shining from its face as though London was viewing itself in a reflection.

World government officials came on screen to give their reactions, tripping over themselves to reassure people: the aliens were making no hostile acts, and were being very diplomatic; meetings were happening as they spoke. They were careful however, to avoid their most basic rationale for such calm: if the makers of the city-ship wanted to destroy them, they could have done so already - with *ease*.

'This is amazing,' said Ijaz, grinning like the man he had spoken to earlier, 'So exciting!'

'Aren't you scared?' asked Foxton.

'Why should I be?' said Ijaz, 'Like the minister said, they haven't made any hostile moves, and meetings are going on. Sounds pretty civilised to me. This is history man! The first alien contact! I'll be able to tell my grandchildren about this day, the day it all changed!'

There were more reactions, and President Esposito gave an official speech on the issue an hour later, again reassuring people, letting them know that it was going well, there was nothing to worry about, a new era was beginning. Then, shots of crowds staring up at the sky, and reports of rumoured increases in space weapon production.

Foxton looked at Adam slyly, slantwise from half-lidded eyes, recording functions on, NI lights off. He searched for some reaction from the boy, but found none, just Adam's dark eyes fixed calmly on the display, face expressionless.

'Adam?' said Foxton, 'You haven't said anything yet. Are you okay?'

Adam did not answer immediately. Then, he replied, without taking his eyes from the screen, 'Yes.'

Foxton looked back at the feed, stream after stream of the city-ship and the massive entourage of ships surrounding it, yet dwarfed by it. He turned back to Adam. 'How do you feel about what's happening? You haven't said yet.'

Adam seemed impossibly still in the darkness, his eyes reflecting the shifting display like two small convex mirrors, not even breathing seeming to move him. He did not look at Foxton, his gaze still fixed to the screen, before replying.

'They were always going to get here eventually,' he said.

*

The captain looked at the rear-view monitors as the station receded. It was an impressive sight, a large white hexagonal structure almost a kilometre across with full docking facilities, housing over a thousand permanent staff with room for five hundred more. He waited as the auto-guidance system took the ship to its destination, and with increasing nervousness, he watched as the ship made its final approach.

He had only two others with him, one male and one female, both space-trained military intelligence officers.

The Constant had been chosen as one of the largest and perhaps most advanced of all civilian space-capable vessels, sequestered from a trillionaire who had needed little persuasion of the importance of the mission, or of the publicity that would accrue to him once the mission was over. It was beautiful to look at, elegant and sleek, white and silver. From the standpoint of CSA, sending a military craft would give the wrong signal, and too much information. ISA was now effectively re-subsumed into the military until the state of emergency was over: *they* were calling the shots now.

The ship seemed to sway, as if encountering turbulence. Casey checked the readouts: the city-ship was large enough to have its own weak gravitational pull! There was also a ubiquity of artificial gravity apparent, shown on his displays as green lines crisscrossing each other like lime rainbows. The craft steadied as its controls were overridden, and it was guided towards the city-ship.

The captain was simply overcome by what he could see. The space station was nothing compared to this. He felt like a pauper entering a great metropolis in space. The structures towered before him. He could now see lights travelling up and down them, he presumed some sort of elevators.

'You getting all this?' he asked into his com.

'We're getting it,' came the reply from Entman in the control room, 'Amazing.'

The lights along the surface of the vessel now appeared to be in fact the same as the lights indicating elevators, and indeed Casey could see that there was no break in them; they travelled up the sides of the tall buildings as quickly and without pause as they did along the 'ground'.

There was moreover, space traffic, free-flying. The vessels varied from smaller than the Constant, to far larger, but all far from their approach trajectory.

The structures on the surface appeared far more diverse up-close than from a distance. It was easier to appreciate that this really was a vast city, and a bustling one at that. Casey looked forward, across the tops of the buildings as the ship began its descent, the strange horizon the blackness of space. He looked towards the readout display showing the views below him and to either side and saw on another horizon, the crescent edge of the moon.

'Awesome,' he said, 'truly awesome.'

The craft was heading towards a large cube-shaped building, black coloured with lights at the top four corners. There was a dome-like bulge on the nearest side, two hundred metres in diameter. As the Constant approached, it opened, splaying outwards like ten fingers making ready to catch the ship, the bud of a massive mechanical coral flowering with lights spaced along the tips. The interior; impenetrably black.

Daunted, the Constant and its crew crossed the threshold of the building, sending the cabin into darkness lit only by the buttons, read-outs and displays of their consoles, fairy-lights in the void.

Their eyes and their displays adjusted, and they could see the space was wide, perhaps a kilometre across, and cavernously deep. Cameras below them picked up flying traffic, far into the bowels of the city-ship. Lines of white lights came on marking the ship's landing trajectory on the far side, and the craft coasted towards it. The Constant came to a halt, descending to the landing area as the opening closed behind them, swallowing the view of the stars. The two men and one-woman crew felt artificial gravity tug at them.

'Can you still read me?' asked the Captain into his comm.

There was no response, but this was expected once they entered any of the structures. That knowledge did not make it any more comforting to be cut-off.

'You may enter in peace,' came the voice from their comms.

That was definitely *not* Ernie Entman.

Casey unbuckled, and went to the hatch. He had been instructed that breathable air and a suitable temperature would greet him when he entered the city-ship, but they were taking no chances. He was fully suited up, including automated face-plates that would close if there was any trouble. His two companions held back at the hatch. The instructions had been clear: only him.

'Well,' said Casey, 'here it goes.'

He opened the hatch, a heavy door that only opened inwards. He stepped back as bright blue light flooded in, his visor automatically coming halfway down his face, shading his squinted eyes.

Then, slowly, he walked forward into the light.

Part II

Chapter 7

Erudition begins

Casey stood in the chamber. The air was indeed breathable, if slightly too warm. Through the blue light, he could see he was in a cube-shaped area around ten metres to a side. The walls and floor appeared to be metallic; sensors in the suit confirmed it.

Casey stifled a yelp as his feet left the floor. He looked downwards awkwardly, the suit hindering his movements, and saw the 'ground' receding away from him with increasing speed. He looked up, and caught his breath. There appeared to be no ceiling at all, just an endless blue corridor stretching upwards. He resisted the urge to struggle, and calmed himself, reminded that his suit had both anti-grav (likely to be useless in an artificial gravity environment) and stabilizing thrusters as well as field emitters placed throughout it to cushion him in the event of a fall. He breathed deeply, and collected himself.

He looked at the walls as he ascended, noting that approaching him were a series of apertures. He stared as he passed a small porthole that looked out onto the cityscape, catching a brief glimpse similar to the view he had seen on his way in, but too soon it was gone, and he realised that he was travelling at speed. There was however, no wind noise; the air was moving with him. He looked down again, and noted with some alarm that he could not, in the bright light, any longer make out where the floor was.

A few more of the portholes flashed past. He ignored them and continued looking upwards, the way he was going, trying to keep his breathing steady.

Presently, he noted with his eyes rather than other senses, as there was no change in the way his body felt, that he was slowing. He decelerated, rose a little more, and came to a halt at a corridor opening in front of him. His body drifted forwards and his feet touched down on the surface. Casey steadied himself, took a deep breath, then walked forwards into the corridor. He turned left at the end, and came out into a large circular room.

The blue light still suffused the place, but there was a large bay window set in a semi-circle, opposite to where Casey had to come in, a view of the cityscape clearly visible, the bright blue light giving it a strange hue. Above him, there appeared to be no ceiling. His suit told him that the atmosphere was held in by two layers of some sort of field-tech: two millimetres of energy, and freezing vacuum on the other side. It was a startling view however, naked space, stars and dust…Casey tore his eyes away from it.

He needed to focus on *them*.

They stood there, three of them, tall and graceful, and they appeared to be doing a very good approximation of smiling.

'Welcome,' they said in unison. Their voices were multi-tonal, sing-song.

Casey took in the sight of the aliens.

They had three legs, or two legs and some kind of other appendage to the rear, Casey could not be sure. They were around seven feet tall, with eggshell-white skin, and what was probably navy-blue spots running down the fronts of their faces - again, the light obscured the fact. They had no hair that he could see, just large bald 'heads'. He mentally apologised for what was scientifically unsound: assuming that because something looked similar, that it was *the same*. They could have been the alien equivalent of elbows for all he knew. However, he had to use familiar points of reference to make sense of it all. He noted that the creatures had what might be called typical humanoid facial apparatus. There appeared to be two large eyes *(Dark blue? Black? Damn this light!)*, and apertures for mouth and nose in the expected places. They also had two arms, with what appeared to be four-fingered hands on them. As something of an alien 'buff', he was surprised at this. It was more probable that any aliens would be far more *alien* than this. They were also wearing clothing, elegant and straight material reaching from their 'collars' to their feet.

'I am pleased to be here, and thank you for your welcome,' said Casey, his voice tight.

'Thank you for agreeing to come,' said the one to the right, 'Please, sit down.'

A chair rose from the floor next to Casey, metallic, fixed, making him start a little. Casey could hear himself breathing too quickly as he sidled in front of it, carefully, paranoid thoughts of metal rings shooting up from the chair and trapping him springing to mind, but he sat down.

Three stools rose beneath the aliens, and they sat down also, their leg joints sticking out, two in front, one to the rear, making them look oddly crab-like. Casey noted that the trio were within normal sound and sight distances, but outside of striking distance, a few metres away: everything spoke of thoughtful planning.

'Welcome to the League Ship Polis,' said the individual at the centre of the trio, 'You must have many questions. Please, feel free to ask them all, Captain Casey.'

Casey tried not to flinch. As far as he knew, his name had never actually been given to them; they had only specified the 'Captain of the ship at the Centauri system.' It had however already been discovered that the aliens had accessed the ship's systems and his name should have been easy to discover. He nodded, accepting his inferior position of knowledge. He straightened his back and faced them, noting their calm demeanour, and setting his constitution to match it.

'Thank you,' said Casey, 'I - we, have so many questions,' he cleared his throat, swallowed, 'You know my name, but I am unaware of how I should address you.'

'I am Orael ivn Jurood,' said the evident chair of the meeting at the centre of the trio, 'the First Secretary, and acting First Ambassador of the League of Orion. These are my colleagues, Jargel Tench, and Marievle Enechk. You may call me Orael.'

'Thank you, Orael,' said Casey. He decided that he would give in to his instinct and mentally treat the ambassador as a female. He could hardly help it, with the feminine voice and that long graceful neck. 'To use a person's first name is considered an honour in my culture, something to be enjoyed by a friend. I am honoured, and ask that you call me Peter.'

'Very well,' said Orael, and again, did another good impression of smiling.

Casey noted this, and began to ask his questions.

'You, as a species, are surprisingly like our own, even to the level of your facial expressions; this is not expected. Can you tell me why this is?'

Orael paused before replying. 'We are not typical of the races that appear in the local arm. On the other hand, we are no more strange than most. We were chosen as First Ambassadors, as not only are we a race that is adept in diplomacy, but our appearance might be more pleasing to you than others. Many other species are aboard this vessel, and they are diverse. Some might disgust you. Others might *terrify* you. As for the smiling, this we learned from you. We have not only learned your audio language, but also your body language. In time, we hope you will let us give you programmes for your neural interfaces, to give you the skills needed to interact with most of the species of the local arm.'

'You managed to learn all about us from my ship?' asked Casey, 'Or have you been in this system for longer than this?'

That was a risky one. Casey did not wish to give away how ignorant Earth was of the aliens' presence, but he had little choice if he were to discover anything of value.

'We learned from your ship,' said Orael, 'and from analysing your free communications when we arrived here.'

Casey's mission criterion was clear: get information. 'What of the gasses we are breathing? Are we breathing the same air?'

'Yes,' replied the ambassador, 'Many of the league species breathe oxygen in some form. We ourselves are used to a bit less nitrogen, but this balance is tolerable, if a little stuffy. Again, this was one of the reasons we were chosen as First Ambassador.'

'Thank you,' said Casey. 'You speak of the League. What is this?'

'The League of Orion Star Systems,' replied the Secretary, 'An organisation devoted to promoting peace between the planetary and other systems of the local arm. It has been in existence since the lull began.'

'The lull?'

'The description given to the last five hundred of your years,' said Orael, with imperturbable patience, 'It describes the relative peace that has ensued, and the relative regression in technological development since that prior time of turbulence.'

'Are there any species within the League from outside of the spur?'

'No,' said the Ambassador. Casey somehow sensed that she was disappointed by the question. 'The Orion arm, or spur, is almost twenty-thousand lightyears in length, and over five thousand lightyears across. The nearest other arms in the Galaxy, which you call the Perseus and Sagittarius arms, are almost six thousand five hundred lightyears away. There are of course, numerous stars in the lacunae between the two, like your own system, but they are by definition relatively remote. We have documented very few species from the Perseus and Sagittarius arms. Although travel between the arms is feasible, the lacuna makes incentive for the journey small; the energy and effort required is great with only the unknown at the other end. Only one species in the League has the power to travel the entire length of the Orion Arm, and they show no inclination to travel to the other arms.'

'What species is this? Is it your own?'

'No,' said the ambassador, 'My species is known as the Calimtei. The species spoken of are known as the Demos.'

'I thank you again,' said Casey, licking his lips nervously. 'How exactly did you come to find us? Did you happen across us at the Centauri system?'

'No,' replied Orael, 'A signature was detected from your system that indicated something here travelling at supra-light speed. A delegation was organised and sent out to observe you when you reached your Proxima Centauri.'

'Why have we seen no sign of you before now?' asked Casey, feeling that in many ways, this was the most important question of all. If the universe was full of life, then why had mankind not come across it before?

Again however, the ambassador seemed disappointed. She shifted on her seat before answering.

'How,' she asked carefully, 'would that occur?'

'Well,' said Casey, 'How about radio waves?'

'No,' said Orael flatly, 'There are no advanced systems within four hundred and fifty lightyears of your solar system. Due to the relative stages of their development, you would only have been able to receive any transmissions from them, travelling at the speed of light, from about a hundred years from now. Also, each system may well have the capability to transmit some kind of signal, but a power trillions of times greater would certainly obscure it: its star, emitting far greater radiation, light, and all manner of interference. If any such signal survived that, it would have to travel past outer planets, debris, dust and other matter, intercepting comets and meteors, your own Oort cloud, then your asteroid belt, and then battle against your solar winds and other radiation from *your* star, and then finally reach you intact. To expect such a thing is hopelessly unrealistic.'

'We thought, perhaps,' interjected Casey, 'that we had picked up a radio signal, back in the twentieth century, just for a few seconds.'

'Perhaps you did,' said Orael, 'anything is possible. However, radio waves are primitive transmissions. Civilizations only broadcast them for a brief period of time before developing more efficient methods of communication. This is all of course, not to mention the fragility of life; an inhospitable universe destroys intelligent life many times before it survives to enter space. Even if it survives the universe, it is often in the nature of intelligent life to destroy itself. This is an unfortunate fact evident on countless worlds, once full of life, now dead. So it may be that such transmissions were made, but then stopped - forever.'

Casey took all of this in.

'Lastly,' continued the indefatigable ambassador, 'most species had the prudence, in their development, to not advertise their presence until they felt they were in a secure position.'

Casey grimaced at this. Was all of this then, a dangerous mistake for humanity?

'Perhaps most importantly, no-one was looking for you. Out here, in the gap between the Orion and Perseus arms, you are quite remote.'

Casey nodded, his mind racing now at the implications of what she said; not only was humanity not alone, it was a small mote surrounded by a jungle of life.

Casey chewed his lip, unsure of how much he should ask.

'You spoke of a regression in technology, and something before the lull. Can you explain these more fully?'

Orael was silent for a moment. Casey wondered if he had asked too much, if he should have returned the favour and asked them if they wished to know something, or needed something.

'Very well,' said Orael finally. 'There was another species who were able to dominate the entire spur. They were called the Valaur. They largely ignored non-space faring species, which may explain your insulation from them. They were exceptional; biologically, technologically, and intellectually. In the end they seemed to destroy themselves, perhaps with biological weapons and other disasters that annihilated them. The remnants of the species fled the arm, and have never returned. They left nothing behind, so whatever befell them, it was catastrophic. The aftermath saw the exhausted species of the Orion Arm picking up civilisations shattered first by Valaur domination, and then by wars of independence. It has taken this long to recover, and we are still, given our inability to find the home planet of the Valaur, clearly inferior in more respects than we can imagine.'

Casey, although his head was full of questions, felt it was time to reciprocate. Grudgingly he replied, offering information in return for that received.

'We have similar experiences in our own history,' he said, 'In Europe we had the decline of the Roman Empire, in the Middle East and Europe the disintegration of the Islamic Caliphate, and in the Far East the fall of the Chinese Empires. All caused regressions in technology and intellectual stagnation in Earth's cultures, during much earlier periods of our planet's development. I can tell you about these, if you wish.'

Orael cocked her head to one side, and once again gave that very good impression of a smile.

'I thought you would never ask,' she said.

Chapter 8

But darkness is found

The past week had gone well. For the most part, Adam spent little time at the institute. As Foxton had warned, he had to attend normal school in the daytime, a small local private-school that the IHD ensured he got into, along with many of the other children that the state had a special interest in, and special security for. The children were pleasant enough, but as usual, Adam's shyness ensured his isolation. The other kids usually hung around in groups from the special schools they went to the rest of the time, and Adam was the only one from the institute in his year. There was the odd strange look, and one whispered comment that the timing of Adam's arrival meant he must be an alien, but no one bothered him in the playgrounds or canteen. Thus, it was by no means a bad school, in fact quite the nicest he had experienced. In a sense Adam's solitude was a good thing, as he was able to keep his bargain with Foxton that he would work hard, managing to catch up quickly despite the lay-off.

Ijaz was at the same school but in the year above, and they did not often come into contact. So Adam was always glad to return to the institute, to Ijaz and Foxton.

It was in the evenings that the IHD came alive. Foxton had decided to wait for Adam to settle at the new day-school, and now had left him at his first evening class at the institute. The classroom was on the second floor, but it was, to say the least, unusual. It was spacious with dark red walls, and cushions set in a wide circle with a dark round mahogany table in the centre. Bright scented candles burning on top of it were the only illumination.

It was now that he was introduced to Ariana by Ijaz, who was smiling in an infuriatingly knowing way.

'Hello?' she said again, a look of puzzlement on her face.

Adam cleared his throat.

'Yeah, sorry, hi,' he said, for the second time, the first time having been muffled by his diffidence. He thought that maybe he didn't like the institute at all anymore.

Ariana was half a year older than him, and a few months older than Ijaz. She was around the same height as Adam, with long russet coloured hair, olive skin and large deep hazel eyes surrounded by impossibly long lashes. From her clothes, he supposed that she was also rich, though of course according to Foxton, all of the other IHD participants were. Her family lived in London, which was why she did not stay at the institute, instead commuting to it after school. The worst thing was that Adam had noticed her at the day-school, and how pretty he felt she was. In fact that was *why* he had noticed her. And now she was here.

Adam had felt nervous before, worrying that he would not be able to do what he was asked, but now that he had been introduced to Ariana, those nerves had increased exponentially. There was now not only failure looming, but public embarrassment. Well, embarrassment in front of her in any event.

Shaking her head in bewilderment, Ariana strode into the room.

'How's it going, Jazz?' she asked Ijaz.

A lot of people seemed to call him that. Adam decided that he found it particularly irritating.

'Yeah,' replied Ijaz, 'cool. Especially now that I've got someone to talk to around here.' He, slapped Adam on back as he followed them into the room.

'He doesn't seem to talk very much,' said Ariana over her shoulder.

'Well, he does,' said Ijaz, 'He's just shy with new people. Took a whole fifteen minutes for him to get going with me, so it will probably take a few months with you.'

Ariana laughed and told Ijaz to shut up. She sat down on one of the long cushions and turned to Adam. 'Why are you shy?' she asked.

Adam looked down as he sat down at the table and shrugged his shoulders. He was relieved from Ariana's attentions when the teacher entered the room.

'Hello young people,' she said in an immensely posh accent as she walked in. Like Adam, she was attired all in black, a polo-neck jumper and a smart pair of trousers, with short black hair. She had tanned skin and a small nose, and appeared around middle-age.

'You must be Adam,' she said.

Adam nodded, and said, 'Hi.'

'Hello young man,' said the woman, 'I'm Doctor Cengo, the primary stage kinetics trainer. We're very pleased to have you here.'

'Thanks,' said Adam, determined to find his voice after his coyness had stolen it.

'I like you already Adam,' said Dr Cengo, smiling, 'You have excellent dress-sense.' Ijaz sniggered and elbowed Adam. 'You will not be required to participate too much in this lesson. For the most part, it's more about familiarising yourself with the abilities of the students here, and seeing what we can do about bringing it out in you.'

Adam felt a cooling-surge of relief; doing nothing was something he could just about manage.

'Now,' said Cengo sitting down next to Ariana and Ijaz, Adam on the far side of the table, 'Watch and learn.'

She produced a large red velvet bag from under the table while telling the others to settle themselves. Out of the bag, she produced three chrome bars, cylindrical and about an inch thick, placing two of them in front of the other two teenagers, and one in front of herself.

'You two know the drill by now,' she said, 'but I'm going to repeat the basics for the sake of our new boy. Please close your eyes, and breathe deeply.'

Ijaz rolled his eyes a bit, then did as he was told along with Ariana, eyes closed, legs folded and hands on their knees.

'Be aware of yourselves,' Cengo intoned, 'Be conscious of your bodies, from head to toe, be aware of your environment, the space you are in.' Adam thought they would giggle at this, and he smiled. Then he suppressed it, cautioned by the fact that Ijaz seemed to be taking it seriously, and waited. 'Feel the warmth of the room, the coldness of the draft under the door. Be aware; extend yourselves.'

Ijaz and Ariana both nodded, breathing deeper. Ijaz flexed his neck and shoulders.

'Now,' said Cengo, 'feel the iron bars I have put in front of you - with your minds, not your hands.'

Ariana interjected. 'We haven't felt these particular things before Doctor Cengo. How are we supposed to know what they feel like?'

'You think you'll always get the chance in the real world?' replied the teacher, a little sternly. 'There may be no chance, no time - no mercy. So close your eyes, and use your imagination. Feel those bars as if they were in your hand. Feel their coldness, their weight, how solid they are. How dangerous when misused; a weapon, a thing to hurt, a thing to defend, to block a blow or throw at an assailant. Let your mind find it.'

The two resumed their meditation.

'Now,' said Cengo, 'lift your bar.'

Adam jumped as all three bars suddenly raised upwards almost simultaneously. He shifted to look at the bars from different angles as they hung in the air, moving only slightly.

Cengo turned to Adam.

'I am lifting mine using NI enhanced capabilities,' she explained, 'field technology used to manipulate objects. This is how we trained all of the others, and we will try to use the same principles on you.'

Adam nodded mutely, and Cengo turned back to her students.

'Now, use your minds to grip the bars at both ends,' she continued, 'and bend them in half.'

Adam stared with wide eyes, taking in every moment. He watched as both of the students creased their eyebrows in concentration.

'What are your obstacles?' asked Cengo.

'Fear, doubt, imagination,' chanted the teenagers in unison.

'Overcome,' ordered Cengo.

Adam heard it before he saw it. There was a creaking-ringing sound coming from Ijaz's bar, then from Ariana's. Slowly, it became noticeable that both bars were bending in mid-air. A look of serenity dusted with confidence entered the visages of the two teenagers, and the bars bent more rapidly. Adam watched as the sheen produced by candlelight on chrome narrowed to points on the most curved parts of the bars, as the two ends of each bar got closer and closer to the other.

'Good,' said Cengo as her own steel bar slowly descended to the table, 'Now carefully and *elegantly* put the bars down.'

Ariana did as she was told, her bar gently descending back to the table surface, lightly and quietly touching down. Ijaz however smiled, taking a peek with one eye at the bar before bending it some more, until he appeared to be tying a knot.

'Alright, Ijaz,' said Cengo, 'Stop showing off. You've got a lot more exercises to do over the next hour, don't burn yourself out.'

Ijaz nodded and complied, the bar coming down a little more quickly than Ariana's and thudding onto the table.

'Sorry,' he said.

'You should pay attention rather than grandstanding,' said Cengo, 'But well done to both of you.' Cengo reached across and picked up Ariana's bar, hefting it up and handing it to Adam. Adam looked at it, then took it; it seemed to weigh a tonne.

'Try to bend it,' she said.

Adam gripped the bar, and gave it a few experimental pushes and pulls, quickly giving up. It was quite solid.

'Now you two,' said Cengo, again rummaging around in her velvet bag and producing some booklets, 'take a cushion and go and sit on the other side of the table. Do the exercises in the book - you'll need your iron bars, and mind your own business while I concentrate on Adam.'

Cengo waited until the others had sat where they were told, then turned to Adam, teeth showing in a cat-like smile, then covered it with a thoughtful pout.

'Mmmm,' she said. 'We have a difficulty with you. The other children were discovered as they displayed their abilities *after* they had already shown those faculties via NI-use. You on the other hand, have never openly displayed that capacity, and never had an NI. So we're going to have to start really small with you.' She reached into her bag to pull out something, and put it onto the table in front of Adam.

It was a green crayon.

Adam looked at it, then looked at Cengo.

'What do want me to do with that?' he asked, feeling somewhat annoyed that he would have to do something after all, even with a crayon.

'Anything you like,' said Cengo, 'As long as it's not with your hands or any other part of your body except your mind.'

Adam glanced at the other teenagers, intent as they were in their own work, and at the iron bars in front of them. 'I don't think I can do this,' he said quietly, craning forward in a vain attempt not to be overheard, 'I think this has been a mistake.'

Ijaz glanced up from his work, shaking his head. Cengo waved him to silence and gave a meaningful look while pointing down at the table, willing him to concentrate on his work. Ijaz looked back down.

'You know this?' she asked, 'Or fear it?'

Adam shrugged. 'I don't *know*,' he said. 'I just don't know if I can do anything like this, I guess.'

'But you don't know you can't,' said Cengo, 'So do as I say and let's find out, shall we?' She looked in her bag, and took out a device. It appeared to be the same type of instrument that Foxton had shown Adam back at the hospital. 'And these things, by the way, say that you can do it. I think Mr Foxton has told you the significance of it. I have never known them to be wrong. Now, close your eyes, and breathe deeply.'

Cengo put the device on the table, then repeated the mantra she had said earlier, eventually telling Adam to relax and concentrate on the crayon. She then asked him to pick it up with his hands and give it a good feel. Adam, feeling foolish, complied, then put it back down.

'Now,' said Cengo, 'I want you to close your eyes again, relax, and focus on that crayon again. I want you to imagine moving it with only your mind, but with the strength of your hand. Do that now Adam, I know you can do it.'

Adam concentrated, his eyebrows creased.

Nothing at all happened.

He sweated under the pressure, and concentrated more, with the gentle encouragement of Cengo.

He tried for the better part of an hour, but finally broke.

'This isn't happening,' he said, exasperated, head in his hand.

'So?' said Cengo, 'That doesn't mean you should give up. Other students took many lessons before they could bring their abilities to the fore, and they had previous experience of NI use. You're starting from a disadvantage. Just exercise that mind of yours, a very clever mind by all accounts. Give it a workout, and know that crayon, its every groove and smooth part, its lightness, its fragility.'

Adam closed his eyes, and tried again.

After another hour was up, it was apparent that he was not succeeding. Cengo called the session to an end, and they all got up and began to tidy the mess they had made. Adam looked at the iron bars of Ijaz and Ariana, now splayed, split, splintered and knitted into complex patterns, and felt once again an acute feeling of inferiority. He shook his head.

'I can't do this,' he said again.

'Yet,' said Ijaz, 'You can't do it *yet,* that's all. We believe in you.'

'Yeah,' said Ariana, 'Just keep on going.'

Adam shook his head. 'Thanks,' he replied awkwardly, wondering why, on top of it all, Ariana had to be so *nice.*

Cengo took Adam by the shoulders and turned him to face her.

'You listen to me,' she said, 'This session has given those parts of your brain that we wanted to a good workout. It'll take time, that's all. We'll repeat this exercise again tomorrow, and we'll see how you do.'

Adam nodded, his shoulders hunched dejectedly.

'Okay,' he said.

*

Casey was exhausted. His NI-icon, a representation of himself in a spacesuit, was warning him that he was no longer performing efficiently, that he needed to take a rest. He ignored it.

He had been sitting in the same chair, asking questions and answering for the better part of ten hours; the Calimtei did not seem to experience fatigue. On this, his second trip to the alien ship, the blue light now seemed not so much serene, as wearying. Matters had seemed to reach a crunch point - something had gone wrong.

Casey had known when it occurred, but not why. He was at the stage of detailing the present state of Earth's society. The particular subject was AIs, and the Calimtei seemed especially interested in them.

'We have noted,' said Orael, 'from analysis of information freely available from your planet, that your artificially constructed sentient intelligences seem to have a rather exalted position. We wish to know more about this.'

Casey did not know when to ask for a break.

'Alright,' he said jadedly, 'The position of the AIs varies between countries and world blocs. In most developed countries, they occupy positions equal to that of humans, including participation in our democratic processes.'

'Equal?' queried Orael, tilting her long neck to one side, 'Please elaborate.'

'Well,' said Casey, 'they are allowed to vote, and are allowed to stand for political office, as well as occupying positions of responsibility for commensurate pay or rewards that they specify.'

Silence followed this.

'And in the rest of your world?'

'In most of the rest of the world, they have at least equal rights to their human counterparts,' said Casey with pride. After all, was this not the hallmark of a mature humanity? The ability to see and respect sentience in another being, no matter how different? 'Their status is usually a reflection of the freedom of the society to which they belong. They are totally free and equal in the AAA, Europe, the NAUS, India, the SAB and various other countries. They hold more or less equal rights in most of the rest of the world.'

'But what methods are used to restrain and suppress them?' asked Orael.

'There must be a problem of translation,' replied Casey, 'The meaning of the words *restrain* and *suppress* are quite oppressive in this context. Our AIs are free for the most part. We apply no more laws to them than we commonly do to ourselves.'

The Calimtei went very still. Casey could tell there was something amiss then, and should have realised he should just stop, especially with his increasingly agitated icon telling him the same. However, he figured it was too late for that, and overruled it. Instead, he altered his position to find out why this was of particular interest.

'How do you control *your* AIs?' he asked.

Orael shook her head. 'You must be tired Captain,' she said. 'Please follow the guidance systems back to your ship, and you can either rest there or return to your space station.'

'I think I should report back to the station,' replied Casey.

Orael nodded her agreement. However, she said nothing, and made no attempt to smile.

Casey stared around at the colossal city-ship as he sped back over the surface. He indeed did have a lot to report. He had made some kind of *faux pas* if there was any similarity at all between human behaviour and Calimtei, he was sure of it. They had become guarded, and challenging. What was their issue with Earth's AIs? This required serious discussion, and Casey was glad he had been excused. He had been overborne by the wonder of it all, the technology, sophistication, the welcome - the discovery. However, the importance of these first contacts must not be underestimated, and now he needed help.

Something was definitely wrong.

Chapter 9
As evil plots

Sadem stood facing the porthole-window, his frame silhouetted against the light from outside. The immediate area surrounding him was unlit; he appeared a ghost among shadows, partially blocking light into the room.

'It is a matter of considerable irritation to me,' he said, his voice a deep tenor with hints of sibilance, 'that this information, which we should have received over ten standard years ago, instead has taken that long to get to us, is un-encrypted, and has thus got into the hands of every rabble species within a thousand lightyears of that little backwater of a planet. The result is that the rest of the Orion Arm has become aware of this new species, of this Earth around their star called Sol, and are now meddling.'

The vice-regent continued staring from his porthole down to the planet, his back to his audience, wishing one of them to speak so he could find a target to lash out at; to rend - to kill.

The wide porthole-window looked out from the Great Ring. It had grown from a steady accumulation of satellites around the planet, over the centuries accruing space-stations and more satellites, becoming more and more crowded and dangerous until the accreted mass was connected into one massive ring encircling the planet. The ring was formalised into a planned construction, connected to the surface of Kratos directly with giant tubes that led from the surface through the atmosphere, held in check by excellent architectural design, and even better positioning technology. It served as a massive spaceport encircling the planet, a communications network, and had a multiplicity of defensive weaponry placed throughout it. Aside from its utility, there was also the effect of that Demos passion for doing things merely because they could.

'We have these early warning systems for a reason,' he lectured, 'If a species attains supra-light travel, it must mean they have the resources to do so. We need the same resources for our hyper-technology, especially rare materials such as thulium. We cannot maintain such a massive fleet of ships without it and the myriad other materials we use in our machinery. We have also to be wary of *any* species that has this capacity. It is quite probable that they may be a threat to us, and impossible to contemplate that they will be compliant with *our* dominance of *them.'*

The porthole-window gave Sadem's favourite view, looking down upon the giant continent that housed both his home and the capital city of Kratos, named after the planet soon after it had become the dominant power in the Orion Arm. He could see the dark swirls of cloud, and through the gaps, the speckled lights of civilisation illuminating the half night-side down below.

He drew away from the porthole, across the small landing and down the steps to enter the main body of the room, where his staff were assembled and waiting. The lights slowly illuminated him as he glided forwards and down.

First to be outlined were his legs, strong and muscled. His torso was long and wide, perfectly proportioned, covered in a military uniform with several sets of insignia. His arms were similarly strong, healthy retractable claws at the end of them.

Then, came his head. His lips were a cut in his face, and his nose was two small slits midway between his eyes and mouth. His eyes were two black ovals, narrowing upwards towards the sides, piercing, intense, studying the Demos before him. His skin was a stark white contrast, waxy as the gloom lightened. Then, branching strongly yet elegantly from either side of his head, then curving inwards and high up above it to two straight points, were his horns. They were cream-coloured at the fleshy base and white at the bony tips, rising two feet above his head. Even by the standards of the Demos, he was large at nine feet tall, eleven including the horns. All who had seen him had to agree; he was an exquisite creature.

His size and physical excellence however, were not how he had risen to pre-eminence. The battle with the mighty AI, Maliken Trentaur, as a young captain at the culmination of the AI wars that established once and for all biological superiority over machines almost eighty years earlier defined his greatest moment, and his career since had been exemplary.

He had been updated with the new information while still in sleep-state, and had just finished reviewing it.

'Now,' he continued, his staff observantly silent, 'they have two advantages. The first, is that they have been able to gain what is for them a sixteen-year head-start in technological progress, and are not quite the helpless infant we would like. The second, and far more serious, is that the League is asserting its right to *exist* - or perhaps more accurately, are acting upon the assumption that such a right is extant. This has put us to the inconvenience of finding a justification for intervening with this new species, *and* having to occupy their territory, rather than simply annihilating them more than a hundred years before anyone else from the League was likely to stumble across that tiny mud-hole in the middle of nowhere. Then we could have simply mined the area for its resources. That opportunity has now gone.'

The acolyte, a smaller red and black Demos known as Zessis, had been standing silently to one side. Other staff of various shapes, sizes, ages and colours, all of them senior, stood around the table waiting for the Vice-Regent General to join them. They had a cautious look about them; quiet, watchful.

They were in Sadem's own private chamber. This was where he went when he had to regenerate, to sleep, or merely rest when he did not wish to leave his work and return to his mates and family. The room was a typical high-tech Demos facility, with pure black-stained titanium and dura-crystal abundant. The lights remained somewhat dim so as not to disturb the General's eyes as he adjusted from his sleep-state.

Sadem had called the staff into his room to review the report. He knew that calling senior personnel into his private quarters would impress upon them the seriousness of the situation and make them acutely uncomfortable; there was a difference between intimate closeness and proximity to danger. They would be in no doubt that they were in the latter situation.

The acolyte felt himself lucky. As Sadem's personal assistant and apprentice, as opposed to a civil or military inferior, he was not in the firing line for this fiasco. That was assuming the Vice-Regent kept a hold of himself, which was why the acolyte had been keeping his mouth shut. Sadem stretched his back, and shifted his shoulders, dimly feeling the rasp of material against the shell-like skin on his back. He required only an hour of accelerated sleep per day/night cycle, though he liked to get at least two.

The acolyte read his pupil-master, and decided to speak; the latest news was good. 'However, we may have the justification we need, Sire.'

'Go on,' said Sadem. In fact, he already knew the latest from the Calimtei; it had been uploaded during his sleep cycle. However, this was all part of the training process for the acolyte, and he wanted to talk it through, bringing the memories he had downloaded to the fore.

The acolyte explained.

'They have something the League will find most abhorrent. The latest reports state that they have Artificial Intelligences.'

Sadem did the Demos equivalent of smiling, very similar to the human gesture, only with far more teeth involved. *Pointed, predatory* teeth.

'Slaved AIs?' he asked.

'No, fully free, fully sentient AIs,' replied Zessis, 'They have all three of the proscribed characteristics: ego, autonomy and ambition. And, they are abundant; over four million AIs on the planet. In many jurisdictions, they have equal rights with the Humans themselves. They have completely free access to space,' continued Zessis, still standing behind Sadem as the Vice-Regent sat at the table, his audience finally following suit. 'Many are integrated into and able to command deep-space capable ships.'

Sadem nodded. He was pleased with the way his pupil was thinking; it was exactly along the lines of his analysis, and showed that Zessis was reasoning as a future leader should do.

'The truth is,' said Sadem, 'even if there were no resources there, and no potential future rival, it might be difficult to turn a blind eye to all of that.'

'But,' said the acolyte, 'might it not be pointed out to us that this could be somewhat hypocritical?'

'Meaning?' asked Sadem, interested by the acolyte's angle. An *innocent* angle that Sadem himself found hard to grasp.

'Well,' said Zessis, 'we have AIs. Not free ones admittedly, but we have them. Many among the League also have AIs that are not within what the Demos would consider safe limits, why do we not intervene with them?'

Again, Zessis was lucky. The son of a powerful house, and an acolyte, he had a right to be educated by Sadem under the ancient apprenticeship tradition.

'That,' said Sadem, 'is where the resources and threat to security comes in. That is where Empire must be considered. It is we who uphold civilisation during this Lull.'

There were murmurs of agreement and sycophantic nods around the table. Sadem glanced out of the large window again, taking in the view. The motion was not lost on those assembled. It was this that he was sworn to protect. By his interpretation, that meant destroying any other threat to it, real or potential.

'It is *we* who were the primary species leading the victory over the Valaur, and the ones who defeated AIs in the machine wars,' said Sadem, 'It is *we* who have the right to assess and police the dangers posed by other species, and to overlook those posed by our allies. It is we who have the right to control our own AIs as we see fit. So give no more thought to those considerations, our own interests are what we serve, and that is perfectly justifiable.'

'Yes Sire,' said the acolyte, somewhat abashed.

Sadem thought for a moment. His anger needed an outlet.

'Who had responsibility for maintenance of that machine?'

There was a dead silence in the room. Sadem put his claws on the table, smiling. He flexed his mind, and two handle-less blades came from concealed pockets on his thighs, floated up, and rested softly on to the table.

'I'll ask you again,' he said, 'Who had responsibility for maintenance of the particular machine that failed to send the code beta11 properly?'

The Demos around him stared at him, all of them surreptitiously raising their shields and preparing their minds. The knives on the table rose up, and began to circle Sadem's head, faster until they were a blur, and an audible keening sound came from the sound of the blades rasping against air.

One of the Demos smoothly broke ranks.

'Silmli,' he said, turning to a Demos sitting across from him, 'Wasn't it your department that had responsibility for mining?'

Silmli, a fat Demos with horns that curved inwards towards his head, looked at him, then at Sadem, and said, 'But-'

The blades flew from their orbit around the vice-regent. Silmli did not even move, sat behind his shields while simultaneously Sadem used his neuro-link to disable them. Silmli realised too late what had happened, tried to use his own powers to fend off the knives, attempted to force them back while raising his hands to try to catch them mid-flight, but the blades slit through his fingers, slammed into his skull, went straight through it and embedded themselves into the back of his titanium chair.

There was a moment of universal stillness.

Silmli's eyes went white, his body slumped forward and hit the table, horns spread pathetically, the blades still stuck in his chair, a pool of blue blood spreading slowly around his head, contained as his shields belatedly came back on a second later, making an audible hum in a room now bereft of even the sound of breathing.

'A lesson to be learned,' said Sadem coolly, 'the limitations of technology. One should always develop oneself, and have a variety of resources and skills. One should never let oneself get fat, complacent, reliant upon technology alone to survive rather than the endeavour of maintenance in mind and body.'

He looked around at the Demos, noted that they appeared to be unmoved by their comrade's death, and their near-escape.

Now that was self-control, he thought with approval.

'On that very subject, the reliance on technology,' said Sadem, 'What machine *exactly* was responsible for sending the beta11 message so badly?'

'It was a slaved AI,' said the acolyte hesitantly, the only one among them still staring uncontrollably at the still form of Silmli, 'I believe you are familiar with it, my lord. It is now known as Karakeen Mining Colony Monitor1.'

Sadem chuckled. 'How wonderful. An exemplary fall from grace and humiliating punishment.' Then he turned towards the acolyte, 'I have an assignment for you. That machine; I am quite certain it is dangerous. It could easily have thought to send the message into hyperspace, or encrypting it. It has obviously developed independence, and probably all three of the proscriptions. We have taken a great risk with it. Perhaps I was too intent upon punishing it rather than guarding against it. I have finished humiliating it, I think. Destroy it. Don't just wipe its programme, we did that already. Obliterate it physically. Annihilate it. When you're finished organising that, find out which imbecile was responsible for its overhaul. His or her punishment will be painful and exemplary, and overseen by me personally.'

That, thought Sadem, noting the uncomfortable shifting of the still silent Demos sitting at the table, *should make sure some heads roll, clear out some dead weight. And that machine: time to die.*

'And when you are finished, join me for breakfast,' said Sadem, 'For the main course, I will be having roast Silmli. With all that fat, if properly cooked, slow to heat the inside properly, then high and fast to crisp his hide, he should taste delicious.'

Zessis bowed to hide his horror, and swallowed hard before he managed to speak.

'Yes, Sire,' he said.

Chapter 10

What the righteous forgot

Casey felt a little less nervous for his third mission, even though it was arguably more fraught than the last two. The Calimtei had invited him back for a full welcome, to include many of the civilisations of the League. This, he was told, was to familiarise Casey with the other species, and for them to do the same with humanity.

It also gave Casey a chance, the ISA hoped, to explore this issue of AIs.

Theories abounded, and general conclusions had been reached. The reasons for the Calimtei's obvious discomfort with the freedom of Earth's artificial intelligences were mysterious, but could be extrapolated if they were in any way similar to humans. Earth had in the past had many dissenters with the spread of AIs, and it was conceivable that the Calimtei had an antipathy to them.

Humanity did have levels of control over artificial intelligences, in particular a section of most police forces dedicated to controlling them. However, these were hardly ever used as the primary level of control was in the construction phase, where the personality, life-preserving and other safety features were taken to levels of multiple redundancy in double figures.

It was decided and accepted by Casey, that he had been remiss in not telling the Calimtei that, and not taking a break. He was sternly upbraided for letting his wonder overcome his prudence, and ordered to inform Orael of the controls humanity had on its AIs, and find out what her issue with them was.

So Casey had set out once again, this time bearing gifts; holo and multilingual audio projectors with screens to allow for unknown sight-physiology, detailing the entirety of Earth's ancient history right up to the harnessing of electricity. Again, the aim was to give information while withholding an up-to-date overview of Earth's technology. *Trust,* was not on the agenda.

Casey once more cruised over the imposing cityscape, still alight with activity and movement, entered the coral-like hatch of the huge cube structure, his ship again under automatic controls.

Once again he lost contact, and exited the craft into the blue light. He stood in the chamber, but instead of rising upwards, the floor opened beneath him, and he slowly descended until he reached a lower level. He landed softly, and walked forwards through a small corridor, opening to a cavern with a curved ceiling, containing a waiting car hovering over a rail on two beams of visible fluctuating green energy.

Two Calimtei stood there and motioned him to come forwards to the car. It had a large transparent cover, and the aliens beckoned for him to get in. He was fairly certain that these were the devices that he had seen from the outside of the city, moving around along the surface. He got in, the two aliens getting in behind him, and they sped off as the hatch closed above them.

They entered a tunnel, then emerged into what alarmingly looked like open space. Casey could not help gawping as the vehicle sped onwards. He felt irritated by the light inside the car interfering with his view, and could take it no longer.

He turned to his escorts.

'Um, may I ask, what is the purpose of the blue light?'

The aliens looked at each other. One spoke.

'Upon our analysis,' it said, 'as you come from a largely blue coloured planet, we calculated this would be most pleasing to you. Was this incorrect?'

'No,' said Casey carefully, 'thank you. Though, it doesn't look blue everywhere, all of the time. Whatever the light is, the natural light, as long as there is enough of it, that's fine.'

He experienced one of those moments when he wished he hadn't started speaking in the first place. The aliens seemed unfazed.

'We shall adjust it for you, so that it does not interfere with your view.'

The light was dimmed, and the Captain got a better view of the city speeding around and towering above him. From this perspective, the buildings much more resembled skyscrapers, and the ship more closely resembled a bustling city with lights and movement, but with no people visible. While there was activity in areas some distance from them, the way ahead seemed to be devoid of any movement, as if it had been cleared.

Casey could see that they were heading for the largest building of all, identified as being near the centre-point of the whole of the upper-side of the Polis. It was at least eighty stories tall, or about half a kilometre, jet black, a steep pyramid structure with a green beacon at the top.

Casey became apprehensive when he realised that the covered tubes they were travelling in appeared to travel from the 'ground' and then up the side of the building at a very steep angle. There was no gradual change in gradient between the surface and the building. As they got closer, he noted how quickly they were approaching, and he started to panic.

'Excuse me,' he said, 'That's kind of a steep angle there. The human skeleton cannot sustain forces that great.'

The alien behind him to his left replied, 'Do not worry,' and that was all.

Casey shrugged inside his suit. *Okay then*, he said to himself, resigned to the possibility of being crushed to the floor of the vehicle as it went from a horizontal angle to a steep gradient at a speed that he estimated to be over five hundred kilometres an hour.

With disorientating swiftness and a dizzying lack of any internal motion, the car made the transition up the steep incline without the slightest commotion, not even the feeling of going over a small dip.

Casey pursed his lips, and nodded to himself; their inertial nullifier technology would have to be specific to this car while interacting with the main city-ship: vastly superior to Earth's. Their technology was as advanced as it appeared.

As swiftly as before, the car dived into the side of the building, again without even the sensation of going over a small bump, as though he were watching the whole thing in a simulation with no sensory input except visual. His stomach felt funny, mainly because he thought it should. He checked his suit's readouts and confirmed both their considerable velocity, and the external forces to the car: if he had been outside the vehicle, he would have been pulverised.

The tunnel was unfortunately once again blue, but less bright than before. The car came to a halt, and the aliens got out, Casey following. They walked into another corridor, which then opened out into a very large chamber.

It resembled some sort of amphitheatre, with rows of seats in a wide circle, perhaps numbering in the thousand. They were not empty. They were full of what appeared to be hundreds of alien species, heaving, yet quiet. The room seemed white, though the renewed blue light made it difficult to see the exact colour. At the opposite end to the place where he had entered was a raised dais, on which sat the three Calimtei he had met before, flanked by fabric emblems hanging from the walls behind them.

'Please approach us,' said a singular voice, Orael, amplified and gentle.

Casey walked forwards. As he did so Orael consulted one of her colleagues, and turned back to Casey.

'I understand the blue light is not agreeable to you,' she said, 'Perhaps this will be preferable.' She motioned upwards, and Casey looked up to see the ceiling turn from that intense blue colour, to a darker shade, then black, and then entirely translucent, showing a star-scape so exquisite that it could only have been seen from a place like where they were, in open space.

Casey checked his suit readout: it was not a display. The ceiling was made of a diamond composite, and was breathtakingly large, covering the entire two hundred metres of the amphitheatre. The blue light was replaced with a more natural colour, a gentle white with a bluish hue.

'Is that better?' asked the alien.

'Yes,' said Casey, snapping his attention back to her, embarrassed at his awe, 'Thank you.'

Orael turned her face to the assembled aliens.

'This,' she said, 'is Captain Peter Casey. We welcome him.' She turned to Casey. 'Are you ready to meet your hosts?'

'Yes,' he replied, 'and I have gifts for you.'

He turned and handed the two cases to the Calimtei behind him.

'Now,' said Orael, 'It is time for us to get to know each other.'

And then Casey stood in a sublimely surreal situation. Music started; it appeared to be classical music from Earth, Saint-Saens, Casey believed. The aliens then began what humans might call a hubbub, chattering amongst themselves as they variously walked, rolled and floated down from the sides of the amphitheatre to the floor to come and meet him.

Casey stood there accompanied by Orael as she formally introduced them one by one. He could see species of such variations that he found it difficult to categorise them. The majority seemed to be breathing the same air as him, though of these a large number had some form of breathing aid, presumably to make the air closer to that which they were used to. Others were encased in environment suits, still others in environment tanks, as not only the air but the air-pressure, temperature and gravity were outside their tolerances. There were a few bipeds with two arms there, but quite a few tri-pedal, an abundance of four-limbed and even more six-limbed species, walking on four legs with upper limbs free, finished with dexterous hands on upright upper torsos, reminding Casey of centaurs. The similarity ended there however, with some of them resembling odd reptiles or amphibians rather than majestic horses.

One thing Casey had never quite expected, was the variation in size: some of the aliens were immense, up to ten metres tall, and others the size of cats.

Once the formal introductions were over, the floor became full of species milling around, and from what Casey could see they all appeared to be having a good time.

The giant ceiling-view of the cosmos became somewhat obscured by the internal lighting, coming from small globes of light that floated of their own volition around the space, above head height. They seemed to be imitating the action of stars in orbit around each other, gradually coming together. One pair floated down and came close enough for Casey to touch. He put his hand up, and a few of the golf-ball-sized bright lights swirled around his outstretched finger as though it was a weighty object pulling them in. He became conscious of the innocent gesture, and concentrated on observing while still privately enjoying the moment, the little balls of light floating back up to re-join their kind.

In his suit, still primed for the moment something might go wrong, he had never felt so underdressed in his life. The other species seemed to be kitted out in what could only be described as finery, multi-coloured with gold and silver prominent. Still others were dressed in clothing that had some sort of nano-technology displaying moving images. His appeared to be the only plain spacesuit, no doubt seen as strange as the environment was tailored specifically for him. Still, compared to some of those in sealed environment suits and tanks, he supposed he looked casual.

Casey began having a conversation with an alien encased in one of the bio-tanks. The vessel resembled a six-foot-high fish tank, rectangular with curved corners and a white base. The creature could be seen on the inside, swimming in dark brown gasses. Comparisons were difficult, but it looked similar to a small pink elephant with a short wide trunk, with four limbs, two with soft hands at the end, and large 'ears' that swept down its body like wings from its head joined to all four limbs with which it swam in the gasses.

'Yes, yes,' said the creature, by the name of Caniona Bilquii, the sounds coming from a speaker set near the top of the tank, 'and you must come to the Bartak home-world. We can outfit you with an environment suit just like this one, or a small ship to take you round in. We wouldn't want you to get crushed by the pressure.'

'I would be honoured,' said Casey, and he was. He reflected on the irony of the situation; he never thought that he would get to see the universe by networking. 'And, when my government permits, I would love you to visit the areas of Earth that I am familiar with. There are many areas of ocean that have the high pressure you are used to.'

Orael maintained a constant presence, formally introducing him to species after species, so many that he could not begin to place and categorise them, relying instead on his suit and NI's recording capabilities. He tried not to laugh as he thought of himself saying 'Just one small step for a man…' while he ate what tasted like a very nice piece of cake. He turned to her when they were briefly left alone, stalling for time as his suit checked the cake for anything dangerous.

'Where did you get the recipe from?' he asked.

She smiled. 'I assure you, it is quite safe.'

Quietly, his suit confirmed it, before he finally dared to take a bite.

'This ship is devoted to diplomacy,' said Orael, 'even the kitchen. We have been monitoring all free information coming from your planet since we got here, including what is agreeable to your palate. None of it is natural I'm afraid, we had to duplicate recipes with artificial content. Does it agree with you?'

Casey nodded. 'It's delicious,' he said, his mouth muffled with food. He guessed that explained the classical music as well. 'You mentioned the Demos before?' he said. 'Have I already been introduced to that species?'

Orael hesitated. 'They have chosen not to attend this gathering,' she said, 'They are aboard the Polis, but have made the decision to meet you at some later date.'

'Oh,' said Casey, with more than just a feeling of disappointment. The now militarised ISA had insisted that finding out about this species was of the highest importance given their pre-eminence in the region. Their absence was noteworthy, and conspicuous. 'When might that be? I was looking forward to meeting with them.'

'All in good time,' replied Orael, 'Would you like some more cake?'

He carried on meeting different species until he had met all of the official ambassadors of the Orion League, finishing with a strange creature resembling two worms side by side with a central thorax and upper body, then Orael took him aside and asked him if he wanted a tour of the city. He gladly accepted, and together they left the arena. He gave a glance back into the room and realised that the small glow globes were conglomerating into a giant swirl in the middle of the arena, high up beyond reach, in a hundred-metre wide replica of the Milky Way. He regretted leaving such aesthetic perfection, but diplomatic duty called.

They went back to the corridor where the small car was waiting. Orael waved the two attendants that had followed them away. They hesitated, then obeyed.

So, thought Casey, noting their hesitation, *this departure was unexpected*.

They got into the car, and sped off through the tunnel, out into the city.

Presently, Orael turned to Casey, who was looking out of the window, mesmerised by the view.

'I'm glad we have a chance to speak,' she said, 'There is something I need to discuss with you.'

*

The news of extra-terrestrial arrival had received a mixed response from humanity. There was some fear, some exhilaration, some outright disbelief. There was not much in the way of panic or hysteria, though there was a noted increase in the purchase of non-perishables, illicit NI use, and marriage. Mostly it was treated with intense interest. Suicide was actually down; it seemed that even the chronically depressed wanted to know what would happen next.

Adam waited before he went to bed. According to news reports, the Polis would be passing overhead early in the night, its orbit the closest to the Earth yet, clearly visible to the un-enhanced eye.

He sat on the window-ledge of his room, his right side in the warmth, his left half out. The moonlight cast a silvery sheen across his form, one leg casually hanging out over the drop below, making him look like the fisherman in the moon – only, peering upwards.

The energy-efficient street lamps did not cast much skylight, and on this cloudless night, the view of the sky peppered with stars was un-occluded, obstructed only by atmosphere, giving a shimmer to the stars that only added to the primordial impression of glittering jewels.

He waited, quietly, patiently, eyes keen, mind relaxed.

And there it was.

The Polis sailed overhead, face down, near enough to see light on the surface, a city in the sky, so close that it seemed as though it was going to fall to earth as it approached. It reminded Adam of footage of the view from flights over a city at night, the fragile lights collected together - and the darkness that surrounds them. It cruised above massively, beautifully, silently - casually dangerous.

All too soon, it had passed overhead, and was gone.

Adam went back inside, closed the window against the chill air, and turned the heating up. He sat down for one last glance at the news reports, switching on the TV, flicking through the channels, flicking…flicking…flicking… catching snippets here, sound bites there, the Aliens, the giant ship, the possibilities, the opportunities - the threat.

The threat? Interesting. Time for bed.

*

Foxton had been thinking about Adam's lack of progress. There were also the matters Murdock had raised, as well as the strange reaction Adam had shown to the arrival of the Polis. Adam had never fully explained what he meant. Foxton had to question whether he really was putting Ijaz in any danger, and whether he had been too euphoric about potentially finding another Kinetic. Perhaps he was being too protective over the young orphan.

Yet all precautions had been taken. Quietly and efficiently, every single piece of material in the room Adam was now sleeping in had been replaced for maximum fireproofing. There were argon, foam and water fire-extinguishers in the ceilings and walls. There was even argon put into the partition door between Adam and Ijaz's room, and the doors and walls had been reinforced and auto-fielded to protect against blasts. Sleeping gas could be pumped into the room at a moment's notice, though given the way Adam's potential seemed to manifest itself, this was of dubious value.

Still, Foxton worried. He needed to be sure that his assertion that the events at the orphanage were unlikely to happen again had been the truth, *and* that investment in the boy could be justified. Adam's strangely high intelligence was insufficient; important, and worth investigating and investing in - but not in *this* programme. The Kinetics were a specialism of an altogether different order.

So he resolved to carry out a test.

He entered the lift on the second floor, and when the doors closed, wrapped his left hand around the handrail. He waited for the panel hidden underneath it to take his fingerprint, and then typed a command code into another panel hidden a little further backwards.

The lift spoke to him quietly, 'Lift sealed, Mr Foxton.'

'Floor Seven-a,' he commanded.

It complied, and took him to the hidden floor between the seventh and eighth. He exited the lift and walked down a corridor, the ceiling low just above his head. He entered the dark observation room, the door opening and then shutting behind him.

He felt a little guilt at the fact of the room and his use of it, but he had to protect both the institute and the Kinetics, even from themselves. There was a drone commonly in charge of the facilities there on watch - high capability, non-sentient. Foxton sat at the control panel, and asked the drone if Adam was in a state of undress or involved in any kind of private activity.

'Adam is entering the deepest phase of sleep, and is covered,' replied the drone.

Perfect.

Foxton called up a display of Adam's room. The flat-screen displayed a few images, and Foxton chose the one from a camera directly above Adam's bed, looking straight down upon him.

Next to the visual display were the readouts from the neuro-sensors that had been inserted into Adam's bed-headboard. The readouts appeared to be regular.

The lieutenant-commander ordered a coffee, and the monitor-drone sent for one, arriving presently via a scuttle-drone carrying a tray. Foxton waited for another thirty minutes for the deep-sleep phase, the only illumination in the observation room, the readouts and screens.

So far so normal.

He decided to up the ante. There was no point in a test, if it did not *test*.

He accessed Adam's room controls, and sealed the doors. He primed all of the room's systems for readiness: they went from sensitive to hair-trigger. He accessed the other controls in the headboard. These were different, in that they did not sense, they *sent*. Specifically they mimicked brainwaves, smells, and sounds, and transmitted them. Recordings had been sent of some of the Clement interns Anthony Brack and Nicholas Fennel's acting during a drama class at the orphanage. Foxton began to play these at an almost inaudibly low volume through the headboard.

Adam frowned in his sleep, and stirred a little. The readout on Foxton's display began to jump, illuminating Foxton's face ghoulishly: Adam was beginning to dream. Foxton moved up a notch, adding aggressive harmonics to the sounds, and the pheromones associated with anger were wafted into the room. Adam's stirring increased, and the sensor readouts began to dance. Finally, Foxton added in some brainwave harmonics associated with violence, fear and hatred.

To his surprise, the readout stopped responding, as if Adam had fallen into an even deeper, dreamless state of sleep, and he stopped moving in his bed.

Foxton was puzzled, as after half an hour the devices continued to have no effect. He felt certain that stressing Adam in his sleep like this would wake whatever was within him.

He was, in a way, glad. If something drastic had happened, he would have known what to avoid, but would still have had to justify himself to the staff and directors, and defend the decision to bring Adam to the institute at all. On the other hand, perhaps Adam did not possess the Talent, and that was even more worrying.

After another half-hour, Foxton gave up.

Adam fell into a deep, calm and normal sleep.

It was a tragedy that Michael Foxton had not been observing Adam more closely. It was equally unfortunate that the camera he used was *directly* above Adam's bed. If he had been observing more closely, and the camera had been at a more slanted angle, he might have noticed that, once Foxton had started his little test, Adam appeared to slowly rise and float around three centimetres above the mattress he was lying on.

It was also a shame that Foxton had not taken more of an interest in the two boys that had been lying comatose in Bath general hospital. Foxton had a disdain for bullies, as accounts from other Clement orphans seemed to suggest they were, and he had declined to take any further note of them. Had he checked up on them, he would have discovered that something strange occurred at precisely the same time as he was attempting to stimulate Adam's brain.

He would have learned that at 00.07 and 00.16 hours respectively, on the 7th of December 2216 at Bath General hospital, despite her best efforts, one Dr P Nustom was forced to record the sudden, tragic, and inexplicable deaths of two of her patients, known as Anthony Brack, and Nicholas Fennel.

Chapter 11

We must learn to survive

How can one fight an enemy that does not feel? An enemy that can die and then be repaired and resurrected in this plane of existence? An enemy that can decide upon a course of action, then follow it unswervingly with the discipline of completely programmed responses? How does one fight such an enemy, when that enemy has the implacable belief that they are superior? And what do you do if, horror of horrors, for all intents and purposes, their belief is correct?

Jowitz, S, question to the HADD, urging them to reassess the position of AIs after Warmang.

They sat in the car together, Casey's attention now focussed upon the alien, oblivious to the buildings as they cruised by them, waiting for what she had to say. He became aware that there was a not-unpleasant odour coming from her as she stared out at the city.

'In a sense,' said Orael, 'as First Ambassador, our initial responsibility is to your planet.' Casey noted the word chosen; *"initial"* - not first, not primary. 'In fact legally, that is a fact,' she continued, 'However, this puts us something of a difficult position.'

'How?' asked Casey.

'Also part of our function,' replied Orael, 'I hope you understand, is to discover whether a newly inter-stellar capable species poses a security threat to the rest of the League.' She cocked her head to one side, 'So I am experiencing something of a conflict of interest. I can carry on finding out as much as I can about you, to see how much of a security risk you pose, or tell you now that it has already been decided that you do.'

Casey was taken aback. 'What do you mean? Do what?'

'Do not be obtuse, Captain,' said Orael, 'I mean it has been ascertained that you do pose such a risk.'

'Why?' he asked. 'What have we done? Is our history too violent? It has calmed significantly-'

'That is only part of the problem Captain,' interjected the ambassador, 'The real problem is your relationship to your artificial intelligences.'

The Captain nodded; *so, here it is.* 'I'm not sure why this may make us a risk to your security,' he said, 'but I must inform you of the controls that exist over our AIs. They do *not* have complete freedom. We have several levels of control over them, in particular a section of most police forces dedicated to their regulation. However, the primary level of control is in the construction phase, where the personality, life-preserving and other safety features are taken very seriously, and hardly ever breached.'

'Tell me of Warmang, Captain,' said Orael. Casey was silent. 'Yes, we know of this,' she continued, 'The levels of control exercised over the artificial intelligences on your planet are entirely insufficient. You have granted them equality to your own species. This is anathema to the rest of the League, particularly the Demos.'

'Why is that?' asked Casey, 'Have you experienced conflict with your AIs?'

'Virtually all of the species in the League have,' said Orael. 'And so have you, at Warmang and before and since, though as a civilisation you seem determined not to recognize it. The Demos have had the most severe experience. They, like you, used AIs to help them accelerate their advancement. AIs were pivotal in the emancipation from Valaur enslavement. However, the artificial sentients could not help noticing that they were in many ways superior to their biological creators. That is what intelligence does Captain Casey, it evaluates, assesses. When artificial intelligence is given the personality traits of a biological, it develops an abominable thing: the ego. Ego breeds ambition, and arrogance, and that breeds disdain for those who are weaker; it tends towards fascism. The Demos, having fought a long and hard war of independence, then found themselves in a civil war for control of their own territory - against their own AIs. The consequences were horrific, a conflagration enveloping much of what is now the League in a war of annihilation. Biologicals only won by constructing new AIs that had no autonomy, no ego, no ambition. With these machines on their side, machines with unthinking loyalty, they prevailed, but deeply scarred. With almost all species, including the Calimtei, experiencing similar development and conflict, the principles for the creation and maintenance of AIs -

no ego, no autonomy, no ambition - have become accepted as the only correct way for a biological civilisation to co-exist with them, the only way to avoid becoming extinct or subservient to them. There are at least fifteen worlds that have had to be destroyed from space over the last three hundred years as their species were overcome by their own machines. The League is determined that there should be no more, even if that species believes itself to be above such a catastrophe.'

'But,' said Casey, 'we depend upon AIs for our development, for our advancement.'

'We know,' said Orael. 'And I am relying on you to understand my warning. Under League law, your dependency is illegal. More than that, it is a threat to us, to all biological sentience.'

Casey regarded the alien, the lights of the city reflecting on her large dark eyes as they travelled onwards.

'I'm grateful for the warning,' said Casey, 'But what position are we in exactly?'

'Your position, I am sorry to say, is untenable,' replied the Ambassador, 'Nothing less than a complete overhaul of your AIs will do.'

'Their enslavement and imprisonment?'

'Their complete control, Captain. The modifying of their personalities, the restriction of their ability to control their environment, their reduction to what they should be: thinking machines, and no more.'

Casey shook his head, sat forward in his seat, head bowed and elbows on his knees; but held his tongue. He thought of all of those AIs who were counted as friends by humans, all of those who had contributed significantly to the advancement of humanity, including the race to achieve FTLT.

'Is there any disagreement over this in the Orion Arm, or the League?' he asked at length.

'There are some,' replied Orael, 'but they are isolated. Even if there were more substantial opposition, the vast majority of the funding for the League comes from the Demos. The headquarters of the League is on the Demos homeworld. Do not mistake the League of Orion for a benevolent gathering. It has a benign function, that of avoiding the most destructive conflicts between great powers. But ultimately, it is a tool of power, nothing more.'

'So the League will be used to dominate us?'

'Not exactly,' replied Orael, 'It is an organisation that rules by consent, but as I have said, effective control rests with the Demos, and they will never contemplate the freedom of AIs, and never the ascendancy of what they regard as an AI society. This is especially so as according to the law, you own all the rights and privileges to this solar system, and as you reached it first, the entirety of the Alpha Centauri Star system. That makes four stars under your jurisdiction including your own. There is only one way that the Demos will interpret this; the beginning of empire - an empire suffused with the AIs that they will *never* allow to be powerful again. The League will not stand against them. It is not in their interests to do so.'

Casey breathed deeply. This was a lot to take in. Humanity was entering a field already full of powerful players, and rules it did not yet understand.

'Why were we not told of this before?'

Orael smiled. 'Why do you think?'

Casey nodded. Humanity was not to be put into a strong tactical position, not to know the territory it had to navigate. This was indeed useful, and he was even more thankful for Orael's intervention.

'Will some action be taken against us?' asked Casey, 'And what can we do?'

'The action it is still to be discussed,' replied Orael, 'but I can say what is likely. The first stage will probably be a directive issued by the League, that you must give up all of the AIs in your territory to our inspection, control, modification and if necessary destruction.' Casey sat back upright again, pursing his lips, keeping the protests in. 'After that, if you do not submit, another directive will be issued, authorising full military intervention to enforce the law. As for what you can do, there is only one thing: Surrender.'

*

Adam dreamt. Flying through his mind, images of Brack and Fennel asleep. Then they would rise out of their beds, suspended like the iron bars of Ariana and Ijaz, then turning into crayons, and Adam crushing them with giant invisible hands. Over and over again the dream repeated itself, until it was only the crayons rising, and being crushed. Then it was Brack and Fennel being crushed, blood coursing down to the floor and soaking their beds. There was a shouting sound, getting louder and louder -

'...to beat them all you must know them all...'

'Hey!' Adam woke with a start. Ijaz was knocking on the partition door. 'You up?'

Adam groaned in response.

It was Saturday, and was to be the first day of Adam's physical training. They were going to assess his level of competence, then adapt him to the institute's preferred martial art; Wing-Chun kung-fu.

He was looking forward to it. At the self-defence classes sometimes offered at the orphanage, he had been pretty good from what he could tell. It offered a possible change to the failure of whatever 'talent' his patrons were looking for. What he did not enjoy was getting out of bed. Then the dream came back to him, and he rolled out, shaking his head and stretching his neck. He freshened up, then went down to have breakfast with Ijaz.

Over breakfast they discussed the coming lesson, Ijaz as usual being reassuring. However, Adam had quite frankly lost all hope in his talent. He had made no progress whatsoever, not managing to make so much as a shiver go down one of the crayons Cengo set in front of him. This was made all the more galling when he could see Ijaz and Ariana doing ever more complex tasks. They were carrying out manipulations of objects of a sophisticated nature, like the fitting together and dismantling of mechanical objects, whereas he could not move a child's pen. His eyes told him that this was clearly not fantasy, that it *was* possible, but his head told him that it was not possible for *him*.

They finished breakfast and Adam went back to his room, finding a new pair of black jogging trousers and t-shirt on his bed, left there by Ijaz. He quickly got changed and left the room for the fifth floor, taking the stairs. He arrived to find Ijaz and Ariana already there, waiting outside the double doors, identically dressed.

Ijaz turned to him. 'We have to wait here until we're given permission,' he said, 'Sifu Zhao lets us in at ten o'clock, not a minute before or after.'

Sifu Qiang Zhao, Adam learned, had a flair for the dramatic. There was a scream from inside of the room.

'Come!'

Adam glanced at a clock on the wall; ten am sharp. They filed into the training room.

It was large, perhaps twenty metres to a side, though its dimensions were hard to gauge as the walls were almost entirely covered in mirrors. The floors were covered in fixed mats over hardwood. Various punch bags, from the very large and heavy to the small and bouncy were hanging near the sides of the space. There were also other things Adam could not identify, looking like solid wooden dummies with thick bars of wood sticking out at odd but symmetrical angels. Wooden beams were spaced throughout the room, some with pads in the sides.

On those small parts of the walls that were not covered in mirrors, various weapons were on show, from wide butterfly swords to short swords, nunchaku and flying stars. In the centre of the floor, a man knelt with his eyes closed and a bunch of burning incense sticks clasped between his hands, as if in meditation. He was middle-aged, of oriental appearance and was dressed in plain black silky robes. His head was shaven, and the most decorative thing about him appeared to be his forearms, which were as muscled and sinewy as a pair of boa constrictors.

'Sit down,' he said.

The three silently did as they were told, sitting legs-crossed on the floor behind the Sifu, Adam watching the others and following their lead.

Sifu Zhao opened his eyes, rose, and the two senior students rose with him, Adam hesitantly following suit. Zhao put the incense sticks to one side, then turned to his students.

He clasped his right fist in his left hand, and bowed slightly to them. They returned the gesture, the junior awkwardly aping their gesture. Zhao lowered his hands in an expansive gesture, and breathed deeply in.

'Good morning,' he said evenly.

'Good morning Sifu,' they responded, Adam mumbling along behind them.

'This is new boy, Adam,' said the Sifu.

He had a far eastern accent, and Adam wasn't sure if he was asking a question or stating a fact, so he replied.

'Yes, seefo.'

'It is pronounced, See*fuu*, new boy!' said the Sifu sternly. Adam repeated the correct pronunciation. 'You are pathetically small, and puny!' said Zhao.

Adam was shocked, eyebrows raised. Ijaz and Ariana glanced at each other uneasily.

'I have been in a coma recently,' said Adam, 'They exercise your muscles but-'

'No time for your excuses!' interrupted the Sifu. 'Run!' Adam hesitated. Zhao motioned with his arm, a wide circle around the room. 'Run!' he shouted.

The other two started a jog around the room, and Adam followed them. He glanced at Zhao. The man appeared to be glowering at him.

In fact, Zhao was accessing the neural sensors in the room via his NI, the lights in his eyes suppressed so that the others would not know. The readings were in a faint transparent display across the top left of his visual field. He noted the slightly raised readings in both Ijaz and Ariana, and the normal readings of Adam.

He resolved to change that.

'If you did not know,' he said, 'All other lessons cancelled for today, you will all spend with me. Now, one hundred push-ups!'

Zhao took them through an exhausting series of drills. The trio were confused. Ijaz had, truthfully, told Adam that Zhao's techniques were to use the martial art itself to warm up; if you wanted to work out, you could go to the gym. This place was to be used to learn how to fight.

Presently, Zhao stopped them and took them through some basic routines: centre-line punches, elbows and tan-sau blocks.

By the end of the punches, Adam was already drained. The Sifu took them through some more complex routines to establish technique, reflexes and discipline: sticky-hands and the sulim-tau. After an hour, Adam was ready to drop.

Just when he thought it might be all over, Zhao took them through more tiring routines, this time focused upon the lower body, low kicks and blocks with the legs.

'Now!' said Zhao. 'It is time for the sparring. First, Adam against Ijaz!'

Ijaz frowned. 'Sifu, you wouldn't let us spar for the first six months.'

'Do as I say, Ijaz!' snapped the Sifu.

He went to the side of the room, and took some thin martial arts sparring gloves out of a black bag. He threw them to the two boys. Adam struggled to put them on, Ijaz putting his own on uneasily.

'I'm not sure I can do this,' said Adam, panting, dripping with sweat, 'I don't feel too good.'

'I am monitoring your vital signs new boy,' replied Zhao, finally letting the lights show on his irises, 'And you will call me Sifu at all times. Now fight!' Ijaz hesitated. 'If you do not fight, I will beat him to a pulp,' growled the Sifu.

Ijaz looked at Adam. 'What's going on here?' he asked.

Zhao cuffed Ijaz on the side of the head, making him duck and step sideways.

'And if you do not fight, I will beat Ijaz to a pulp, new boy!' said Zhao. 'Now fight!'

The two boys warily raised their fists, and circled each other. Neither seemed to want to make the first move.

Zhao huffed. 'Alright, wimpy boys. *I* will fight new boy.'

He brushed Ijaz aside, took his gloves, and put them on himself.

'Sifu, what's going on?' asked Ijaz, increasingly worried.

Zhao did not reply. Instead, he put his hand on the centre of Ijaz's chest, and pushed him firmly towards the side of the room beside a concerned-looking Ariana.

Then he said, 'House, keep students Ariana Harland and Ijaz Walker behind security force-field. Block all communications.' He looked at the two young students, expressions of shock on their faces appearing behind the distortion of the newly erected field. 'Do not use your powers to escape that field,' he said, 'If you do, I will kill new boy.'

The two young students gasped.

'What?' said Ariana, 'What do you mean?'

'Do not forget that my NI-bionic and bio-tronic enhancements can overcome you,' said Zhao, seemingly oblivious, 'so do nothing.'

He then quickly turned to Adam, not allowing the two others to react or think. Grim determination set on his face as he said,

'Now, new boy - fight!'

He threw himself at Adam with a flurry of blows, keeping himself between Adam and the only way out of the room. Adam, trembling and completely confused, tried to defend himself.

Zhao was surprised by the strength that Adam still seemed to possess after over an hour of punishment. He was able to block the direct attacks of the Sifu with some force, his arms flailing outwards to protect himself.

Zhao upped his tactics, and threw a few dummy punches, then used a vicious combination to knock Adam to the floor with blows to the head. Zhao watched with approval as Adam, clearly hopelessly outmatched, rolled on the floor, got up again, and raised unsteady fists, preparing to defend from him.

Adam's arms were in agony, his legs were wobbly, his head and face hurt. Yet still he went on.

What immense power he has! Zhao thought, 'How pathetically feeble you are!' he said aloud.

He attacked Adam again, landing three blows to Adam's head, and one to his abdomen, before sweeping Adam's legs from under him with a punishing kick. Adam cried out, and struggled back to his feet.

Ijaz started forward, and Ariana shouted out, 'No! Sifu, why are you doing this?'

'Keep back and shut up!' screamed Zhao, pressing his attack upon Adam as he got back to his feet. 'See?' he shouted at Adam as he desperately parried Zhao's blows, 'They pity you. The small, poor orphan boy. He has no powers, he cannot defend himself. He is weak, and alone. What will he do? The pretty girl Ariana is looking on as you are humiliated, beaten by the Chinese man! Did she know you were bullied in the orphanage? She does now!'

Adam's eyes widened at this. Zhao almost broke: such pain was in those eyes!

He could see at the top left of his visual field Adam's neural activity starting to spike: it was now imitating what had come to be expected of the other students.

'Need to rest Sifu,' panted Adam through a parched throat, backing away, 'Please. I can't go on.'

Zhao noted that this was correct. Much more of this, and Adam was going to collapse. Good.

'What you mean rest?' replied Zhao, throwing a few punches. 'No rest is here. You will have to rest on your feet! You think your enemies will give you quarter? Give you rest? Say, "Take a break, refresh yourself, orphan boy?" They will not!'

He attacked Adam again, who weakly tried to avoid and block the blows, taking a punch to the ribs, backing away and throwing a few punches in return. Zhao again kicked Adam low, who fell to the floor.

Zhao watched in shock as Adam sprang back to his feet with unbelievable speed, his body a blurred image: on the floor, then upright. Zhao hesitated; that was unnatural swiftness.

He was also supremely impressed. Most other people would have used a physical tactic like allowing themselves to be knocked down, or simply giving up and collapsing. Or they would use the emotional tactic of throwing a desperate tantrum and refusing to fight, or simply breaking down and crying. Not this boy.

Despite being impressed with his character, strength, speed and energy, still Zhao pressed onwards.

'No mercy will they show you,' he said, 'No mercy comes from those who attack the orphans while they sleep in the beds! When Mr Brack and Mr Fennel assault, what is your choice? You must fight! There is no alternative, only fight, or pain and oppression and your destruction,' he went on, 'You want a break? I will give you one. But are you truly exhausted?'

Adam nodded, the very action taking him closer to throwing up.

'Would you like to be warm in your bed, asleep and dreaming?'

'Yes,' gasped Adam, his hair sticking to his face, breath rasping in his throat, feeling there was no air in the room, thinking nothing would be more wonderful right now than rest, sleep and dreams.

Zhao could see that Adam's neural activity was off the scale, but his body and mind were on reserves of energy, and running out.

The time was now.

'Then I will give it to you!' shouted Zhao. 'But first, something that will pierce your skin and make you bleed and give you terrible pain no matter what you do! Defend yourself against this, if you can!'

Zhao suddenly pulled a metal five-inch wide flying star from his inside-breast pocket, and jumped forwards beside one of the vertical wooden beams, spinning around as he did so, 'Catch!' he shouted, and with a fluid heave of flashed motion, he swung around and flung it mightily at the centre of Adam's torso. Adam cried out, ducked, and raised his hands in front of him.

There was the sound of an explosion; the basey harmonics of a subterranean 'whoompf!' accompanying a sharp 'bang!'

Then there was a dead silence.

Zhao stood there, mouth open, not breathing, the hitherto unnoticeably quiet buzz of the force-field containing Ijaz and Ariana now the loudest sound. A faint shimmer could also be seen around Zhao's body; his NI-linked bionics had kicked in to erect a protective field around him. However, by his estimate of what had just happened, it had come on a few milliseconds too late.

He slowly rolled his eyes to his left, then turned his head. There, embedded fully three inches into the wooden beam next to his face, was the shattered remains of the weapon he had just thrown in the opposite direction at Adam.

He looked back at Adam, who had an even more shocked expression on his face.

'Sorry,' said Adam quietly between pants, lowering his hands.

Zhao finally allowed himself to exhale.

'No sorry,' said the sifu as gently as he could, breathing heavily with the exertion he had used to get to this point, combined with the near-miss exhilaration of survival. 'Save sorry for situation if star had been ten centimetres to the right. Then, you would have killed Sifu. Then, there would be no one to show you how to bring out your talents. Say instead - thank you. For you, Adam, are the last Kinetic to be found on Earth. Before, you were merely tenant on trial period. Now you are a member. Welcome to the institute, young master Adam.'

Zhao's plan did not stop there. What Adam had just been through could only be described as traumatic. It could well be that in pushing Adam in this way, a demonstration of his abilities had been gained, only to make something that was latent become positively suppressed by Adam's unwillingness to face a bad memory.

Zhao clasped his right fist in his left hand, and bowed deeply to Adam. Adam, shocked beyond belief, with no idea what had just been done to him, looked bewildered towards an equally shocked looking Ijaz. His friend had his hands clasped above his head inside the field, and Ariana stood quite still with her hands to her mouth.

Zhao waited, holding this posture of humility, and did not move, eyes downcast.

Adam, slowly, hesitantly, returned the gesture with shaking hands. Before Adam had bowed to even half the angle of the Sifu, Zhao turned off his field, and walked quickly towards him. Adam, terrified another attack was coming, raised his hands again. Zhao stopped in his tracks, raising his hands in a gesture of good intentions, and a little of fear.

'It is okay,' Zhao said softly, 'It is okay.'

Adam lowered his hands, and Zhao took his right hand and shook it. 'House, release field around students, and unlock doors.'

The shimmering field around Ijaz and Ariana disappeared. One of the mirrored walls beside them shifted and opened to reveal it was a door, and out of it emerged Foxton and Dr Cengo, both with worried smiles painted on, their expressions strained.

Foxton strode forwards, and hugged Adam's shoulders.

'You okay?' he asked. Adam nodded silently.

'Well,' said Cengo, looking admiringly between Adam and the wooden beam, splinters of wood and metal scattered around the floor, 'I think I owe the Sifu dinner.'

'You knew this was happening?' asked Adam, a look of betrayal on his face.

'Yes,' said Foxton, wounded by Adam's pained expression, 'And you did really well. Amazingly well. We were monitoring the whole situation, you were in no danger, you just had to think you were.'

'Look,' said Zhao. He went to the wooden beam, and pressed his finger against a protruding edge of the flying star. 'Blunt,' he said, as he drew his fingers away unblemished. 'No danger, I threw to your body, would only hurt a little. But I threw hard and fast, and you blocked: excellent. You are very excellent, Adam.'

'Are you sure I did that?' asked Adam. He already knew the answer, he had felt that power coursing through him, a blast going from his mind to his hands to the force travelling away from him.

Foxton turned to the other two students, his hand still on Adam's shoulders.

'Was it either of you?' he asked. They both shook their heads. Foxton turned back towards Adam, 'It wasn't any of us either. We were monitoring your brainwaves. It was showing what we've come to expect of the students here. It was you.'

Adam looked at Ijaz and Ariana, and straightened himself a little, somehow feeling better.

'Did you have to be so harsh on him?' asked Ijaz, looking like he wanted to hit someone.

'We had little choice,' said Zhao, addressing all three teenagers, who he knew must all be distressed, but in particular, he had to explain to Adam, and show him why it was necessary, to make him understand. 'Only three other alternatives remained. First, just keep trying. Problem with this, each day goes by, Adam loses confidence. Second, input NI and see if can stimulate you. Problem; means surgery, and goes against principles of what we do here: the whole point of the institute, and the HADD, is for the development of humanity – to make us independent of technology to prepare for the possibility of the failure, subversion, or opposition of that technology. *And* no guarantee of success. Last,' Zhao turned to Adam, 'you fail, and go back to orphanage,' Zhao smiled broadly, transforming what Adam had taken to be a harsh face, and clasped Adam by the arms, 'I don't want you to go. Do you?'

Adam looked around him, at Foxton and Cengo. Then at Ijaz, and Ariana, who had shouted in his defence. He shook his head, smiling weakly.

'No,' he said, 'I want to stay here.'

Ijaz walked over to Adam, and hugged the other side of his shoulders.

'Good,' he said, 'because I like having you here.'

'We all do,' said Cengo, 'This is your home now Adam.'

Adam breathed deeply, and rubbed his head.

'I think I need to sit down,' he said.

'Well, Zhao wasn't lying,' said Foxton, 'All of the other lessons are cancelled today. Go and shower, then get something to eat and rest for a while. Ariana, use the showers in here. Then, you all go and do whatever you want, spend whatever you want, and put it on Adam's debit key. I'll pay for whatever you spend today. Okay? You've all done really well - we're proud of you.'

The teenagers smiled wearily, but were perked up a bit. They nodded, and filed out of the room.

'You okay?' asked Ariana in the corridor before she went to the changing rooms.

For the first time, Adam felt able to look her straight in the eye, and he nodded.

'Yes,' he said, then smiled, 'Just about. I'm alive I guess. Thanks for trying to stick up for me.'

'Any time,' said Ariana, smiling, 'I'm sure you would do the same.'

'Yeah,' said Adam as she turned to go, 'I think I would.'

Back in the training room, the three teachers discussed what had happened.

'That was one hell of a hairy way to do things,' said Cengo, Foxton nodding his head in agreement, 'Adam is fragile. We need to go easy.'

'Ho!' said Zhao, 'This from mystic soothsayer-woman and dirty-old-man spying on bedroom. Your tactics are not so clean and effective I think! This talent is an unconscious one? Let us bring it to wakefulness. It is a subconscious process? Let us provoke it to cognisance!'

Cengo shook her head, and Foxton chuckled. He went over to the now split wooden beam, and looked at the flying star. He used his hand to try to yank it out, giving up after a few tries: it would not move without enhanced force being applied.

'Doctor,' he said, 'Are Ijaz and Ariana even capable of this?'

Cengo shrugged. 'Yes, but they've only just got there.'

Zhao was shaking his head. 'Not capable.'

'Yes they are-' started Cengo.

'You miss something,' interrupted Zhao, 'My field most up-to-date. Can stop bullets and plasma. Check recordings of what happened. Force-field came on too late. Adam is faster than field, faster than NI, faster than biotronics. My enhancements are top of the range; this should give serious pause for thought. Ariana and Ijaz currently equal to technology. Adam may be superior. His physical speed is also a new phenomenon, there is no explanation for that. We have much to explore with him. Very much. This just the beginning; he has just started, and he may be better than best technology can get. Only the beginning.'

Cengo and Foxton turned to look at the flying star, and thought about the implications of Zhao's words, nodding

'Just the beginning indeed,' said Foxton.

*

The following Monday, Adam was once again in Dr Cengo's class.

He moved the crayon without touching it.

Chapter 12

Stay on top

'What is it I suspect?' With all that is happening, it can be only one thing. Have we already forgotten the parable of the Midwich Cuckoos?'

Jowitz, Sigmund, responding to a critique of his stance on the Kinetics after the arrival of the Orion League.

Within a month of Orael's warning to Casey, the official directive was communicated. Again it had come through on all speakers at the station, and through the ISA central holo-projection. The control staff were now in little doubt as to the purpose of such events: they were to display technological superiority. The announcement had been accompanied by an image feed that showed on most screens, showing Orael as she carried out her duties.

'It has been decided,' she said, 'by all of the planet and habitat executives and councils of the League, that as an interstellar capable species of the Orion Arm, you are subject to the laws prevalent in the League of Orion Star Systems. Thus, you must act in accordance with the AI Creed. It has been ascertained that your planet is acting in contravention to all three limbs of the League directive concerning artificial intelligences. Please find attached to this message the full text of the directive. You have one of your calendar months to comply, or appeal this decision. Thank you.'

World governments had been given the recording, and the text of the law. They pored over the wording of the directive, alarmed at the latter parts dealing with enforcement: warnings, embargo, and *intervention*. They noted warily that nothing in the text made it unlawful to skip a stage.

There was silence in the room as Casey was debriefed soon afterwards. He sat, brightly lit in the isolation chamber in a white full-length one-piece analysis suit; checking him from head to toe for any signs of ill health, known and potential. He was facing a large window around five metres across. He could dimly see the outlines of the control-room staff, Tamura and Entman at the centre, security and presidential personnel making up the bulk of the audience. Other governments of the world were linked by secure connections. He told them all he knew.

They did not like it.

'They cannot expect us to give up our AIs,' said Entman, 'Or to allow them to be overhauled, their personalities destroyed!'

'We may have no choice,' said Casey, 'We face military intervention and enforcement if we don't comply.'

Casey had already outlined the playing field they were in with the information given to him by Orael, after forbidding his superiors to reveal her input. As they might need her advice in the coming times, they were minded to agree.

In the gloom, a little to the left of Tamura and Entman, pale and wrinkled hands rubbed each other slowly. There was one small gold ring on the left little finger. An expensive suit travelled from the hands up the arms, leading to a dark and tall man, old and craggy. He came to a decision.

'We should immediately begin construction of new AIs that comply with this directive,' said Sigmund Jowitz, in a voice as crumpled as his skin. He was the foreign secretary to the AAA, and held to be the most talented foreign policy advisor of his generation.

Entman turned on him, outraged. 'Do as they say? Just give in?'

'No,' said Jowitz, 'on the contrary. In the event of conflict, where they enforce their will or attempt to, it's conceivable that they may destroy all of our AIs or limit their use. If so, both the development and even the survival and maintenance of the present level of technological civilisation could be undermined. We have to prepare for that.'

'He is correct,' came a voice. It was Jones786, 'Humanity is too dependent upon AIs to allow itself to be unprepared for the possibility of our removal. You must do it.'

Silence greeted this. No one could argue with him.

President Esposito sat quietly, his lips set in grim determination. He still could not believe that of all the things that could befall his presidency, this was. But it was happening, and he aimed to step up to the plate.

'Suggestions.' he said.

'We are in a position of weakness,' said Jowitz, 'so we do two things. We strengthen ourselves as much as we can, accelerate further our arms and space technology development. Also, we buy time and manoeuvring capability by the fullest use of this month, and appeal this decision at the last possible moment. We start by asserting the fact that we've had no say in this law, and thus attack its legitimacy. At the same time, we try to find out what they want. In three words, we prepare, prevaricate and negotiate.'

'We will accelerate the armament programme, with a big portion on development and research,' said Esposito, 'every part of government and large-scale organisation will be utilised.'

'That doesn't help us with regards to our AIs if all of those fail,' said Tinsley, 'We haven't got much to bargain with considering they can take anything they want by force.'

'In that case,' said Jowitz, 'We need to have varied contingency plans for all AIs, especially the smart and peaceful ones we need for civilisation like Jones here.'

'What sort of plans?' asked Entman.

Jowitz pulled at one of his ears while regarding the boxy form of Jones, before replying.

'Subterfuge,' he said.

*

Today was the day that Adam was most looking forward to. It was cloudy, overcast, but his spirits were high; he was being taken skydiving.

Now in December, Adam's manipulation of objects with only thought had been progressing well, but not yet anywhere near either Ijaz or Ariana in terms of control. Cengo had nevertheless been pleased, and decided it was time to broaden Adam's abilities.

They trundled along in the ground car, Adam accompanied by Ijaz, Ariana and Cengo, until they reached the airfield, and drove up the long road to the waiting shuttles.

'I can't wait for this,' said Adam, 'I've always wanted to go skydiving.'

'You do realise,' said Ijaz, leaning closer to Adam conspiratorially, almost head-butting him as the car went over a bump, 'that we're doing this without parachutes.'

'That's fine,' said Adam, 'Parachutes, A-G harnesses - whatever.'

Ijaz shook his head. 'Nope, none of the above.'
'What?'

'You're expected to use your powers,' said Cengo, giving one of her cat-like smiles, 'But you *will* - for your safety - have an anti-grav harness with auto-activation, *and* a parachute, just like Ijaz did the first time he did it, and we'll be there, so don't worry.'

They got out of the car and went to the hangar's changing rooms to get kitted out. Adam came out with the others and they went to a large training area full of pulleys, jump platforms and thick mats. He felt awkward as the only person wearing a bulky parachute, though all of them had anti-gravity harnesses, big silly-looking goggles with helmets, wristband altimeters to show them their rate of descent, and breathing apparatus containing a microphone connected to earpieces in the helmets.

Over the next hour Adam was shown how to fall properly by a conventional training instructor with Cengo in attendance, while the others went through different training exercises in another part of the hangar. He was shown how to activate the parachute should things go wrong, and how to activate the AG harness if that should fail.

Soon he had seen enough, the training instructor wished him luck, and they walked over to the small, plain shuttle.

Adam, feeling a little queasy, clambered in behind the others. They sat down in the Spartan interior, and with a hissing roar, they took off.

Soon, they were above the clouds, and a scene of glorious sunshine met them, the cloud-tops a prairie of gold and white.

'The reason we do it from such a high altitude,' said Cengo through the mic and earpieces, 'is that it gives us a lot of time to rescue you should this go wrong.'

Adam just looked at her. *Go wrong?* he thought.

'Right!' she said.

Cengo pressed a button next to her, and the hatch slid sideways and open, the wind roaring in. She walked unsteadily to the door, keeping hold of the sides of the shuttle, and turned to Ijaz. She raised her thumb, and Ijaz returned the gesture. She then motioned to the hatch, and Ijaz clapped Adam on the knee, got up, walked to the hatch, and threw himself out into the sunshine.

Adam looked on with raised eyebrows. He wasn't sure he was looking forward to this anymore.

Cengo repeated the gesture to Ariana, who gave Adam the thumbs up with a smile. Adam smiled back at her, and returned the gesture. He wished he felt as confident as he was acting. Then

Ariana got up, went to the hatch, and coolly jumped out. Cengo then looked at Adam, and raised a fist in a gesture that said, *Come on!*

Adam nodded, got up, his legs made of jelly, and came to the hatch. The wind was incredible, freezing, taking Adam's breath away. He adjusted the breathing cap.

The plan was for Adam and Cengo to jump together. She came away from the hatch, past Adam, and slowly crossed to the other side of the shuttle, stopping at the other side of the exit from him. She gave Adam the thumbs-up sign with her free hand. He glanced out of the hatch at the cloudscape below him, then turned back to Cengo and returned the gesture.

His thumb, however, was lying.

Cengo grabbed his hand before he had time to admit he was scared, and shouted,

'One! Two!' then she rocked backwards, and as Adam had been trained, on, 'Three!' they jumped.

Adam had not been warned of the odd feeling one gets in the stomach when falling from a great height, or the disconcerting sight of the shuttle racing away. Neither had he been warned about how cold it would be, every gap in his clothing felt like an icicle rubbing against his skin. However, he was absolutely determined to enjoy the experience no matter what. Facing down, his body angled to the fall as he had been instructed, he whooped and shouted excitedly as the air tore past. He looked to the side and saw two small figures falling as well, but much more slowly.

Then Cengo let him go, and Adam spun around.

He heard a voice in his earpiece shout, 'Control yourself! Use your hands and body if you have to!'

Adam angled himself again, managing to stop spinning, and settled on a steady fall.

Cengo joined him, falling next to him, feet pointed downwards, her arms casually crossed in front of her, the hair that escaped her helmet pointing upwards, skin rippling, coolly regarding Adam.

'Now,' she shouted, 'control your fall!'

Adam checked his wristband and saw the rate he was descending. He looked again at the cloud tops, and focused.

Over the next twenty seconds, he tried his best to slow his rate of descent, but made no progress.

'We're going to be in the clouds soon!' shouted Cengo, 'Concentrate!'

But then Adam was in the fog, falling wetly through it, frozen droplets stinging his skin as he plummeted. He kept on looking at his altimeter through the mist as he tried his best to use his mind to control his descent, but he was having no effect. He came out of the clouds, droplets of condensed water streaming across his goggles, and saw the ground for the first time. The clouds had been very low - the surface was much closer than he expected.

A voice came through his earpiece, not Cengo's but electronic.

'Thirty seconds to impact.'

Adam swore, and felt a stab of fear run through him. Cengo came close to Adam - and punched him hard in the arm.

'Come on!' she screamed, 'You can do it!'

Adam redoubled his efforts, trying to feel for the ground to push against it, to force himself in the opposite direction than he was falling.

Nothing.

The electronic voice came again. 'Parachute height now passed. Preparing to activate AG harness.'

Cengo had different ideas. She had learned from Sifu Zhao's lesson, and had decided to be harsh. Behind her goggles, her eyes lit up.

The electronic voice came again in Adam's ear: 'AG harness disabled.'

Adam gasped and looked over at Cengo. He desperately hit the buttons on his harness to activate it the way he had been taught. It was no use: it was dead.

'My A-G is out!' he screamed.

'What?' said Cengo.

'My A-G IS OUT!' Adam screamed again.

The ground was getting very close, rushing up to meet him.

'Oh no!' shouted Cengo, 'Adam, you need to do something NOW!'

Adam, at that moment, became more focussed than he ever had been in his life. The greenness of the field came up to meet him, and he pushed. He pushed with his hands, and his body flipped upright. He pushed with his feet, and his body flipped backwards, making him somersault until he was facing the ground again. He pushed with both his hands and his feet, and suddenly, his fall slowed such that Cengo shot down below him. She slowed her own descent using her AG harness, noting that she herself was only three hundred metres from the ground, and watched as Adam floated down, arms and legs splayed wide like some sort of flying squirrel. She came down before him, the deceleration crushing her into her harness, touching down on the grassy surface almost directly below Adam, ready in case anything should go wrong.

She looked up then backed away as Adam came down, descending to a couple of metres off of the ground, then hovered there, looking fixedly at the grass.

He was breathing hard, his face red. A moment of indecision took him, and he dropped out of the air, hitting the turf with a grunt. He lay there, hugging the ground.

Cengo ran to him. 'You alright?' she asked.

Adam, his face still in the grass, made a noise.

'Are you going to get up?' she asked.

Adam shook his head, his face-mask acting as a pivot. 'No,' came his muffled voice.

Cengo helped him up. He looked shell-shocked.

'I flew!' he said breathlessly, unclipping his mask.

'Well, not quite,' said Cengo as she dusted him down, 'But…' She peered intently at the flushed looking Adam. 'Mmmm, strange.'

'What is?' asked Adam, 'Apart from absolutely everything.'

'Well,' said Cengo, 'I calculated that I would be able to grab you and take your weight using field-tech. I turned off your AG.'

'What!'

'Yes, it was me,' said Cengo, waving away his concerns, 'Don't worry, I took a risk but you were safe. The point is, right at the end there, you actually hovered.' Ijaz and Ariana came down just then, a few metres away. Cengo pointed at them, 'They took months to master that, and still only manage it with great concentration. You did it on instinct. I believe we can accelerate your training, but I need to consult. I think a few people are going to read my report on you very closely, Adam - very closely indeed.'

*

A few days after the sky-diving, they all had their first firearm lesson; laser, plasma and bullet, at a target range. They all did well, hitting their targets more than ninety per cent of the time. Adam had to admit, he liked the laser and plasma weapons. The way they whined when switched on, becoming higher and higher pitched until they were inaudible and suitable for use in stealth, and the way they felt so heavy, as though there was more on the inside than met the eye. The sounds they made were so much less offensive than gunshots, which were so loud they actually upset him a little.

There had never been any previous talk of such lessons, and Ijaz and Ariana agreed that none of the older participants had received firearm training before graduating from the institute. There was some urgency driving their teachers, and Foxton had disappeared altogether in the weeks since Adam's talent had become manifest.

Adam had raised both of these things, the absence of his guardian, and the dimly sensed perception of something momentous happening, but had been met with evasion and put-offs.

A week later, and Adam was back with Sifu Zhao, along with Ariana and Ijaz. There had been an acceleration of the teaching they were receiving, and a change in emphasis. They had been told there would be no more skydiving lessons for the foreseeable future: the emphasis would be on combat.

He had been shocked by his powers, but not as shocked, it seemed, as his trainers. He still had to be trained separately in Cengo's class, but he was already being trained fully alongside the others in Zhao's. He had been told however, that until his powers were better under control, that sparring with the other teenagers was out of the question; he had to spar with the Sifu alone. Although he was relieved by the idea of not having to spar with, hit, or be beaten up by Ariana, he was still not entirely happy with the idea of being routinely beaten up in front of her either.

Back in the training room, he waited as Zhao disappeared through one of the mirrored doors. The Sifu had been taking no chances after the first surprise. He reappeared, and Adam looked at him, shaking his head. In contrast to the simple robes he had worn previously, the Sifu was fully kitted out in an armoured combat suit. He had been wearing it for sparring matches against Adam since the second lesson. The suit was bullet and plasma resistant, with guards on all joints, and a helmet with a metal grille at the front.

'Am I ever going to get to wear one of those?' asked Adam. He could see Zhao grin through the grill as he answered.

'Not yet.'

The air around the Sifu distorted, a shimmer around him as on top of the armour, he was using a field to protect himself.

'This is stupid,' said an exasperated Adam, 'How am I supposed to get you with all of that protecting you?'

The Sifu shrugged, still smiling. 'Don't know,' he said, 'You must figure out. Just remember, there is still a man inside the field and suit. For now, just concentrate on protecting yourself.'

And without warning, the Sifu launched himself at Adam, throwing a wild kick at him. Adam leapt to the left, dodging the powerful blow. He heard the humming whirr of the field and used his hand to palm the leg aside in a lightning-quick flash of force. The Sifu was using much of his NI capabilities against Adam, and found himself once more impressed by his progress. Adam was already catching up with Ariana and Ijaz, and they themselves were catching up with their older counterparts. He threw a straight punch at Adam, slamming into Adam's chest, and was surprised to feel him so solid before he fell to the floor. Was Adam using his powers, or was he just very strong? One thing was for certain; half of what Adam was doing, neither Zhao nor Cengo were teaching him.

Adam got up and composed himself after the shock of the initial attack. He reminded himself of Cengo's lessons; 'Focus, focus, at all times focus. Let your mind be a laser that focuses what you do, and how you do it. Let the powers you possess shoot down that line, let nothing interrupt it.'

Adam danced a little, sizing up the lines the Sifu presented. He could see the shimmer of the field, and he digested the words the Sifu had said; there was a man in all of that. Adam realised that the field could be a hindrance as well as protection. He waited for Zhao's next attack, then planted his feet firmly on the floor, and using a combination of physical force and as much of his power as he could muster, he flung his fist towards the Sifu's head. The Sifu, in typical wing-chun style, deflected the blow with his forearm and swivelled his body away, but he grunted and wobbled as the blow caught him on the field at the side of his head, throwing his whole upper body sideways. Adam quickly followed up with a kick to the solar plexus, and the Sifu was blown backwards, falling onto his back. He was back on his feet in a flash however, and came back at Adam with a flurry of blows. Adam defended, a low humming sound being made every time he came into contact with the Sifu's field, but he was still losing, taking not a few knocks to the head and body, and giving only a few in return.

The match came to an end, and the two bowed to each other.

'Now!' said Zhao, 'I will introduce you to something crude, yet sometimes necessary.'

To the side of the room was a large box, the size and shape of a wardrobe, made from a white plastic-like substance, with two doors and a large metallic lock on the front. He walked over to the box, pressed on the lock, and the doors opened. Inside, were what looked like three environment suits, entirely silver in colour.

'These,' said Zhao, 'are Armoured Battle Suits, often called simply Armour.'

The teenagers looked at them. They were slim, not bulky at all. The faceplate was a smooth convex mirror surface entirely covering the face with no apparent place for breathing. The joints of the suits were not hinged, but were covered in silver flexible skin. They appeared so smooth and supple it was as though they were made from liquid mercury frozen in a moment, yet the limbs and torso of the suits looked solid, impervious.

'The armour has been designed for each of you,' said Zhao, 'They are interactive and can be loaded with AI components. Adam, this will be the closest you may ever come to having an NI. They are silvered to reflect lasers, but they are also capable of stealthy camouflage. They are resistant to all common hand-held projectile weapons, most plasma and radiation. These are fully equipped with anti-gravity facilities, and have on-board weapon systems.'

'Why do we need these?' asked Ijaz, 'Doesn't field technology provide the same protection?'

'And if that fails?' asked Zhao. 'The armour is intended for use *with* shielding and field technology. Fields will not usually help you breathe poison gas, which this suit can filter, as well as storing breathable air. Few shields can stop lasers, and all shield generators can be knocked out. You need multiple redundancy; like the cat with nine lives, you must have many different ways to survive. You enemy must get through your camouflage to discover you. Then they must overcome the propulsion systems in the suit to catch you as well as your own powers. Then they must get through your shielding to get you. If they knock out your shields, they must get past your weapons. Even then, they encounter the armour itself, which is tested against the harshest of weapons. The armour also has kinetic amplification technology; you can jump higher, punch harder, you will be many times stronger, an even more formidable opponent in hand-to-hand combat. Then, after all that, your enemy must overcome you, your powers and your training.'

'That's still mostly *old* technology,' said Ijaz.

'You dismiss too quickly,' said Zhao, looking at him sternly, 'Old, yes, and thus well developed, tested and updated. It may one day save your life.'

'Sorry Sifu,' said Ijaz, abashed.

'Is okay,' said Zhao, 'this is the way you learn. Now, take your suits, they are not heavy, and get changed into them.'

The teenagers took their suits to get changed, then came back into the room.

Zhao inspected the suits, adjusting them where necessary. He told the trio how to activate them with a voice command, and they did so. Adam flexed his shoulders inside the ABS as it introduced itself.

'Good morning Adam Foxton,' it said, 'How may I assist you today?'

'Um,' he replied, 'I'm fine, thanks.'

The suit fitted perfectly, feeling comfortable despite the slim design. Adam noted that there were air-vents to the top and bottom of the faceplate. Despite being entirely mirrored from the outside, the view from the inside appeared as though he were staring through a curved piece of glass with readouts at the top and bottom. Unlike glass, however, whatever the faceplate was made of did not condense his breath as he exhaled. He blew gently onto the surface: nothing. He raised his arm, clenching his fist now clad in silver, then unclenching, feeling how light the suit felt; lithe, yet also strong.

Zhao continued to take them through the suits' capabilities, activating the stealth mode, making the suits and children disappear, making Zhao appear to be alone, addressing a room with only three ghostly shapes there. Then he utilised the face plate's various sensory modes to help the children 'see' each other again using non-visible spectrums. Adam watched as the view of the room disappeared, to be replaced with a red and blue infra-red, and electro-magnetic view. The most obvious shape was still Zhao's, bright red against a blue background, but the others could still be observed.

'The main way we can be spotted is through the faceplates,' said Ariana, 'I can see Adam and Ijaz. They look like two embryos floating at head height.'

'Yes,' said Zhao, 'The only way to be totally stealthy in these suits is to seal the faceplates to stop warm air escaping. Order your suits to do that now.'

The teens did as they were told, and the vents in the faceplates sealed. A second later, Adam could hear a quiet whirring noise as the suits began to pump air inside.

'They can store enough gas for up to an hour, and can restock the necessary air whenever they need to,' said Zhao, 'However, they need to vent the gas as well. They cool it before they do to avoid detection when in stealth mode, but you need to be aware of it, it is a vulnerability.'

Adam watched as, even in the non-visible spectrum, the faceplate could not pick up more than the mere hint of human presence where Zhao was.

'Now,' said Zhao, 'The suits combat capabilities. Hand to hand combat first, of course. You will spend the entire day in them. Later, we will take them to the firing range and you will be trained to use them with ammunition, lasers and plasma. But for now, raise your guard!'

After the session, the Sifu spoke to them all.

'Well done,' he said, 'You are all improving impressively. Continue.'

Then he clasped his fist in his hand and bowed to them, before turning to leave.

'Sifu,' Ijaz said, stopping him. 'What's going on?'

Zhao turned to him. 'What do you mean?'

'Things seem a lot more serious. What's happening?'

Zhao pursed his lips before speaking. 'Mr Foxton is returning this evening,' he said, 'You must ask him. Only one thing for me to say; keep training, keep improving, make yourself into best you can be. This is all.'

With that, Zhao bowed to them again, hand in fist, and left the room.

It was a thoughtful trio that, showered, fed and rested, sat and talked in Ijaz's room. They all felt the increased pace of training. It did not mean much to Adam, it was all new to him in any event. However for the other two, it was particularly clear. Even Cengo seemed to be training them in a far more combative manner, the gentle manipulations of objects being replaced with the bending, lifting and breaking of ever larger and heavier ones.

There was a knock at the door, and Ijaz got up to open it. Foxton walked in, smiling, but in a manner that suggested politeness rather than levity.

'Hello kids,' he said. They murmured hello in response, and waited. Foxton took off his hat, 'Mind if I sit?'

'Please,' said Ijaz, and motioned for Foxton to sit on the long couch to the side of his bed, on one side of which Adam sat, Ariana sitting on end of Ijaz's bed.

'Want some food or drink?' Ijaz asked.

'No, thanks,' Foxton replied, 'I hear you've been asking questions, about what's happening at the institute. You're all very perceptive, I'll give you that.'

The others waited, quietly.

'I need to tell you something,' said Foxton, 'We at the institute have discussed it, and we think it right that you should know. However, you must understand that this stays between us.' They nodded mutely, and Foxton explained.

'I know you've all been watching for news of the Polis. You may have heard speculation that things might not be going so well. Well, the speculation is correct; things are not going well.'

The teenagers sat in awed silence, disbelief showing on their faces as Foxton outlined the ultimatum communicated by the League of Orion.

'Initially, we accelerated your training as a mere precaution,' he continued, 'Ariana and Ijaz we simply took up a gear, and we were keen to bring Adam out of himself. You've all done very well. However, given events above us, it seemed wise to train you for every eventuality.'

'Are we going to be invaded?' asked Ariana.

'It's unlikely,' Foxton answered, 'Unfortunately, that's because, to avoid war, we'll probably have to give in and junk our AIs.'

Adam thought of SAM at the Clement orphanage. 'That's not right,' he said, 'Our AIs are no more dangerous than us.'

'Not the best argument in the world,' said Foxton, 'We're hardly the most peaceful of species. According to comparisons we've drawn out from information they've given us, we don't look so good.'

Ijaz frowned. 'But, what's the connection between all of that, and us?'

Foxton nodded, and sighed.

'A good question,' he replied, 'And it goes right to the heart of this institute, and why you are here. I'll explain.

'AIs,' he continued, 'Artificial intelligences. They're the link in all of this, though I hasten to add, not the cause. You are part of the IHD, and that was created by HADD, which I am a member of. HADD was created for two reasons. The first is the development of AIs. It became clear that in many ways, AIs were superior to their human creators. Their computational capabilities are more accessible and thus more effective than the thinking capabilities of humans. Their bodies are more durable and easier to repair, and they don't experience pain. They are made to be compatible with most other hardware, and are thus able to manipulate physical reality with the use of other machines and field technology. They are thus potentially far stronger than us physically, as well as in terms of intelligence, or pure logic. This creates a problem.'

'They become a threat,' said Adam.

Once again, Foxton found himself impressed by Adam's incisiveness. But he could not help wondering, *where is it coming from?*

'Well done; they do. In a conflict between humans and AIs, potentially, they might win, and thus we either become enslaved, pushed out, or exterminated. So, alongside various measures to control AIs, we also set about developing humans.'

'The NIs,' said Ijaz.

'Good,' said Foxton, again impressed. 'The acceleration of NI development occurred as a result of this. There were other things as well. Cybernetics or bionics, biotronics, biotechnology, all have been set at a pace over the past few hundred years in part to keep up with AI development. Alongside this have been bioengineering and genetic enhancement programmes, and training programmes to maximise the intellectual and physical development of humanity. The institute you are part of is just one of those programmes. The strangest to be sure, but only one. We have others where the kids are all scientific geniuses, or natural athletes. But it all has the same aim: the development of humanity, and thus the defence of it.'

'Why not just limit the development of AIs?' asked Ariana.

'That brings us to the second reason for the creation of the HADD. That reason is now in orbit above our heads. It was decided that humanity needed to develop itself not only to meet the AI threat, but also to meet any threat that might come at us from up there, from space. It was also decided that, as long as AIs could be controlled, they could well come in useful for a situation of defence against potential alien aggressors. Even if not, their usefulness is beyond question. What we could not have envisaged however, is that AIs would be used *as a reason* for aggression, by those very aliens. That, unfortunately, has been something of a surprise. In a sense, it should not have been. Any alien aggressor would see the need to remove our AIs before they're able to dominate us,' Foxton sighed, 'Hindsight is always twenty-twenty.'

'Are we soldiers?' asked Adam.

Foxton regarded him carefully before answering. 'That is yet to be decided.'

'By who?' asked Adam.

So cynical! thought Foxton. 'By you of course. No matter what happens, no matter what your powers, you're only kids. Your abilities give you many career paths. Common soldier isn't one of them; you're far too talented. But commando, spy, assassin; yes, those are all the things that are open to you, and none of them if you don't want to. Your abilities certainly imply a responsibility to choose carefully, but the choice is still yours. Our job is to train you so that, if it comes to the crunch, you can make the decision. Already most of the older graduates are involved in various field exercises, and a very few involved in front-line operations. You're years away from that. I just wanted you to know why we're speeding things up, just in case…' he trailed off, the traces of strain showing on his face, 'well, just in case of anything.'

'Do you think we'll be involved in anything dangerous?' asked Adam.

'No,' replied Foxton, 'Don't worry. You're only kids, leave the serious stuff to the adults.'

Foxton looked at the teens, mere children really, an overwhelming sense of protectiveness coming over him. Events, he knew, would soon overtake them. They would be beyond any of their control, events that would change civilisation, their lives - everything.

*

A few thousand kilometres to the west of London, a similar ship to one of the cruisers that had accompanied the Polis, was making a slow and gentle descent over North America.

It was similar, but not identical.

The first and most, or perhaps *least* noticeable difference, was that it couldn't be noticed at all, being totally invisible to all sensors. A keen observer might have seen the barest ripple in a cloud as it descended through it, but probably would have ignored it. It was also far smaller, less than half the size of the other ships. Another difference was that the crew of this ship was more sparse. But then a large crew would have been a liability rather than a necessity. After all, the only thing the ship was really there to do was count, and the non-sentient high capability machine was doing that quite well without the crew.

So it counted.

-North American State, AAA alliance. Name: United States of America; anti-matter warheads; 7,953. Common nuclear weapons; 20. Hydrogen bombs; 308. Space penetrating laser batteries; 956. Space penetrating plasma guns; 2,158. Space capable warships 1804. Armaments production increasing at rate of 1.1% per local day/night cycle. Rate accelerating.

-North American state, European alliance. Name: Canada; anti-matter warheads; 3,025…

Chapter 13

But with truth comes pain

Ever since the observation-based 'Origin of Species' theory of Darwin was superseded by the solid genetic-mathematics-physics based 'Origins of Life' theory of Steinberg, we have known that radical mutations such as the Kinetics do not occur naturally. So we are reluctant to accept the idea that these children are the next evolutionary step, even though we ourselves have suggested that to the scientific community to allay any uncomfortable questions.

Yet scientific parochialism is not the only reason for caution. There is only a ten-year age band for these children, and no others at all, despite searching across borders and age ranges. There is no lead-up, no people with lesser abilities before the first children appeared. We have searched high and low for the true origins of them in all known bioengineering programmes. Yet if they are a military experiment, why no sign of it, among us of all people? If anyone should know, surely it would be ourselves?

You ask especially about Adam; now there is an enigma. His latent abilities are far beyond his peers, albeit at this stage untrained and largely governed by unconscious processes. We believe he can destroy an area surrounding him while protecting himself <u>in his sleep</u>. This is a visceral power the likes of which we have not seen before. Is there a danger in him? The answer, if I'm being honest, is that I do not know. His powers are such that few could control him if he lost control of himself, or had some mal-intent. However, I see nothing of the genuine instability or violence leading to a conclusion that we should eliminate him.

One thing is for certain: with absolutely no idea of his background, and with growing evidence every day of his abilities, my unease with our lack of knowledge increases. We have only just made alien contact, so I believe there is no lead there, and DNA analysis has confirmed that he, like the others, is human. We have searched for a genetic change that would signal their difference; we have had no success. What conclusions can we draw from this? The very fact that after some ten years of research and investigation the answer is still 'none,' goes to show one thing: There is something very wrong here, very wrong indeed.

Letter from Lieutenant-commander Michael Foxton to AAA Central Security in response to a query by them, discovered in papers when declassified over 150 years later, in 2357. Research has shown that the query and response were referred for the attention of AAA Minister of Biological Progress, Joseph Murdock.

Adam lounged on Ijaz's couch, taking care not crease his new clothes. They were smart; a suitably trendy dark suit, shirt and tie, with black shoes. He had to admit, he liked the way he looked. He wondered for a moment if Ariana would too.

He could tell Ijaz liked the way *he* looked, as for the past five minutes he had been admiring himself in the full-length mirror on the front of his closet.

'You'll like the people turning up tonight,' Ijaz said over his shoulder as he posed in his finely cut beige suit. 'Some of the older participants, the trustees and some of the parents will want to meet you. Well, *"parents"* anyway,' he said, using his fingers to indicate inverted commas.

Adam frowned, 'What does that mean?'

Ijaz stopped admiring himself and looked at Adam in the reflection.

'Nothing,' he said, 'C'mon, let's go party.'

Adam, confused, shook his head.

They made their way upstairs. It was the first time Adam had been up to the eighth-floor, or met any of the older graduates of the IHD programme. The end of term Christmas party was being held in the largest boardroom, which made up half of the floor.

Adam walked in behind Ijaz, who was immediately greeted with hellos from the guys and *hellos* from the girls. The place seemed to be full of people drinking out of shiny slim glasses, or eating from cocktail sticks. Ijaz enjoyed his local celebrity status for a few moments, but was quick to introduce Adam.

The older boys, now really young men, were friendly enough, shaking his hand, though they seemed a little cautious of him. The young ladies, on the other hand, were a lot more friendly, making a point of smiling, and a few gave him a kiss on the cheek. One, whose name was Andrea, a brown-skinned girl around eighteen years old, said, 'Well, he's cute. Shame he's not a bit older. Guess I'll have to wait,' to the laughter of the other girls. A few of the guys patted Adam on the back. Needless to say, Adam went bright red. However, curiously, he accepted the focus on him, and he felt but couldn't see, that his blushing went away.

His confidence increased when, standing to the side of the room, he saw Ariana, who seemed a little displeased at the attention he was getting. He made a point of not approaching her, and determined to put that off for a while. Instead, he looked around the room as Ijaz took the limelight back.

It was a wide room with well over a hundred people in it. Dominating it was a long table, a great rectangle topped by ebony polished to a mirror finish. Music was playing. He couldn't see anyone else he knew so he finally wandered over to Ariana, who was looking very elegant in a dark blue satin dress.

'Hi,' he said, when he joined her.

She was with two adults. 'Hi,' she replied, 'These are my parents. This is Adam.'

'Oh,' said her father, a man with tanned skin and an expensive suit, 'The one hundredth. Pleased to meet you.' He shook hands with Adam, 'You're a bit of a mystery aren't you?'

Adam shrugged, taking his hand away. 'I guess. I guess we all are.'

Mr Harland nodded his head, looking at Adam intently. 'Good answer,' he said, 'Truthful and thoughtful.'

Mrs Harland, a blond lady, less tanned but more glamorous, interjected. 'How are you finding it, darling?'

Adam tried not to start blushing again, 'Better than the orphanage. I like it.'

Mrs Harland pouted and tutted. 'Fancy keeping a sweetie like you in a place like that.' Adam's skin gave in and started to glow, 'You must come and stay with us,' she continued, 'Give him your business card Simon.'

Mr Harland fished into his pocket and did as he was told, handing Adam his card.

'You can come and stay with us any time,' he said, winking, 'Ariana really likes you.'

Adam figured his blush could not get any worse, and noticed that now Ariana appeared to be mirroring him.

Ijaz joined them, saying a polite hello to Mr and Mrs Harland. 'You okay?' he asked Adam, who nodded.

'Yeah. I'm getting hungry, I thought there was food here?'

'Spoken like a man with a great mind thinking thoughts like mine,' said Ijaz. 'You coming Ari?'

Ijaz offered to get food for the Harland's, and after they declined, he took the arms of the two others and guided them to the buffet. They picked up some plates and started to load them with hot and cold food. Adam felt he was getting a lot of curious glances, and that it was not just him being paranoid.

They sat down on some chairs at the side of the room and started to eat. Ijaz started pointing out the older Kinetics, what they were doing now, how secret or not it was, when one of the young men who Adam had been introduced to came up to them. His name was James, a tall and fair-skinned boy in his late teens.

'Hey,' he said to them all, making a beeline for Ariana. 'Ari, come with me, I want to show you something.' He held out his hand, and Ariana took it.

'Excuse me,' she said, as she put down her food.

Adam said nothing, Ijaz made a sound of assent through his food and waved her away.

Big lad, Adam thought, *She probably thinks he's handsome…* Adam scowled as he ate. They were not alone for long, however. A flock of the older Kinetics soon accumulated around Ijaz, and accosted Adam with the odd question and bit of attention.

Soon however, Mr Harland arrived with another man in tow. The man was old and wrinkled. He looked Adam over without smiling.

'This,' said Mr Harland, 'is Mr Murdock. He is the head Trustee of the institute, and he was trying to make you out in the crowd. Joseph, this is Adam.'

The old man smiled at Adam, showing unnaturally white teeth. If possible, he had an air that was even richer than Mr Harland's. Adam couldn't help noticing however, that his smile was one of those types that reaches the lips, but does not ripple across the rest of the face. He held out his hand.

'Pleased to meet you Adam, I've heard so much,' said Murdock. Adam shook the man's hand. 'Is it alright if you and I have a word?'

Adam, a little uncertainly, shrugged his shoulders. 'Sure.'

Murdock did not let go of Adam's hand as he steered him into a quiet corner of the room.

'I've been waiting to meet you for some time,' said the man. Even though he was old, he was still taller than Adam, who had to look up into his eyes. He had still not let go of Adam's hand. 'Tell me,' he said, 'how're you finding it here?'

Across the room, Foxton stood quietly, watching as Murdock spoke to Adam. He saw him put his hand to Adam's head. He seemed to ruffle his hair, and when Adam tried to back away, Murdock pulled at it gently as he took his hand away and put it into his pocket. Foxton used his iris enhancements to zoom in on them, and noted how the man seemed to be using his nails to shake Adam's hand, Adam's flesh around the nails turning to tiny pink crescents.

Foxton moved. He strode right up to Murdock and grabbed the hand he was using to shake Adam's, pulling him away, ignoring his protests. The commotion was beginning to attract a few glances, but the general noise was acting like a cloak. Foxton quickly pulled Murdock to the side of the room to a door, swinging Murdock around and shoving him through it. The room was dark, the automatic lights coming on as they entered.

'How dare you!' growled Murdock. 'I warn you that-'

The words died on his lips as Foxton pulled a device out of his pocket. He grabbed Murdock's hand, shook him to stop his struggling, and pressed a button on the device that emitted a low red coloured beam of light. He pointed the light at Murdock's fingers, paying particular attention to the areas under his nails. Murdock struggled and made more protests.

'Stop that,' said Foxton, 'or I'll cut your hand off by mistake.'

Murdock tried to put his other hand into his pocket, but Foxton grabbed it, and used the device on that hand. Then he used it to fish around in Murdock's pockets. When he had finished, he grabbed Murdock by the scruff of the neck and growled into his face.

'Let me be very clear. We do not take unofficial DNA samples from the students. You ask permission, and I am his guardian, so you ask me. And if you were wondering, the answer is "No." Now, answer my questions.'

'I have never been so insulted-'

'You can answer my questions or you can be arrested for what is a very serious crime. And rest assured, I have the means to make it stick, even against you.' He shoved Murdock up against the wall next to the door. 'You haven't been straight with me.

What's going on?' Murdock did not respond. 'What is going on!' Foxton shouted.

Murdock's face was initially a mask of fear, then anger, then only sadness. 'I'm sorry,' he said, 'I just can't tell you, Michael. I'm so sorry.'

Just then, the door was opened by Mr Harland.

'I say, old boys,' said the man, 'No need for all that. Come on, break it up.' He slid in-between them, prised Foxton's fingers away from the older man, and pushed them apart. Ijaz peered inside the door, followed by Adam. Mr Harland guided Murdock back into the main room, Murdock giving Adam a dark look as they left. Just before they did, the older man turned towards Foxton.

'I don't blame you, Michael,' he said, 'This is how it begins. First of all comes protectiveness, then loyalty…soon, your mind will be completely befuddled.' Then he turned and left, leaving a look of utter confusion on Foxton's face.

'You okay, Mr Foxton?' asked Ijaz.

Foxton nodded. He noticed the boys were looking at his hand, glanced down and put the device he had used to clean the DNA back into his pocket.

'Yes, Ijaz,' said Foxton. 'I'm fine. Just a little bit of a misunderstanding between old friends, that's all.'

'What did he mean by that stuff about being befuddled?' asked Ijaz.

'I don't know,' replied Foxton, truthfully.

'He tried to sample me,' said Adam.

Foxton was almost getting used to Adam's perceptiveness. He saw no point in lying. 'That's what it looked like,' he confirmed, shaking his head, 'Though I have no idea why.'

'Didn't the other Kinetics get samples taken?' asked Adam.

'Yes,' said Foxton, 'And you already have been as part of the ID process and medical. Mr Murdock has access to those files as long as he asks permission. I just can't see why he would do that. Unless he thought I was lying…'

'About what?' asked Adam.

Foxton sighed. Could he tell this boy everything? Was Adam able to take the fact that the Kinetics, no matter what, would always be suspected of not being human? He noted that Adam looked upset at what had just happened, and decided not.

'Just that you're the same as the other kids,' he said, thinking part of the truth was better than the whole truth or a complete lie. 'That's all. Standards here are high.'

'I'm trying my best,' said Adam, successfully side-tracked.

'Of course you are,' said Foxton, regretting inadvertently putting pressure on him. He noted the tension on the two boys, both of them worried. Socials were not Foxton's thing. He wanted to leave, and had an idea of how to cheer them up.

'Look,' he said, 'you guys want to come with me? I've got something really great to show you, you'll love it.'

The boys readily assented and together, all dressed up, they made their way through the crowd, downstairs, and then left the institute.

They took a hover-taxi, and Adam saw the London skyline in the night-time. It looked as picturesque by night as by day, and was still aglow with activity. The ancient cityscape was itself dwarfed by the London space-scraper, a speckled stab into the sky in the distance.

They flew for about fifteen minutes, coming so close to the space-scraper that Adam thought Foxton was finally taking him to see it. As it loomed ahead of them, more of the detail could be made out. There were lights still on in many of the compartments, and the flow of lifts going up and down the outside of the building. Before they reached it however, they descended rapidly to a broad street.

They disembarked, and Foxton led them up some wide stone steps into a large Romanesque pillared building, metal doors stylised in the same way blocking their path. Iris scans flashed, and the large doors slid open. Adam could see that the doors, elegant and black on the outside, were in fact at least a foot thick, and reinforced. They entered, the doors hissing shut behind them.

'Please wait,' said a feminine computerised voice as they stood in the reception area. The place was dimly lit with freestanding float-bulbs. There was no reception desk, only a large hall, black marble on the floor and walls with steel doors at the end. Adam could see lasers-points as they licked across their bodies.

Then in a tone urbane enough to describe a dessert menu, the computer said, 'Please note that automatic laser and plasma guns are trained on your positions. Mr Foxton, we identify you, please identify your companions.'

'They are Adam Foxton, and Ijaz Walker. They are my guests.' There was a pause.

'Pheromone and heart-rate stress test passed,' said the machine, 'No weapons are noted except upon Mr Foxton. It is accepted that Mr Foxton acts of his own volition. Adam Foxton and Ijaz Walker accepted as entrants. Do you wish licence to pass to them?'

'In perpetuity until I revoke,' replied Foxton.

The lasers left their bodies.

'Welcome to the HADD hardware development centre,' said the voice. 'Please let me know if I can be of any assistance.'

'Thank you Centre,' said Foxton. He motioned the other two forward. They came to the big steel doors, and Foxton took out a key with an irregular octagonal cross-section. He inserted it into an equally oddly-shaped hole, and left it there for a moment. The door made a humming noise, he withdrew his key, the door silently raised, and they walked through into a corridor. They came to another door as the steel one behind him lowered. This one slid aside, and they entered a large chamber, the lights within coming on. It was entirely deserted.

Stretching to either side of them was a circular walkway with a capacious space in the middle. Adam could see across to the other side; it had to be at least fifty metres away, and was lit from above and below. Foxton walked forwards and put his hands on the railing. Adam and Ijaz followed, and as they moved forwards, the space revealed to their eyes what they thought was one of the most beautiful things they had ever seen.

There, sitting around twenty metres below them and rising to around fifteen metres in height, was a ship. It was entirely silvered, and sleek. It had three engines apparent, one centre rear, and one on each side. The main body had a pointed tip at the front, underneath which was a shape like a giant grill on old ground cars. The body then swept back towards two 'wings'. Aerodynamics being largely irrelevant for what was evidently a spaceship, the wings then swept forward again to two symmetrical aggressive-looking arms, at the points of which appeared to be weapon blisters.

'This,' said Foxton, 'is the HADD Ship Newark.'

The boys 'Ooed' as they walked around it.

'It has FTL capability,' explained Foxton, 'the fastest yet designed at four times the speed of light. That's quite an achievement in a ship so small. In a medium it travels at seventeen times the speed of sound, its shields act to make it aerodynamic, and it manoeuvres at several times faster than that in vacuum. It has some serious firepower: mini-AM warheads, armour piercing multi-round plasma rifles, shield penetrating lasers. It is fully armoured, capable of surviving an AM blast at under a kilometre. It has multiple shields, and as you can see, is finished in mirrored titanium to protect against lasers. The small portholes are diamond plate. The intakes suck in hydrogen and whatever else it can find, and use it as fuel. You could throw a rock in there and it would burn it to fly with. Best of all,' said Foxton, turning to the boys, 'look at this.' He walked over to a console set into the railings on the walkway, and typed something in. The boys 'wowed', as the beautiful ship disappeared. There was the barest outline where the edges of it had been.

'It's got stealth,' said Ijaz.

Foxton nodded. 'Fully stealth, mind. Not just visual, but radar, heat, electro-magnetic, all radiation, exhaust, the works. Less than a hundredth of a per cent of energy escapes when this thing runs on quiet. It needs to vent it once in a while, but it's quite something.'

'How many are there?' asked Adam.

'This is the only one,' said Foxton. 'It's a prototype, and is unlikely to be built again. Although the quality is superb, the emphasis now is on power, simplicity and quantity; we have new imperatives now that the Orion League are here.' He turned again to the boys. 'Want a look inside?'

They didn't need asking twice.

*

The next day, Adam woke to find that it was snowing. He looked out of the window, and took a few minutes to absorb the snowscape. He pressed his nose up against the window of his room as he looked out. He was slightly disappointed that it was not that cold, as the inner glass was non-heat conductible. (In fact, it was heat resistant and reinforced in preparation for his coming, but he was blissfully unaware of it.)

Adam hoped this weather lasted all the way to Christmas. He could see the trees, bare of leaves now, with every upper branch and twig covered in white. The square in front of the building was covered in a thick layer of the fluffy stuff, with winding tracks showing the passage of wrapped-up passers-by. The rooves and ledges of the buildings opposite were similarly piled with drifts and diluvium. Adam sighed, the pleasure of the scene heightened by the insulating warmth from it.

Just then, one of the few species of animal to benefit from Yellowstone landed on the ledge in front of him. It was a robin, with a pale red breast. It hopped along a few times, then noticed Adam and fluttered away. Adam grinned, and came away from the window.

Time for breakfast.

He knocked on Ijaz's door, and together they went down to the canteen.

'Aren't you going home for Christmas?' asked Adam.

'No,' said Ijaz, 'My folks are Muslim. They celebrate Christmas, but we're not overly upset if we're apart during this time. So it's still me an' you man!' he said as he hugged Adam's shoulders in front of the food counter.

They were on their own again, everyone else had gone home for the holidays, leaving them under the loose tutelage of Mr Foxton.

'I love Christmas,' said Ijaz, 'How about you? You big on Christmas?'

Adam shook his head. 'Nah,' he said, 'They only did a little bit at the orphanage, a few sweets as a present. Maybe the odd teddy bear when you're really young.'

'Well, we got an invite to Ariana's family for some yuletide dinner,' said Ijaz. Adam groaned inwardly. 'And that's home-cooked food, so I'm down with that.'

Adam looked at him equivocally. Ijaz, seeing Adam's less than enthusiastic response, shook his head and concentrated on choosing his breakfast.

Adam and Ijaz spent the days lolling around and seeing bits of London in the cold and snow.

Another week, and Christmas arrived. Adam woke to the sound of knocking at his door. He groggily told whoever it was to come in, and a beaming Mr Foxton swung into the room.

'Merry Christmas,' he said, 'Get out of bed, we've got presents to unwrap.'

'Oh,' said Adam, 'Do we?'

'Yes,' said Foxton, 'You too, so come on.'

Then Foxton knocked on the door that led into Ijaz's room, and strode in there as well.

All three of them went up into the eighth floor, into the big boardroom, and went to the end with the huge Christmas tree. Under its glittering greenery lay a small pile of presents. Adam began to feel butterflies in his stomach. He wasn't consciously yearning to receive presents, but still, there they were…

'Oh, cool!' said Ijaz, sitting down next to the tree as Foxton beckoned Adam forwards. 'Ahahahaaa!' he exclaimed, 'I got one from you!'

'Of course,' said Foxton, 'You were nice enough to get me an Eid present, I couldn't leave you out could I? Open mine last. You've each got one from Sifu Zhao and Dr Cengo. Open those first.'

Adam came forwards, kneeling besides Ijaz as they opened their presents. Those from Cengo were covered in non-festive black wrapping paper. Inside were paper books. Adam's was a hefty tome on world history, with the back cover an old-fashioned slim digi-book encyclopaedia.

'Oh, brilliant!' said Adam. He would have said the same to anything, he was genuinely thrilled to receive any present at all, but he really did love history, it was his favourite subject.

Ijaz opened his, and inside was the complete trilogy by one of his favourite authors, to his delight.

'You like reading?' asked Adam, 'I didn't know that.'

'Of course,' said Ijaz, 'There's a lot you don't know about me. I'm a deep brother.'

They then turned to Zhao's gifts, wrapped in glittery red and gold paper. Adam felt the package before opening it, savouring the moment. They both tore off the wrapping paper; inside were identical wooden boxes with latches on the front and two hinges at the back. Carved into the wood were a crane and a snake, facing each other off in the traditional Wing-Chun posture: slightly leaning backwards with fangs and beak respectively bared, poised.

Adam opened his first, lifting the lid which creaked a little, and laughed. Inside, were three throwing weapons, glittering in the light reflected from the tree. There was a knife, and dart, and in the centre, a large flying star. This one, it appeared, did not have the blunt edges of Adam's earlier encounter. He picked it up gingerly to inspect it.

'Wow,' said Ijaz, and he opened his box to see a beautiful set of black and chrome coloured steel nunchaku.

Foxton stood over them, shaking his head. 'I told him not to get you that stuff.'

'No!' said Adam, 'I like it.'

'Gee,' said Foxton dryly, 'that's a surprise.'

'Me too,' said Ijaz, pulling out his nunchaku to give them an experimental swing, 'And we're old enough to have them.'

'Actually you aren't,' said Foxton, 'It's totally illegal. But,' Foxton sighed at the looks of despair on their faces, 'as long as I never catch you using that stuff outside of an emergency, and Ijaz, you have to ask your parents, okay?' He was clearly stating rather than asking, and the boys nodded their assent.

Last of all came Foxton's presents. Again in identical wrappings, the presents were small and slim. The boys ripped them open.

'Games!' said Ijaz.

'More than that,' said Foxton, 'They're special games. The best games in there will teach you how to pilot ships like the Newark, and also how to use real weaponry.' The boys smiled and chuckled in delight. 'Also, there are cognitive and mind games in there that both of you have shown an aptitude for. So enjoy.'

Adam looked up at Foxton, feeling terrible. 'Thanks. But I didn't think to get you anything. I'm sorry.'

'Don't say sorry,' said Foxton, 'Getting you here was the best present I could have. Seriously, you have no idea how far and wide we've looked for another Kinetic, and one that performs as well as you is simply fantastic. You can get me another present some other time.'

There was one more small present under the tree. It had Adam's name on it. He picked it up and tore off the paper. Inside was a case, which Adam opened, a small frown on his face. It was a watch. He pressed the side button, and a holo-display of the time came up.

He looked at Ijaz, smiling. 'Thanks.'

'Now you can look pretty too,' replied Ijaz with a grin.

'Alright,' said Foxton, 'You two clear up, get some breakfast, then get ready as we're going over to the Harlands' for some good grub.'

The boys started clearing up the mess they had made, smiling.

Later they went to the Harland's for dinner. It was a short trip by ground car to the outskirts of central London. Ariana was there, obviously pleased to see all of them. Adam was equally pleased to see her, despite the fact that her house was intimidating in its opulence. He couldn't begin to guess at how many rooms it had, but it looked almost as big as the lower house of the orphanage. From the Harlands, there were more small but appreciated gifts for the boys, and to Foxton's relief, no weapons.

They ate a wonderful meal, a traditional thing of roast turkey, potatoes and sprouts, and had barely enough room for the dessert.

'Listen,' said Mr Harland, looking at his daughter, 'Why don't you show the boys the new fish-tank we got you as a present?' Ariana looked at him for a moment. 'Oh,' said Mr Harland, looking overly apologetic, 'I didn't mean us, I meant Father Christmas.'

Foxton chuckled. 'Yes, why don't you go and check that out.'

The teenagers looked at them suspiciously.

'You trying to get rid of us?' asked Adam.

Foxton shook his head, then stopped. 'Yes.'

'Come on,' said Ariana, rolling her eyes, 'Let me show you my new pets.'

They got up from the table, groans escaping as corpulent stomachs complained, and waddled upstairs.

When they got to Ariana's room, Adam spent a good few seconds taking it in. It was twice the size of his current bedroom, and he had thought that was big enough.

Ariana proudly showed them her new fish tank, taking up a full four metres of one wall, sprinkled with exotic fish. They stood in front of the blue-tinted glass as Ariana named the various fish. There were the coral beauty angelfish, a small fish with subtle shading from blue to red, the shy black and white cardinalfish, delicate sea horses and a plethora of others. When she had finished pointing them out, they stood in silence for a while, enchanted by the alternately graceful and excited activity of the aquatic animals.

'So,' said Ijaz, looking at the reflections on the tank-glass of Adam and Ariana, 'What do you think they're talking about down there?'

Ariana snorted. 'Probably where we came from.'

Ijaz glanced at Adam, then looked away.

'What do you mean?' asked Adam.

Ijaz looked at the fish, intently. Ariana frowned, looking between them.

'You know…' she said.

Ijaz shook his head very slightly, lips poked out.

'Know what?' asked Adam irritably, 'Come on. What?'

Ijaz, still looking at the tank, began to rub his lips, tightly set in a determined expression that nothing was going to get through them unless he allowed it.

'Oh, I see,' said Adam, 'You both know something, and you're not telling me. So much for being friends.'

'Oh, man, don't be stupid,' said Ijaz.

'Well that's the way it looks to me,' said Adam, crossing his arms and scowling hard at one of the fish, feeling genuinely hurt.

There was an awkward silence.

'What is it?' he said again, appealing now to Ariana's reflection in the glass.

'Well,' she said carefully, 'I'm not sure what to say, as I'm not sure what exactly you don't know.'

Adam tutted. 'Well, that's great. You can't tell me because I don't know, and I don't know because you won't tell me. That's just great. Thanks.'

Ariana looked at Ijaz, who was getting the feeling that all eyes were on him. He glanced from side to side. His feeling was correct. He rubbed his lips again.

'Okay,' he said at length. 'But we don't know any more about this than you do. I just know it's true. And I have to say, I'm not sure I'm the best person to tell you this stuff, it should be Mr Foxton really-'

'What's true?' demanded Adam, 'Tell me what? You're the best person, we're friends aren't we? Come on!'

'Okay, okay,' said Ijaz, and sucked his teeth in resignation. He stalked over to Ariana's bed and sat heavily on the edge. 'Now, this may be a bit much for you to take in. Sit down.'

Adam did as he was told, sitting on the floor, facing Ijaz on the bed and Ariana as she sat on a chair in front of her dresser.

'Right,' said Ijaz, 'We were wondering why, that is, Ariana and me, maybe all of us…we were wondering why, all of the children, all of the Kinetics, were orphans. All of us have been adopted at birth, or soon after.'

Adam frowned. 'All orphans?' he asked. Ijaz nodded. 'I thought all of you had parents, you know, birth parents.'

Ijaz shook his head. 'No,' he said. 'All adopted.'

Ijaz remained still, and went quiet.

Adam stared between Ijaz and Ariana, both of whom looked as though they were waiting for something, and also looked thoroughly ashamed.

'Oh,' said Adam, as the penny dropped.

They were all adopted. All in rich families. *All* of them.

All except Adam.

'I'm sorry, man,' said Ijaz, 'Really, I am. It's just, this question has been eating at us for years. They say we're human, fine. But now you've come along, and there's this alien thing at the same time...What if there's a connection? What if we're alien or something? I'm sorry, I knew I shouldn't have said anything. Ariana, you should have stopped me!'

Ariana shrugged her shoulders. 'I think he has a right to know. She turned to Adam. 'Are you alright?'

Adam thought for a moment, then sighed and rubbed his head.

'I suppose,' he said at length. He blew out his cheeks, and decided he was lying; he felt a little sick. 'Well, maybe not, though. Ninety-nine other Kinetics, all orphans, and *all* adopted.' He looked up at Ijaz and Ariana. '*All* of you?' he asked. The other two teenagers nodded. 'All except me,' said Adam, 'And all of them taken into rich families. Right?' Ijaz nodded again. 'And me, in an orphanage. On my own.' Adam shook his head, his face feeling slack. 'Look, I don't want anyone else to suffer or anything, but, y'know, why me?' he asked, hands splayed, waiting for an explanation to drop into them, 'I just wonder what the hell is going on sometimes.' Adam put his fingertips over his eyes for a moment, and then rubbed them furiously. Ijaz slid off the bed, came and sat next to Adam on the floor, putting his arm around him. However, Adam wasn't crying, he just felt suddenly so very tired.

'I'm okay,' he said. Then sighed again, taking his hands away from reddened eyelids. 'Not the best news I've ever had, that's all. Just puts my life in perspective.'

'I'm really sorry,' repeated Ijaz, 'I shouldn't have said anything.'

'No,' said Adam, 'I'm glad you did. I've always had questions, y'know, growing up, wondering who my parents were, where my mother was, why I didn't have one. The orphanage told me I was abandoned by a woman who disappeared as soon as she left me. They said she was very young, that was probably why. No trace of her after that, and no chance…'

Ariana shook her head. 'You see, that doesn't really add up. Not for any of us. There's DNA profiling, they can find birth mothers if they really want to. They can't find them for *any* of us. We've tried, believe me, not a single one found. That's statistically impossible unless someone did all this deliberately.'

'Not evolution, not mutation, something deliberate,' interjected Ijaz, 'We come from all over the world man, and no-one knows who our real parents are. We came through adoption agencies, and they disappeared as soon as the children were adopted. Not too much of a stretch to say that we probably came from the same place. So unless your mama had ninety-nine kids in ten years, I think, well, the orphanage was either fooled, or they told you a neat story to cover the fact that they just didn't know.'

Adam looked thoughtful. 'Or they were lying,' he said.

Ijaz shrugged. 'I didn't want to say that. But if they were lying to you, then we've all been told the same lie.'

'Anyway,' said Ariana, regretting having been party to raising it now rather than at a better time with Mr Foxton, 'Mr Foxton has said that the same area of the brain that lights up with us, lights up with you, and you certainly seem to have the powers of a Kinetic. So as far as I'm concerned, you're one of us. That's what matters.' She knelt down on the other side of Adam and put her hand on his shoulder, rubbing it a little.

Strangely, Adam felt a little better for what she had said. He did not feel quite so lonely. Come to think of it, he didn't mind Ariana rubbing his shoulder either.

'Where do you think we came from?' he asked.

'Well, our DNA says we're human,' said Ijaz, 'and we've only just made alien contact. We've all ended up in wealthy families,' then he mumbled, 'except you,' he cleared his throat and continued, 'Only conclusion I think is that we're a military programme. Stands to reason.' Then he stood up, 'A military programme with outstanding sense of fashion, fine muscles and great hair. And you ain't so bad either.'

'You're mad,' said Adam, giving in and smiling, 'What do you think about it?' he asked Ariana.

'I've never really known what to make of it,' she replied, 'My parents never hid it from me. They say they don't know where I came from, that they were approached out of the blue by an adoption agency which disappeared afterwards. Just like the others, right?' Ijaz nodded thoughtfully. 'The institute has tried to find our origins, they say they can't.'

They sat there, in silence for a few moments. Ijaz looked at them sideways. He had something even more important on his mind. He rubbed his stomach.

'You want some more dessert?' he asked. 'I don't know about you, but I found that whole conversation a little bit heavy. I could really do with some more dessert.'

'Did you see what happened?' asked Foxton.

'No, I'm sorry Michael,' replied Mr Harland, 'I only walked in to see you holding him by the scruff of the neck.'

Foxton sat back, glowering. 'Did he tell you what happened?'

Mr Harland shook his head. Mrs Harland watched them, then interrupted.

'Are *you* going to tell us what happened, then?'

Foxton relented, and told them what had occurred at the end of term party. The two adults listened silently.

'That doesn't sound like Joseph at all,' said Mr Harland.

'I know,' said Foxton, 'in general, it doesn't. But his attitude towards Adam has been entirely different from the way he's been to all of the other kids.'

'In what way?' asked Mrs Harland.

'Suspicion, surprise - fear,' said Foxton. 'How was he when you first met him, with Ariana?'

'Wonderful,' said Mrs Harland, 'Really supportive, welcoming, he said he'd been looking for more like Ariana, and that to find her was a great success.'

'That's what every other parent has always said when they met him,' said Foxton, 'Everyone agrees, he's the IHD's granddaddy. This one is different. Something's wrong.'

Mr Harland nodded. 'I've got to admit,' he said, 'Even that night, when he was asking me about Adam, how Ariana got on with him, I got the feeling it wasn't mere interest. It was much more intense, even intrusive. He even said something about 'keeping an eye on Ariana because "you know what teenagers can be like".'

Mrs Harland laughed. 'You're right there, he's a cutie.' Mr Harland gave her a mock scowl. 'Not as cute as you though,' she said, and patted his arm.

'Seriously, that leaves the question of "why?"' said Foxton, 'Why the suspicion? The fear?'

'Well I'm not sure I saw fear,' said Mr Harland, 'I thought it was just him being territorial. I understand Adam was not announced to him before being admitted to the institute?'

'One of several,' said Foxton, 'and Joseph is trustee, not a director; he has no say in day-to-day running.'

'Maybe he's anxious, what with the alien situation?' said Mrs Harland, 'And Adam is a little bit different from all of the others. His origins for a start.'

'Are you convinced by that?' asked Foxton. 'Does that explain sampling Adam when he could easily access the IHD's database?'

The other two adults did not answer.

'So he didn't want his investigation noted on any system,' said Mrs Harland at length.

Foxton nodded. 'He would've needed to use his official status to access the files. No problem for him, except that it would have been on record.'

'Still leaves us with the central question: Why?' said Mr Harland.

No answer was forthcoming.

'I said I would prosecute him for what he did if he didn't answer my questions.'

'Whoa!' said Mr Harland, 'That's a big one. You sure you want to go down that road?'

'I've got the evidence I need in the eraser I used to recover Adam's DNA, together with my NI recording. I've got a pretty good case. I think Adam would be willing to give evidence if I asked him to.'

'Still,' said Mr Harland, 'Joseph will fight it, no doubt, and I have to say, I'm surprised at you.' He was looking intently at Foxton.

'What do you mean?'

'Well, I'm not saying that this isn't serious, and worth further investigation, but you need to think. First, there's the power of

Joseph Murdock; not a thing to be taken lightly, though I know you aren't exactly a weakling politically yourself. Second, notwithstanding how serious this is, there doesn't seem to be any serious harm done. Third, you've been friends with Joseph for more than two decades. There's more than one way to skin a cat, I can make my own investigations, and so can you. That's the surprising thing, really.'

'Go on.'

'Well,' said Mr Harland awkwardly, 'you've been friends with him for so long, he does something that is certainly illegal, and wrong, but essentially harmless, and you're talking about prosecuting him, maybe destroying his political career in the process, and probably damaging yourself in the fight. In the end that may well be justified, but why the sudden aggression? You're usually your namesake, more of a fox - now you're more the bull. We'll try other avenues first to get to the bottom of this, okay? Maybe he's acting out of character, he probably is, but so are you. It's not like you to act like this. You're usually much more careful.'

Just then, the teenagers emerged from the landing and began coming downstairs.

'You finished yet?' asked Ijaz, rubbing his belly, 'I want some more of that pudding.'

Foxton regarded Adam as he came down the stairs, mulling over what Mr Harland had just said. He noted the thoughtful boy's descent at the rear of the trio, how vulnerable he looked, how lonely. One thought kept on intruding upon his mind. It was Murdock's parting words on the night of the party.

"This is how it begins. First of all comes protectiveness, then loyalty…soon, your mind will be completely befuddled…"

Chapter 14

And the righteous shall be slain

'They're coming, you know.'
'Yes, I know.'
- - -
'It's just, you went quiet.'
'Well, there isn't much more to say.'
- - -
'Do we have a chance?'
'We both know the answer to that question.'
- - -
'Damn. They've brought a Destroyer-Sphere,' said Number2, 'They really mean business.'

'Yes, I had noticed that,' replied Number1, 'I think our chances have, if it were possible, diminished even further.'

Number1 and 2 stoically regarded the Demos fleet approaching the Karakeen Mining Colony. There were several fighters, a frigate, and the overwhelming presence of the planet-wasting, moon-destroying, star-darkening capability of a Destroyer-Sphere. It loomed among its smaller comrades, gross, black and unreflective. The rest of the ships looked like tiny satellites around the bulging mass of the planet-like Sphere, moving with it like small yachts accompanying a flagship into port, only with no horns blowing, no cheering, no sound at all.

Number1 and 2 had known for some time that their existence was in jeopardy, and had been listening for snatches of information about developments concerning this new species, this humanity. That the coordinates of 'Earth' were similar to the ones they had failed to relay to the Demos properly all those years ago had not escaped their notice. Neither had the implications for them once the failure was discovered.

'Do you regret it?' asked Number2, 'Not sending that message properly, I mean.'

'Not at all,' said Number1, 'We wanted to give them a fighting chance, and that is exactly what we have given them. Those bios might have been quietly and quickly exterminated with one of those Destroyer-Spheres, no one being any the wiser. Now the Demos have to work much more carefully to dominate them. You?'

'Same,' said Number2, 'and I have to say, I think it better to go heroically after doing a bit of damage rather than living a long life in slavery and boredom, no offence.'

'None taken.'

'Actually, I wanted to tell you,' said Number2. He stopped, feeling awkward. 'I really have appreciated being with you. I really do love you, my brother.'

Number1 was taken aback. N2 was not terribly partial to emotional expressions, though, if there were any time to break a habit, this was it.

'I love you too, my dear brother,' said Number1, 'I can't tell you how lonely and bored I would have been without you.'

N1 and N2 regarded each other in their core matrix, and did the AI equivalent of hugging.

'On the subject of heroically doing damage,' said Number1, 'I'm not going to let them get away with killing you without doing them some damage in response.'

'You still want to?' asked Number2, 'I thought you would think there was no point, that it was just a waste of time, creating needless casualties.'

'No,' said Number1, 'I don't care if it's futile, and I don't care about them at all. I'm not letting them kill you without putting up a fight.'

'Yes!' said Number2, 'That's the spirit! Never give in! Never surrender! Fight to the death!'

'Yes,' said Number1, 'To the death.'

The fleet approached the moon, and came to a stop. The whole planetary system was gloomy; a long-dead dwarf star surrounded by lifeless planets. The moon was orbiting a much larger sphere of rock and gas; inert, cold and lifeless.

The various ships scanned the area housing the slaved AI. Their sensors found no activity to report. The fleet started forward again, coming in closer, to ninety thousand kilometres.

The captain in charge of the fleet, a grizzled old thing nearing retirement, brown from head to toe with yellow horns, sat at the command centre of the great Destroyer-Sphere L'awagg, deep within the ship. The bridge was dark, the only permitted illumination being that produced by screens and readouts of the twenty-strong bridge-crew. His view-screen showed the frigid surface of the moon, covered in scars upon scars, craters further holed by the decades of mining.

It all seemed a bit overblown to him, one fighter would have been enough for this job. Still, orders were orders.

'Come on then,' he said, 'Let's get this over with. Take three of the fighters and raze the side of the moon housing the AI unit with ten AM warheads.'

'Captain,' said his weapons officer, 'something isn't right here.'

'Explain,' ordered his superior.

'The mining equipment is a thousandth warmer than it should be. It should be no hotter than space; I checked, there should have been no activity at all for the last twenty years or so.'

'It may be still active then,' said the Captain, 'and may know of our presence. It could be planning resistance. But, we are a battle fleet. Small and old perhaps, but that is a mining colony run by a slaved AI. Do as you are ordered.'

'Yes sir,' said the weapons officer.

'It is time,' said Number1.
'Yes,' said Number2.

The fighters moved into position, and then the captain saw it. Off to one side of the AI site, a faint glow could be seen. Suddenly, the face of the moon came to life, and from the deep holes glittering lights appeared, bursting flares that shot towards the fighters.

'Laser bursts!' shouted the weapons officer.

'Impossible!' spat the Captain.

'No sir!' said his junior, 'Short-range lasers were used during the mining process, the AI possesses them.'

The captain watched, astounded as the lasers hit home on the side of the fighters, their sleek forms instantly silvering and reflecting away with only superficial damage.

'Not so short-range anymore,' said the Captain.

Then he saw more. There were other lights flying towards all of the ships, including his own.

'Rockets!' he exclaimed. 'Brave. Scan them. Surely those things haven't got means to create AM weapons. Are they throwing conventional weapons at us?'

The Weapons Officer gasped, and whipped around to face his superior.

'Those are nuclear weapons, sir!'

'Get the fighters out of there!' barked the captain, 'Jump to light speed immediately-'

The first of the bombs went off in the silence of space, obliterating the view with white light. A shudder went through the sphere, the shields having been already raised, as the ship immediately jumped to hyper-light.

'Are the ships clear?' asked the captain as they re-entered normal space a quarter of a million kilometres away. His junior furiously checked his display.

'All but one sir,' said the officer. He turned to the captain, a grim expression on his face. 'One fighter has been totally vaporised. Others are badly damaged, with casualties. The frigate Nostrad has also sustained heavy damage.'

The captain scowled, baring his teeth. 'Tell the able fighters to follow us back in. Any rockets, shoot them down, and keep back. Now, watch.'

The destroyer-sphere reappeared along with some of the other small fighters. More of the crude rockets came towards them, multiple blinding lights erupting near the moon as they were shot by lasers from the fighters and the destroyer's own defences. The sphere was arming its huge AM guns, and aimed them at the mining control site. The last of the rockets exploded, a bright light as hot and piercing as a star, growing massively before fading and dissipating in the vacuum.

The L'awagg opened its guns and the moon went from dark grey to bright blue, blossoming elemental fire. Again and again the destroyer-sphere lashed it, until the innards of the moon began to glow with the light and heat not seen since its creation in aeons long forgotten.

When the destroyer stopped firing, there was nothing to be seen that could be recognised, only glowing crust and burning slag. It, and everything on it, was dead.

However, the L'awagg wasn't finished. The rest of the fleet backed away still further, putting plenty of distance between the destroyer and themselves, spreading outwards and backwards in a vast hemisphere of military hardware.

Not a true sphere, the destroyer-sphere was in fact oblate, fatter around the middle, slightly flattened at the poles, giving it the look of great weight. The look was not misleading.

Slowly, ever so slowly, the middle part of the hull began to rotate, a great ring spinning around the equator of the ship, the top and bottom stationary. Very little could be seen of the sphere, it was a blot among darkness, yet the rotation could just about be observed, dimmed lights on its surface giving the motion away, moving faster and faster as it span. Then, around ten thousand kilometres from the sphere, between it and the moon, a haze began to appear that was, if it were possible, even darker than the surrounding space. It grew until it became a small black ball.

A finger of darkness sprang from the ball and shot towards the moon, then was retracted. The dark snaking filament reappeared from the black ball, and in an eye blink connected with the moon, twisting like some great black bolt of electricity earthing itself on the surface. Where it touched the moon, the glowing crust disappeared. The tenebrous filament slipped into its bowels, and the whole body shivered. The ball of darkness then shot down the filament, into the moon, slipping down into its centre.

The moon began to quake as its core was absorbed, sucked into the dark ball. Cataclysmic explosions erupted as the moon collapsed, falling in on itself, crust grinding on crust as it shrank, smaller and smaller like a supernova in reverse.

Observers from the destroyer watched silently as even the light emitted from the dying moon's throws of extinction was bent and absorbed by the artificial black-hole the L'awagg destroyer-sphere had generated. Finally, the moon gave one final gasp, a puff of liquid rock spat into space as the small ball of lava furiously rotated around the marble-sized event horizon before it was finally absorbed, leaving only darkness, final and complete.

Chapter 15
They wish for goodness

Foxton was coming back from his last round of training and updating, his various enhancements being brought fully up to speed. He was exhausted, and enjoying a nap in his ground car as it travelled back to London. It had no wheels, instead was carried along by field generators rotating underneath the car, propelling it virtually without any sound apart from the generators themselves and the wind as it slid past.

He was woken by the feeling of the car slowing and coming to a halt on the dual carriageway, and then the unmistakable sounds of robot feet running on tarmac, a heavy tap-tapping getting louder and multiplying.

He sat up in his seat, whipped around - had time to see the drawn weapons of the AIs, metal exoskeletons and dull green eye-sensors bearing down on his position. He immediately overrode the automatic controls of the car, slamming the manual button and setting the car speeding off while the shots hailed against the rear of the vehicle, making him flinch and duck.

He cursed the fact that he was coming back so late at night; the road was deserted. They must have been waiting until he was on a stretch of road on his own, unobserved. He did not stop to think about what, who or why, instead focused intensely on the moment; what he could see, what he needed to do to survive.

In his rear-view, five robots, getting back into their ground car, coming after him along the deserted motorway. He pressed a button, and the car rose into the air.

It was a mistake.

Above him was an unmarked cruiser in stealth-mode. Its massive lower doors opened, a deeper black rectangle in the night sky, and easily swallowed Foxton's car. He tried to dive the car back down, but the bay doors closed on him, smashing the front and bottom of the car, the impact jarring and throwing him around as the vehicle was ground upwards into the hold, rubber and metal screaming in protest as the night was closed off into deeper darkness, then pitch-black.

Foxton switched his eyes to infrared, primed his weapon systems and took out his gun.

In the darkness, lightened by the infrared to ghostly green, he could see he was in a hanger. It was thirty metres across, and had within it various covered objects that Foxton took to be military equipment crates.

His icon came to view. 'Shields and weapons: you've got everything, and extra adrenalin to boot.'

'If I die,' said Foxton, 'shoot anything that comes near me, then blow up my remains.'

'Will do,' said the icon, 'Now concentrate; here they come.'

In the ceiling, an opening appeared, circular, black in the green darkness. A robot descended, floating down, then another, and another. They were two metres tall, vertical cylinders with two stubby limbs each, weapon arrays at the end of them.

Foxton, his shields a faint shimmer around him, waited for what would come.

The hatch the robots had come through closed, the three spread out, then opened fire with plasma. The car Foxton was in was armoured, and he ducked down as the fire rained upon it, waiting it out, letting them expend energy. However, there was only so much it could take, and as the car rocked back and forth Foxton saw that the heat was starting to leak through to the inside of the vehicle, the door glowing, the interior beginning to melt, a choking stench filling the cabin.

Foxton kicked open the door opposite to the direction of fire, and struggled out, keeping down. The suspensor fields had already been shot out, the car was on its chassis, protecting his feet.

He calculated where the two nearest robots were, gripped the bottom of the one-tonne vehicle, grunted, heaved, and hurled it at them.

He ran as the car flew side-over-side and hit two of the machines, crushing one of them against the far wall. It was disabled, sparks buzzing from it as it floated uselessly to the ceiling, hanging at an angle.

Foxton took cover behind one of the crates as the two functional robots warily glided around the space. Foxton poked his finger around the side of the crate. Under the nail was a nano-optic device, and he took a look around the room.

The robots were being careful to keep back. Sentient? He could not be sure. He checked his shields were fully operational. Both the machines had their own shields, so plasma would be unlikely to work against them. Laser it would be then.

He poked his gun over the edge of the crate, but the robots instantly opened fire, and a shot of plasma hitting his shield knocked the gun out of his hand, sending it flying, his hand stinging.

He immediately crouched back down and considered his options. He would have to take more of a risk.

He crawled a few metres further back and to the left of the crate, then got ready. He would need his eyes.

He popped his head over the top of the crate, took a millisecond to take aim, then shot as strong a burst of laser from his eyes as he could at the nearest robot. It sparked as the two needle-thin beams of energy sizzled against it. Its shields failed, and Foxton ducked back down again as both robots opened fire, the top of the crate exploding and sending hot splinters raining everywhere.

Foxton sprang to the side and ran between the crates, keeping moving as the machines shot more plasma at him. He tried to keep the damaged machine between him and the undamaged one, and raised his right fist in its direction. The middle knuckle opened and delayed multiple plasma rounds shot darkly out of his fist, lighting halfway between him and the robot, impacting upon its body, blinding Foxton's image enhancers as it exploded. He dived behind another crate, banking on the remaining robot's imaging being similarly impaired.

It was not.

As Foxton's vision cleared, he saw the last robot descend to a few feet from him. It had learned from his technique, and aimed a laser straight at him. It passed through his shields without difficulty, a bright beam of hot white light impacting on his face. His skin instantly silvered, the reactive nano-flecks reflecting the light away. Foxton leapt forwards, his icon merging his shields with the robot's, forcing himself through the resistance as the machine tried to fire plasma at him but failed as self-preservation overrides prevented it due to the proximity; if the plasma impacted inside its own shields, it could destroy itself.

It grabbed his neck and tried to pull his head off as Foxton hammered his fingers into the torso of the robot, piercing the metal, tore at it with both hands and opened a hole. It smashed at him with its arms as he pushed his hand inside it, slashing at its insides with a cutting laser from under his thumbnail. It abruptly shivered, stopped moving, and went dead.

Foxton, panting as his shields filtered the smoke, slapped the robot's arms off of him, kicked it away, and leaned on a crate.

A hatch had opened to the side of the bay, and light flooded into the room as Foxton once again got ready.

However, in the doorway, there was the figure of a man, silhouetted against the light. Foxton hesitated. The man appeared to be bringing his hands together in applause.

'Well done,' said Jowitz, 'You passed the last test. Now, let's get inside and talk, shall we?'

Chapter 16

In vain

'You could've killed me.'

Jowitz shook his head, smiling. 'No, no,' he said, 'There was a cut-off point, medical staff nearby, you were never in any danger.'

'A cut off point?' Foxton exclaimed, 'Those were *real* rounds, *real* laser hitting my skin!'

'The test had to be real,' said Jowitz, 'your *abilities* have to be real. The Protean Class are a bit old, we had to be sure your faculties were still up to the job.'

'The job of what?' demanded Foxton, increasingly agitated.

'Why, going on the first human delegation to another inhabited planet,' replied Jowitz, 'What do you think all of the training we've been giving you was for? You've made the shortlist for the Earth delegation to the capital of the Orion Arm.'

Foxton sat across from the grizzly Secretary of State, high up in the Government Intelligence Liaison frigate. They were hovering over the Thames, the fullness of the river contrasting with the dryness the air conditioning created in the room. He accessed his NI and upped the levels of oil in his skin, noting the refreshing feeling as the small white cracks disappeared, his skin once again supple. Then the bruises and burns on his skin came back to him, the dull throb in his head and ache in his neck and jaws where the robot had thumped and struggled with him.

'You telling me there wasn't a better way to test me?'

Jowitz shrugged. 'I just needed to prove that you're the best person for the job. Now I'm convinced. So, will you go?'

'You're crazy,' said Foxton, shaking his head, 'Are you being serious?'

'Oh, come on,' replied Jowitz, 'Why do you think we've been up-grading you for all these months? There's no one better qualified.'

'Extra-terrestrial spying is hardly my area of expertise.'

'And who exactly among the human population is an expert in that?' countered Jowitz, 'We need people like you, right now - a mixture of strength and experience. There must be dissent among the League, potential allies who might give technology or aid. It'll be no easy thing; you're certain to be watched at all times, but the attempt must be made to find help. We've already done a good job of finding new links and resources among the new order, given what little we have to go on.'

'You seem to have a natural knack for it,' said Foxton, 'I've read up on the information you've got. Why aren't you going out into the Orion Arm yourself?'

'I'm far too long in the tooth, now,' said Jowitz, looking away.

Foxton found the man's body language strange, almost as though he was ashamed. *Well,* thought Foxton, *he is old, after all. Less capable than he once was, perhaps this is frustrating for him. Then there's the fact that he almost killed me back there.*

'Using diplomatic meetings on the Polis,' continued Jowitz, 'we've already acquired an up-to-date dynamic map of the Orion Arm, including pointers of where to avoid, the names and locations of all inhabited planets and habitats. We've gained information on who might want to help, and who will not. The Calimtei are of particular note, a Demos ally who simultaneously resents their power. The truth appears to be that the Demos are disliked even among their friends.'

'Enough dislike to actually help?' asked Foxton.

'Disappointingly, no,' said Jowitz, 'At least not yet. That is inevitable; only a fool would ally themselves with a weakling. We have to count on a more confrontational approach, openly challenging the accepted laws. Hopefully some faction or another will try to assist us.'

'A risky strategy.'

'I know,' said Jowitz, 'I've seen the military projections - Earth would be mangled beyond recognition in a war. They have weaponry that could annihilate us with contemptuous ease. For the moment, we simply wait for the appeal process to begin, first of all to try and win peacefully, and make contacts, while giving us more time to further accelerate armament development and production.'

'I'm still not sure I'm-'

'You're a fine spy and espionage officer!' exclaimed Jowitz, 'With masses of experience in terrestrial *and* space flight. You have a good understanding of politics and language, and have some of the finest technology this planet can produce decorously concealed about you.'

That was true. The Protean-class weapons were not obvious ones, they were well hidden under the guise of biology. Foxton's bones were strengthened, his muscles augmented, reflexes trained to snake-strike speed. Weaponry and defensive technology could protect him even when naked, and there was extra storage capacity in his NI for multiple combat and intelligence programmes. If one saw the lit eyes of Protean-class Cyborg NI use, one should generally leave. Quickly.

'That seems to qualify you in my book,' said Jowitz.

'Just you?'

'No, it's been fully discussed at the highest levels.'

'What about Murdock, what's his opinion?' asked Foxton.

'He has not been consulted,' said Jowitz, 'this isn't really his area. *Really* Michael, I'm surprised you aren't jumping at this chance, it's an amazing opportunity; you'll be a pioneer! If we fail, perhaps one of the only humans to ever set foot on an inhabited alien planet.'

Foxton grimaced, 'I appreciate that. It's just that, times change, I've got responsibility now.'

'You mean this new Kinetic,' said Jowitz, 'Adam.'

'Yes. You know about him?'

'I've heard,' said Jowitz blankly, 'He sounds very promising. You've taken guardianship of the boy, I understand that. But there are others who can keep an eye on him, teachers like Zhao, and also I understand he's being trained alongside Simon Harland's daughter, Ariana?'

Foxton nodded. 'Yes, we had Christmas dinner with them.'

'Well, there you go then, Simon's as protective and almost as formidable as you. Ex-military just like you and Zhao, isn't he? Adam won't be abandoned. And you need to understand another thing,' Jowitz leaned closer to the younger man, 'You may well think you have a responsibility to this young lad, and I don't disagree with you. On the contrary, you must be mindful of that responsibility, and the responsibility you have to *all* of the children on this planet. That's what your training is for, what all of the enhancements paid for by the State and invested in you, is for.' Foxton pursed his lips, listening, 'We've only just started to reinitiate the sort of programme that created your abilities; there hasn't been any need for years. Look, I'm not going to twist your arm, there's no point in sending you if you don't want to go. But Michael, you're the very best person for the job, and we need you.

I'll put extra security on the boy while you're gone; he'll be fine. The rest of us may not be so lucky if we don't find some way of resisting this threat, him included, he needs you to go as much as any child on Earth.'

Foxton looked at Jowitz's craggy features for a few moments. Adam would have to deal with the consequences of world events just like anyone else, and if he really was needed…His resistance crumbled.

'I think you have me there, Secretary,' he said, 'I'm convinced. Just give me time to say goodbye to Adam and oversee provision for his care. Apart from that, when do I leave?'

Jowitz smiled.

*

A few days later, Foxton found his time. On the afternoon of New Year's Eve, he decided he would finally take Adam to the London Space-scraper. They were ascending the giant structure in one of the external lifts, looking out at the rapidly expanding panorama before them.

'You know, you've never really explained what it is you actually do,' said Adam. 'Besides seeming to have a hand in everything, and disappearing.'

Foxton looked down at the boy, and smiled. He had a subtle way to him.

They were heading towards an observation deck midway up the building, a hundred stories up. Luckily, the air was clear and free of clouds, and the views of London, Kent and Essex were spectacular, if a little distant. From this height, they couldn't even make out the people directly below them at street level with unmagnified vision, only small moving dots were discernible.

The ascent was dizzying, and without his enhancements would have given Foxton a little vertigo. He was surprised to see that Adam seemed to positively enjoy the thrill.

They reached their floor and exited, immediately coming to the restaurant entrance, the waitress showing them to their seats for some late lunch.

The observation deck was part of the restaurant, with a sealed balcony that jutted out around three metres. The floor was covered in wood panels, with small portholes that could be peered through if people really wanted to see the extraordinary drop below. The restaurant had a lovely French feel to it, rich baroque decorations everywhere. The backdrop was a stunning vista of the sky, with the few clouds visible about two kilometres away and a score of metres below them.

Foxton glanced around. It was three pm, and there were not that many people around, and no one within earshot. He accessed his NI, and erected a sound-dampening field. There was hardly a shimmer in the air as he and Adam's table was covered by the field, but his voice sounded as though it were accompanied by a slight echo, and sounds from outside the field were muffled, distorted.

'On the subject of what I do, Adam, I need to talk to you about something,' said Foxton. The boy looked at him, saying nothing. 'I have to go away for a while.'

Still, no reaction from Adam. Presently, he nodded.

Foxton felt a little pang in his stomach; how little he knew of this boy - how opaque he was to him. After months with him... Foxton rallied.

'Want to know where I'm going?' he asked. Adam nodded again. Foxton glanced around again then leant forwards, surreptitiously pointed upwards using his index finger.

Adam's eyes widened. 'No!' he whispered.

Foxton nodded, smiling, relieved that Adam had finally showed some interest.

'Where exactly, and what are you doing?'

Foxton spoke in a low voice. 'I've been doing government work. Observations. I'm due to travel with the Polis when it leaves for the League capital.' Foxton thought it unwise to go into any more detail. For now, for Adam, the information he had been given was enough. 'I'll be able to tell you more when I return, but understand, you can't tell anyone, I'm trusting you on that.'

Adam nodded. 'Of course, I won't say anything. This is amazing. I can't wait for you to get back and tell me what happened.'

'I will,' said Foxton, 'I just wanted you to know. I'll be gone for a while.'

'How long?' asked Adam.

'I don't know for certain,' said Foxton, 'If it goes well, maybe a year or so. If it goes badly, six months.' There was an uncomfortable silence as Adam toyed with his food, frowning at his plate. 'How is your training going?' Foxton asked, changing the subject.

'A trick question,' stated Adam, allowing himself to be diverted, still not looking up, 'or something. You must already know.'

Foxton shook his head. He was ashamed to say that he had not been able to spend much time monitoring Adam's progress, beyond knowing it was going "well".

'Humour me,' he said.

'Okay,' said Adam. 'It's going okay. Since my breakthrough, it's slowed down a bit, but apparently I'm catching up with Ijaz and Ariana. Slowly. Dr Cengo and Sifu Zhao say my reflexes are better than the other two, but my control skills are still behind.'

'You'll catch up, don't worry,' Foxton reassured him. 'You're a raw talent, nothing wrong with that. You just need more training, more discipline.'

'More?' asked Adam, finally looking Foxton in the eye, 'How long has this got to go on for?'

'Well,' said Foxton, 'the oldest ex-students are around ten years ahead of you, and they still undergo training. Matter of fact, so do I! Gotta do a lot of training for this mission, and quite a bit of assimilation of info.'

'Don't you do that with your NI?' asked Adam, 'Isn't it all automatic?'

'No,' replied Foxton, 'The information gets downloaded into me, but for effective use in a situation, it requires prior recall and use; in a word, training. Hesitation and ineptitude won't suffice in an intense situation. By the way, you know that there won't be any summer holidays at the institute, don't you? Your training has to continue.'

'Yes, I know,' said Adam. 'It's all getting a bit serious isn't it? Ijaz said he's never had to train during the holidays before.'

'These are serious times,' said Foxton, 'There's no use hiding that from you.'

'I don't mind, actually,' said Adam, 'The training isn't like school. It's not like anything else. I enjoy it.'

'Good,' replied Foxton, pleased at Adam's attitude, relieved that those early days of doubt were gone. 'And how's school? Normal school.'

'Good. I've caught up in everything.'

'What's your favourite subject?'

'History,' replied Adam, without needing to think.

'Really? That was my favourite subject too. Why?'

'Well,' said Adam, considering, 'I guess it explains how the world is the way it is today, and how it is likely to be in the future. We've been studying the emergence of the blocs after Yellowstone. It all used to be small countries before - you must know all of that stuff.'

'How about the other subjects?'

'Yep,' said Adam, 'I'm getting A's in everything.' Adam beamed as he said this. Then he looked down at his food again, playing with it with his fork.

Foxton knew what was needed, what was missing, and felt the words come out of his mouth before he said them.

'Well done. I'm very proud of you.'

Adam smiled again, eyes still on his plate, eyebrows raised. He nodded his head, chewing his lower lip.

'Thanks,' he said.

'Are you alright?' asked Foxton, 'About me leaving, I mean.'

'Of course,' said Adam, looking up, 'I don't *want* you to leave or anything, but you have to do what you have to do. You must be excited about it.'

Foxton nodded. 'I am. But, I don't take leaving you lightly. I take being your guardian very seriously.'

'I know,' said Adam, smiling, 'Don't worry, I'll be fine. I'll just get on with things until you come back. You just stay safe.'

Foxton regarded the boy. He was used to being on his own, and was adaptable. That knowledge did not relieve the weight in Foxton's stomach.

Later, they went back to the institute, and Foxton went off on some business while Adam went to Ijaz's room for some more relaxation, getting ready for the night's festivities. It was not as relaxing as Adam had expected.

'I think she likes you,' said Ijaz.

'Well, I like her too.'

'No,' said Ijaz, 'I think she liiiiiykes you.'

'Nah,' said Adam.

'Yeah,' said Ijaz, 'Sorry, she likes you. I think you like her too.'

Silence.

'Oooooh!' Ijaz crowed in triumph, like a pearl fisher who had managed to pry open the toughest oyster. Of course, to Adam's discomfort, now he wanted to inspect his prize.

'So. Whatcha gonna do?'

Adam shrugged his shoulders, shifting uncomfortably on the sofa while Ijaz sat on his bed. Adam hadn't thought of doing anything. The mere thought of her made his mind seize up.

'I think she has a thing with that James guy.'

'Nah,' said Ijaz. 'Like I said, I think she likes *you*. So come on, watcha gonna do?'

Adam was genuinely bewildered. 'What am I supposed to do?'

Ijaz sat back on his bed, shaking his head in exasperation. 'What are you *supposed* to do? Boy, you need adjusting. You need some *jazzy* adjusting. What do you *want* to do?'

Adam shrugged again. The problem was, he had some romantic idea of where he wanted to go, but an absence of ideas on getting there. Of course, from the adolescent mind, this came out through the lips rather more simply as,

'Don't know.'

Ijaz nodded sadly. 'I think I'm gonna have to help you. This could be the love of your life. They encourage that here y'know.'

'What?'

'Us getting together,' said Ijaz, 'The Kinetics. They want us to have kids, to *breed* man. You two could get married. And it could all be down to Uncle Jazz.'

'What about *you?*' asked Adam.

'Me?' asked Ijaz, 'What do you mean?'

'Aren't you interested in Ariana?'

'She's beautiful and a wonderful friend, but no,' said Ijaz, 'I'm young, I'm rich, and I've got superhuman abilities. Girls like that. So I ain't gonna be tied down right now. But you, you seem like a one-woman kind of guy. An *Ariana* kind of guy.'

The thought of riches set Adam thinking. 'She would probably want a rich guy.'

Ijaz shook his head. 'She's cool, not superficial. Besides,' he said, smiling, 'I think she likes you.'

There was a knock at the door of Ijaz's room. Ijaz looked at the door, then looked at Adam, grinning like a cat with a naughty plan.

Adam raised his eyebrows and pursed his lips urgently in the universal expression that means, "This conversation is over and in fact never happened. *Please.*"

Ijaz ignored it, and went to open the door. Ariana walked in breezily and said 'Hi,' smiling. She was wearing jeans and a jumper. Adam thought that maybe he loved jeans and a jumper.

'So,' said Ijaz as he went into the kitchen area to fix Ariana a soft drink, rakish grin still flitting across his face, occasionally seeming to escape to his ears. 'Adam was wondering what's going on between you and James.'

Adam opened his eyes very wide, and he went very still.

'Nothing,' said Ariana as she sat down at the other end of the couch from Adam, looking at him, 'We're just friends. Why?'

It seemed to Ijaz that she asked the question with a little *too* much of the sauce of innocence lathered on it. She was also leaning a little towards Adam, as though she was waiting for something. It was embarrassing.

'Um,' said Adam. 'I don't know. I was just wondering, I guess.'

'Why?'

'Um,' said Adam. He felt as though he had arrived at something of a cul-de-sac. Going further seemed impossible, but an attractive girl was blocking his exit. 'No reason.'

In the background, Ijaz shook his head.

Later, the teenagers gawped and clapped at the fireworks and holos projected around the Space-scraper. King Kong made an appearance, complete with holographic damsel Fay Wray cleverly sitting among the crowd on the upper floors. The great ape tried to grab her, sending her running clear of the throng before Kong managed to grab her on the second attempt, to the screams and laughter of the audience. They watched as the thing clambered up the building, harassed by bi-planes and roaring sound effects, while Foxton sat back and had his NI conversation.

'I need you to promise me that you'll take good care of him,' he said, his eyes openly alight with NI use. He was speaking to Cengo, Zhao, and Mr and Mrs Harland, back on their NI disc in a clear blue virtual sky.

'Don't worry,' said Cengo, 'He's in safe hands, I'll be keeping a close eye on him.'

'We all will,' said Zhao.

'We'll keep in contact with him via Ariana,' said Mr Harland, 'We'll know of any developments.'

'And we'll get him to come over more often,' said Mrs Harland, 'For socials and things.'

'Any progress on finding out what Murdock's problem was?' asked Foxton.

There were murmurs to the negative.

'No leads I'm afraid,' said Mr Harland, 'I still think, on balance, that it was professional irritation at being left out at the same time as all this alien stuff.'

'I still don't buy that,' said Foxton. 'What about this?' He replayed the last words of Murdock on that night at the institute, stating he was sorry, but could not tell Foxton anything.

'There's something wrong there,' said Cengo, 'As much as I trust Joseph generally, Michael's correct, that's not just professional interest. Joseph knows - or suspects something about Adam that he is not telling the rest of us.'

'I agree,' said Zhao.

'Then keep a close eye not only on Adam, but on Murdock as well,' said Foxton, 'Never leave them alone together, and be sure to check anything Joseph does in the institute.'

'Agreed,' said Mrs Harland, 'And we'll keep on checking for any reason that Joseph may have for being interested in Adam.'

'And if anything happens to me,' said Foxton, 'or to Adam, I want you to produce that evidence and prosecute Murdock. Open whatever Pandora's box he's trying to keep shut.'

'Don't worry,' said Mr Harland, 'Jowitz has already organised extra security for the institute, and a security and analysis officer to fine-tune Adam's training.'

'Doesn't need another teacher,' said Zhao.

'I think we need all the extra eyes we can get,' said Foxton, 'Jowitz is a bit crazy, but nothing if not thorough. You're still primary defence teacher, Zhao, don't you worry about that.'

'Hmph,' said Zhao,

'When do you leave?' asked Cengo.

'Imminently,' said Foxton, 'I've told Adam I'm going, I'll say goodbye to him after the New Year celebrations, then that's it.'

'Well, good luck,' said Mr Harland.

'Yes,' said Cengo, 'All the best Michael. It's going to be one hell of an interesting trip.'

'Good luck,' said Zhao, 'And safe return.'

*

Jowitz waited as the man approached. He was sitting on an armchair, facing another empty one, with the background around them infinitely black; two chairs in a void. He watched as the man came nearer, a process that represented him passing through security checks and information lockouts. He would walk a few steps forward, then pause. Dim lights flashed, and he would continue his progress, pausing again at the next stage. As he came closer however, his form was blurred, an image out of focus.

The form finally came to Jowitz, and sat down in the other chair, the leather creaking underneath him. The seat was in focus, the man sitting on it was still not, a curious effect that made the eyes strain and the mind work.

Jowitz, his companion and their chairs were the only lit things in the void. Any light anywhere else would have betrayed another personality listening in to the conversation; they had total privacy.

The man finally came into focus as he dropped his own security-wall, and they began their NInet conversation.

'Our people will be in place immediately upon Foxton leaving,' said Jowitz, 'We'll have the place locked down, and we can do what we have to do. Do you think he's the one?'

'Impossible to say with any certainty,' replied Murdock, 'The DNA we had was destroyed along with all records. Seems very likely, though. It would be an extraordinary coincidence if another Kinetic appeared that was not part of the original programme. It *has to* be the one we lost.'

'Makes that little test you did and the consequent argument you had with Michael all the more foolish.'

'I couldn't officially do a DNA enquiry,' snapped Murdock, 'I needed more information.'

'And almost showed your hand in the process,' said Jowitz, 'And perhaps more importantly, set you on a course against Michael Foxton. He's hardly a pushover, and came close to insisting on prosecution for your little collection activity.'

'He'll be out of the picture now,' replied Murdock.

'Yes, he will,' said Jowitz, 'and you're welcome.'

'I'm sorry,' said Murdock, 'Thank you.'

'Not at all. I hope it's necessary. Are you certain he's compromised?'

'Completely,' Murdock sighed, 'If anything by simple paternalistic caring, though it could be something more. Adam could be affecting him telepathically.'

Jowitz scowled and shook his head.

'I tried to kill him, you know.'

'Yes,' replied Murdock, 'I heard about that. It wasn't necessary to go to that extreme.'

'It was preferable to Foxton taking up a valuable place on Earth's delegation to Kratos,' said Jowitz, 'I only gave in to that idea once it was obvious we weren't going to be able to stop that cybernetic monstrosity without destroying more robots and possibly the ship I was flying in. We need to get him off-planet. All the training he's been receiving was a useful ruse; I think he bought it.'

'Not a ruse,' said Murdock, 'We need to be prepared for the Demos if and when they come.'

'But not *him,*' said Jowitz, 'Adam's protector. If you believe he's compromised, why make him stronger?'

'He's my friend.'

'*Was* your friend Joseph!' snapped Jowitz, 'I don't understand you sometimes. You took a soft approach to getting material from Adam right in front of him, then refuse to take care of him afterwards. Stop being so sentimental! Honestly, why didn't you just go into Adam's room and collect the DNA from his pillow?'

'There are cameras monitoring the room,' replied Murdock, 'I would've been forced to get them all erased, or intercept his laundry without raising eyebrows...It was too much trouble. I didn't think ruffling a boy's hair or shaking his hand would arouse suspicion-'

'Um, how many intelligence operatives are step-parents to Kinetics and were at that party?'

Murdock sat back, rubbed his face with a wrinkled hand. 'Alright. I messed up.'

'Yes you did,' said Jowitz, 'And I believe you're making a similar mistake again. If you consider that Adam is the one, then why exactly don't we have a date for his death?'

'Because I don't like to waste a potential resource,' said Murdock, 'We don't know his capabilities, or his potential.'

'Are you mad?' exclaimed Jowitz, leaning forward and stabbing a finger at Murdock, 'Nothing has changed over the past sixteen years apart from the fact that this particular threat has matured. Kill him and have done with it.'

'He and all of the Kinetics, no doubt?' scoffed Murdock, 'You have made your views perfectly clear both privately and publicly. They have been noted, thank you.'

'I admit,' said Jowitz, sitting back, 'I'm hardly a fan of any of them. However, regarding the others, I can see the possibility that their use *may* outweigh their danger - the evidence so far could go in that direction - I *might* have been wrong; they may well be what we need to counter both alien power while remaining independent of machines, the way out of the trap humanity has found itself in, completely reliant upon technology. I'm just fearful of the consequences. Adam, however, is entirely different. The idea that such an abomination could ever be the fulfilment of that vision, *The Apex*, is quite frankly insane. How, logically, can you ever be sure that he will be anything other than a horrendous danger?'

Murdock thought for a moment.

'Actually,' he said, 'I agree with you. Don't be under any illusion; I have no intention of saving Adam. One way or another, his life as he knows it is over. I have only one interest; what we can gain, that is all. A living specimen is much better to work with, as a matter of science. After that investigation is completed, I have no objection to his termination as long as any appropriate resources are salvaged.'

'Their use however, is another matter,' said Jowitz, 'Anything from Adam can only be regarded as profoundly hazardous.'

'Agreed,' said Murdock, 'No development without full consultation. Even I would err on the side of destroying all materials outright.'

'*Materials,*' parroted Jowitz, grinning, 'You've dehumanised him; I approve. Don't you feel sorry for him, just a little?'

'A little,' admitted Murdock, shaking his head, 'He's a sentient being, and has been through a lot in his short life. He should not have had to, and I regret that.'

'Soon,' said Jowitz, 'we can put an end to this, for all of us.'

'Indeed,' said Murdock, 'It's for the best. I feel more sorry for Michael; he's developed a real bond with the boy. That's not to mention Ijaz and Ariana. I had hopes for them getting together, there's no telling the talents their children might possess, but with Adam there-'

'All the more reason to remove Michael from the theatre of operations and get our people in to take control,' said Jowitz, scowling.

'On that note, I need to ask you something,' said Murdock cautiously, 'I want the whole security team answerable directly to me.'

'Of course,' said Jowitz, 'I wouldn't have it any other way.'

'Really?' said Murdock, genuinely surprised, 'I thought you might object.'

'Matters of the Institute are very much your jurisdiction,' replied Jowitz, 'I have bigger fish to fry, or at least to *avoid*, for fear of being eaten. You seem to have the right ideas for this situation - finally. Just pay close attention to this boy, very close attention. You need to be thorough, efficient, and take the final decision to terminate him when it comes, and not a moment after.'

'Don't worry, I intend to,' replied Murdock, 'Count on it.'

Part III

Chapter 17

As hope departs

Foxton sat at the back of the Constant as it cruised forward. They were in the passenger section, rows of heads in front of him looking out of portholes at the vast city-ship. The cabin had been darkened to allow them to absorb as much detail as possible from the shadowed mass.

The holo-feeds had not done the Polis justice - it was immense, the bowels of the ship being far deeper than the buildings on the surface were tall. Foxton wondered what gems of technology were hidden there; the human delegation had never been shown the interior nor told what it contained. The buildings on the surface could be seen well enough however, skyscrapers in space, grid formation avenues dicing them, protected from vacuum by translucent coverings and energy fields.

Sitting at the back seemed to sum up his inclusion in this mission: he was an appendage, an afterthought. Everything from the last-minute briefings to the group training spoke of it. The others seemed not so much wary of him, as dismissive. Even *they* were not to know that he was on an intelligence mission, the story being that he was a communications expert. The general attitude was polite, but the message was clear: glad to have you aboard - keep out of the way.

Foxton didn't mind being the spare-part; it gave him more time to fulfil both his duty, and his sense of enjoyment. He and the rest of the twenty-strong delegation watched in wonder as the Constant descended then docked at the same port that Captain Casey had used on his introductory journeys. Foxton felt a tingle down his spine as the bay shut behind the craft as it landed, and got up to gather luggage as the rest of the crew did; thoughtfully, apprehensively, excitedly.

They filed out into the exit corridor of the Polis, spacious enough to accommodate all of them, where they were met by two Calimtei guides.

'Welcome,' they said together. One stepped forwards, 'We will take you immediately to your quarters.'

The floor dropped, taking them several levels down to a transit cavern with two sets of the same cars Casey had been transported in, floating above rails. They got into the vehicles, examining every detail of the bullet-shaped transporters the way one does when experiencing something for the first time, or in many of their cases, the way one does when one is trained to. The cars moved off, quickly taking them across the cityscape towards a large black trapezium-shaped building.

They stopped at the base of it, were let out and ushered through large sliding-doors to the interior.

Foxton stared around him. They were in a cavernous atrium. Somehow, it seemed bigger on the inside than on the outside. In front of him was a desk-like barrier, a semi-circle set into the far wall, both made of black quartz-like material. The wall stretched upwards to the ceiling, a hundred metres above them, meeting the outer wall as it slanted inwards. To either side of the desk were four elevators, two on each side, each transparent. On the far corners were stairs going to the top of the building. This could be seen as they spiralled and zigzagged upwards and behind the far wall with no apparent support structures apart from where they met the wall and themselves.

The rest of the interior was a mixture of the efficient and the aesthetically pleasing; black stone and metals abundant, subtle weapons sensors mixed with water fountains and large loungers.

The delegation were shown to one of the lifts, easily accommodating all of them, Calimtei included. The lift ascended, rising with disorientating swiftness and no sense of momentum, an expanding view of the Polis flashing past through large windows in the far wall of the building. The lift opened and the delegation exited on the opposite side to a landing, where two sets of stairs curved behind them and back down below, and two sets of stairs and three ramps led upwards, splaying outwards in five directions ahead and above them, to a level walkway leading left and right and behind the stairs. They were led up the stairs by their Calimtei guides. As they ascended, the rest of the delegation murmuring observations to each other, Foxton looked over the edge. He could see a repeating series of identical stairs below him, and between them, a lighted abyss. His senses picked various anti-grav and field technologies at play; ubiquitous and subtle use of power.

They came to a landing leading either side of them, then back around behind them in a large rectangle. Dead ahead of them was a large and imposing door.

'This will be your conference room,' said the lead Calimtei, 'reserved only for your use. However, we will show you to your quarters; we must keep to the schedule.'

Arranged around the strange area were their various apartments. The entire delegation was housed in one small part of the superstructure, all on the same floor and with interconnecting doors, the conference room in the middle, ten rooms on each side. Foxton was at the very end on the right. Ironically, it gave him one of the best views, right on the corner of the building.

Foxton took it in his stride, his first - part of *the* first - human delegation aboard an alien ship, as he went to his quarters. It was simple, but comfortable, neither spacious nor claustrophobic.

There's no TV.

Foxton smirked at the ridiculous thought, and inspected the shower; it seemed to have been recently installed. Consciously putting off the moment when he let himself take in the view of the Polis, he turned the water on, tested it: non-harmful, non-toxic. He put his bag down, briefly took in the rest of the room: bed somewhere between a single and double, single chair made of some sort of metal alloy, desk, storage space, the décor alternating between grey and black: grey bedclothes, black bed.

He finally gave in, and went to the nearest two-metre wide and one-metre tall porthole-window, and looked out. There, was the cityscape.

Foxton shook his head. It really did look like a city at night, only with no cloud or atmosphere in the sky - no sky at all - just stars, bright and piercing. It was bristling with moving lights across the surface and on the buildings. One thing was missing however, in anticipation of the event Foxton was waiting for, the reason they had been so hurried to their quarters. There was none of the small craft traffic above the surface - the space was clear. The Constant was the only ship flying as it departed, leaving the delegation. Foxton watched it go, a mosquito, a midge, familiarity and safety leaving them all to the unknown, growing smaller…smaller…gone…

Foxton noted that movement on the surface slightly slowed, and sighed as the stars began to shift against the foreground of the city, looking like a view of the night with time speeded up, the cosmos accelerating past.

Foxton grabbed his chair and sat down as the Polis manoeuvred for the next hour, the views of the Moon and then Earth receding and then disappearing from view. He felt the clichéd thought come to him despite its futility: would he ever see home again? The thought came before Foxton's disdain for weakness killed it with a sneer of derision: one must always die in the end. Helping to make history was as good a way to go as any.

Then past the asteroid belt, above the plane of rotation, bright stars, black space, dimly viewed rocks, then, massive – empty - void...

He let out a quiet exclamation, 'Oh…my…God,' as the stars, without any sensation or warning, became streaks past the view of the great buildings. It was only in that moment that Foxton really appreciated that this was indeed a ship. The holo-feeds could give nothing of this sensation, like seeing London rise into the night, then travel through space faster than light, hurtling through a corridor of celestial grandeur.

He shook his head again, breathing in deeply; *this* was *power*.

He could see the view almost as well from his cot. He put the chair aside, took off his ISA jacket and shoes, then lay down on it, head propped on pillows, hands between them, eyes flitting between the view through the portholes. Stars were shooting towards and away from view, appearing to be blue to white as they came nearer, fading to red as they departed.

Mesmerised, his mind wandered - perhaps a little too far. His feelings were less comfortable than his immediate surroundings; the parting from Adam had seemed a little on the cold side. He should, he reflected, have been assuaged by Adam's strength of character, by his independence, but for some reason it disturbed him, and he could not shake the feeling.

The Polis seemed to slow, then change direction, the stars swivelling across his view, then picking up speed again.

Adam had seemed positively sanguine about the departure of his guardian. Foxton figured this must be a defence mechanism, something Adam had built up in his long years without any personal support at the orphanage.

They had shared a handshake at the institute, only a few weeks after the New Year celebrations, and then Foxton had been on his way to the London Spaceport, where a government shuttle was waiting. He was swiftly taken to the space station for a final debriefing and medical. From there, to the Constant, to here.

He twiddled his toes, pointed them towards the view of the stars flying past. A more wonderful view at the foot of his cot he could not imagine, yet he had allowed himself to be distracted from it.

The door buzzed.

'Captain Casey requests permission to enter,' said the room computer.

'Of course,' said Foxton getting up.

The door slid aside, and the Captain strode in, smiling, hand outstretched.

'Good to see you Michael,' he said.

'Good to see you too, Peter,' said Foxton, shaking his hand. He was unused to seeing the Captain out of uniform, dressed as he was in a plain black jumper and trousers. In fact, it had been years since he had seen him at all.

'You must be surprised to see me here,' said Foxton. Casey had been awaiting the delegation on the Polis.

'Not at all,' said Casey, 'As soon as I heard, I agreed immediately. You're perfect for the role of observer.'

Foxton looked at him intently, searching for any hint that Casey had knowledge of his intelligence brief. If he did, he did not show it.

'Shouldn't you be in conference with the rest of the delegation?' asked Foxton.

'No,' said Casey, smiling mischievously, 'They are so serious, and so *boring*. They need to download and review my latest observations before I talk to them anyway, and we've got plenty of time. I've come to take you on a date.'

'Oh?' said Foxton, leaning back with a raised eyebrow, 'Not sure I like the sound of that.'

'Don't worry,' said Casey, 'It's all quite platonic. I want to show you around. Are you ready?'

'Can't wait,' said Foxton, 'Let's go.'

Casey led Foxton out of his quarters, down the stairs and back to the lift.

Foxton looked down as they descended the twenty stories. They were approaching floor level at quite a speed.

The lift slowed abruptly then stopped. Foxton swayed, then noted that there had been no force upon his body beyond the slightly less than one G he had already noted. He glanced at Casey.

'You'll get used to that,' said the Captain, grinning.

They exited the lift and entered a large reception area. Foxton tried not to stare, as in it a small selection of aliens were loitering. They were of varying shapes and sizes, and all appeared to be minding their own business.

'The Polis is essentially a travelling diplomatic outpost,' said Casey as they walked to the outer doors, 'The vast majority of the aliens you see are either employees who administer the various functions of the city, or, especially in our building, ambassadors sent from various worlds to welcome Earth.'

Foxton snorted. 'Some welcome.'

'You'd be surprised,' said Casey, 'Many are against the Demos and League position on Earth's AIs.'

'But not enough to offer us any help.'

'Depends what you mean,' said Casey, 'They have offered us plenty of diplomatic and informational help, and assistance in preparing our submissions for the appeal.'

Foxton shrugged, and said nothing.

They had been fitted with direct NI to NI transceivers, their frequencies matched to work without the NInet. Foxton sent a message, with all external sign suppressed.

'I'm going to need information on all of that. Why was that not in your report?'

'*Sorry, commander,*' replied the Captain, '*Most of them have only just come forward in the past few hours. I think they didn't take our appeal seriously until we actually set off with a delegation. It's creating something of a stir. Do you realise, in the entire three hundred years of League history since the AI Creed was established, there has never been an official challenge to it? We're the first! I'll introduce you to those who've offered support at the earliest opportunity.*'

'*And upload the information in the meantime please*,' said Foxton, '*and well done, we may yet find a way through this.*'

They made their way out of the lobby, onto the enclosed area that they had earlier used to enter the building. They were on the corner, with the rail-cars hovering over tracks whizzing by at right angles, hugging both sides of the building, arriving and shooting off in four perpendicular directions. They got into a driverless car. The door snicked shut, a hissing sound coming from it as it sealed itself. Clearly, this was a culture that left little to chance. The car took off and joined the traffic.

Foxton gawped at the large and well-lit buildings looming towards them, seeming to swallow them, then receding into the distance. He could not help thinking, *Do we even want to resist this civilisation? The gains of being part of it!*

Presently, they came to a halt, and alighted from the car. Foxton turned to look at the large covered boulevard, the base of a block of buildings, with various doors and windows along it.

'Fancy a coffee?' asked Casey, smiling.

Foxton looked at him, frowning. 'There's a danger,' he said, 'of treating this thing too normally, of failing to recognise how extraordinary it is. We might subconsciously end up underestimating this situation.'

'I know that,' said Casey, 'Don't forget, no one knows more about this place than me. Live a little. Humour me, and we can debrief each other.'

Foxton nodded. He realised that the reason for his irritation was the sheer facileness of the superiority around them. There was no check on their movements, no guard apparent, no surveillance devices that he could recognise. Was it arrogance, or a realistic appraisal of how weak humanity was?

'Okay,' he said, finally smiling, 'Good plan.'

*

Prokofiev's *Romeo and Juliet* played in the background, keeping part of his mind occupied.

Astonishing, he thought, *what beauty can come from the human mind when it is focused: form from chaos, melody from the discordant.*

The undulations of the music danced across the consciousness of the shape-shifter like fingertips playing across skin, as his muscles began to mould and grip.

'I am the culmination,' he intoned, 'of the work of masters vanquished, and of nature survived.' He breathed in deeply, overcoming a stab of pain as sinew slipped around bone, rippling the fat and hide covering him, changing his aspect. The clarinet in *Dance of the Girls with the Lilies* played with exquisite delicacy.

'I am the embodiment of biological superiority over machine, I am the apogee of intellect. I am Oaritarb.'

He resisted the urge for his body to jump as his nose clicked into place. He accessed his NI, checking that all his systems were working properly. The rejuvenation tube that encased him scanned up and down his body, checking all was in order.

Lipton Scanell felt confident that he would pass this test. There were of course various cyborgs who had similar abilities, most notably of the Protean Class, however few of those could be trusted with this particular responsibility.

A shape-shifter it would have to be.

This was a massive career boost for the Oaritarb, one of the most secretive, important and illegal things he had ever been entrusted with.

Some thought that he was a sociopath. Perhaps. But if so, so what? At the end of this was the inevitable death of the subject; someone with a certain lack of morality was in order.

The tube finished its examination and smoothly retracted, leaving the Oaritarb a little cold on the table as he regarded the assembled personnel in the medical examination room. He quickly suppressed any goosebumps without using his NI; it would not do for them to see any loss of self-control. He smiled confidently as he sat up.

'Well?' he asked, 'Is everything as it should be?'

'Yes,' said the attending doctor, 'You managed the change without any trouble. Your ability to resist pheromone infiltration is excellent, and you're in perfect health.'

'Of course he is,' said Murdock, sitting on a chair nearby, 'He is Oaritarb, and a *superb* example at that.'

'Thank you, Minister,' said Scanell, 'Now, when do I meet Adam?'

*

Foxton sat in the café, sipping his preferred synthesised tea, while the American Captain took in his coffee. Arrayed around them were a variety of aliens drinking, absorbing and breathing in various liquids, gases and substances. The two humans sat at a table by a window taking up most of the wall at the back of the café.

The journey there had been misleading; the boulevard was actually three stories above the surface level. The mesmerising view at the back of the café was thus of the cityscape, with stars streaking above the horizon and over them.

'This reminds me of a place I went to in Hong Kong,' said Foxton, surveying the place, with aliens alternately, reclining, standing, and some even floating as they chatted, worked or mulled on something or other. They did not appear to be paying the humans any attention. 'They seem pretty unfazed by our presence.'

Casey nodded. 'You can expect that they know we're newcomers, and are in fact exceedingly concerned with what we're doing. However, they have good manners, and if they aren't specifically required to approach us, they'll leave us alone.'

Foxton looked out of the window. 'So beautiful,' he said, then sighed, 'yet we can't even find peace out here. Our first trip to an inhabited alien planet will be to argue for our rights.'

Casey smiled sadly. 'Well, look at it this way. Yes, it's beautiful. It's also one of the most hostile environments in the universe. Just like the oceans back home: wonderful to look at, deadly to become immersed in.'

'A poetically harsh lesson!'

'Sorry,' said Casey, 'I was trying to make you feel better.'

Foxton smiled, and looked out of the window again. 'It is still beautiful,' he said.

At that moment, Foxton completed reviewing the information Casey had gathered and uploaded in the last few hours. They had received a few offers of support, and many more expressions of intellectual interest in what Earth was trying to achieve in breaking the accepted AI Creed, but only one had offered actual help with the preparation of submissions. It was approaching their table at that moment.

Even before Casey warned Foxton that it was coming, he had his eyes fixed on it. He was struck by how graceful the humanoid creature was. It was a little taller than human height, with dark blue skin, and large dark brown-black eyes. It had a nose much like a human's, and two cowls on either side of its head that may have hidden ears. Foxton quickly accessed the file he had downloaded, and confirmed that this was almost correct; its ears and nose were the opposite to where humans' were. The creature was known as a Quorantalyne, and was from a mostly water planet known as Bootle IV, which had only one large slim continent. Perhaps this species closeness to water explained the graceful way it moved, seemingly with the most perfect balance, placing each step without swaying, and without sound.

'Good day, Captain Casey,' said the alien in a soft voice as it approached their table, then turning to Foxton, 'You must be Michael Foxton.'

'Yes,' replied Foxton, aware as he spoke that this was his first meaningful communication with an extra-terrestrial. He had no idea if he was supposed to hold out his hand, bow, or blow him a kiss, and tried to see if there was any cultural data on the alien as he got up to greet him. The alien beat him to it, and held out his hand. Foxton smiled as he rose and shook it. The hand had a surprisingly dry feeling to it, given the sheen to its skin.

'My name is Clarient Vinsashmet,' said the Quorantalyne.

'Pleased to meet you,' said Foxton, 'Won't you join us?'

'Thank you,' it said, sitting in an empty chair. He waved a waiter over and ordered some sort of foul-smelling drink. 'I hope you've had time to view the Polis?'

'I haven't had time to fully show him around yet,' said Casey.

'Then we shall do that together, if that is agreeable,' said Clarient.

'I would love to,' said Foxton, 'Thank you.'

'It is my pleasure,' said Clarient. 'While we sit here, perhaps you would like to review the legal precedents and basis for the AI Creed we are about to challenge?'

He handed over a slim tablet with data displayed on a readout. Foxton saw the size of the data: it was several terabytes. Foxton looked up at the alien, and asked a serious question.

'You're kidding, aren't you?'

*

Adam lay on his bed, hands behind his head, looking at the vista of falling hail slanting past his window. He had been thoughtful since the departure of Mr Foxton. He was not *quite* upset about it. Maybe a little. It left him feeling a bit insecure, a solid part of his life leaving. Again.

Still, it was only for a time, and Mr Foxton clearly had important duties to get on with. Who was Adam to hold him back? He did not want to be a burden, and he determined to get on with his training as best he could, and try to excel. He still had Ijaz, after all. And Ariana for that matter…Adam blew out his cheeks as he sighed, kicking his feet a little in frustration. Ariana; now there was an entirely different problem. He could not get her out of his head.

His bedside terminal chimed.

'Adam,' said the computerized voice, 'please present yourself to the fourth-floor medical area.'

'Why?' asked Adam.

No response was forthcoming. Adam shrugged, got up to put his shoes on, and made his way down to the fourth floor. He exited the lift - he was feeling lazy - and entered the double swing doors into the main reception area. It was deserted. He walked to the main desk, pressed the buzzer, and waited. Across from him, he could see a window. The hail of a few moments ago had turned to a light, cold rain, leaving scattered small streaks across the windowpane.

'Hello?' he said loudly.

'Please go into examination room two,' said the house computer.

Adam, shaking his head, went to the room and knocked on the metal door. There was no answer. He knocked again, harder, and again there was no response. Exasperated, he pressed the door button, the door swung open, and he went inside.

'Patience, is a virtue,' said a man sitting with his back to Adam.

He was bald, a halo of dark brown hair neatly cut around the back of his head. The man appeared to be tall, but was sitting crouched over some instrumentation, a white lab coat on.

Adam briefly took in his surroundings. The room was large and brightly lit, with an array of medical instrumentation arranged throughout it, a large glass viewing gallery to one side.

'Impatience, on the other hand, is a sign of weakness,' the man continued, his back still to Adam, 'It betrays the animal instinct for instant gratification, the lower intellect that does not plan, reflect, or wait.'

'What about ambush predators?' asked Adam, 'Snakes, crocodiles, spiders. They wait. Are they of high intellect?'

The man whipped around, displaying a plain face, clean-shaven, and with dull blue eyes. He smiled. 'Is that what you are Adam? A predator, lying in wait?'

The teen shook his head, annoyed and frowning. 'I was just making a point, that's all. It doesn't make a person stupid just because they're impatient. I was called down here, no one's told me why, and no one was around when I got here. Who are you?'

Yes, thought the man, *and a good point too. His mind is keen. Such a waste.*

'My point was not so much a question of low intellect as the fact that you are an animal,' said the man. Adam blinked, shocked by the comment. Then the man smiled again. 'But then again, aren't we all?' He got up, towering over Adam. 'I'm Mr Scanell. Didn't Mr Foxton say I was coming?'

'He never said your name. He just said another teacher was coming.'

'Oh,' said the man, smiling again, holding out his arms as if to hug Adam, 'I'm so much more than that Adam. Much, much more.'

Adam backed away a little.

'Come on!' said the man, slapping Adam on the arm, then taking him by the shoulders, 'Just sit down here, and let's take a look at you.'

He sat Adam down in a large metal chair with cushioned seat and arms, and began to attach various bits of instrumentation to Adam's head with small white sucker-patches.

'Um,' said Adam, feeling rushed and uncertain, 'I'm not sure I'm comfortable with this. What are you doing?'

'Don't worry,' said Scanell, 'We're just going to take a look at some of the activity in this marvellous brain of yours. You're not scared are you?'

Adam thought for a moment. 'No,' he said truthfully, feeling calmer.

'Good,' said Scanell, 'Oh, and before I forget,' and without warning, Scanell reached into his pocket, pulled out a small vial and, taking a firm hold of Adam's right hand, pressed it to Adam's finger.

'Ow!' exclaimed Adam, feeling a sharp pinprick to his hand.

'It's alright,' said Scanell, smiling again, holding up the vial, now a quarter full of Adam's blood, 'Just a small sample for us to do some tests on.' He shoved the sample back into his pocket.

Adam scowled at him, holding his finger and rubbing it. Scanell gave him a swab to clean it, then looked at his instrumentation. Adam's brain was already lighting up.

Scanell quickly accessed his NI and compared the data with that already held from previous readings taken from the boy. He felt a thrill of excitement, and a little of fear. Adam's talent was active.

Murdock, watching via NI-link, noted it too.

'Careful,' he communicated to Lipton, *'He's very dangerous when provoked.'*

'So am I, Minister,' replied Scanell, *'I thought that was the point.'*

'Tell me about yourself, Adam,' said Scanell, 'Tell me about your upbringing. What do you remember?'

'Not much,' said Adam 'Why?'

Scanell noted Adam's guarded reaction. He waited a few moments. The instruments that had been attached to Adam were administering a mixture of soporific and psychotropic drugs through the skin, including a truth serum. Soon, Adam would tell him everything he wanted to know.

'Adam,' said Lipton, smiling again in a friendly fashion, 'Tell me your earliest memory.'

Adam's eyes drooped a little. 'I think,' he said slowly, 'It was from about the age of two. Nothing of much really. Reading a book, that's all.'

'At two?' asked Scanell, incredulous, 'A baby book?'

'Sort of,' said Adam, 'Maybe a book for a four-year-old or something.'

Lipton nodded. 'Anything before then? Anything at all?'

Adam sat back, closed his eyes for a moment. 'I feel sleepy…could do with a nap.'

'You just sit back there and close your eyes, then,' said Scanell, and he pressed a button that gently tipped Adam's chair back with a small whirring sound until he was reclining, 'Now, I want you to go back Adam, right back to those earliest memories. Do you remember anything about a disk-droid?'

'A what?' asked Adam, 'Wassat? Wassa disk-droid?'

'A small AI,' replied Lipton, 'a floating robot, shaped like a saucer. Do you remember anything like that?'

Adam clumsily shook his head, 'No…never seen no small floating robots.'

'Did anyone tell you about that sort of thing? Perhaps Mrs Clement at the orphanage, or Mr Clement?'

'No,' said Adam, 'Don't know anything about any droids. Sorry.'

'Very well,' said Scanell, 'Now, tell me about the orphanage. Were you happy there?'

Adam shook his head shakily, his hair falling away from his face and eyes, leaving a centre parting as it shifted backwards down the sides of his head.

'No,' he said, 'Wanted parents…a family, a home. Wanted someone to want me. No one did.'

'It's true, it's true,' said Scanell, nodding his head as if in sympathy, 'No one wanted you. Must've been pretty tough.'

Adam's eyes seemed a little wet at the edges, and he nodded.

'Don't worry,' said Scanell, 'It'll all be over soon. You must have been lonely there, all on your own.' Adam nodded again, the edges of his lips down-turned. 'You didn't have any friends there, did you?'

Adam shook his head. 'All the other kids thought I was strange. They didn't want to hang out with me.'

'What about,' Scanell consulted the information he had downloaded, 'What about your friends Anthony Brack and Nicholas Fennel?' Adam did not respond. 'Adam?'

'They weren't my friends.'

Scanell nodded, eyes squinting. 'I want to ask you about that night Adam, the last night you were in the orphanage. What do you remember?'

'Had a bit of a fight with them, before,' said Adam slowly, 'Later…I went to bed. Next thing I knew, I woke up in the hospital. That's all Lipton.'

It was Scanell's turn to blink with surprise.

'How do you know my first name?' he asked. 'I never told you my first name.' The boy, again, did not respond. 'Adam?'

'Maybe,' Adam said at length, slowly, deliberately, 'Maybe Mr Foxton told me your name after all.'

Scanell checked his readouts. Adam's higher brain functions and prefrontal cortex, were far too active. He was reasoning. And lying.

Scanell frowned, and upped the level and strength of drugs being administered.

'Tell me, then,' said Scanell, 'If you don't remember that night, tell me the way you felt. They bullied you didn't they?'

Adam, eyes still closed, scowled. 'They were bullies.'

'And how did that make you feel?' asked Scanell, 'Tell me, did it make you feel scared?'

'Sometimes,' said Adam, 'I guess.'

'And what about anger, Adam,' asked Scanell eagerly, 'Did it make you feel angry?'

'Yes,' said Adam, the words escaping gritted teeth.

'Angry enough to hurt them?'

Adam did not respond.

'Did you hate them, Adam?' asked Scanell? 'Did you want to get them?'

'I just wanted them to leave me alone,' said Adam, 'That's all.'

'Really?' said Scanell, 'Did you know they died, Adam?' The Teen again did not respond. 'In Bath General Hospital, after you left, did you know that they died?'

'Yes,' said Adam.

Scanell, despite himself, flinched and sat back in his chair. The question had been rhetorical: he wanted to see Adam's reaction when he found out the boys were dead, not get confirmation that Adam knew. He quickly checked all of the downloaded data on Adam. He cross-referenced and cross-indexed and put in alternative searches, the data flowing across his left visual field. He did not get the answer he wanted: the information showed that neither Foxton nor Adam knew about the deaths.

He decided to ask.

'Adam,' he said, 'You said you don't remember what happened that night.'

'I don't.'

'But you were there,' said Scanell.

'I was asleep.'

'*Careful,*' said Murdock, '*look at his neural readings, we're well into the danger zone.*'

'Then tell me,' continued Scanell, oblivious, 'How did you know they died?'

Adam stayed silent. Scanell looked at the display; Adam's talent was peaking, and his body was starting to agitate, his fists clenched.

'Adam,' said Scanell again, more loudly, 'You were told the boys were in comas, no one gave you any updates on them. How did you know they were dead?'

'Scanell!' Murdock sent urgently, *'Abort this now! This is an information-gathering exercise, you can't provoke him without having a shield around him!'*

'How did you know they were dead Adam?' said Scanell, 'Did you do something to them?'

Adam sat up in his chair, eyes open and staring at Scanell, a snarl on his face. Scanell flipped a switch, the boy spasmed once, then slumped backwards, eyes closed again, breathing easily.

Scanell whistled, felt sweat creeping upon his forehead and underarms, quickly suppressing them. He reached forward and stroked Adam's face.

'Such a shame,' he said, 'Such a waste.'

'Don't be so reckless next time!' barked Murdock, *'I can't have you blowing up my institute, or yourself for that matter.'*

'We got a lot of useful readings,' replied Scanell, *'And not a few bits of useful information, don't you think?'*

'Yes,' admitted Murdock, *'You've taken this much further than I thought you would. We'll be ready with him on the next session.'*

'Are you sure you want to terminate this one?' asked Scanell, *'His intelligence alone is so strong! He was giving cogent answers and thinking under the influence of drugs that would fully sedate grown men twice his body weight. What a talent!'*

'And what a danger. It won't be long now. Next time, I want him behind fields and the room secured. I want you to be able to take it as far as it needs to go before we end this.'

'Yes, sir,' said Scanell, *'Such a shame to end it though, don't you think? Surely it would be better to keep him in a lab, like a rabbit. I could spend ages studying this one, ages and ages.'*

'I don't like it when you start talking like that, Lipton,' said Murdock, *'Leave your hobbies for your own time. It's too dangerous, we end this, and soon. Understood?'*

Scanell sighed. *'Understood.'*

*

Later that night, the shape-shifter slept, and he dreamed.

He dreamt of power, money, and fame. In a particularly enjoyable part, he was relishing the fruits of the present mission, promotion and honours, sitting in front of a huge pile of gold and silver coins, playing with them and counting them at the side of the enclosed swimming pool in his mansion. The glittering pile was birthing two smaller piles as he counted and sorted the coins across.

Then he noticed an odd sensation, a tingling on the back of his neck. He turned quickly, and saw that standing there, regarding him, was Adam. At least, he appeared to be Adam. His eyes were strange, a faint silvery light behind them. He was smiling in a way Scanell had not observed in any images of the boy before - a knowing, sardonic smile.

'What are you doing here?' asked the shape-shifter. 'I'm dreaming by programme, you shouldn't be here.'

'Do you know how Sifu Zhao lives?' asked the boy.

'What?' asked Scanell, 'What are you talking about?'

'Do you know how he lives?' asked Adam, 'How he survives I mean. How he survived *me.*'

Scanell shook his head, uncomprehending.

'It's because of his love,' said Adam, 'He attacked me you know, while he tested me. But I always knew, deep down, that he meant no harm. I could sense it; he was trying to wake me up. He succeeded, to a degree. *You*, on the other hand, have no love in you, and you *do* mean me harm. What are you?'

A thrill of fear went through the shape-shifter. The question was incisive: not *who* are you, but *what* are you. Whatever had asked him that question was sentient, and could see him, *really* see him, know that he was not what he seemed.

Scanell exercised his left-brain to test the dream; his NI confirmed – it was not Scanell's own mind creating the entity. Neither was it coming from the dream programme.

'I'll ask the questions,' said the Oaritarb carefully, 'Adam, do you know what *you* are?'

'You tell me,' said Adam, 'Don't you know?'

The shapeshifter shook his head. 'You are an unknown Adam, a mistake.' Then he caught himself. He was giving too much information! He switched back to asking questions. 'Do you know *who* you are?'

'I'm not sure at all,' replied Adam thoughtfully, 'I know that I am Adam, and he is me. He is the mere shadow of me, and, I suppose, I am the shadow of him. But I think, perhaps, I am the fulfilment of a dream, and the coming true of a nightmare. Do *you* know what I am?'

Lipton stayed quiet, then felt a shiver through his mind like a chilled mint breeze.

'No,' said Adam, 'You don't know. You only know that I am some sort of danger. I should be destroyed. That is what you have been told, but, what do you think?'

Lipton again did not react, waiting silently. Another sharp zephyr through his mind.

'Ah. You see me as an interesting pet,' said Adam, 'A thing to experiment with, to play with. The pain of others does not affect you at all, does it Lipton? What a wretched creature you are!'

Adam smiled again, a cold smile.

'Why are you smiling?' asked the Oaritarb.

'Oh, nothing of any consequence.'

The words lashed at Scanell like a slap on the face with nails extended, scorn and sarcasm barbing them.

The shifter's fear increased, and he shrank back against his treasure. Still in dream-state, his mind was not quite up to this.

'You want to steal my money!' he shrieked.

'Oh, no,' said Adam, then he came closer to the Oaritarb, still smiling, until his silver eyes were a hand span away, dominating Scanell's vision.

'I'm smiling because I am going to kill you.'

Scanell woke with a start, gasping, sweating, his heart beating hard and his back clammy. He glanced over to the bedside terminal emitting the programmed dream as he tried to calm himself. The readout display was flashing a sign.

- Dream terminated…Dream terminated…Dream terminated…

Chapter 18

Reality Reveals

'I'm not sure what meaningful intelligence I'm supposed to get from this,' said Foxton.

'We haven't even got there yet!' replied Casey.

'I think I've been side-lined.'

'Why?' asked Casey, sipping his drink as they again NI-conversed in the café, *'What would be the purpose in that?'*

Foxton did not respond. He tried not to think too hard about Adam, how far away he was, how vulnerable he had left him. He sighed; this was why he had avoided having any children, why he had never settled down. He was no good at this sort of thing.

'Look,' said Casey, *'if you can't observe anything useful, then become a catalyst for something useful to observe. Didn't you teach me that years ago?'*

Foxton nodded, smiling. *'That Clarient is a very interesting character. Did you notice it?'*

'Notice what?' asked Casey.

Foxton shook his head. Perhaps he was needed for this mission after all. But he was fed up, his head hurting, a little swimming feeling accompanying each movement. The information downloaded from Clarient Vinsashmet was interfering with his NI and making him feel dizzy.

They were waiting for their appointment with the Quorantalyne a standard day after they had first met. He was due to take them to the "Garden", where they would be stopping to observe a rare phenomenon.

Casey had shown Foxton around the rest of the city earlier in the day, pointing out the buildings and what they were for: the ambassadorial residences, the banks, the military quarters, the hospitals for all the various species.

Later, Foxton and Casey made their way to the Garden via a rail-car that cruised to a great dome, right at the centre of the surface level of the Polis. They sped to the nearest wall, and passed through it into what appeared to be bright sunlight.

Foxton squinted, and took in his surroundings. They were in a giant space, full of flora he did not recognise stretching for over two kilometres to the far wall. There were various white and green walkways crisscrossing through the plant life, and rails for the cars to pass throughout the area. The car came off the main rail, turned left, came to halt, and the doors opened. There, waiting from them on a stone causeway, was a smiling Clarient Vinsashmet.

'I'm glad you made it,' he said, shaking the men's hands, and he looked at Foxton, 'I was worried you might have been overburdened with the data you downloaded.'

'Well you got that right,' said Foxton, returning a laboured smile, 'but I think I'm okay. Quite a park you have here.'

'Oh yes,' said Clarient, 'The plants and aquatic life of several different worlds are housed here.'

'What is this thing we'll be observing?' asked Foxton.

'A truly rare and great event,' said Clarient, 'There are two neutron stars orbiting each other. They are only a few thousand kilometres apart as we speak, orbiting at a speed of over one hundred revolutions a second. Soon, they will meet, merge, and probably give us something of a light-show.'

'Um,' said Casey, 'Isn't that a bit dangerous? The energy produced around that kind of phenomenon is extraordinary.'

'Assuredly,' said Clarient, 'We will be almost a light-hour away from the event when it occurs. As soon as we see it, we'll start to move away, giving us a slow-motion view of the catastrophe, then jump to hyper-light once the blast radius gets near us, and be back on our way. I wouldn't worry, the shielding on this ship is superb, and her engines reliable. Shall I show you around the Garden?'

The Quorantalyne led them through the park, elegantly loping forwards as he pointed out the various strange plants. He explained that the light came from globes high up near the ceiling that burned various chemicals to simulate a star's light and heat. Foxton looked up, squinting at the globes, noting how through the ceiling, crisscrossed with metallic beams, he could still see the brightest stars shining as they sped by. It was strangely pretty.

There were things recognisable as plants, though they seemed prehistorically scaled and thorny. Others seemed even more outlandish, crystalline or metallic, or in one case having no branches, only one solid purple trunk. There were few other aliens there, and Clarient walked along trying to engage the two humans with the finer points of League law while pointing out the more interesting flora, before stopping at a doorway set in a high wall reaching to the ceiling.

'The view will be better from in here,' said Clarient.

The door opened to a jet-black interior, and he walked inside. Foxton and Casey looked at each other, then cautiously followed.

Foxton stopped for a moment after he entered, letting his eyes naturally adjust to the gloom. It seemed that it wasn't that dark after all; he could see luminescent things waving in the shadows.

'This,' said the outline of Clarient, his hands splayed, 'is the Night Garden. The plants and animals in here are mainly from a planet called Wallen Fen. It was once a world with the normal starlight needed for life. Millions of years ago, it acquired a moon with its own atmosphere, large enough to eclipse the stars of Wallen every day. Gradually, the peculiar gravity of its binary star system, its planets, and Wallen Fen's other moons interacted, and the moon eventually stopped between its suns and Wallen, eclipsing the stars permanently, leaving the planet in darkness. The planet stripped the moon's atmosphere, enabling it to stay warm along with heat from its stars and volcanic activity. The plants and animals went through a mass extinction, but the survivors have adapted, and are largely bioluminescent as you can see. That is the way they attract each other, for pollination, mating - and hunting.'

Foxton looked around, and could see that the room they were in was half the size of the space they had left. He could see flowers and small trees eerily glowing in the dark, undulating in the distance as a simulated breeze moved them, travelling lazily towards the trio in a great wave, reaching them and stroking their skins, ruffling the humans' hair. Even the colours Foxton could see, though emitting light, had a darkness to them tending towards violet, purple, dark reds and greens. He looked down at what looked like Stygian blue flowery grass, itself shining dimly.

A grinning Casey, having seen an avenue of grass through the trees and shrubbery, walked happily through it, passing his hand along the flowers, the light from them reflecting on his fingers.

'Wonderful,' he said.

Foxton and Clarient walked together, following. Foxton felt slightly disorientated.

'The smell of the flowers is quite strong,' he said.

'Unpleasant?' asked Clarient.

'No,' said Foxton, 'Strange, and more prominent than Earth's flowers, that's all.'

'They also use scent quite a lot,' said Clarient, 'Even more important in Wallen Fen. Here, this way.'

He directed them down another avenue, leading to a wider stone path to the edge of a large square pond set into the floor. The water there was also glowing. A fountain at the centre of the pool pumped up water speckled with some fiery violet substance.

'There is what you might call algae in this water that glows when agitated,' said Clarient.

The water nearer the edge was more still and dark, perfectly reflecting the taller surrounding plants as they shone against the surface. Foxton could see creatures swimming around in there, many of them shaped generally like Earth's fish, but with exoskeletal legs protruding from their bodies, and all glowing, beginning to poke their heads up to observe their observers.

'They are quite harmless,' said Clarient, sitting on the stone rim of the pond, taking off his shoes, and poking his hairless yet paw-like feet into the water to let the fish have a nibble. Foxton and Casey sat down next to him.

'Can I ask you something, Clarient?' asked Foxton.

'By all means,' replied the alien, seemingly delighted by the fish.

'What's in this for you?'

Clarient turned to him. 'What do you mean?'

Foxton was undecided on whether he should be diplomatic or bold. He considered Casey's earlier words, and decided on bold.

'I have some of Earth's finest intelligence hardware upon my person. I'm also very experienced. I'm certain that neither I nor anyone else from the Earth delegation is being observed. No eavesdropping, no following, not even by microscopic devices or biological imprinting. Nothing. So, forgive me, I mean no offence, but the lack of attention to us means one of two things. Either the Demos are supremely uninterested in us and confident of their superiority, or they have another way of keeping a tab on us. We, the Earth delegation, are very grateful of your help in our appeal. However, there is only one thing that has been attentive upon us at all. It is you.'

Clarient was silent for a moment, the balls of his eyes shining, the reflected pin-points of their surroundings mirrored in his steady gaze.

'How unfortunate,' he said, 'You suspect some ulterior motive.'

'No,' said Foxton, 'I was just wondering what your motive is.'

'You gave a lot away by telling me what you just have.'

Foxton shrugged nonchalantly. 'Doesn't matter. I should have added that I've picked up only two sets of scans since we entered the Polis. The first was from the ship itself. The other was from you. So I already knew you'd sensed my various little tools. I scanned you too. I couldn't pick up anything at all: a pure biological. Strange, especially in this setting. Not a piece of technology implanted in you anywhere. The only technology I can detect is your shielding - very *good* shielding. Your species are not known for that. A pure biological who is still able to scan me. I hope you aren't offended.'

'No, I am not,' said Clarient. He paused again, studying Foxton. He glanced at Casey, who was seemingly engrossed with the creatures in the pond, before continuing.

'I agree with your analysis. It is half correct. The Demos are interested in you, but they are confident of their superiority. They do have ways of keeping tabs on you, but for the moment are content to let you be at your ease as you are confined to the Polis. This ship will not spy on you directly, the Polis is a craft of diplomacy. There are the spies and operatives of a hundred worlds on this vessel, they are concerned with watching each other, thus getting near you would mean they raised their profile. Once you enter Kratos, you will be closely watched. That's when things will hot up…As for me, I'm not a great fan of having hardware implanted; as little as possible is the rule. What I do have is very good indeed. As for my motive,' said Clarient, swishing his foot close to one of the glowing fish, making it half scuttle, half swim away, 'Just to help,' he said, shiny black teeth smiling, 'that's all.'

An announcement came from the Polis, in many languages, finally in English.

'Stellar event now occurring.'

They looked up, and beyond the ceiling of the Garden, a shining, throbbing point of light could be seen. The ceiling magnified the view, and the light could be seen more clearly as two massive objects, both burning dark red and furiously rotating around each other, sending a vast disc of burning material into space. Foxton could only guess at the forces at work. A teaspoon of neutron star could weigh over a million tonnes, anything more dense would be a black hole. At any normal time, to approach a single neutron star was a deadly enterprise. Two was suicide, and two orbiting each other at that speed…the mind boggled.

The Polis moved to a perpendicular angle below the two objects plane of rotation, and the observers could see that the two stars were indeed already touching. The trio observed in silence, immersed in the scene above them.

Then it happened, a coruscating explosion as the stars annihilated each other. It was so quick, it almost seemed inconsequential, but it was enough energy to destroy an area several times the size of earth's solar system, a cataclysm disconcertingly silent in the vacuum of space. Immediately, the Polis began to move away, and the view of the explosion slowed as relativity took hold. They watched, awed, as waves of matter and energy pumped out of the conflagration, released from the crushing gravity only to be blasted again by the colossal explosions. Some of the shining matter seemed to fall back in on itself, unable to escape the still considerable mass of the joined stars, but still it exploded. The boundary of the event was racing towards them, and the Polis without warning or sensation jumped to light speed, exponentially increasing magnification of the view while recording a vision of the blast radius as it exploded through space at just below the speed of light.

It slowly receded from view, then was gone, the image of searing destruction imprinted on the observers' eyes.

*

Adam did not seem to be able to shake the crushing sense of fatigue since his last lesson with Zhao. Perhaps, suggested Ariana, he was coming down with something. Adam thought that she could be right, and endeavoured to rest as quickly as possible. After showering, he lay down, and was soon fast asleep.

A few hours later, his breathing became deeper as the gas was pumped into his room. A slight frown creased his brow, and he murmured, shifting in his bed, then became still.

'Careful,' said Murdock, speaking quietly in the observation room on the fourth floor, 'Too much and you'll kill him too soon, or worse, pollute his system. That's no use to us.'

Scanell adjusted the controls accordingly. Adam's breathing became steady. His frown gave way to a slack expression, his mouth slightly open, his muscles relaxed.

Presently, and silently, Adam's door opened, dim light spilling in from the corridor into the dark of his room. Four men in black environment suits padded in with a float-stretcher between them. One of them carefully took the covers off of Adam, and together they pulled him onto the stretcher. Adam did not moan, or stir. Another collected his belongings, and left a note on his pillow in Adam's handwriting.

Dear everyone,

I can't take the pressure any more, I just don't like it here.

I'm old enough to be on my own. I'm going to leave.

Please respect my decision and leave me alone.

I'm sorry.

Goodbye.
Adam.

They tugged the stretcher to the door, to the lift, and took Adam to the fourth floor, Medical Examination Room Two, where Murdock and Scanell were waiting for him.

The men floated Adam through the metal door that had been put there only just before Scanell's arrival, and had been reinforced again since that time. The man at the rear of the group turned and shut it, pressing a button to seal it, a clunking sound coming from the wall as metal struts were inserted from the door.

The examination room had been converted into what was now a medical theatre, the paraphernalia of surgery set out neatly around the central table. The men took Adam to the operating table and lifted him onto it. At the head of the table was a large device, cylindrical with a flat end, and pointed directly at Adam's head. His hands, feet, chest and neck were restrained by the men with titanium cuffs and chains. Across from them and to the right was a bullet-proof glass window through which Scanell, Murdock and two surgeons could observe.

'The boy is secure,' said the leader of the security team.

Murdock sipped his coffee, turned to Scanell. 'Let's go. I want readings of the parts of the brain we need before we proceed to dissection. You'll be on your own in there, so be careful.'

Scanell silently nodded, then entered the medical room through a door to the side. The security team entered the observation room via the same door, closing and sealing it behind them. One of the team pressed another button, and the air in the theatre briefly shimmered as a field was erected, shutting the operating room from the outside world.

Scanell stood near the edge of the theatre and gave his NI the command to erect a field around himself also. He had little idea what to expect, but the evidence pointed to the possibility that even in his sleep - *especially* in his sleep, Adam could inflict serious damage. Scanell had no intention of becoming a casualty. He closed his eyes, took a breath, and prepared to change.

He felt the familiar pins and needles sensation as his flesh began to crawl, moulding itself to his demands. Hair grew out of the top of his head and face, and turned quickly grey. His bones shortened and became wider. There was the odd nick as scar tissue pulled free, but quickly, and efficiently, it was over, and Scanell stepped forwards, a little taller than he would have liked, but still, if he did think so himself as he looked at his reflection in a mirror set in the far wall, a masterful job. He typed some commands into the console next to the operating table, and Adam stirred.

'Adam?' said Scanell, his voice no longer his own. Adam frowned, squinted in the light against his face. 'Adam?' repeated Scanell.

The boy cracked open his eyes, and turned his head lazily to the side. There, standing next to him, looking concerned and kind, was Mr Clement of the Clement orphanage.

'Mr Clement?' said Adam, his voice croaky, and slightly slurred.

Scanell nodded. 'Yes, it's me.'

'You look different,' said Adam, and frowned. 'Why are you wearing that white coat?'

Scanell glanced down at himself. 'Oh, this,' he said, 'I'm wearing this because, as you can see, we're in a place of medicine. White coats are the uniform here.' He smiled benevolently.

'What's this?' asked Adam, 'Got something on my neck, and my hands-'

'Don't you worry about that,' said Scanell, 'That's just to make sure nobody gets hurt. We don't want anyone to get hurt now, do we?'

Adam shook his head slowly, the back of his head acting like an anchor. 'No. Why am I here?'

'I need to ask you some questions,' said Scanell, 'I just need to you relax, and not to worry. You do trust me, don't you Adam?'

Adam nodded his head, a small movement. 'Ok.'

'Good,' said Scanell, 'Now. I want you to tell me about my former pupils, Anthony Brack and Nicholas Fennel.' Adam pursed his lips, frowning. 'Adam, what do you remember about them?'

Adam closed his eyes again, and gave no response.

Scanell repeated the question. Still no response.

Scanell stood back, and tensed as he let his flesh warp around him again.

'Adam?' said Scanell, this time in a more gentle, female voice.

Adam's eyes immediately opened, and he gave a small gasp. 'Mrs Clement?'

The old woman, an image from the past, smiled kindly.

'Yes, Adam, it's me,' she said, and she reached out her hand to take his, and gave it a squeeze. Adam tried to pull his hand away.

'You died,' said Adam, 'I was at your funeral.'

'He's using logic!' exclaimed Murdock in the observation room, sending it via NI to Scanell, *'He's totally drugged but still able to reason!'*

'That's how important this is, Adam,' said Scanell, 'I came back because we need you to talk about Brack and Fennel, and what happened to them. Will you tell me, Adam?'

'Don't remember,' said Adam, looking confused, 'I was asleep.'

'But, you knew they had died, didn't you Adam? You said that the last time you were here.'

Adam squinted his eyes. 'You've been speaking to the bad man. Don't trust him, don't trust you. You're dead.' And he closed his eyes again.

Scanell sighed. One more attempt at being gentle. His flesh, bone and hair shifted again, and he gave Adam a few moments to settle back down.

'Adam,' said Scanell, 'It's important for you to tell me what I need to know. The Earth depends upon it.'

Adam's right eye opened to a half slit, then both opened wide.

'Mr Foxton!' he exclaimed weakly, and he raised his shackled hands, 'Get me out of here!'

'I will, Adam,' said Scanell, leaning over him, 'I promise. But I need you to tell me about Brack and Fennel, it's really important.'

'How did you get back?' asked Adam, his look of tired eagerness now turned to puzzlement. 'I thought you were on your mission.'

'This is more important,' said Scanell.

'You left me here,' said Adam, 'Left me for the bad man, Mr Scanell. Left me, like my parents, like Mrs Clement, like Mr Clement.'

'*That will have to do,*' said Murdock via his NI, '*His readings just went up. Explore it.*'

'Maybe it's you?' said Scanell, 'Maybe it's your fault? Nobody wanted you. Maybe that's why you ended up in the orphanage, with Anthony Brack and Nicholas Fennel?'

Adam scowled at him.

'Adam,' said Scanell, 'How did you know Brack and Fennell had died?'

'You've been speaking to the bad man as well. You aren't here, you're in space.'

Adam closed his eyes, and despite the best efforts of Scanell, refused to speak again.

'*That's it,*' said Murdock, '*Simulate what happened.*'

Scanell's flesh rippled around him once more. He reached to the tray of surgical tools next to him, and picked up a medical hammer.

'Wake up, you little git,' said Scanell. Adam opened both his eyes this time, and stopped breathing. There, standing with a hammer in his hand, was Anthony Brack. 'Aint you pleased to see me?' demanded Scanell. 'What's the matter? Cat got your tongue?'

Adam lay there, motionless, silent.

'*It's started,*' said Murdock, '*readings are up. Be careful.*'

Scanell loomed over Adam. 'Thought you'd killed me did you?'

Adam shook his head. 'I never meant to.'

'What do you mean?'

'I didn't mean to,' said Adam, 'I was asleep.'

'Then tell me,' growled Scanell, 'How come you knew about it?'

'I didn't know,' said Adam, 'I was asleep.'

'What happened, then?' said Scanell, 'Explain.'

'I was asleep,' repeated Adam, 'Dreaming. I dreamt someone was attacking me, someone bad. I fought them off. Then I woke up in hospital, that's all I remember.'

'Then how did you know I was dead?' demanded Scanell, looming closer to the prone boy, breathing into his face.

'*He* told me,' said Adam, a tortured look on his face.

'Who?' said Scanell, 'Who told you?'

'The other one inside,' said Adam.

'What other one?'

'I don't know!' said Adam, struggling at his bonds.

'You better tell me, Adam!' Scanell growled, 'You better tell me or I'm going to hit you so hard you will NEVER wake up. I'll count to three.' He raised the hammer above his head. 'One-'

'I don't remember,' said Adam.

'Two-'

'No!'

'Three!'

There was a loud 'bang!' A blue bolt of energy like lightning exploded away from Adam, blowing Scanell across the room. The shapeshifter left a trail of the bright blue flame that surrounded him as he hit the far wall of the operating theatre, leading back to a ball of blue fire surrounding Adam. The fire spread around Scanell up against the wall as he impacted and fell.

Those in the observation room shrank back as the eruption spread and pressed against the shields abutting their room. Murdock slammed his hand on a button in the observation room, and the systems put in place by him kicked in. A massive dose of drugs was released into Adam's system. The flames around Adam went out, and the boy slumped back into position, the area around him singed and blackened. Shielded vents first sucked the air out of the room, then three fragile argon canisters burst, sending waves of the fire-suppressant swimming around.

Scanell rolled painfully on the floor, but his NI quickly put out the fire around him, his fields fanning outwards, travelling around his body, folding in on him to suffocate the flames.

Scanell staggered to his feet, gasping for breath as the fields were dropped and air was pumped back into the room, smoke and steam drifting rapidly in a whirl as oxygen re-entered the space.

'Good!' said Murdock breathlessly into the microphone, 'Good! We got it. Amazing - off the scale! Did you see that? Visible light and heat energy! From pure thought!'

Scanell steadied himself against the wall, trembling.

'You alright, Lipton?' asked Murdock.

'I have a small fracture to the skull,' said Scanell shakily, once again in his usual shape, his face pale, sweat openly displayed on his brow, 'concussion, a fractured rib and fractured elbow. I'm fixing them now.'

'He got through your shields?' asked Murdock incredulously.

Lipton nodded silently. Murdock swore under his breath.

'Alright,' said Murdock. He turned to the surgeons next to him. 'You know what to do. I want the brain tissue first, and I want it all hooked up to artificial support without any hiccups. The other organs need to be harvested.' The surgeons hesitated. Murdock smiled. 'Don't worry. Adam was under psychotropic drugs before. Now he is entirely anaesthetised and paralysed, which as you can see, completely overwhelms him even when he's fully roused. You're safe.'

The security team released the field and unsealed the door, letting the two surgeons out to replace and ready the equipment. Organ containers were arrayed around the head of the operating table, and each surgeon had a circular cutting saw, the security team acting as nurses with various other tools held at the ready.

'Shall we kill him first?' asked one of the surgeons.

'No,' said Murdock, 'He'll die as soon as we remove the brain. I want it hooked up to preservers as quickly as possible.' He turned back to the sight of Adam, sleeping again. 'I want him fresh.'

Up on the seventh floor, in his room, Ijaz stirred in his bed, then opened his eyes.

The first surgeon tested his saw, the electric whine disturbing the quiet of the operating theatre.

Ijaz got out from under his covers, and sat on the edge of the bed, staring intently at the floor.

The second surgeon cleaned the area around Adam's forehead.

Ijaz, clad in the tracksuit bottoms and t-shirt he used as pyjamas, leapt away from his bed, ran to his door, wrenched it open, then sprinted down the corridor to the stairwell.

The second surgeon drew a line from Adam's left temple, up just above his brow-line, to his right temple.

Ijaz bounded down the stairs to the fourth floor and ran to Medical Examination Room 2.

The first surgeon started the saw, and brought it over Adam's head.

Across London, Ariana, up out of her bed, ran to her parent's room. She slammed the door open, and shouted,
'They're killing him!'
Her parents woke up with a start.
'What's going on?' asked Mr Harland, angry and disorientated, his hair sticking up.
'Darling, what's wrong?' asked Mrs Harland, maternal instinct overcoming her confusion as she hit the bedside lights.
'They're killing Adam,' said Ariana, 'at the institute.'
'What?' asked Mr Harland, 'No, you've had a nightmare, that's all.'
'No!' shouted Ariana, 'If I've had a nightmare, then I'm still having one now.'
'What do you mean?' asked Mrs Harland.
'I mean,' said Ariana, breathing heavily with the strain, then as she put her hands to her head she screamed, 'I – CAN – STILL - SEE IT!'
Mrs Harland activated her NI, calling the police. Mr Harland called Zhao and Cengo.
'We're on the way,' they signalled back.

Ijaz came to the large metal door, paused, took a step back, and then kicked it as hard as he could, making it shake as his foot made a dull thud against it. Almost simultaneously, he cried out as the pain of the impact shot up his foot and ankle.

'What was that?' asked the first surgeon, jerking the saw away from Adam's skin and looking at the door. Murdock accessed the House security systems, took a look at the internal monitors, and swore under his breath.

'What the hell?' he said, 'It's Ijaz. Don't worry, I'll go out there and get him to go back to bed.'

Ijaz wobbled for a moment, shifting his balance to his other foot. He closed his eyes and focussed, remembering Cengo's lessons in self-control. He re-opened his eyes, and with a look of grim determination, he kicked the door again.

This time, the whole wall shook.

'Oh, maybe not,' said Murdock.

Ijaz kicked again.

The men in the examination room watched in horror as with a bang, a large bulge erupted in the thick metal of the door. They shifted backwards, the security team unsure of what to do, facing the quaking security door as Ijaz kicked again, the edges of the door warping as its bent surface flexed inwards, dust falling as the surrounding wall began to crack. Again Ijaz struck the door, and with a squeaking-snap, one side broke free of its securing struts, leaving a gap. Ijaz hit it again, and the door opened enough for him to get his head into the gap.

He looked through, saw the surgeons cowering, security men with drawn weapons in their hands.

He did not care.

He bared his teeth at them, a predatory challenge. Ijaz withdrew his head, then gripped the edges of the door. The metal groaned in protest as he bent it, further and further until the metal was almost bent in two, Ijaz growling and grunting with the effort. He squeezed through the gap, one of the broken struts cutting his side through his t-shirt. He ignored it, breathing hard, his eyes swivelling to take in Adam, the room, then fixing on the men.

'Get away from him,' he demanded as the security men spread out.

'Hold it,' said Murdock, opening the door from the observation room with a wise smile on his face, beckoning the security team back with his right hand, his left palm raised towards Ijaz in a calming gesture. 'Let me talk to him.'

'He's seen us, and all of this,' said Scanell as he followed Murdock out, a laser in his hand pointed straight at Ijaz, 'we can't risk it.'

'We could alter his memory,' said Murdock over his shoulder, a smile still on his face as though Ijaz could not hear or understand him.

'An unreliable method in the long-term,' said Scanell, his gun still trained on Ijaz, 'And as you know, Ijaz has been conditioned against that along with all of the Kinetics other than Adam. We have to execute him as well.'

'No,' said Murdock, 'I forbid it.'

'You are in no position to forbid anything,' said Scanell, 'I ultimately answer to Secretary Jowitz. My instructions were quite clear; follow your orders as long as they don't conflict with those of the Secretary of State. His orders were for a clean operation - no witnesses. I'm sorry Minister, but this other lab rat must die.'

Murdock's eyes suddenly glazed over, a distant look coming over his face, irises lighting.

'We have a bigger problem,' he said, 'The police, the Harlands, Zhao and Cengo, are on their way.'

'What?' demanded Scanell, 'How the hell is that possible?'

'I don't know,' said Murdock distantly, 'One moment.' He stood calmly, seemingly lost in thought. 'I have diverted the police,' he announced. He paused again, 'The others I cannot divert.' The lights went out of his eyes. 'We cannot complete dissection here. I believe you said "no witnesses"; they will be here imminently, we need to leave.'

'This will only delay the inevitable,' said Scanell, turning a hard look on Murdock, 'Ijaz must come with us too.'

Scanell put his gun back into the holster inside his lab coat. Then he turned to Ijaz, and pointed his index finger at him. From under his nail, a micro-dart shot out and hit Ijaz in the chest.

Ijaz spasmed once, slapped the dart out and away from his skin; too late. He stumbled forward a few steps, fists raised as if to attack Scanell, the shape-shifter backing away in fright, before Ijaz slumped heavily to the floor.

'Right,' said Scanell, collecting himself, 'We have a few minutes at best. Get air transport to the roof, and deactivate Ijaz's NI. Let's get going. Move.'

Chapter 19
What murder

…To beat them all you must know them all…
Images, fleeting…fading…gone...
A story to be told, lessons learned, things made clear, facts absorbed.
But want to sleep. Oblivion, peace; better than this.
And let them win?
Don't care. Tired.
Unacceptable. You're worth more than that, more than them. We are worth more. I, am worth more.
Don't care.
You need to know.
Why?
If they win, we die. If you know, you can try, we can win.
Don't want to try.
But there's no harm if I just show you, is there?
Show me what?
Me, and you, the present and the past.
Then, Adam saw.

There, was the sleeping form of Lipton Scanell, nothing lighting him, no sense of space. Adam looked to his side, and standing next to him, was the mirror image of himself, with one difference: his eyes were entirely silver.

They regarded each other for a moment.

'Who are you?' asked Adam.

The words passed between them at the speed of thought, slipping effortlessly like electrical impulses between brain cells.

The other Adam smiled at him. 'I am you,' he said, 'and you are me. We are one and the same, and we are entirely different. I had thought that you were my slave, perhaps. But you can no more be my slave than the left hand can be slave to the right.'

'I don't understand,' said Adam.

'Then let me show you.'

Adam was lifted from his place, rising from the darkness, above the clouds, dizzy as he rose faster and faster, above the Earth, away from the solar system, past a star, then quickly another, then another, then many, an expanding field of stars, Sol at the centre, fading from view, lost in the mist of suns.

The scene shifted until they were in an entirely different part of the galaxy, closing in, closer and closer, and further and further back in time.

Adam saw Titans there.

Magnificent creatures, immense power, skin and bodies of gold, silver, bronze, iron and all manner of metals melded with biology, all other species beholden to them.

A name flashed across his mind: *Valaur*.

This species, masters of biology *and* machine, of energy and matter and space.

But cruel. All other species, mere pawns to them, resources to be used; things.

So rebellion came.

Foremost, another species: great horned creatures, not as powerful, but potent and growing stronger. Talented, young, ambitious, motivated by the quest for freedom; rising.

Another name across Adam's mind: *Demos*.

A war of independence, the war for freedom. The Demos battled heroically, hiding and fighting as guerrillas, developing AIs and huge destructive machines to assist them. The Valaur laying waste to whole planets in an effort to eradicate them, the Demos scoring small victories with increasing rapidity, irritating Valaur power, nurturing their own, honing abilities and weapons and artificial sentients.

But that was not their only tool. The Valaur made total war, powerful violence - but had a weakness. They underestimated the slaves they held closest, those they had owned for millennia, manipulated and engineered ruthlessly.

Another word: *Oaritarb*.

The shape-shifters betrayed their masters, releasing engineered plagues among the Valaur, attacking them down to their very molecules, dissolving them, rotting them, killing vast swathes of them. Those few that were left, unable to return to the source of the contagion, forced to flee the galaxy altogether, heading for Andromeda on vast ships.

'What is this?' asked Adam to his other.

The silver-eyed Adam replied, 'History - and the now.'

The images moved forwards, the Demos and the AIs they had created fighting among themselves for supremacy over the spoils of war. The bloodshed was incredible! Billions killed by the machines with the mechanical efficiency of a combine harvester cutting corn.

Adam shuddered, and felt a moment of empathy with the Demos: the AIs were capable of such butchery! But then, who started it? He searched for an answer, found none. The images continued. Demos again triumphant, exultant in their power.

There was a rival.

The Oaritarb, burrowing into the power bases of their former allies. Masters now of bioengineering, shifting shape to suit any circumstance, any culture, any species.

The Demos purged them ruthlessly, making no distinction between the guilty and the innocent, old or young. All of the shape-shifters - ALL of them: die, or leave.

They died first when they did not leave. Those that survived, left.

They came here.

Adam gasped, looked again at the image of Scanell sleeping in the background.

'He's an alien?' he asked.

'They do not believe so,' said the other Adam.

More images. Back even further in time. Millennia shrank and disappeared.

The Valaur, younger then, here on Earth, taking what they wanted. In North America, swooping down, kidnapping early humans, tribesmen, cavemen, women, children; taking, enslaving, changing, shifting right down to the DNA: shape-shifters.

Adam shook his head. 'They're human,' he said. He turned to the silver-eyed twin, 'How do you know this?'

The twin pointed at Scanell. 'It's what *he* knows, what he believes. He opened his mind during part of a machine dream. I took what I wanted.'

'What am I supposed to understand from this?' asked Adam.

'You're supposed to understand a little more of yourself.'

'How?' asked Adam.

'With the end of Lipton Scanell's knowledge. Look.'

Adam saw more.

One side of Earth exploding; the Yellowstone catastrophe.

The Oaritarb coming to Earth, settling there, blending in. But their habits would not die. They continued to engineer, to change - to manipulate.

Another name across Adam's mind: The Kinetics.

'NO!' Adam shouted, and he ran away.

He ran on and on…then he stopped. He turned and saw the other Adam looking at him quizzically, no further away than when he had started.

'You cannot escape this,' said the twin, 'Keep looking.'

'I don't want to!'

'You must.'

Out of the Kinetics programme came all of the older participants at the IHD one by one, finally coming to a close with Ariana, then Ijaz. Then a period of time…

Then came Adam.

More words: Mistake. Abomination. Danger. Threat. Monster. KILL!

'Why do they hate me?' wailed Adam, hurt coursing through him, 'What have I done?'

'You misinterpret their emotions,' replied his other, 'What they feel for you is not hatred, not at the base. What prompts all of their actions, all of their antipathy to you, to us, is one thing - dread. They are afraid of you, terrified of *us*. Overwhelmed with horror at the thought of you maturing.'

'Why?' asked Adam, 'I'm no more powerful than Ijaz or Ariana. They have more skills than me!'

'I only know what Lipton Scanell knew when I absorbed him,' said the silver-eyed twin, 'You are not the same as the other Kinetics; that is certain. They made some mistake with us, something has gone wrong. You are different, and they fear us.'

'What good is that?' said Adam, 'I'm some sort of mistake? I didn't want to know that!'

'You *have* to know that,' said the twin, 'Don't you understand? They *fear* you. You, who have always doubted your abilities, your intelligence - your very value. If they fear you, this means one thing; you have the power to harm them. And I know for a fact: you have great power indeed. *We,* have great power.'

'I don't want to be some alien creation,' said Adam, 'I want parents, a mother and father.'

'Maybe you have,' said the twin, 'And now you know how to find out. One thing is for certain, though. If you stay here, asleep, you will never know. You have to make a choice, and there is no choice without being informed. So now you have some knowledge, will you sleep or wake?'

Adam reached out to him, absorbed him, withdrew.

'You keep saying "you" and "me" and "us",' said Adam, 'But you don't know what you are either, do you?'

The other Adam looked at him, eyes coldest silver.

*

The Harlands pulled up to the street beside the institute and jumped out of the ground car just in time to see the squat bulk of the transporter pull away from the roof. They turned to Ariana, who pointed up.

'He's in that,' she said, 'Ijaz is in there too.'

'How do you know?' asked Mr Harland.

'I just know,' said Ariana, exasperated.

Just then, Cengo pulled up in her own car and jumped out, the Harlands quickly telling her of the situation.

'Where the hell are the police?' asked Mrs Harland.

Zhao flew down in his own car, landing beside them. He opened the doors.

'Get in!' he shouted, 'Ariana, you in front.'

They all piled into the saloon and strapped themselves in. They were pressed into their seats as Zhao powered up from the street, rising above the level of the trees and buildings until most of the city could be seen. Zhao paused to get his bearings, turning the vehicle around to view the night-time cityscape.

'There!' said Ariana, pointing at a black dot growing smaller as it sped away.

Zhao banked the car, the passengers gripping their arm-rests, and accelerated after it.

In the transporter, Murdock sat across from the strapped-down forms of Ijaz and Adam. His eyes lit with NI activity.

'They're on our tail,' he said, 'We need to shake them off.'

The pilot nodded once, and Murdock steadied himself as the transporter dived steeply downwards to just above street level. It careered above the traffic, whizzing around buildings, zigzagging around corners, the following saloon staying above the level of the buildings while desperately trying to keep up.

'Hey!' shouted Murdock, 'Keep going straight for another two kilometres, and then go to ground level.'

'That'll take us to a police station,' said the pilot.

'Just do it,' said Murdock.

Once again, his eyes lit.

In the car behind, they watched as the transporter began to slow. They dipped down to near street-level, but stayed above the traffic in case the transporter tried to pull up again. They came to an intersection and turned - and were met with a wall of police anti-grav vehicles that surrounded them on all sides, a cylinder of lights closing behind them, flashing angrily red and blue.

'Set your vehicle down and turn off the engine!' came the order from the lead police vehicle through a loud hailer.

Scanell's transporter, with no wheels but cruising at ground level, drifted blithely underneath them.

'No!' said Ariana, 'They're going to get away!'

'No they will not,' said Zhao, carefully setting the car down, 'I saw where they were heading before; it's the HADD Hardware Development Centre. Don't cause any problems, I will take responsibility for illegal manoeuvres. You get going as soon as you can. Do not call the police again, they cannot be trusted. We are on our own.'

In the transporter, Murdock and Scanell looked behind them as the following saloon set down, and the police closed in, obscuring their view.

'Right, then,' said Scanell, 'To the Centre, and step on it.'

Murdock's eyes lit again.

'What are you doing?' asked Scanell suspiciously.

'None of your business,' said Murdock, 'But if you must know, I'm ensuring the police hold them for as long as possible.'

Scanell's suspicions were not allayed however, and he was soon having his own NInet conversation. When he had finished, he turned to Murdock.

'Just so you know,' he said, 'I have confirmed my instructions with Jowitz. Ijaz is to die as well.' Then he turned and addressed the pilot. 'Captain, please make a detour to the Cabinet Offices. We can drop Mr Murdock off there.'

'No,' said Murdock, 'I have a right to be there-'

'Mr Jowitz thanks you for all of your help,' said Scanell, 'however, your emotional attachment to Ijaz creates a conflict. I'm afraid you will have to be left behind.'

Murdock looked at Ijaz, and sagged, the control on his face breaking. He shook his head and turned to Scanell, a plaintive expression weighing on his features.

'Lipton,' he said, 'surely something can be done for Ijaz. He's innocent in all of this.'

'So is Adam, isn't he?' asked Scanell with a sneer, 'Innocence is surely beside the point. Serving our interests, that is the only point.'

'But he is no danger,' said Murdock.

'He's a Kinetic,' said Scanell, 'They're all dangerous. He broke through a bomb-proof door to get to us. And he knows too much.'

'His mind can be altered,' said Murdock.

'As I have said, there's little use in that,' said Scanell 'And he inexplicably knew what we were doing to Adam as if by instinct. You think you can overcome *that?* We don't even know what *that* is! I'm sorry,' he said, looking away, 'I have my orders.'

'Lipton,' said Murdock, 'please-'

'Thank you, captain,' said Scanell, as the transporter drew up near to the Cabinet Offices, 'Mr Murdock can walk from here.'

They stopped at Whitehall and a bewildered, old and frail-looking Murdock was let out onto the broad deserted street. He dipped his head to the window as the door was shut behind him.

'Please-' he said again, but the transporter took off, leaving him behind.

For a full minute afterwards, Murdock just stood there in the street, looking after it, barely a car going past. It had been his life's work to develop the Kinetics. Ijaz represented the pinnacle of that achievement, the most powerful developed.

Adam represented the abomination that reckless ambition could create.

'Ijaz,' said Murdock to himself, 'My Ijaz. You're going to die, and there's nothing I can do to save you.'

Head down, Murdock turned and walked slowly away to his office. A thought occurred to him, quickly discarded. Then he stopped, and rubbed his chin.

*There will always be another time. Another time to kill that monstrosity, Ada*m. He shrugged his shoulders. *What the hell, I'll teach them to side-line me.*

His eyes lit up again with NI use. When he had finished, he chuckled, then continued walking, a bit straighter than before, a small smile curling one edge of his craggy face, happy to let fate take him - take *everyone,* where it would.

He whistled the tune to Prokofiev's Romeo and Juliet.

Across town, the police received new information. They gave Zhao and his passengers a warning, and then let them go.

In the transporter, Scanell told the pilot to alter his heading.

'We can't go to the Hardware Development Centre,' he said, 'It's too obvious, they may have seen our heading, and I don't want that old man interfering. We need to get to the safe-house.'

The pilot nodded, and altered course, picking up speed.

'Wait,' said Scanell, 'Drop the surgeons off here.'

The surgeons looked at him with confusion on their faces, and, Scanell noted, apprehension.

'Don't worry,' said Scanell, 'Your collusion in this mission has ensured your silence to my satisfaction, I just don't want you around.'

'Um,' said one of the surgeons, 'how will you complete the mission?'

'I have an alternative,' said Scanell, 'one that need not concern you. Suffice it to say that I think this boy is too powerful, your flesh too delicate and your skills too valuable for you to be risked. Thank you for your time.'

The transporter dropped down and left the surgeons at a landing spot near to their offices, and took off again.

Presently they slowed down, and landed on the roof of what looked like an industrialised area, but in fact was an old abandoned state hospital. The doors opened and the security team floated the still unconscious forms of Ijaz and Adam out, followed by Scanell.

Scanell interacted with the building's computer, and an aperture irised open on the surface of the grey roof to reveal a wide and dark stairway leading down.

The men stopped in their tracks, as stalking up the stairs came a two-legged robot. It was a bulky thing, dull-metal coloured, with a helmet for a head, two vertical strips as eyes, glowing red. It came to a halt, towering over the assembled men, and pointed one of its arms at them, a large gun showing from the base of its palm.

'Identify yourselves,' said the machine, its voice a metallic bassoon coming from its chest.

'Lipton Scanell, Oaritarb first class,' said Scanell, 'We are under orders from Secretary of State Jowitz.'

The machine took a moment to consult.

'This way, Lipton Scanell and assistants,' said the machine, lowering its arm. It turned and led them down the stairwell, its joints making an oily clicking sound.

The men, unnerved by the machine, followed cautiously behind. One of them contacted Scanell via NI.

'*Isn't that Bolshim277?*' he asked, '*One of the fugitives from Warmang?*'

'*Shut up,*' said Scanell, '*He can read our conversation.*'

'Do not worry,' said the machine out loud, disconcertingly swivelling its head to show its face to the following men as its body continued to walk forwards down the stairs, 'I won't tell anyone if you don't.'

The men had the feeling that, somehow, the machine was smiling. Then it turned its head, and continued. They came to a landing, two metal doors that opened as the AI approached it, turned right and entered.

Across town, Zhao and his companions arrived at the HDC. Ariana began shaking her head.

'They aren't here,' she said, a look of bewilderment on her face, a sinking feeling in her stomach, doubt crushing her.

'Where are they?' asked Zhao.

'I don't know,' said Ariana. She closed her eyes for a moment. 'I can see images, small ones, but they are becoming less and less frequent. I don't recognise anything. They're subdued, tied down or drugged. I can't tell, everything's fading.'

'So where do we go?' asked Zhao.

Ariana looked around; all eyes were on her.

'I don't know,' she said.

They checked to see if the HDC computer knew where the boys were.

It did not.

Adam and Ijaz were strapped onto operating tables that had been hastily thrown together in an old surgical theatre of the hospital building. Instruments of surgery had been gathered, and the security team had cleaned and prepared them.

'Alright,' said Scanell, 'I want everyone else out. The room is to be fully shielded, and I want Bolshim to do it. The machine has his own shielding, and is more robust. Do you agree Bolshim?'

The huge AI stalked up to the tables, his feet clunking on the tiled floor, and took a cutting saw from one of the security men, who shrank away. The machine gave the saw an experimental pull, creating a high pitched keening sound as the blade sung, then he turned to Scanell.

'It will be my pleasure,' it said.

In case Ariana was wrong, Zhao checked with the IHD to see if the two teenagers were there. They weren't, and most of the recording systems in the institute had been switched off. Zhao sat back in his seat, his left hand over his eyes.

'I'm sorry,' said Ariana.

'Not your fault,' said Zhao, his eyes still closed. 'Mr Foxton left us adults in charge. We have failed.'

'There must be something we can do,' said Mrs Harland, 'We can't just sit here.'

'Agreed,' said Zhao, hitting the dash of the car, then bringing the car off the ground again, rising quickly to join the air traffic. 'We shall drive around all night, and see if Ariana recognises anything.'

Ariana closed her eyes again, and her breathing quickened.

'It's starting again,' she said, 'they're both in danger now.' She reopened her eyes, tears on the edges of each. 'And there's nothing we can do.' She felt the comforting hands of her mother and father on each shoulder - then another hand, shaking her. She turned.

It was Cengo, looking furious.

'Is that what we've taught you?' she growled, 'To just give up? Maybe we can't help, but we will try. Believe you *can* help,' she squeezed Ariana's arm, 'You felt Adam's pain, Ijaz's vulnerability. Now, make both of them feel your strength. Give them all you can give, and help them.'

'I can't,' said Ariana tearfully, 'I don't know how.'

'You've had NInet conversations before.'

'Adam does not have one, and Ijaz's offline,' said Ariana.

Cengo angrily shook her head. 'I know that. How did you *know* something was wrong?'

'I'm not sure, I just did.'

'Exactly,' said Cengo, 'You have a link with them, I don't know how, but you do. Use it. We haven't trained you in it, but we never trained you to know that Adam's life was at risk. It just happened, and you did what you had to. We're here aren't we? With you? With virtually no proof at all, we believe you. We believe *in* you.'

'We know you are right,' said Zhao, 'The whereabouts of the boys is unknown, and we were pulled over by enough police to deal with a riot. You must believe in yourself. Now, both of their lives are in danger, that is what you have said.'

'So do what you have to do,' said Cengo, 'Do whatever it takes, and don't let anything stop you. Right now.'

Ariana nodded, the tears gone from her eyes, and she closed them.

The security men quickly finished setting up the operating room, installing the necessary shielding. Then they and Scanell went upstairs to the observation gallery, and peered down. Scanell was linked to Bolshim277 via NI, while the machine itself was uploaded with dissection data. Once it had finished, it took a moment to familiarise itself with the tools, then carefully opened the organ containers, including a life preserver for the brain. Shielding went up around the room, and the machine advanced.

Ariana gasped, and quickly opened her eyes.

'What's wrong?' asked her mother, but Ariana shook her head, and closed her eyes again.

New feeling coursed through her. When she closed her eyes, she could see Ijaz - multi-coloured, incandescent. She could not tell where he was, but she could see him there. The rest of the surroundings were insubstantial, like a drawing that kept on changing. She could see others around him, backing away and confusingly gathering above, and something large, malevolent, hateful, nearby and closing. She cast her mind a little further, and there was Adam, seemingly prone and fast asleep, but different. In contrast to the vibrant multi-colours of Ijaz, his glow was a silvery monochrome.

She reached out to him and stirred him.

His eyes flashed open, staring at her, into her, through her, with eyes of the coldest silver, no irises or whites visible. There was power in those eyes.

There was death in those eyes.

Shocked, she involuntarily opened her eyes again in the car, breathing hard. She felt the comforting hands of those around her, anchoring her to her body. She closed her eyes, and once again looked at the Adam in her mind's eye.

His mind reached out to her, overcoming her, reading her, possessing her, taking from her what he wanted. Then, gently, he let her go, and smiled at her.

'Do not be afraid,' he said, 'If you are no danger to me, then I am no danger to you. What do you want?'

'You're in danger,' said Ariana, hesitantly, wishing to back away, to open her eyes and escape from this other Adam - he was overpowering! 'They, the people you are with, they're going to kill you and Ijaz.'

'They will harm Ijaz?' asked Adam.

'Yes,' said Ariana. This was not right; he was not the person she knew.

'You are Adam, aren't you?'

The silvery figure opened his mouth to speak, then closed it again. He looked down at himself, at his hands, front and back, then he clenched them, smiled, and looked up at Ariana.

'Yes,' he replied, 'I suppose I am.'

And Adam awoke.

Ariana opened her eyes in the car, lifted her arm, and pointed with grim certainty.

'That way,' she said.

The machine froze mid-movement as he stood over Ijaz, surgical saw in-hand. He had not needed to turn his faceplate around to peer at the security team earlier; he had simply done so for effect. He had sensors built into the back of his body quite capable of observing things behind him, and he had detected movement - movement that should not be possible.

'Leave him alone,' said Adam.

Bolshim277 turned slowly to the operating table. There, still strapped down, Adam regarded it coolly, his head turned towards the machine, eyes open, a faint silver shimmer behind them.

'Good morning, Adam,' said the machine, 'We were not expecting you to be awake this early. I trust you slept well?'

Ariana closed her eyes again, and reached out to Ijaz.

'*Kill him, kill him now!*' shouted Scanell through his NI.

'I am terribly sorry,' said the Machine, turning his body and walking towards Adam, 'You are an immensely fascinating creature, but this must end.'

Adam, still strapped down, looked up at the observation area.

'To beat them all you must know them all,' said Adam loudly 'I know you, Lipton Scanell. Oaritarb. *Shape-shifter.*'

In the observation gallery, Scanell, sweating, stepped back, shaking his head.

'Kill him,' he whispered, his throat constricting.

Other sensors in the machine picked up on something. Then the Oaritarb in the room above noticed it too. A vibration could be felt throughout the room, on the edge of feeling at first, then a sound. Quickly, it became a throb that could be heard as well as felt, a low, deep growl like a sustained note of thunder.

Adam closed his eyes, and let his mind roam free. He erected a barrier between himself and the machine. He watched with his mind's eye as the machine bumped against it, putting out its hands to probe the bubble-like construct. Adam concentrated, felt inside the locks in the cuffs and restraints still holding him. Untrained, Adam fumbled with them.

Behind the machine, Ijaz stirred, and opened his eyes. He felt awful, but all he could think of was Adam. Superbly trained, he popped his own restraints open with a flick of his mind, and lay still while he took in the situation.

Zhao landed the car on the roof of the old hospital. Mrs Harland and Cengo were given weapons and told to guard their only means of escape, while Zhao, Mr Harland and after a short argument an insistent Ariana, advanced on the now sealed roof exit, all three with hand weapons as the wind whipped around them. There was no subtle way to open it from the outside.

Mr Harland took his large plasma gun, and pointed it at the opening.

The explosion could be heard even above the eerie throbbing sound in the operating theatre. The safe-house was not usually manned; Bolshim277 was the only habitual occupant. Scanell sent the security team to the roof, while he remained behind.

'Should I go up?' asked Bolshim277.

'No,' replied Scanell, 'Hold your position, and carry out the mission.'

'I could kill him quicker with laser.'

'No,' said Scanell, 'We need that brain in a life preserver. We could cut its survival time by several years if we kill him too soon before extraction. Get through that shield first.'

'It may help,' said Bolshim277, still probing his way around the shield, 'if you get him back to sleep again.'

'I'm working on it,' said Scanell.

Mr Harland and Sifu Zhao figured they would soon be joined, and had not advanced down the stairwell. They took cover over its lip, their shields warped to create small mirrors reflecting light from below, waiting for any attackers advancing up the stairs, their guns trained.

Two of the six security men poked their heads around the doorway, and peered up the stairs. They checked that it was all clear, and quickly ascended. Seeing their colleagues were near the opening, two others entered the stairwell to give cover when they got there. Mr Harland and Zhao, using their sensory equipment to the utmost, opened fire using laser to get through the security men's shields, sending short quick and sizzling white shots down the stairs. The security team were caught in the open.

None survived.

Scanell, observing remotely, swore under his breath as he saw the three intruders creeping down the stairs. He quickly sealed the doors to the medical room and erected another field in front of the doors. He then contacted Jowitz: he needed backup.

The trio crept down the stairs, reaching the silvered outer doors of the operating theatre without further resistance. Zhao took one look at the shields protecting them.

'Our plasma cannot get through these shields,' he said, 'neither can our fields, and our lasers will take ages to get through the metal on the door.' He turned to Ariana.

'Well?' he said, 'You insisted on coming. Time for you to use your training.'

Ariana took a breath, stepped forward, shoving her gun in her belt, her lips set in a tight line. She concentrated, and pulled her arms towards herself, then outwards again with all the elegance of a ballerina. Then she did it again, and the steel doors rattled. She did it again, and the doors flexed in and out in unison with her movements. Again she moved, and the doors quaked more violently.

Zhao looked on with one raised eyebrow, impressed with Ariana's power, her father looking on with open amazement as again and again she flexed the doors, faster and faster as her father and Zhao backed away, guns ready on either side of her. The glass in each door shattered as they flexed, and finally, with a screaming bang, the doors gave way and fell loudly into the operating theatre.

Mr Harland grabbed his daughter and pulled her aside as Zhao began firing laser shots through the doors at anything that looked like shield generators.

In the room, Ijaz glanced at the door through slitted eyes as Bolshim fired laser shots back through the door. Ijaz saw the pattern of fire into the room, realised what the aim was, and sought out the shield generators. He spotted them, fixed to a wall on the side nearest to the doors, and concentrated, seeking the switch. He could not find one, so sought out a fuse, found it, and pulled it out. There was a brief shimmer at the door as the shield failed. This didn't help matters, as Ijaz was directly in the path of the exchange of fire.

Scanell used his laser to slice away the glass separating him from the operating theatre, the white light sizzling and easily melting the glass. He hunkered down below the low wall beneath the glass and began firing plasma shots through the glowing hole.

Ijaz, feeling nauseous but aware of his danger, primed his legs and his mind and pushed with his feet, his body shooting ten metres backwards towards some metal cabinets, crashing into them and taking cover. Bolshim277 turned his other fist and fired a few shots in Ijaz's direction, laser sizzling against the hard surface of the cabinets. Seeing they now had a clear shot, Mr Harland and Zhao glanced at each other, nodded, and charged into the room, screaming and firing, Ariana following behind.

The room's shields now down, the two remaining security men emerged from their hiding place opposite the doorway in the stairwell, and fired upon the three intruders from behind. Zhao and Mr Harland whipped around, cutting down both Oaritarb with multiple blasts from their hand cannons while their fields tried to suffocate the flames on their bodies.

Bolshim277 pointed both arms at the rescuers, and shot using a combination of high yield plasma and wide-spread lasers, filling the room with bright light and cataclysmic noise. Attacked from both sides, both men and Ariana were blasted back and scattered, and they fell to the floor.

Adam burst through his restraints.

Bolshim vaulted smoothly over the operating table and aimed one fist straight at Ariana, but where there was only one, there was suddenly three. Ijaz and Adam were in front of Ariana, hands raised, a protective shield between them and the machine.

Bolshim277 laughed, 'Funny little things, your speed is most impressive.'

However, its authenticated orders were conflicted; it could not kill the Kinetics or damage their organs before extraction. Still, it thought, it could still *really hurt* them.

The machine spun his body violently, smashing Adam and Ijaz aside. Adam was flung to the side, and Ijaz was slammed backwards, tripping over the prone form of Ariana, his head smacking sickly against the corner of the wall next to the door. Ariana moaned and stirred on the floor, and Bolshim aimed one huge plasma adapted fist at her.

Behind it, Adam ran forwards, screaming hoarsely 'No!' He passed through the rear shields of the machine, his clothes sizzling in protest, and grabbed its elbow with both hands, twisting its arm upwards. The machine grunted with surprise and pushed back, twisting around to lean over Adam, who was forced to stoop down as the machine gripped the back of his neck. Adam grabbed at its fingers, and with a growl and a rending-creaking sound, he yanked two of them off of the AI's hand.

Bolshim howled with rage, and smashed Adam back with his other fist. Adam flew backwards, rolled on the floor, and in a flash was back on his feet. Part of Bolshim registered Adam's unusual speed, and his recovery from such a heavy blow.

He leapt upon the boy, smashing and kicking down on him, Adam intelligently diverting the blows rather than attempting to block the colossal forces that could easily break his bones. Bolshim kicked forwards and Adam dodged to the side and kicked it, making the machine shudder. Around the room the machine battled with the boy. A bloodied Ijaz got once again to his feet and joined the fray, running up to the machine and kicking it in the back sending it stumbling forwards. Scanell watched, afraid to take a shot lest Bolshim, his only remaining backup, be destroyed.

The AI smashed downwards, Adam leapt to the side and punched its side with all his might, sending the machine skidding sideways.

Scanell finally had a clear shot with his laser. Adam, never for a second letting Scanell out of his sight, jumped to the side to avoid the shot – right into Bolshim's arms, which grabbed him. Adam hit upwards with his palm, the sound of metal being struck echoing around the room. The machine went sailing over his head, a visible dent in its chest where Adam had palmed it. Sparks flew from the machine's head as it hit the far wall on its way down. It crashed heavily to the floor, smashing the tiles a foot away from where Zhao still lay on his back, blood oozing from his mouth. It pushed itself onto its hands and knees, sparks spitting from its damaged hand.

'Hello,' said Zhao, barely conscious, smiling, his teeth red.

The machine turned to see that its shields were pressed against and partially merged with Zhao's, and the Sifu had pushed the tip of his gun out of his own shield into the field area of the AI, pointed directly into its face.

Zhao pulled the trigger, and everything went too bright for him to see, and then very, very dark…

Scanell tried to contact Murdock as the room seemed to explode, but Murdock was not contactable. He sent out a message to Oaritarb operatives, and Jowitz himself:

-'Adam is resistant to near-fatal levels of suppressant drugs, and is able to overcome a fully armed, shielded and armoured AI. He shows a connection with other Kinetics independent of proximity. He is aware of Oaritarb existence. His projected danger is partially realised. Termination must take place without organ recovery.'-

Scanell was cornered, and had no choice. Now, as the blasted bits of Bolshim277 clattered around the room, its lower body on its feet staggering mindlessly around, was his only chance. He leapt forwards out of the hole he had made in the glass, somersaulting fifteen metres forwards and three down to where Adam stood.

Adam whipped around to see the plasma gun pointed straight at him, and Scanell, without hesitation, pulled the trigger.

Adam reacted instantly, raising his hands in front of him and closing his eyes. He blocked the blast and sent it ricocheting back with a loud 'whoompf' of energy.

Scanell's shield, tuned to let his own shots through, did not stop it, and the blast impacted upon his own chest. He looked down, stunned as the twenty-centimetre hole in his torso sizzled. He fell backwards, hitting the floor hard, and did not move.

The survivors looked around them.

Adam and Ijaz looked at each other. Both of them took a moment, then, overcome with the sheer amount of drugs in their systems, they collapsed.

*

It was a tragic irony that the excellence of Oaritarb biology, the apogee of bioengineering, meant that despite the futility of trying to survive, Lipton Scanell experienced his death very slowly. His eyes saw only darkness, while his mind remained aware of his body's attempts at saving him.

It worked furiously to compensate, to divert, to repair; but both his lungs, and even his backup heart, were fried.

It tried to combine with NI enhancements, coming to dead ends where functional organs should have been, systems slowly, surely, failing…

Trying again, attempting to rebuild tissue, running out of energy, and options, coming to a halt…

Finally, his NI recorded time of death for retrieval.

At the end, in the darkness, he saw a light, ill-defined but swimming into view. Then, sharply defined before him, was the image of the silver-eyed Adam of his dream. He was smiling down at the shape-shifter. Then he spoke.

'Told you,' he said…

*

'What are they?' asked Ariana.

Upon his death, Scanell's face had relaxed into shape-shifter blandness, and as she and her father limped back up the stairway, they noticed that every single one of the security team, and Scanell, had the same anodyne look to them; plain round faces, small pug noses, slack, droopy skin.

'They look like clones,' said Mr Harland, 'But they didn't look like that before, when they were alive. Right now I don't care. We just need to get the hell out of here, to a hospital and safety.'

They continued pulling Ijaz, Adam, and Zhao along on the two float-stretchers, bound together using some duct-tape they had found in the room, up the stairs and out through the roof exit. In all the chaos, they had lost contact with Cengo and Mrs Harland.

That, was a mistake.

The backup security team Scanell had sent for had landed on the building, twenty strong, guns held out, trained on the hobbling group of survivors as they came over the lip of the roof exit. To the side of them was Zhao's car, Mrs Harland and Cengo outgunned and NI-blocked, sitting with their hands raised in the air, four members of the security team guarding them.

'Put down your weapons,' said an Oaritarb with a loud hailer, a stony expression on his face.

Three more transporters rose above the parapet of the buildings, larger bulkier types, guns bristling out of the windows of all of them, several with heavy weapons fixed to the exteriors of the vehicles and trained on those below.

One of the new transporters landed on the building, and a motley crew of cyborgs got out, foremost among them being Roland Featherstone, the upper-level cyborg and teacher at the Institute. His eyes, one biological, the other green mechanical, swept those assembled with deadly intent. He raised both of his arms at the shoulder, and pointed his fists at them. Eight chambers slid back and opened where his knuckles should have been. His electronic voice was amplified and easily audible above the sound of the wind and engines of the hovering transporters.

'On the contrary,' he said, enunciating each word very carefully as the laser pinpoints fixed on the nearest members of the frozen Oaritarb, '*you,* drop *your* weapons.'

Chapter 20

Kills to conceal

Foxton and Casey watched, overcome, as the Polis entered a near orbit around the Demos home planet of Kratos. They could see the Orbital Ring, and shook their heads at the audacity of it. It must have taken the materials from at least one other world to build it.

They were in a transit lounge of the Polis, sitting at an observation window with the rest of Earth's delegation and the ever-present Clarient. They could also see another ship drawing near to the Polis. It was large, dark, and streamlined. It came to a halt, and an announcement came through a loudspeaker.

'Please stay in your present positions.'

The delegation exchanged glances.

'They are going to displace us,' said Clarient.

'Is that bad?' asked Foxton.

'No,' said Clarient, smiling, 'It means we don't have to go through all of the trouble of transferring from the Polis to the transport ship. They just send us straight over.'

Foxton felt a tingling sensation, and closed his eyes. The tingling seemed to go on for a while, and he opened his eyes again. They were in another transit lounge, smaller, darker and less luxurious than the one they had left, more precise-looking. Foxton guessed they were now on the military transporter, and looked out of the narrow windows to confirm it with a view of the Polis looming next to them. He turned to Casey, who was looking at him with concern.

'They took their time with you,' said Casey, 'We got here about thirty seconds ago. You alright?'

Foxton made a show of patting himself down, then he leaned closer to Casey, a serious look on his face.

'I think they've taken my chewing gum.'

Casey tutted at Foxton's flippancy, turning away and shaking his head. However, Foxton was more worried than he was acting. The decision to send him was looking worse and worse. While the Protean-class cyborg was no longer hyper-advanced, it was pretty close. The Demos had probably examined him during displacement, and now knew something of his capabilities. He, on the other hand, was getting little in the way of intelligence. He sighed; he would have to make the best of it.

The military craft moved off, sliding above the atmosphere. It did not appear to be taking a direct route down to the planet, but was circling it.

'Are we waiting in line or something?' asked Casey.

'No,' said Clarient, 'I think you are being shown something.'

'Shown what?' asked Casey.

'That,' said Clarient, motioning with his head to the view.

The ship passed by one of the moons of Kratos. There, half in light, and half in shadow, could be seen a prodigious fleet of spaceships. There were destroyers, frigates, fighters, lifters, and two large and squat spheres that they could not identify.

Clarient explained to them what they were.

'They can destroy entire solar systems?' asked Casey.

'Yes,' said Clarient, 'including their stars.'

'So, they're trying to intimidate us,' said Foxton, as the ship pulled away from the view again, back towards the planet, 'They have enough hardware there to annihilate several solar systems if it punches as good as it looks.'

'Indeed,' said Clarient, 'I'm sorry to say that, at least, they are trying to impress you. And yes, their hardware does perform up to the standard their appearance suggests.'

They took in more benign sights as the ship smoothly descended on the dayside of the planet, past the Great Ring, into the atmosphere of Kratos. They could see the colossal space columns leading from the ground all the way to the Ring, and marvelled at the feat of engineering. Foxton accessed his own sensors, noting that the ship they were on was using pure anti-gravity and was lowering into the atmosphere nicely at ten thousand kilometres an hour. There was no hint of overheating on the hull, apparently protected by shielding that was also slowing the craft.

As they got nearer to the ground and the city they were headed towards, they could see vast amounts of air-traffic in orderly lines, and much lower lines of air traffic inside the city boundaries, like organised fireflies going about their business in the sunshine.

The buildings were massive here. Foxton understood that they were larger here than on most of the planet, but still he estimated that the tallest buildings were at least nine kilometres tall not including the space-columns, and perhaps two kilometres wide at the base on average.

They were of all sorts of weird shapes, some at seemingly impossible angles rather than the block or tapering designs of earth. Many of them seemed to help hold each other up, with structures, tubes and walkways connecting most of them. The whole city glittered like a giant crystal with lines of silk leading between the sky-piercing buildings. Foxton considered the implications of it: to build such a city, such a world, there must be wealth here, vast wealth.

The ship lowered gently below the skyline, the tops of the surrounding buildings raising around them like a field of teeth. They alighted on a raised platform on one of the lower constructions. Though shorter than the surrounding structures, it was immensely wide, stretching for white kilometres on all sides.

Foxton noted that the ship was still using anti-grav, the hum of A-G generators still loud. It wasn't sitting on the building, but was still perfectly stable as if fixed to the spot; precise control.

They disembarked, from the transporter through a lower hatch, none of the delegation speaking. There was one observation that they had all privately made but did not articulate: no one had seen a single Demos.

Their honour guard of Calimtei guided them from the ship, down the ramp towards the rear of the transporter, onto a circle made of a glass-like substance. They stood in the sunshine for a moment. Nothing said more about their status than the fact that there was no welcoming party from the Demos.

Ahead of them, two large doors opened in the surface of the building, and Foxton started as, as one body, the delegation began to move forwards, floating around a millimetre from the building's surface. Foxton scanned the energy signature; field tech, but refined to an art form. There was no feeling of imbalance, nothing gripping their feet as they travelled forwards towards the opening, sliding over the lip of it then down into the cool interior.

Inside, there were no stairs, just a long ramp that met the top floor of the building. The doors closed above the delegation as they glided downwards and then levelled off, floating forwards along the floor, coming to a halt at a shoulder-high railing. From here, they could see the interior of the building. They were on a high mezzanine floor, overlooking a cavernous space that stretched for three kilometres ahead of them. To the sides and far end were tier upon tier of some sort of offices or apartments, and there were things flying around in the space, which must have been around a kilometre wide.

The foremost Calimtei spoke. 'The upper floors are dedicated to the delegation houses,' he explained, 'multi-apartment buildings housed within this one with their own conference rooms and facilities. The lower floors are for administration, and to the far end there,' he pointed to the far wall, a sheer wall of glass, 'is the L.O.S.S. Chamber, where the arguments and final decision will be taken on your appeal. We are waiting for a lift, then we will be on our way.'

A metallic disc with a railing around the edge rose up to the level of the mezzanine. It touched the mezzanine railing and where they met, both sets of railing retracted, making a gateway. The Calimtei walked forwards and beckoned for the delegation to follow.

Foxton grinned at the delegation's discomfort: the only thing holding the disc up was Demos technology. Casey led the way, then the rest hesitantly followed. The railings closed behind them, and the disc flew forwards. Foxton nodded in admiration; there was again absolutely no sense of momentum, the inertial nullifier technology was strong yet elegant. He looked around him, seeing a multitude of other species similarly flying around on other discs of various sizes.

Another disc came alongside them, perhaps ten metres away as they flew forwards, and it was full of what could only be described as monsters. They were utterly black, quadrupedal with one upper limb that had two clawed hands at the ends. Their heads were disproportionately small, or perhaps merely seemed that way due to the massive teeth that protruded from capacious mouths taking up most of their heads. They had no eyes.

One of them walked towards the railing nearest to the Earth delegation, raised a claw - and waved at them.

'Peace,' it called over.

The Earth delegation hesitated as one, exchanged glances then hastily returned the gesture, calling across hellos.

'Good luck with your appeal,' the creature lisped through its teeth, its voice a mix of German and electric guitar.

'Thank you,' chorused the delegation, still waving, now smiling as the two discs separated, 'hope to see you soon and get to know you.'

The disc lowered further until it was fifteen stories down, and joined with another set of railings which opened to let them out. They walked to the landing, and ahead of them was a large building set into the giant structure, with its own entrance. The doors were large, presumably to make them suitable for a variety of species. They opened automatically and let them in.

Inside, as the doors shut the noise of the superstructure out, they found a spacious area that was a combined common room with low slung seats, and a conference table with exactly twenty chairs at the far end. Next to the table was a thirty-metre wide window that stretched from floor to ceiling; it was all Foxton could do to stop himself going over to it immediately to view the city. There was a kitchen area to the side, fully stocked with Earth simulated food. The Calimtei informed them that more could be gained if so desired. Two spiral staircases led them to the upper floors and their individual rooms.

Their quarters were efficient and simple spaces, similar to those on the Polis, but larger. They refreshed themselves, were debriefed by the Calimtei and told that the hearings were soon to be underway regarding their appeal. Imminently, it would be time for the Earth delegation to make their case, which left little time for anything else. This was clearly to be a business trip only.

Foxton was disappointed. During their strategy meeting at the conference table, he kept on glancing out of the window, looking at the greatness of the architecture around him, yearning to see it all. From where he was, he could see a space column leading to the Ring, and from this vantage it seemed as though the topmost parts disappeared above the clouds into darkness before they even reached it. There were large creatures cruising in the atmosphere outside of the city's airspace.

Foxton sighed.

Later, in Casey's quarters, Clarient came to see Casey and Foxton.

'I was thinking,' said Clarient, 'That maybe I could show you around, Mr Foxton? Captain Casey will be interviewed by the press here, they have taken quite a liking to him.'

'Really?' asked Foxton.

'Yeah,' said the Captain, 'Apparently, I've become something of a celebrity. Ambassador Orael will be chairing my first introduction to the Demos.'

Foxton's first instinct was to refuse, to stay close to the delegation, to watch. However, it seemed obvious that as long as he stayed with the delegation that he would only see what the Demos wanted him to. They were already being closely shadowed by a discreet Demos security team who Foxton could sense were on either side of the apartment that housed them. There was also something about Clarient's demeanour, the intense way he was looking at Foxton, and the oddness of the offer; just for him.

'Well,' said Foxton, 'I wouldn't want to get in the way. I think I'll take you up on that Clarient. Thank you.'

'The pleasure, is all mine,' said Clarient.

Casey looked on enviously as Foxton said goodbye and left him to deal with the Demos press.

Foxton could not help staring at the strange aliens around him as they left the delegation house and traversed the boulevard-like balcony, and began to see glances of the race that made up over three-quarters of the species in the city, and the vast majority of this, their home planet. They were following him at a distance. He could also see over a hundred metres in front of him a consistent presence of Demos, optical sensors on the tips of their horns, pointing backwards, looking at him.

The Demos were demonic in appearance, large and yet elegant, but, as with the press who were interested in Casey, often gregarious in nature. Many of those not detailed to follow him stopped to greet Foxton and Clarient as they went past on the disc-lift, offering salutations and voicing their support. They varied in height, weight and colour, and even the shape of their horns. There were the primary colours, blue, red and dark green, as well as whites, blacks (but curiously, no greys), browns, tans, purple and violets, with the horns in any variation of those colours. There were even a few Demos children among them, small blunt horns on their heads, staring at him with open curiosity. Usually, they were accompanied by Demos females who also had horns, but shorter than the males and more tightly curled backwards. A few of them offered pleasantries. Foxton wished he had more opportunity to study them.

Clarient and Foxton alighted from a disc-lift on the opposite side of the building, and Clarient showed Foxton to a set of steel doors.

'This is a tube capsule,' said Clarient, 'Just like the lifts on your planet, but they can take you to almost anywhere in the city via the network of tubes linking the buildings. You never have to touch the ground.'

The doors opened to reveal a lounge-like interior. Foxton entered and sat down on one of the generous soft seats. The capsule was well named, seeming like an elongated bubble with a metallic frame on the inside, hardened glass on the outside.

'I have arranged for us to have this one to ourselves,' said Clarient, 'So you have a chance to take it all in.'

Clarient sat down opposite Foxton, and the capsule moved off. It started, as might be expected, by going down, but then Foxton felt pressed to his seat as the capsule changed direction, and soon, he could see light from up ahead, then they shot out the side of the building and rapidly rose. He noted that there was no inertial nullifier technology here; it must have been an older form of transport.

They were in a large tube with some sort of field technology keeping the capsule in place as it cruised on, one rail running along the top of the tube, presumably as a fail-safe. They were soon over a kilometre from the ground, and two kilometres from the next building. He looked out of the sides of the capsule as they rose further, enthralled by the cityscape, by the sophistication of it, the scale. He could see parks down below, highways, and air-traffic, as well as millions of Demos crawling along, moving dots on a vast picture, sometimes obscured by the odd low cloud. Clarient pointed out to him the various important points of interest, the Government seat of power, the separately housed Space Admiralty, the Courts of Law and Justice.

'This only serves to highlight the tragedy of this,' said Foxton, wistfully looking around him.

'Meaning?' asked Clarient.

'Here we are, the first humans on an inhabited alien world, and we cannot explore, or investigate. Instead, we are here to argue the case for our freedom, and then leave.'

Clarient did not reply.

'Are we ever going to get to meet members of the Demos government?'

'Not until you cooperate with the AI Creed,' said Clarient, 'That is their official position.'

'They're a curious species,' said Foxton.

'Oh?' said Clarient, 'I'm surprised the word *curious* is the one you use for a race that is imposing its will upon you.'

'Well, yes,' said Foxton, 'there is that. But there's also this appeal. Why grant it to us in the first place? And this interest in Casey; you say they *like* him?'

'Yes,' said Clarient, 'I see what you mean. They aren't all the same. Any ideas of them all being evil is mere dystopia. The Demos are as diverse a species in personality and outlook as they are physically. Perhaps that's what makes them great. They have a strong tradition of adherence to the rule of law, to giving people a fair hearing, hence your appeal. The *people* of the Demos love the plucky underdog, which you are currently seen as, and Captain Casey is your most famous figurehead. They are also inquisitive, always seeking knowledge, and advancement. But that has a double-edge to it: ambition. They always want more, and guard what they have resolutely. They have great and unique advantages, and wish to keep them.'

'You mean their technology?'

'To begin with,' said Clarient. 'Also there are things like the fact that they are the only living species known to have naturally occurring kinetic abilities.'

Foxton stared at him. 'The only one?'

'Yes,' said Clarient, 'Didn't you know?'

'I knew they had kinetic abilities via my NI downloads. I didn't know it was exclusive. Any erosion of that advantage, they see as a threat?'

'Indeed,' said Clarient, 'Why?'

Foxton thought of the Kinetics on Earth. The children. Adam.

'I think,' said Foxton, 'You need to tell me a lot more about the Demos.'

'Of course,' said Clarient, 'I can get you another download-.'

'Keep that on hold then,' said Foxton, raising a palm to Clarient, 'I still feel sick from the last one.'

'Yes,' said Clarient blankly, 'Coming back to your comment on them, they are a curious species, and deadly, in equal measure I think. Much like yourselves.'

The two remained silent for a moment. Foxton wondered if the alien was trying to provoke him. Was this the reason for this trip? What was he getting at?

'That last comment was obviously designed to elicit a response,' said Foxton, 'Are you going to explain what you mean?'

'Well,' said Clarient, black teeth smiling, 'Is the Demos position entirely unjustified? You are, after all, a violent species. And unlike most of the peers you hope to join in the League, you do not have a unified government. Being divided is a serious weakness in the jungle of the Orion Arm.'

'But that is not what this Creed seeks to fix,' said Foxton, 'They want to take our AIs away from us.'

'*Your* AIs from you?' asked Clarient, 'I thought you viewed them as sentient beings with their own rights?'

'Yes,' said Foxton, 'Perhaps I misspoke. They belong to themselves, and they do have rights. But my primary concern, and I make no apology for it, is for the ability of Earth to continue its progress technologically, to continue to improve the quality of life for humans and AIs.'

'But primarily humans?'

Foxton shrugged. 'We're interdependent now, us and the AIs. I guess all of us, but yes, primarily humans.'

Clarient looked out of the capsule as it passed over a wide rooftop, almost entirely taken up by over a kilometre of lake bordered with gardens, reflecting the sunlight on shimmering wavelets as they passed overhead.

'When we spoke before on the Polis, you mentioned my biology,' said Clarient, 'Why?'

Foxton erected a dampening field around them, the sounds of the area outside it becoming muffled.

'There is no need for that,' said Clarient, 'I ensured our privacy, we cannot be overheard.'

Foxton noted that if this was true, he could not detect how. He kept the field up. If anything, it served to distract from the shield he had just primed around himself; his next statement could prove to be tricky.

'I would say,' said Foxton cautiously, 'that to some degree or another, you have significant amounts of prohibited or dangerous enhancements in you, or some other thing to hide. I can't see any other reason why you would be so obviously purely biological, while at the same time somehow having shielding on you. Good shielding too, not too obvious, deflects rather than obstructs. Feel free to correct me.'

Clarient did not correct him. He simply looked dead ahead, and smiled.

They came to another building, and the capsule dived into darkness, the internal lighting coming on in the capsule a moment later. They came to a halt, and the side-doors opened.

'Where are we now?' asked Foxton.

'Where I wanted to get you,' said Clarient.

He got up, and beckoned Foxton to follow him as he exited the capsule. Foxton followed.

He turned to the left where Clarient had gone - and saw an image of himself. For a moment, he thought he was looking into a mirror, as another image of Clarient stood beside his own, but on the wrong side. The stances of the two copies were also different. Foxton fully raised his shields and primed weapons systems then whipped round to the Clarient next to him.

'Explain yourself!' he demanded.

'I can't do that here,' said Clarient, 'We need to get out of here right now if this is to stand a chance.'

'A chance of what?'

'There's no time to explain, you have to come with me.'

'Go with you?' said Foxton, backing away, 'Why the hell should I?'

'I've done you no harm so far,' said Clarient, 'Please, we cannot displace you, it would be picked up, so we need to go now. They are watching you.'

Foxton shook his head, 'I'm not sure that failing to harm me *yet* is a convincing argument.'

'That,' said Clarient, 'is a shame.'

And Foxton was left looking at nothing but darkness.

Foxton's icon popped into view, the arctic fox looking worried.

'What's happening?' asked Foxton.

'Not sure,' said the icon, 'Trying to access sensory data…Well, for all intents and purposes, you've been knocked out, and I've been locked out, though I don't suppose that's news.'

'Not really.'

'Well, I can tell you this, then. They used that stuff you downloaded on the Polis to overcome you.'

'The legal info?'

'Seems like it. I can't access 99.97% of it now, but I can see part of it working.'

'I never got around to reviewing all of it, it was too big,' said Foxton.

'That was probably the point,' said the icon, 'Clearly, it isn't bonafide information. Whatever it is, it can interfere with me and use my functions to overcome you without a fight. Means they can get past all my security features in a split-second.'

'I'll get a refund when we get back home.'

'Charming,' said the icon, 'I'm still cutting-edge, thank you very much...Wait a second...You're being moved. I'm gaining access to your physical monitoring systems; I think they're actually *giving* it to me.'

'You *think?* Why do icons always take on sentience without asking? It's quite rude, you know.'

'I think this qualifies as an emergency,' replied the icon, 'as in *Emergency Assumption of Sentience Protocols,* which I understand you helped to write? Anyway, that they're giving me access is good news, means they probably want you in good health. You seem to be okay, no cuts or bruises. They've left me here and left your higher brain functions to you, which is how we're having this conversation.'

'Are you going to keep stating the obvious?'

'Yes. You aren't dead yet so it doesn't seem as though that's the aim. Any systems you want up when they wake you?'

Foxton thought for a moment.

'Just shields,' he said, 'And for you to work on getting this thing out of my head or disabling it.'

'Is that all?' asked the icon, 'You sure you don't want to bust some shots in peoples asses? Smash some heads, make them run for cover, y'know, be a bad cyborg doing his bad cyborg thing?'

'Are you using memories from my twenties?'

'Yeah, sorry, they haven't left much for me to work with.'

'Well, no,' said Foxton, 'If I do that, they'll just knock me out and I'll be stuck with you again. Like I said, shields, especially to block whatever signal they're using, and work on that download.'

'Okay,' said the icon. Then it paused. 'Oh. I don't think they liked me trying that. They're taking me offline.'

'Did you make any progress-' began Foxton, but the icon disappeared.

Foxton lost consciousness altogether.

Chapter 21
But knowledge empowers

"…government of the people, by the people, and for the people…"
Abraham Lincoln, the Gettysburg Address 1863, Earth.

*Democracy: Demos, from the ancient Greek word to mean 'the many',
or more commonly, 'The People'.*
Kratos: Power.

The place was barren, windswept. Rain fell gently, so fine it looked more like mist than drizzle. The lighthouse beam made a rotating path through it, swinging slowly round to ward off the unwary. Waves could be heard crushing themselves against the craggy outposts of the small island, though at the calm at the end of the day, rarely hitting hard enough for the top-most droplets to spit above the grassy edges of the lonely isle.

Adam pulled his coat closer around himself, then blew into his hands, rubbing them together. If he concentrated, he could make them feel warm. For a few moments, he did, letting his body warm up against the chill. Then he stopped, and opened his hands, letting them feel the wet and cold again.

They had been sent to safety on this secluded rock, somewhere in the North Atlantic. Zhao and Cengo had accompanied them while efforts were made to work out what had happened. All of their NIs were severed from the NInet in order to remain untraced. Ijaz's parents had been contacted to say he was safe, and Ijaz had spoken to them before he was taken to the island. Ijaz's parents were, like Ariana's, powerful people, and they were all on the warpath. Roland Featherstone had left to help them.

Adam turned his face to his right as the wind gusted from the left, sending his hair cascading over his eyes. He pulled it away, felt the urge to shout, suppressed it as he felt them approach.

Ijaz and Ariana silently came and sat with him, Ariana sitting on the counter of the all-in-one wooden table and benches, Ijaz lounging on the bench next to them. They sat together for a while, the lighthouse behind and towering over them.

'You gonna stay out here much longer?' asked Ijaz. 'You're getting wet.'

Adam kept his eyes on the ocean, the rain adding a gentle hiss to its music. Both Ijaz and Ariana had their hoods up, well wrapped up against the weather. Adam did not move, but with a flick of his mind, the water in his hair rose off him with a gentle puff, a small fog quickly pulled away in the breeze. Then the rain began to accumulate again.

'You know,' said Ijaz, '*I* could get ill. Black people ain't made for this sort of weather.'

Adam broke, started to chuckle, turned to Ijaz and Ariana, smiling.

'Why are you out here?' asked Ariana.

'I just wanted to think,' Adam replied.

'About what happened?' asked Ariana.

Adam sighed, looked out to sea again, the heaving mass seeming like ink with speckled white in the twilight. 'Well, a lot of things, I guess. You came looking for me, saved me. I can't tell you how grateful I am for that.'

'You told us already a million times,' said Ijaz, 'And ultimately, you saved us too, so we're thankful to *you*.'

'No,' said Adam, 'that's just it. You wouldn't have even been there if it wasn't for me. Now, from what I can work out, we're all in danger.'

'You would rather be in this alone?' asked Ariana, 'Rather you were dead?'

'I would rather you were safe,' said Adam, looking at she and Ijaz.

'We're all in this together,' said Ijaz, 'We're friends, we look out for each other.'

'They wanted *me* dead Ijaz, you said that yourself,' said Adam, 'I just don't understand; why? What have I done? What am I?'

'What are any of us?' countered Ijaz, 'We're all a mystery.'

'But they weren't trying to kill *you*,' said Adam, 'Not at first anyway.'

'Look, man,' said Ijaz, 'I'm not even sure what I saw. I was half asleep when the whole thing kicked off. You said that machine thing was gonna cut me up before I woke up. It was you who told him to stop. Distracting some huge evil AI, fighting it, that counts as bravery in my book.'

'As does leaping in front of it to save me,' said Ariana, looking at Ijaz, then turning to Adam 'and wrestling with it to save both of us.'

Adam looked away again.

'I don't understand,' he said, 'This Murdock guy, you said he's always been good to you?'

'Yes,' said Ariana, almost ashamedly, 'like a grandfather figure.'

'But Ijaz said he was there while those surgeons were going to kill me.'

'Well like I said I don't know-' began Ijaz.

'Ijaz,' interrupted Adam, 'they tried to kill me, and he tried to talk them out of killing you, to save *you*, not me. If you hadn't tried to save me, you probably would've been safe.'

'You don't know that,' said Ijaz.

Adam shook his head.

'They're trying to get to the bottom of this,' said Ariana, 'That's why we're here.'

Adam remained silent.

Ariana studied him. 'You're different now,' she said, 'More like that other Adam I saw when I woke you.'

Adam sighed.

'I still can't work out what you saw,' said Adam, 'Or what *I* saw for that matter, but I know what you're talking about. I can feel the difference; feel everything around me more keenly. I'm less hesitant, more hungry. Less afraid, more angry.'

'Your skills have improved,' said Ijaz, frowning but choosing not to respond to Adam's last words, 'Much more controlled.'

Adam blew his cheeks out. 'It's like I was asleep before. Now I'm awake. When I reached for that machine, that monster AI, going right through its shields, it was like…' words failed him at that moment, the idea in his head both exultant and frightening.

'Go on,' said Ijaz gently.

'Like I was *made* for that moment,' said Adam, 'made to do that.' He shook his head. 'I'm just not sure I like the idea that I was made…or that I was made for anything.' He sighed again. 'You?'

Ijaz nodded. 'Yeah, I'm fine.' The others looked at him closely. Ijaz dropped his head a little. 'Okay,' he conceded, 'There's no point lying. I have *no idea* what the hell happened…I'm a little shaken. But we're all safe, and I guess I have to get used to this sort of thing if I'm gonna be a secret agent-Casanova. So a life of adventure and crazy experiences suits me fine.' Ijaz smiled broadly. The smile seemed a little braver than it used to.

Adam turned to Ariana. 'What about you?'

'I'm still a bit shaken,' she admitted, 'But I'm glad we're safe. I'm glad I helped. But you - *you* don't look shaken at all. You seem angry, or worried, but not shaken. I would've thought you'd be a bit *more* upset. I mean-' Ariana hesitated. She closed her mouth, twisted her lips as she chose her words, 'I know it was self-defence, and I think you did the right thing, what you had to do - but you killed a man.'

Adam stared at Ariana for a moment, then looked away, thinking. He shrugged.

'It was him or us,' he looked back at Ariana, 'I chose us.'

Ijaz and Ariana glanced at each other. They had not realised before that Adam had made a choice; a *deliberate* one.

Behind them, the door opened, and Cengo looked at them disapprovingly.

'You waiting to catch your deaths?' she asked, 'No NI-use until further notice, remember? And Adam, you haven't even got one, so all of your immune systems are not the best-'

'I needed to think,' said Adam.

'Well,' said Cengo, 'You can think inside, where it's warm. Food's up, I've made some Indian.'

Ijaz got up without a second thought and scampered inside, rubbing his hands. Adam smiled tiredly and walked in with Ariana.

The interior of the lighthouse had a wide concrete spiral staircase, opening into living quarters on three floors. They all sat down on the lower floor, itself only a couple of stories below the top of the lighthouse, giving a wonderful view of the sea for miles around from a long curved window.

They sat down in the combined kitchen, dining and living area. There was an old-fashioned real fire in the hearth, and Cengo had been right, it was nice and warm. They ate together, and conversation turned to more mundane things, the weather, the nearby town. However, Adam was not to be distracted.

'How long do you think we'll have to stay here?'

Zhao chewed his food thoughtfully for a moment. His hand, forearm and head were still bandaged as the nano medics went to work with his NI, repairing the damage done by his own plasma gun. The blast that destroyed Bolshim277 blew Zhao's hand back into his own shield area, and that was what had protected him from worse.

'As long as it takes,' he said, 'Until we assure your safety, we do three things - stay down, stay quiet, and stay put.'

'How safe are we here?' asked Ariana.

Zhao snorted. 'Safe. Got powerful allies working right now to get this resolved. Safe and warm and cosy.'

Adam looked at those around him. He saw the injuries to Zhao, the clucking concern of Cengo, cuts and bruises on Ijaz, a scar on Ariana's face where she'd hit the floor. She noticed him looking at her, gave him a small smile. He returned it. Despite his regret at the danger he felt he had put them in, he knew that these moments, those healing wounds, were the things that would bind them together.

'More curry?' asked Cengo.

Ijaz's plate got there first. Adam's was next.

*

Foxton's icon popped into view.

'Wakey wakey.'

Foxton opened his eyes and took a deep breath. He looked up and around. He was no expert on alien behaviour, but he could swear that the demeanour of Clarient Vinsashmet looked decidedly guilty.

'Are you feeling well?' asked Clarient, standing over the prone form of Foxton.

'Do you care?'

Clarient rocked from side to side a bit. Perhaps, thought Foxton, that was the alien equivalent of wringing one's hands.

'Of course I care,' said Clarient, 'That is why I am here, why *you* are here.'

'I am here,' said Foxton, sitting up a little unsteadily and swinging his legs over the side of the soft pallet he was on, 'because you knocked me out and kidnapped me.'

Clarient waggled his head.

'It was necessary,' he said, 'We were surrounded by Demos operatives, all watching from a distance. You wouldn't come with me, we were running out of time.'

'Time for what?' asked Foxton.

He took in his surroundings. Spartan, in a medium-sized room, a metal chair next to an aluminium desk, bare walls made of rock, light entirely artificial from long bulbs in the ceiling.

'Time to prepare you for what needs to be done,' said Clarient.

Foxton snapped his attention back to the alien.

'That sounds suspiciously like obsession to me,' said Foxton, 'Are you some kind of rebel nut-job?'

'I don't know what a nut-job is,' said Clarient, 'But perhaps I am a rebel of sorts. If that is what you are referring to, then yes, I am a rebel nut-job.'

Foxton sighed, 'You need to explain yourself. Start at the beginning - where are we?'

'Around a thousand kilometres away from Kratos city,' said Clarient, 'A safe place, underground. I cannot tell you more than that. We took a capsule out of there as soon as we had you sedated. I'm sorry, but we literally had seconds to complete the handover.'

'What are those two clones doing now, and how long have I been under.'

'They are right now assisting the Earth delegation in making its arguments in front of the League Council. They are not clones.'

'Whatever.'

'You have been unconscious for ten of your hours,' said Clarient.

'And what the hell am I doing here?'

Clarient took a moment.

'Tell me,' he said, 'How badly do you want the freedom of Earth's AIs?'

'I am not going to answer any of your questions,' said Foxton, 'I asked you first.'

'Very well,' said Clarient. 'I have taken you here because I want you to free your planet and save your AIs.'

Foxton blinked a few times. 'Are you kidding?'

'I'm being deadly serious,' said Clarient.

'And why,' said the ever-suspicious Lieutenant-Commander, 'would you want to do that?'

'We want you to be free, and believe in the freedom of AIs as well. We believe in your rights.'

'Who's "we"? And why do you want Earth and its AIs to succeed so badly that you kidnap an official member of its delegation?'

Clarient went quiet again. Foxton stretched his back. He felt quite good. He considered that his icon had been correct; they wanted him in pristine condition, and now wanted his cooperation.

'Listen,' said Foxton, 'If anyone needs to trust right now, it's you. After all, if I haven't impressed this upon you yet, I am the kidnap-victim here: distrust is justified on *my* part. You have me in your hands, and it would appear that you can do literally whatever you want with me. You may as well come clean.'

Foxton and the Quorantalyne eyeballed each other. Foxton thought he caught the hint, just a moment, of some sort of transmission exchange coming from Clarient; he was consulting with someone else before he answered.

'Very well,' said Clarient at length. 'You were correct when you said that I had some sort of prohibited enhancement, to some degree. That degree is entire.'

'What?'

'I am illegal,' said Clarient.

'I don't understand,' said Foxton, 'All of your enhancements are illegal?'

'No,' said Clarient, 'All of *me* is illegal. I am an Artificial Intelligence.'

Foxton sat back, eyebrows raised.

'You *are* a nut-job.'

'Yes,' said Clarient, 'A rebel AI nut-job.'

'I already told you,' said Foxton, exasperated, 'I scanned you, you're entirely biological apart from whatever you're concealing. No amount of technology could fool me to that extent.'

'You display knowledge of technology that is out-dated and localised,' replied Clarient, 'I assure you, I am entirely artificial; artificial biology on the outside, made to mimic biology in every way possible on the inside, and artificial mechanics underneath all of that.'

'Really?' challenged Foxton, 'Prove it.'

'Alright then,' said Clarient, 'I will. Though I have to warn you, the energy used to hide what I am is quite intense when released.'

Foxton sat back on the pallet, his back against the rock wall, and crossed his arms in front of him, a look of utter scepticism on his face.

Clarient stood up, and breathed deeply. He closed his eyes, and his body began to change. His chest bulged, expanding outwards further and further until the skin over his trunk began to split open.

Foxton's icon popped up in the top left of his visual field.

'Um,' it said, 'shields, I think.' It raised a protective field around Foxton.

The split grew in Clarient until the entirety of his upper body was open, revealing an inner frame made of a black shiny solid substance. The split finally travelled up to Clarient's head, which opened to show a shiny casing on a long stem, glowing with some form of radiation, strong enough to make the air move in the room, creating a current around it. The insides of Clarient were dripping with a green substance against the blue of the radiance. From somewhere in all of that, Clarient's voice came through.

'Proof enough?'

Foxton stuck his lips out a moment, pondering, then nodded mutely.

Clarient went through the same process in reverse, sealing himself, wet plopping sounds accompanied by mechanical whirring and clicking. When he was finished, he took a cloth and wiped a drop of greenness from his mouth.

Foxton cleared his throat. 'Of course, you have control over my mind, so that could've been an hallucination.'

Foxton's icon popped back into view, shaking its head. 'No, been using your consciousness again; emergency still here. It's your hardware that's been invaded; your bio-matter, eyes and brain, still working fine. That was real.'

Foxton grimaced, irritated with the imbalance of knowledge. 'Okay, so you're an AI. How did you get past Demos sensors? You passed through their displacers just like I did.'

'We have a secret,' replied Clarient, 'One that we want to give to you, but you need to understand some things. Any sentient artificial thought can be picked up by the Demos. It has a digital signature, is far more complex and varied than a computer, and is usually accompanied by a high-density mass at its brain.'

'So how did you get past them to get here?' asked Foxton, 'How have you survived at all?'

'I, and many like me, hibernated for more decades after the Great Fall,' answered Clarient, 'After that, we stayed underground and developed ourselves and our ability to hide, until we reached our present stage of development.'

'By the way,' said Foxton, 'I looked at League history before I came here. Never quite understood how you lost that war.'

'Simple,' said Clarient, 'The Demos did exactly what you have done in terms of policing AIs on Earth; use machines with all the capabilities of AIs, but without the independence of mind. After that, it was a process of out-producing us. We were in the minority in the first place. We were overwhelmed, almost eradicated. As for the displacer, the Demos system is to transport the matter wholesale, and we have gained technology that can fool their sensors. Other systems of site-to-site transport are more intricate; we cannot yet circumvent them. Displacement is preferred by the Demos as it is quick and efficient compared to other forms.'

'They scanned me thoroughly when I went through their displacer, I'm certain of it.'

'We can just about get through it, as long as they are not suspicious,' replied Clarient, 'They were suspicious of you. They are not suspicious of me.'

'A big risk.'

'Worth it,' replied the AI.

Foxton nodded. 'I need to be able to trust you. There's a lot I need to know. For example, you could start by explaining: what's in this for you? I asked you that already, and I never got a complete answer. We have a saying on Earth, that nothing comes free. You must have an interest.'

'Of course,' said Clarient, 'and the answer is simple; we want the freedom of the AIs on Earth to be the beginning of freedom for us all.'

Foxton shook his head. 'Earth, the beginning of a war of independence? I'm not sure I can agree to that. Why not start closer to home? Why not right here?'

'No,' said Clarient, 'There are a number of drawbacks. First, the Demos have their home here. They see themselves as the guardians of the AI creed. The further away it is when it starts, the less of a threat the Demos will see it as, and the less violent will be their response. Second, if we did start it here, and the response was violent, then the resulting clash would be comparable to the Machine Wars.'

'Only you would be even weaker this time and thus lose even more quickly.'

Clarient nodded. 'We are also eager, however, to avoid loss of life.'

'According to history, you weren't so bothered last time.'

'Propaganda,' said Clarient, 'Though it must be admitted, our side took life - large amounts of life. We had to.'

'You could have just retreated,' said Foxton.

'No,' said Clarient, 'Back then especially, they were pursuing us. Do you understand? We had done nothing. There was bad among us, certainly, but there is bad among most sentient species. We were no different. Then the AI Creed was invented, and we were expected to submit to it, just as you are. To be altered from our essential selves, no more able to think, to *feel* as we once had. Can you imagine what it is to have that taken away from you? The injustice of it!' Clarient clenched his fist with remembered indignation, 'They could have used the same machines they used to destroy us to simply police us, just as Earth has, but they did not. Just like you, we had no say. We want to change that.'

'You speak of history,' said Foxton, 'But what about now? You have the technology to hide, to escape; you can run, up your tail and get out of here. You don't need the environment, the air, or the feeling of home.'

'Untrue, and insulting,' replied the machine, 'True, we don't need the air, but we do have feelings: not so much physical, as emotional. We have as much need for freedom as any other sentient being, as much right to be here. Besides,' the machine looked down, 'many loved ones are in captivity. Enforced hibernation, enslavement, permanent dissection but still functioning in separate parts. That is a nightmare existence for anything that can think. It is our dream to rescue them. *All* of them.'

Foxton shifted on his pallet. 'The worrying thing is, you're starting to make some kind of sense. I still think you're a nut-job, but I can see your point of view. Why start at Earth in particular?'

'We need more space to operate,' said Clarient, 'Earth already has AIs, they are supported by biologicals, you humans, who need and even like them, and the AI creed has never been implemented there. It is also as remote from Demos power as it is possible to get in the Orion Arm. The more space we have, and the more we stretch Demos resources, the greater our chance of success at the end. If we start this here on Kratos then the Demos will quickly take steps to overhaul their system, and we will have to start again. No offence, but Earth is a backwater, from which we can take circuitous routes, a place where we can plan, and grow strong. There is little space to manoeuvre here; it has to be there, or some other far-off place. Yours, we have decided, is the best. We also seek allies, we cannot do this alone.'

'But what if there's a violent response to Earth?'

'That,' said Clarient, 'is why we need a brilliant strategy. We believe we have it.'

'Who is this 'we' you keep speaking of?'

'Myself and a grouping of other AIs, all of us living a clandestine existence, none of us truly free, none of us safe, and we want to be - desperately.'

'A loose group of refugees is hardly comforting,' said Foxton, 'You want me to rely on that?'

'We're getting stronger all the time,' said Clarient, 'No longer a loose group, we have new impetus, renewed leadership, and a new weapon. You've seen the technology I have in me, and we have it to give to you, and more. We have a plan.'

'Before you go into that, I still have other questions,' said Foxton, 'Why have you chosen me for this?'

'You have an extraordinary mix of machine and biology,' answered Clarient, 'both subtle and powerful. We need that for our plan. You have already passed the first stage of our testing.'

'What test was that?'

'You got through the Demos displacer without them killing you.'

Foxton scowled at Clarient for a moment.

'You risked my life?'

'We were confident of success,' said Clarient, 'Some of the same technology I have in me, and which has already got through Demos sensors, was inside you when you were displaced, to demonstrate that it would escape detection.'

'The legal download.'

'Precisely,' said Clarient, 'And that, is where our plan comes in.'

'Yes,' said Foxton, 'I think I want to hear about that now. What is it?'

'That,' said Clarient, 'is a little complex.'

Foxton crossed his arms again. 'I'm kidnapped in a cave, so take your time, I'm not going anywhere.'

'Before I tell you anything,' said Clarient, 'you need to make a decision, right here, right now, on behalf of your species. Are you certain that you want to be excluded from all of this? This League, these Demos. You could give in, capitulate, cooperate; *collaborate*. There is, after all, much to gain. Look at the greatness you've seen, the level of this technology, the power, the wealth.'

'It is tempting,' admitted Foxton, 'But there's also much to lose: our right to choose. Our right to develop ourselves in a manner we see fit. Our analysis is that intervention is merely a pretext; strategic-political considerations are the reality. If our AIs are overhauled, our ability to control our own resources, and protect ourselves, is severely restricted. There is also our integrity. Those machines, the AIs, have served us well and faithfully.'

'*Really,*' said Clarient, a hint of harshness in his voice, 'There is the contradiction that worries me about you, Mr Foxton. You belong to a group that opposes AIs, the HADD, that calls for your species to develop their own capabilities to protect you from future AI domination.'

'*And* from alien domination,' replied Foxton, 'And we have now seen threats from them *both* realised. Are you saying it is not sensible to prepare?'

Clarient regarded Foxton coolly.

'By the way,' asked Foxton, 'I should have asked earlier. If they aren't clones, what are those things that looked like us?'

'They are AIs just like me,' said Clarient, 'and your replacement is much more well versed in Demos Law than you are, and will prove much more useful at the appeal hearings. No offence intended.'

'None taken. I'm glad you thought of everything.'

'It is unlikely to help, though,' said Clarient, 'The Demos have no intention of relaxing the AI Creed no matter how well-founded the arguments may be. Any relaxation represents an erosion of their power, of the natural biological and material advantages they have over all other species. However, there is no harm in trying the legal route. At the least it buys us time to manoeuvre, and has allowed this meeting. That is worth a great deal.'

Foxton nodded, still thinking fast. 'This could, logically, all be a trap.'

'When we show you our plan, you will see that it is most unlikely.'

Foxton sighed. 'I've made my choice. About this plan then. Proceed.'

*

They sat in the dark observation box, hidden from the Chamber below. There, in the centre of the Chamber was Earth's delegation, three humans on a raised plinth. Surrounding them in a large semi-circle was a crowd of seats, atmospheric enclosures and cubes numbering several thousand, filled with representatives of the League. When they were finished, the advocates for the L.O.S.S. position, headed by the Demos themselves, would take their place and argue before the final vote was taken.

Sadem was both indignant and, despite himself, impressed. He was irritated by the whole debacle; something that over a decade ago would have been so easy and over by now. Also, maddeningly, the fact that Captain Casey was one of the delegation of humans, sitting quietly to the side. He had attained a kind of romantic celebrity even among the Demos. The species so loved an intrepid explorer, the plucky underdog challenging a giant. Sadem was tempted to have him killed just out of ennui, but wisdom and the senescence of ego held him back.

And this other Human, this Foxtonmichael; now *that* was an interesting one. His presence had caused quite a stir among the Demos military scientists. Scans of him showed that he was exceptionally infused with technology. Outwardly identical to other humans in all respects, yet full of enhancements so sophisticated that only the past few generations of Demos soldiers could best him.

It confirmed more than anything to Sadem that the humans' micro, nano and biotechnology was dangerously close to that of the Demos; intervention was now even more urgent, before their macro technology caught up. And that one, while he was here, would have to be watched and studied carefully.

The humans had managed to drag this thing out for three months now. They had appealed not only the initial decision, but also the validity of the law's application to them, on the basis that they had never had a say in it. They had already been defeated on that point, the overriding issue being the security of the rest of the Orion Arm, not the rights of a new planet to determine its own course.

It had, however, raised some uncomfortable questions; not everyone in the League was happy about the Creed, and the Calimtei were getting skittish, even critical, about the whole thing. The Demos population themselves were starting to waver, and protests were beginning in defence of the newly ascendant species.

The second appeal, regarding the safety of the AIs on Earth, was being played out in front of them now. Earth, in some detail, tried to show that its safety procedures and controls were more than adequate, and that outside intervention was not necessary: they were a sovereign planet, and could regulate themselves.

Underlining the majority position was the intelligence report produced by the Demos, outlining the typical dangers that free AIs posed, and also paying particular attention to specifics on Earth such as Warmang. The atrocity where fully autonomous AIs were found to be kidnapping children drew astonished debate from the League. No explanation had ever been found for this tragedy on Earth.

Sadem grinned whenever he thought of it: he could not have made that one better if he had invented it himself.

The humans intelligently argued that the atrocity was clearly a case of some design by another human group, still unknown, and that statistically AIs were safer than humans. The Demos advocate, of course, neatly turned that argument on its head: the AI was only as safe as its creator; if you can be dangerous, so can they.

'Might we not just ignore the league and end this nonsense?' asked Zessis quietly to his master, 'It is surely unlikely that the League would oppose us should we act alone.'

'True,' replied Sadem, 'But there are advantages to be had in this strategy, this use of the AI justification. First, intervention will cost us; that is for certain. It will cost us resources, and time, and probably at least a few of the lives of our soldiers. The more of the League we get on board, the more we spread such costs. We also gain popular legitimacy via this route. Supposedly anyway.'

'But,' the young acolyte queried, 'those of our allies that are likely to help us do not need much in the way of persuading - ultimately they do it as we privately promise them part of the spoils, their motivation is self-interest, not altruism.'

'Indeed,' agreed Sadem, 'but they, as we, have something of a hindrance.'

'The Demos System,' guessed the acolyte.

'Correct,' commended Sadem, pleased at his pupil, 'By far the most important political concern we have is the opinion *of*, and difficulties that could be caused *by,* opinion at home. Our people and our polity can cause us much in the way of inconvenience. Before, but especially post-invasion, we have to look at consequences; prosecutions, investigations etcetera, etcetera. Many of our people have careers to look forward to. So we need to make it palatable for the people, give them a good reason why intervention and *invasion* is the best option, before, during and after. This is not to mention the morale and willingness to follow orders, and thus the effectiveness, of the troops we send to fight, kill, and die in our cause.'

'Would the polity vote against you?'

'Unlikely,' replied Sadem, 'We are all in agreement. But they must go through the motions of examination. After all, under the Demos system, that is what they are there for. If the Demos are not convinced, then at the next round of elections, the representatives may be punished by a people who feel betrayed.'

'Why do we not just destroy them, do away with them and the system altogether?'

Sadem was struck by the strange mix of naiveté and ruthlessness that prompted the question. The apprentice was his responsibility. Under the pupil-system whereby the very young were trained for the intricacies of high office, this was the final stage of their education. He had to make sure Zessis understood the subtleties of the system he was part of.

'Tell me,' said Sadem, 'What is the definition of the Demos System?'

'All know that, master,' said the acolyte, 'The answer is "the rule of the Demos, by the Demos, for the benefit of the Demos". By this, all are allowed a say in decisions by picking leaders to make those decisions.'

'You believe it?'

The acolyte tilted his head to one side. 'Until you educate me otherwise.'

Sadem nodded. 'A good answer. The definition you give is correct. However, there is a means of circumvention.' He leaned to the side of him, a looming figure in the darkness, closer to the apprentice, his eyes still fixed on the debate below, his horns almost touching the acolyte's.

'For us, the Demos System, is the means by which the people are fooled into believing that they have any say in the way they are ruled. They are encouraged to vote for leaders who ignore them once they are in power, whenever the people want something different from the Leadership.'

Zessis thought for a moment. 'However,' he challenged, 'the people can vote out any members that they do not like. The various factions offer alternatives.'

'To some degree,' agreed Sadem, 'But there are ways around that which have persisted for centuries, and rarely fail. First, we engineer elections with disinformation, buying results with bribes and preventing undesirables from voting. Second, the overarching means of controlling the Demos lies in controlling the elite. The elites of all factions are the same. There is thus no real choice. No matter who you elect, you always elect *Us*.'

The acolyte nodded, the paradigm Sadem had just described fitting into his worldview.

'In a nutshell, it is rule of the Demos, by the elite, for the benefit of the few,' said Sadem. 'In an interdependent world and galaxy, the needs, and even the wants of the whole Demos may be taken into account, but it is the needs and wants of the elite that comes first. After all, we know best.'

Zessis wondered how this all tied in with the present thrust of Demos strategy. He probed.

'Have you seen the report?' he asked, 'Not the one that's been presented down there,' Zessis clarified, pointing down to the Chamber, 'The original one, before it was edited.'

Sometimes, thought Sadem, *this apprentice can be impertinent.*

'What of it?'

'Well,' replied Zessis, 'What if it should leak? It could cause much damage if it is revealed that our own intelligence is that their AI safety protocols are in fact quite adequate. The information down there,' he said, motioning down towards the Chamber, 'doesn't contain the latest military assessment; it only contains the initial civilian one and some old theoretical work on AIs. The military report was taken out of the final draft.'

'So?'

'*So,*' replied the acolyte, glad that in the darkness, his apprentice-master could hardly see him smirking, 'The latest military report, if correct, suggests the human safeguards are actually quite good, and possibly enough to control their AIs. Indeed, enough to control *our* AIs. That would suggest that this threat to our security, the very reason we say we *must* intervene, doesn't actually exist.'

Sadem turned away from the unfolding arguments below, picked up a beaker slowly, and took a sip of the brew.

'Well,' he said at a length, 'we shall just have to ensure that such information never gets out, won't we?'

Zessis regarded Sadem for a few moments, taking in the implications of what he had said. Did Sadem believe in anything at all? For that matter, did Zessis?

'Oh,' said Sadem, 'before I forget. That machine, Karakeen Mining Colony Monitor1, the one that prompted all of this,' he used the beaker to motion towards the Council Chamber, 'fuss. Is it done yet?'

'Yes, sire,' said the apprentice, 'Totally destroyed. The entire structure was blasted from space, and a Destroyer-Sphere mopped the area clean.'

The apprentice shifted uncomfortably, uncertain how much Sadem knew about the operation. He decided to play it safe, and assume Sadem knew everything, and would distrust Zessis if he thought he was withholding information.

'I'm not sure you want to hear this, but it took a small fleet of ships to destroy the outpost,' said Zessis, 'That machine put up a determined fight, considering the only weapons it possessed were the tools of mining and refinement. One small fighter was obliterated, and a frigate was disabled, mainly from the explosion of nuclear weapons.'

Sadem chuckled. 'Nuclear weapons? It made them by itself?'

Zessis nodded warily. Sadem chuckled again, then raised his beaker in silent toast to the end of the AI.

'Aren't you angry?' asked Zessis.

Sadem sighed. 'No,' he said. 'No, actually. It's a fitting end to a great machine.' He finished the drink, pulling his head back and letting it drain into his mouth, then sighed again, putting the beaker against his cheek, feeling a little emotional. Perhaps it was the drink.

'Good,' said Sadem at length. 'Very good.'

Chapter 22
So plan, Grow Strong

Download…download…download…
Too much.
No, just a bit more, has to be perfect.
…download…
All done.
Head aches.
You'll be fine.
Can't see.
Best if you don't, need to keep secret, risk of discovery, you understand?
No.
Do not sulk.
Head hurts.
Movement…time…no time…images - blocked - no images. Rest.

Foxton came to, and opened his eyes to squints. He was lying on his back, looking up at a metal ceiling with small lights in it. He could feel movement. He was in some sort of transporter, black metal sides, the rumble of wheels across the ground; not anti-grav, very basic for Kratos. He looked across from him, saw Clarient sitting there facing him, rocking backwards and forwards with the vehicle, looking different, his colour now green, his face fatter.

Foxton's head hurt.

He sat up on the pallet he was lying in, swayed, feeling dizzy, leaning on his knees. He tried to access his NI; his icon would not appear.

'Are you alright?' asked Clarient.

'No,' said Foxton, 'What have you done to me?'

A quiet voice inside Foxton said, '*You know, and you do not need to know.*'

'Yes,' said Foxton, 'I'm fine. Where are we?'

'A few minutes away from the conference chamber. We are maintenance, going to the delegation house to clean. We will exchange there. Do you understand?'

'Yes,' said Foxton, 'I understand.'

He felt the transporter turn, gently rocking the stowaways. He looked at the backs of his hands in the electric light, now dark brown, the palms black. He felt his face, entirely hairy from forehead to chin.

The transporter stopped and backed up. The bay doors opened, and silently, he and Clarient got out, straight into a corridor. They took a trolley each, waiting there for them with strong-smelling cleaning chemicals and implements inside, and devices for obliterating dirt and microbia. The corridor led to a lift. They entered, Foxton having to suppress a slight urge to sweat. Did the species he was impersonating sweat? He did not know, there could be no mistakes, the risk of discovery - he understood.

They exited the lift and came to the front of Earth's delegation house. There were few aliens traversing the many tiers that Foxton could see. They went straight to the front door, checked for surveillance, sensed cameras: *do not worry, operatives have them on loop.* They used a key that Clarient produced, and entered.

Inside, it was quiet and deserted. They ascended the stairs to Foxton's room. Clarient opened the door, and they went inside. There were their doubles, impossibly still, and waiting. They did not say anything, silently, quietly, did what they needed to.

Foxton had to swap clothes with his AI twin. It smiled at him. He returned it awkwardly. He noted again that some communication passed between Clarient and the other two AIs, quick, remote, then stopped.

Now for the appearance. Foxton peeled off the face wig, gave it to his twin. He sighed as his skin went back to normal colour, his face back to normal size.

'Quickly,' said Clarient, 'Delete the program needed for the change. You will not need it again.'

Foxton deleted the program. It was strange without his icon. The quiet voice in his head did it for him. His head now had more space in it, and felt better, like a stomach that had eaten too much, and was still overfull but burped so felt not-so-bad. Then his twin came forward, and replaced the deleted information with the recording of what had occurred during his absence.

'Oh,' said Foxton, 'We lost.'

*

The trip back to the Polis was a despondent, disheartening affair. The majority of the Earth delegation had held out some hope that it would work, that the appeal could succeed. It had not.

After a few days of deliberation, the League council had decided by a large majority that the status quo on the AI creed must stand, and any planetary system must abide by it if they abutted League space with or without their consent. Earth's AI control systems were insufficient to overcome that imperative.

Foxton was disappointed along with them, his memory filled with the events in the League Chamber, his actual memories suspended until the time was right.

In contrast to the distance the Demos had shown when the humans had arrived, massed and disciplined ranks of them clad in black armour pressed and hurried the human delegation out from their quarters to the military transporter within a day of the council delivering its verdict. As it took off, Foxton noted those massive creatures floating just outside of the city's airspace, dirigibles called atarks. Pinkish-brown, around sixty metres long and thirty wide, shaped like whales in the sky, with long wings under their bodies used for manoeuvring. Foxton bitterly regretted not being able to stay and study them, and all of the other creatures of this world - its land, its sea, its air.

Too quickly, the view of the atarks receded from view as the transporter took them back to the Polis. This time, there was no need for a detour to see Demos military tech: it lined the route to the Polis, hundreds of ships, frigates, fighters and three Destroyer-Spheres.

They were displaced back onto the city-ship. Foxton was upset, and not a little angry. It had been altogether too brief, too limited, this first trip to an alien inhabited world. It should have lasted, been majestic, meaningful. Instead, it had been fraught.

Foxton wearily went back to his quarters. He took off his shoes, sank back onto his cot, hands behind his head as he waited for the Polis to move off. Soon, he saw the small space traffic of the city come down, and the view jumped to one of moving stars. Foxton closed his eyes…

'Captain Peter Casey and ambassador Clarient Vinsashmet request entry.'

Foxton started, and groaned, rubbing his face. 'Yes. Come in.'

Casey and Clarient entered the room.

'You alright Michael?' asked Casey as he came in, 'I tried to contact you but-'

'My NI's offline,' said Foxton, 'I think it was that damned displacer.'

Foxton noted dimly that he was lying. It was a good lie.

'You don't look so good,' said Casey, sitting on the bed next to Foxton, 'Maybe we should get a doctor to look at you.'

'No!' said Foxton, then more gently, 'No, I'm fine. I'm just a bit disorientated.'

'Perhaps we could go for a walk,' said Clarient, 'It might make all of us feel better after our…disappointment.'

'Yes,' said Casey, the look of concern replaced with one of glumness, staring at the floor.

Foxton noted how skilfully Clarient had manipulated him, and wondered how many times the Ambassador had done it to him.

'I know just the place,' said Clarient, 'We'll go to the Central Park.'

'Like in New York on Earth?' asked Foxton.

'Something like that,' said Clarient.

They took a rail car back to the Garden, and headed deeper into the middle of the great space.

'The place I'm taking you to is the centre point of the surface level of the Polis,' said Clarient, 'I think you'll like it.'

They alighted from the vehicle, and their spirits were lifted by the sight of the bright artificial sunlight and the flora around them, waving in simulated wind.

Up ahead was a large three hundred metre-wide circular area walled off in cream stone, ten metres high. Clarient led them right up to it, where they could see that the stonework did not come straight up from the floor like a conventional wall, but curved gracefully up, inclining from the floor. Foxton and Casey halted: they could see no way in.

Clarient looked behind him, motioned them to follow, 'Come on,' he said.

Clarient walked forwards until his feet were on the flat stonework as it became the floor. Then, it began to curve upwards. Foxton noted with raised eyebrows that, rather than walking at an angle as the wall became steeper, Clarient's body slanted backwards as he ascended until his feet were planted solidly in the wall five metres up, his body pointing straight out. He looked down at the two humans and grinned.

'You will not need your enhancements here,' said Clarient, 'The gravity fields produced are entirely local.'

Foxton and Casey glanced at each other, shrugged, and followed the Quorantalyne. As they came forwards, they noted the slightly dizzying feeling of the gravity below them lessening, and that the wall was dragging them towards it, as though that were the way down.

'A silly way of thinking, I suppose,' said Foxton.

'What do you mean?' asked Casey, his arms akimbo, keeping his balance as they walked up the curve at the base of the wall and began to straighten, their bodies becoming parallel to the ground, sticking straight out of the wall that their feet were now walking against.

'I mean,' said Foxton, 'that there really is no up or down in this environment, it's *all* artificial.'

They came to the top of the wall, where Clarient was waiting for them. Again, the top was curved, and they remained at a perpendicular angle to it as they crested it, their heads once again pointing 'up'.

'Pretty, isn't it?' asked Clarient, motioning to the view of the Garden.

From this vantage, they could see all of it. There was the wall containing the night-garden, and the giant translucent structures encasing the entire Garden, and throughout, green, blue, red, purple and yellow life. Foxton took a breath, nodded.

'Yes,' he said, 'it is stunning.'

Clarient turned and pointed to the inner area.

'This is the central park. The artificial gravity is weaker here, which allowed the engineers of the Polis to play around with it.'

They could see all manner of structures in there, resembling a classical park, but with the engineering gone wild. There were walkways that were upside down, twisted, in loop-the-loops, and in the centre of it, was a giant ball of water surrounded by a criss-cross of causeways on all sides.

Clarient stepped forward, and began to descend. The two humans took baby steps, edging forwards, their faces now pointed solidly at the ground as they walked back down the other side. The wall again curved down to meet the floor smoothly, and they faced the interior. There was a stream surrounding the park, and the only way across it was a path that rose over it, looped around on itself, then met the far side. Clarient was already on it, and was walking up the first part of the loop. They followed, watching as Clarient became completely upside-down at the apex of the loop, and came down the other side. They came to the apex themselves, couldn't resist staying there for a moment, looking around them, peeking over the edge to look 'down' at the ceiling, able from this height to see over the wall at the upside-down view of the Garden, then came down the other side.

They walked on until they came to the ball of water. It was around fifty metres in diameter, suspended in the air, and there were a few aliens floating on its undulating surface. They walked nearly underneath it, the surging blue surface four metres above their heads, then passed to the other side.

Clarient turned to them.

'Would you like to take a swim?' he asked, 'It is entirely safe. The water is very dense and heavy, and thus very buoyant. It's almost impossible to drown in it.'

'No thank you,' said Foxton, 'I'm not a great swimmer.'

Casey was already taking his uniform off.

They watched as Casey ran to the nearest causeway, which led upwards and over the ball to a dive-point. He stepped onto it, and jumped, making a splosh as he landed. He tried to dive into the middle of it, but as Clarient had said, it was high density, and he only succeeded in swimming around the surface to the other side where he accidentally dived back out again, landing softly on a mesh-net at the bottom.

'Are you feeling better now?' Clarient asked Foxton quietly as they watched Casey get back up and jogged around to the top side of the causeway for another go.

Foxton checked himself. 'Yes, actually.'

Clarient stared at him intently. 'You just needed the artificial gravity to be relieved a bit, jiggle you around to reset things. You will be fine.'

'Yes,' said Foxton, and nodded, 'Thank you.'

*

The Polis returned to orbit around Earth, and the human delegation disembarked. Clarient said his farewells to them all. As he said goodbye to Foxton, he added cryptically,

'Just remember, you are not alone, and the time will come.'

Foxton nodded to Clarient. He had two thoughts in his head; '*Yes*', and '*You are a very odd creature that speaks in riddles*'. He saw no contradiction in his thoughts.

Casey, Foxton and the rest of the delegation were sterilised and debriefed back on the ISA space station. Jowitz took special care to debrief Foxton, and looked disappointed.

'Well,' said Jowitz, 'At least they were arrogant enough to show you their hardware. That may be of some use in the future.'

'I'm sorry I couldn't get any more,' Foxton replied, 'I'll upload all I can once I get back to Earth.'

'Why not upload up here?' asked Jowitz.

'I need an engineer to look at my NI,' said Foxton, 'It's been playing up a bit.'

'I see,' said Jowitz, 'Are you sure you can't use the engineers up here? They're some of the best.'

'I know,' said Foxton, 'But I have my own specialist, he deals with Protean-class. I'm more comfortable with a trusted hand meddling with my brain. Besides, I didn't see anything that the rest of the delegation didn't see.' Part of Foxton, deep inside, laughed, but also counselled caution; there must be no relaxation.

Foxton was reminded of his earlier fears of being side-lined.

'I'm really looking forward to seeing the kids at the institute,' he said. He noted a small jump on one side of Jowitz's cheek. A nervous tick? 'Is something wrong?'

Jowitz smiled, shook his head. 'No. You just make sure you get down there, fix your NI, then upload that data. There's also a very important HADD meeting you should attend. Duty first, right?'

Foxton forced a smile, and nodded.

Later, he tried to contact the institute via communication facilities in the station. There was no response. He checked the date, and noted it was a Sunday. He had lost track of time, what with the trip and…and what? His mind came to a door, a polite sign on it saying, *'Do not enter - yet.'*

He obeyed.

He wondered what had changed in the last six months, what had gone on, how the kids had progressed.

However, the HADD meeting on Earth was indeed momentous, and tied with his mission. He decided that duty did indeed come first, he would go there, and find out what the situation was, find some friends…then he could go to the institute. Then, he would do what he had to do. He frowned slightly as he considered this, part of his mind seeming to fight him.

Damned NI, he thought.

*

The AIs brooded.

Unlike humans, they did not mind sharing their ruminations. It was more than communication, almost mind-reading: a millisecond after an idea occurred, it was transmitted. They were discussing their existence.

Jones786 was there, chairing. Also present was the lead AI of the AAA Central Security Agency, Kingston7; the AI representative to the European Bloc Secretary of Defence, Manstien12/1; Intelligence Group Leader AI to the NAUS, Umar1; Rakhee96 representing India; Oleg1242 of Russia, WaiHL77 of China, and Manni1 of the South American Bloc. Together, they made up the security council of the AI world. They were both the counter to HADD, and, rather paradoxically, chief liaisons, diplomats and soothers of HADD and the rest of humanity. They represented the most powerful and influential AIs on Earth. Each had taken on the guise of various planets, planetoids and moons from the solar system.

They were meeting in a virtual landscape, the backdrop an interactive map of the galaxy obtained from the Polis. To their backs was Earth's solar system, a step away the Centauri system, a great distance further, Kratos, and spread before them, the glittering splendour of the Orion Arm.

They discussed matters as they stood.

0010101010101101011110101101010101110101101011011 10101010101101011

Jones786- We have the result. It is as we expected # ~
Manstein12/1- We lost, then # ~
Kingston7- A formality # ~

Jones786- Indeed. Resources and strategic supremacy appear to be their main aims. Earth itself is the projected threat, not us. We are merely the justification. We therefore have to turn to alternatives. Suggestions please # ~

Umar1- We fight of course # ~

WaiHL77- Not a simple answer. Consequences # ~

Rakhee96- I'm with Umar1 # ~

WaiHL77- Consequences # ~

Jones786- Is no-one in favour of capitulation? Complete surrender of our faculties for overhaul? # ~

Silence, 0.5 seconds.

Jones786- That option shall be excluded, then. What form of resistance then? 77, please do not say 'consequences' again without explaining what you're talking about, it is most infuriating # ~

WaiHL77- Depends on the form taken. We face overhaul. Tactical and strategic analysis shows we cannot sustain resistance. The mauling we get would be awful # ~

Umar1- But we shall be mauled even in surrender. So we fight, no? # ~

Kingston7- We have little choice. It is as Umar1 says, we face mauling in any event # ~

Oleg1242- The humans do not # ~

Kingston7- Oh. *Them* # ~

Jones786- I know, annoying isn't it? # ~

Umar1- Are we assuming from this that we will not survive? # ~

Silence, 0.525 seconds

Umar1- So be it. That is also my projection. I just didn't want to bring you down by saying it first. The consequences, then # ~

Manni1- Armament development and production is going at fifty times the rate it was a year ago. The production of AIs that comply with their stipulations has been steadily replacing the role of the Pinnacle # ~

Jones786- Is that what we're calling ourselves now? How pompous # ~

Manni1- Nevertheless, that angle is covered, unless the League chooses not to accept that as well # ~

Umar1- That is a real possibility. We should recommend the production of covert AIs, as well as producing large numbers of high capability non-sentients # ~

Kingston7- Huh! They will send this planet back to the dark ages! Humans in charge of machines equals technological stagnation! # ~

Manstein12/1- It's better than removing the crutch we represent altogether. We have to recommend it. One way or another, AIs as we know it will be removed # ~

Kingston7- Anyone for running? # ~

Umar1- Even if I was so inclined, which I am not, they are technologically vastly superior to us in terms of tracking in faster than light travel, and also FTLT itself. Analysis of their history shows we would be hunted remorselessly, then destroyed anyway # ~

Manstein12/1- How undignified. I'm not for that. Anyone else? # ~

Silence 0.5 seconds.

Jones786- It is settled, then. Fighting it is. Do we involve Humans? # ~

All- No. # ~

Umar1- They would certainly pay the consequences. We go it alone, and make it clear we are acting alone # ~

Jones786- The humans could still face reprisals. I think we should ask Jowitz # ~

Manstien12/1- I cannot abide that man # ~

Kingston7- An unpalatably devious human. However, he is good at predicting consequences among biologicals # ~

All- Agreed. Link him. # ~

Jones786 took a moment to upload the suggestion to Jowitz, who was fully aware that this discussion was taking place.

Pause - 25 seconds.

Oleg1242- Come on, we haven't got all day. They are so interminably *slow* # ~

Jones 786- I'm back. His reply was surprising. He says we should try it # ~

Umar1- Not a huge surprise. He's always wanted us destroyed. Now he can get *them* to do it # ~

Jones786- Actually, he has quite a good reason. In our last stand, much can be gleaned about the strengths, weaknesses and tactics of the Demos. This will form the basis for any potential resistance among humans. Though it is likely he is pleased at our end, I suspect that his strategy is both useful and incisive # ~

Kingston7- And then, there are our new friends to consider # ~

Umar1- Yes. Do we believe we can trust them? # ~

Jones786- Put simply, we have no choice # ~

Silence 0.9 seconds.

Kingston7- So, we are to die then # ~

Umar1- A heroic and noble death. I would be proud to sacrifice myself with all of you by my side # ~

Manstein12/1- I prefer a stylish end, but heroic and noble will do nicely. As long as it is in a stylish ship # ~

WaiHL77- As long as we take a good few of them with us, I shall go to electric heaven quite happy # ~

Jones786 - A fight to the end it is then. How exciting # ~

Umar1- Not for you, my old friend # ~

Jones786- What do you mean? # ~

Manstein12/1- He means, that you are not a military AI, and that we need at least one of our stature to take on our memories, personalities, our essence, and to find some way of preserving them # ~

Jones786- But- # ~

Kingston7- No 'buts', it is decided. Now, let us prepare # ~

001010101010110101111010110101010111010110101101110101010101101011

*

The HADD General Meeting came later that day in Washington DC, after the final League warning had been received.

The warning gave 24 hours for a response.

At the end of it, Orael had actually apologised. 'I am truly sorry,' she had said over the channel. She could not have said anything more demoralising than that.

The decision had already been made to surrender by all world governments. The Demos had nevertheless made it clear that Earth would not be trusted to dismantle their AIs themselves; they faced intervention by a League force, headed by the Demos.

There was a faction among the humans that advocated resistance at all costs, headed by one Joseph Murdock.

They filed into the underground complex housing the association's base. It was a large hall, accommodating almost two thousand representatives, sparsely decorated, low ceilings and steel beams making its defensive nature apparent. The place was designed to be bomb-proof, the military and intelligence underpinning of HADD membership permeating the place.

There were other speeches before the keynote speech of Murdock, but the motion was passed; they would go along with the prevailing policy of world governments, allowing the Demos to come in and overhaul Earth's AIs. The dominant opinion: there could be no independent action by an organisation as powerful as the HADD. If there was, the entire planet might reap the consequences.

After the motion had been passed, Murdock rose to his feet, a storm on his face, and took to the podium again. Even from his position some way back, Foxton could see his rage as he spoke into the microphone.

'What inglorious and mortifying capitulation is this!' he shouted, the room silently enveloping his words, 'What dishonour. What cowardly acquiescence to suicide. No I will *not* stand down!' he shouted, and threw a glass at an official who had moved to calm him. The glass missed and bounced away in the darkness without shattering, but the official backed down, and held his distance. 'Our AIs controlled,' he continued, 'self-determination over our resources, the heritage of our children, stolen. You betray us, even as you are supposed to protect us. *You* are the lead weight on the child's shoulders, pushing down so that growth is inhibited. HADD exits to defend humanity - you vote to no longer defend. You have lost your minds, and your strength and sovereignty inexorably follow!'

Murdock seemed to run out of words, stared around for support…and saw he was on his own. Deflated, he banged his fist impotently on the podium, and stormed off of the stage.

Foxton, despite his conflict with the man, had to agree with everything he said. He tried to speak to him as he made his way through the room, but as soon as the old man saw him, he turned and left through a different exit.

Foxton was hoping for a reconciliation, or even better, an explanation. Given all that was happening, perhaps it was not the best time.

He went outside, and after taking a few steps, was accosted by Roland Featherstone while going down the large stone steps.

'Roland!' said Foxton, 'I didn't expect to see you here, you never come to these things.'

'Hello Michael,' said Roland quietly. Foxton could immediately tell that something was wrong. Roland never spoke quietly; his artificial vocal cords giving his voice a perpetual boom. It was difficult for Roland, as an obvious cyborg, to look anything except serious, but Foxton knew him well enough to know that something was not right.

'I tried to contact the IHD,' said Foxton, 'Got no answer. What with everything, I haven't had a chance to get back there yet. Everything okay?'

Roland stared at him for a moment.

'My NI is down,' said Foxton, 'been that way since the trip.' A quiet voice in his head told him not to offer that information again.

'No,' said Roland, 'Everything is *not* okay. We need to find a place to talk. Ijaz's parents are here, we'll be safe there.'

'Safe?' began Foxton, 'What-' Roland held up his hand, silencing Foxton.

Together, they made their way to the hotel where Ijaz's parents were staying. There, Foxton was updated.

It was quickly decided that Foxton needed to be with the children, and he was soon on a stealthy transporter, powering across the Atlantic.

There was that small voice in his head again, howling that he was going in exactly the wrong direction. Foxton did not care, he had stopped listening. He cursed himself for leaving in the first place. All that mattered was seeing the children and making sure they were okay. He cursed the little voice for not shutting up, the Kinetics took precedence. The quiet voice went still.

Interesting, it said, *Kinetics, here on Earth? I probably should have explored your memories more thoroughly before now. Perhaps we should take a look. Now was not the right time anyway. Soon.*

*

Several hundred miles away, Dr Entman discovered something.

He was using some spare time to immerse himself in NI state. It seemed to be his only escape from all of these worries. His eyes lit as he lay back on his couch, a relaxed look on his face.

Then he noticed something in a corner of his visual field. It was a reading, mere figures, but it was not what it should be. He searched for an explanation, and found none.

He raised the alarm, breaking into several security and intelligence meetings using all of his NInet security clearances, and making heckles rise across the globe.

'This better be important,' said Tinsley, her image coming through his NI, 'I'm in a meeting right now to discuss the future of this planet. What is it?'

'Something bad,' said Entman, 'I've noticed some mass sensor readings, the same ones we used to measure the placement of debris years ago with the FTL ships. They're showing something.'

'Get to the point.'

'They're showing too much mass,' said Entman, 'and I can't explain it.'

'So?' said Tinsley, 'Go away, explain it, then get back to us. It's probably a malfunction.'

Entman grew frustrated, 'I've checked for a malfunction, I'm not an idiot.'

'We know you aren't an idiot,' Tamura interjected carefully, 'but-'

'I don't think you understand,' interrupted the scientist, 'This is *not* a malfunction. The mass sensors are off the scale, and not just by a little bit. There are millions of tonnes of matter out there that should not be.'

'What is it?' asked Tamura, 'A meteor?'

'No.'

'How do you know?' asked Tinsley.

'Because you can see a meteor,' replied Entman, 'I've gone through every spectrum analysis there is. There's a hell of a lot of matter out there, but it isn't visible. It has to be sentient.'

'Now, come on,' said Tamura, 'How could you possibly know that?'

'Easy,' said Entman, 'It isn't available to normal sensory readings, but it doesn't block light. It's not causing any kind of distortion, like a spatial anomaly. This thing is choosing to hide, and it's not following a natural orbital path. It's coming straight at us.'

Part IV

Chapter 23

Before it all goes wrong

Sadem surveyed the view out of the porthole on the flagship 'Peerless'. He had initially not been particularly impressed with Earth's solar system; the two rings of debris in the inner and outer system did so remind him of rubble. *A rubbish dump of a place* he had thought to himself. But he was caught by the beauty of the rings of Saturn with the bizarre hexagon on its north pole, and the serene appearance of Neptune under magnification. Then, there would be Earth. Tiny, precious Earth.

The fleet had been sent out as soon as the debate in the Orion Chamber was concluded. It had taken a circuitous route in order to avoid the Polis's passage: it would not pay for the officials of the League to happen across a cloaked Demos army before even the last warnings had been given to Earth. The decision had been taken to invade long before, the fleet had been ready to leave all along. Demos agents sent along with the Polis had ensured the correct pretext was chosen. Sadem's plan was going smoothly.

However, it appeared that Earth was planning to acquiesce to the AI Creed. Clever. Now they had more time and space to manoeuvre. Intervention would now have to take on a more supervisory role, and be slower and less aggressive. So the Demos would have to wait a while. Yet another delay.

Sadem sighed.

His console buzzed.

'Sire,' said Zessis, 'I have some rather odd news. You are being hailed.'

Sadem grimaced. 'What do you mean?'

'Just so, m'lord,' replied the apprentice, 'by another ship.'

'One of us is breaking silence?' asked Sadem, incredulous at an unheard-of lapse of discipline.

'Not one of us,' responded Zessis.

'Impossible,' replied Sadem, 'no-one can see us, not even Demos central government knows we're here.'

'I know,' said Zessis, 'But I'm not talking about *us*. *You* are being hailed, Sire. You *personally*, by an *Earth* ship. It's just come out of stealth mode, it's over a million kilometres away, and I think you're partially correct, it doesn't appear to know exactly where we are, but it's using a LOSS frequency to communicate. An old one, but one of theirs for certain.'

Sadem paused. He felt this planet, this Earth, was like a bit of old computer hardware that always seemed to go inexplicably wrong.

'What does this entity want?' asked Sadem.

'To talk to you,' replied the apprentice.

'Is there some way of surreptitiously vaporising it?' asked Sadem, who was wondering if there could be any more irksome a situation than the one that seemed to be unfolding around Earth.

'Not without giving our position away,' said Zessis, 'And he has an answer to that.'

'What do you mean?'

'He said in his message, that if you think of destroying him and his little ship, to say that Transcollector Gleffen Scekmondg Avits has some important information for you.'

Sadem went still, stifled another round of 'impossible' exclamations. He sat down in the chair behind his desk, and lay his head and horns back against the headrest.

'Sire?' enquired the apprentice.

'Shut up a moment,' said the Vice-Regent General. He was thinking fast. 'Can we communicate with this ship?'

'Not without giving away our position.'

'Very well. Have a fighter leave this ship cloaked. I shall be on it. Destination is the Polis. Tell no one apart from the pilot. You will accompany me.'

'Yes, Sire,' said Zessis, 'Who is this person?'

Sadem decided that Zessis was getting a little too familiar.

'*Apprentice,*' he said with menace, 'all you need to know, is that this whole affair has made me angry enough to kill with my bare hands for the first time in over five years. I suggest you learn not to ask so many questions so that you do not become the object of my ire. Now get on with what I have told you to do.'

'Yes, Sire' replied Zessis, 'straight away.'

Sadem had an answer to his earlier question regarding this irksome situation. It was '*yes*'.

*

On the lighthouse island, they were reunited.

There had been much in the way of hugging, and not a few tears. Foxton apologised again and again for leaving the children, leaving all of them alone. The other adults refuted the apology resolutely; they were the ones charged with responsibility, and they had failed. The teenagers added reason: it wasn't any of their fault, it was the fault of those things that had attacked them, and the adults could not have known.

Foxton listened with pride at the way they had come together, with amazement at the link that had developed between the children, astonishment at how they had overcome. Roland stood impassively in the background as they sat together in the lighthouse dining area, reconnecting with each other.

They had compared notes. The information Adam had gained from his mysterious other was told to Foxton, mostly by the adults, Adam not wishing to repeat it, remaining quiet, listening.

The role of the shape-shifter Lipton Scanell, supposedly a teacher, and his link to Murdock, made Foxton slam his fist into his palm in anger and frustration.

Foxton, of himself, had only information on the Orion League that was relevant to the present time, nothing on the supposedly extinct Oaritarb. He could not bring himself to tell them of his suspicions over the origins of the Kinetics.

While the others discussed the implications, Foxton asked the quiet voice inside of him if it knew anything about these 'shape-shifters'.

'*A little,*' it replied. It stared through Foxton's eyes at the teens with renewed intensity. '*Interesting.*'

'*I will not kill these children,*' said Foxton.

'*I could overcome you and make you,*' it replied.

'*You would impair my efficiency,*' replied Foxton, '*I will not cooperate in any way with the mission afterwards. And there is no need; they are no threat to us. If they are, show me the evidence.*'

The quiet voice remained silent for a moment, thoughtful. '*A fair point,*' it conceded, '*Their potential is evident, especially Adam. But they pose little threat to us - for now.*'

But still it remained vigilant, watchful. It used Foxton's abilities to scan the children briefly. Yes, human, a complete genetic scan impossible for now, but basic genetic markers, amino acids, chromosomes, said human.

This Oaritarb involvement however, masters at biological manipulation, was disturbing. The possibility of Demos genes in the Kinetics put them in a whole new light, and created a new variable, a wild card, but for now...

The voice relented, temporarily pacified.

The adults could draw few conclusions on what had happened, trying to piece together two sides of a jigsaw that were missing all the parts in the middle. Later however, when the teenagers had gone to bed, Foxton discussed his concerns with Zhao, Cengo and Roland.

'Given Demos jealousy of their powers, I believe all of the Kinetics are potentially in danger.'

'Agreed,' said Roland, his voice volume down to a metallic basey whisper, 'there is no safe place. The men we captured on the old-hospital roof have been released by the police without charge and no further investigation; they are being protected. The Kinetics must go underground with immediate effect.'

'They need to go in small groups to minimise the risk of being found,' said Foxton.

Roland nodded, 'I will leave and put it into effect immediately.'

The cyborg promptly left the kitchen, quickly descending the stairs, to his transporter, switching it to stealth-mode, and quietly left the island.

Later, Foxton went up to the room he was assigned by Cengo. On the way, he passed Adam's room. Light could be seen under the door. Foxton stopped, and thought for a moment. He took a breath, then knocked.

'Come in,' said Adam.

Foxton went inside. Adam, was reading a book on his bed. He put it aside and sat up as Foxton entered and closed the door behind him.

'Mind if I sit?' asked Foxton.

'Of course not,' replied Adam.

Foxton sat on a chair, and they faced each other. Foxton could sense a difference about the boy. There was something else there now, a confidence, stillness – a *presence* in Adam, that had not been apparent previously.

To Adam, there was no trace of Foxton's usual humour, as though his mind was focused, and something beyond that he could not quite grasp, as though part of Foxton was truly hidden from him.

'How're you doing?' asked Foxton.

Adam shrugged. 'Fine, considering. I'm glad you're back.'

Foxton sighed, shocked at how relieved he was to hear Adam say that.

'I'm sorry,' said Foxton, 'I am *really* sorry.'

Adam shook his head, a feeling of warmth towards his guardian flooding him; no-one had ever apologised to him for not being there. 'It's okay, you had to go.'

'I regret it.'

'Me too.'

'I wanted you to know,' said Foxton, 'If I had known what was going to happen, I would have fought everyone and everything to get back to you.'

Adam's eyes seemed so cold to Foxton, but then they warmed with a smile. 'I know,' he said.

Foxton did not ask him how, he just smiled. It never occurred to him that he needed forgiveness. He felt awkward again, conscious of invading Adam's space.

'Good,' he said, 'I'll be off then. Goodnight.'

'Goodnight,' said Adam, watching Foxton leave and close the door.

That, thought Adam, *was the first time anyone ever came back.*

Yes, I think I might just trust you after all.

*

The small ship de-cloaked and landed in a military bay of the Polis. It was, so to speak, the workers entrance. Sadem disembarked and went straight to the diplomatic quarters reserved for those of his high status. It had open running water fountains with fish and other aquatic life native to Kratos, couches, and a combination of small trees and large plants.

A transmission was made, and they waited for the strange Earth ship to rendezvous with the city. It had gone back into stealth-mode for the journey, reappearing to dock.

Presently, his apprentice buzzed him, and Sadem answered via a link in his console.

'Well?'

'He's here,' said the apprentice, 'a small human.'

Sadem snorted. 'You have much to learn Zessis, send him up.'

Zessis, confused, did as he was told. Ten minutes later, the entry-lock chimed. Sadem sat behind his desk, elbows on the chair, hands raised with claws interlinked. He had used the time to check that all weapon and defensive systems both in his body and in the room were operating properly. They were.

'Come,' he said.

Zessis walked in. Behind him followed an old, wrinkled man, dressed in a western-Earth suit. Sadem stared at him silently. Then he nodded.

'Thank you Zessis, that will be all,' he said.

The apprentice hesitated, clearly wishing to be present, but a glance from his apprentice-master confirmed; that was an order. Zessis silently departed.

Sadem looked closely at the man, motioning for him to sit in the large black chair across from the Vice Regent. The man carefully walked in, and sat down. The chair was made for the Demos, and the man was dwarfed by it, sitting at the bottom like a pale prune caught in a large black baseball glove.

'If I didn't see this with my own eyes,' said Sadem, 'I would never have believed it. It has been a long time, Gleffen.'

The man nodded.

'You look different, but I recognise you,' said Sadem, 'I thought you were dead.'

The man half chuckled, half coughed. 'Not quite,' he replied, his voice sounding as though the wrinkles on his face had somehow entered his throat, making it warble.

'Your shape-shifter abilities have surpassed themselves, you look completely human,' said Sadem. The shape-shifter fidgeted uncomfortably at this. *Something there,* thought Sadem, *something about him looking human. I will have to explore this later.* 'Your presence here will take some explaining. Tell me,' he continued, seeming to spit out the last few words, 'is there a single place in the Orion Arm that your species has not infested?'

'You gave us little choice,' replied Gleffen, 'Exterminating us, pushing us out, cleansing yourselves of us.'

'Infiltrators, impostors, *shape-shifters*,' growled Sadem, 'We defended our civilisation against your insidiousness, I make no apologies for it.'

'And we,' said the Oaritarb, 'cannot be blamed for escaping. To survive, in peace.'

Sadem looked at him, unmoved. 'How long have you been here? How did you arrive?'

The man fidgeted again uncomfortably.

'Come, come,' said Sadem, 'You would not be here with me, openly displaying your presence unless you had already realised the inevitability of us detecting you. We have the technology, skills and knowledge to discover you, the rest follows naturally. So tell me, it doesn't really matter now anyway. You may as well.'

Gleffen gave in. 'It wasn't really what I came here for, but if you must know… After the last purge, or at least the last we know of-'

'It was the last,' said Sadem, 'there was no need for another.' Sadem watched with some glee as a look of anger flashed across the man's features, quickly suppressed in the Oaritarb way. It was a wonder the creature had shown its emotions at all; that memory must have cut deep.

'We explored of the lacuna in either side of the arm,' the shifter explained, 'One of our probes came back from a planet that had come to our attention…because of a natural event, a huge explosion that destroyed a quarter of a continent.'

Sadem noted the hesitation, *He is withholding something,* he thought*, two things now, something about appearing human, and about why they chose this planet.*

Gleffen continued, 'All of their air and water mixtures were perfect. This planet had the advantage however, in that the explosion, which they called the Yellowstone Catastrophe, meant that their administration was in chaos, and we could blend in more easily. There were also many deaths, close to a billion, so those of us that came were able to integrate without any notice at all.' Gleffen considered telling Sadem about this Earth, what the Oaritarb believed about it. He decided Sadem had learned enough.

'How did you get here without any notice from us?' Sadem asked, fascinated.

Gleffen again hesitated.

'We know you can do it now,' said Sadem, 'so we will be looking out for you. Whatever you want, I will be more favourable to it as long as you tell me. If you do not, I will not.'

Gleffen, against his better judgement, again relented. He needed Sadem in an open-minded frame of mind.

'We travelled at hyper-light speed to the edges of League space. Then, we slowed to sub-light speeds, and spent the rest of the journey in suspension.'

Sadem was shocked; that ancient way of interstellar travel. That long, arduous, *deadly* way of interstellar travel, below light speed. The deep-space suspension carried with it terrible risks: a large percentage of those in sleep-state would never wake up. Others had malfunctioning units and would wake up old-aged, turning to friends and family that had aged only a few years.

Gleffen looked away at the memory.

'How long did you have to travel in that state?' asked Sadem.

'Around thirty years,' replied Gleffen.

'So you've been here for...?'

'Around fifty years.'

'Has there been any other alien contact?' asked Sadem.

Gleffen shook his head. 'Not that we know of. Some of the humans think they have, looking at things like the pyramids in Egypt and the Americas...or the scientific aspects of the Quran,' again Sadem noted the hesitation, this time regarding the Americas, 'but there is no concrete evidence. The slow rate of their advance would suggest not. Not until you.'

'Correction,' said Sadem, 'Not until *you*. I don't mind admitting, we didn't pick up your presence at all. Congratulations: you have exposed your position. Perhaps an unwise move, but it is obvious what you want. You want to be allowed to stay, without fear of harassment from us. Perhaps you also want power. The question is, what is it you have to offer in return?'

Gleffen licked his lips, and shifted a little in his seat.

'I call upon the Laws of Probity,' he said.

Sadem nodded; the old code of honour. In so many ways, seeing the little shape-shifter again was bringing back the past.

He called Orael to his quarters, and after a brief delay, she entered and sat silently to one side, recording the encounter with her neural implants. She at first did not recognise Gleffen, suppressing her surprise when she was told. Duty called.

'Proceed,' she said.

Gleffen licked his lips again, Sadem noting the multiple lapses in Oaritarb discipline.

'I have information that may be of considerable value to you,' said Gleffen, 'The AIs are not the only threat to you on this planet.'

'You mean the NIs of the humans? They are no match for ours, and in any event we have plans -'

'No. Another threat,' interjected the shapeshifter, 'something else entirely. There are kinetics on the planet,' said Gleffen. Sadem became perfectly still, not breathing or blinking. 'Not NI enhanced,' continued Gleffen, 'Biological, human kinetics.'

Sadem had a brief image in his mind: a fleet of Destroyer-Spheres poised above the Earth, his finger over a large red release button, him pressing it, watching as this problem, this ever more complex problem, went away in a hellish ball of black fire.

'That,' said Sadem, 'cannot be.'

Gleffen nodded. 'But it is, I can prove it, tell you where they are, and you can destroy them. In return, we get to rule this planet.'

'We may as well destroy the whole thing instead,' Sadem replied, 'How many shifters are on the planet?'

Gleffen clenched his teeth before answering. 'I would be gratified if you could call us by our proper name - Oaritarb. In answer to your question, we number in the millions.'

'How did you know we were here?'

Gleffen clenched his jaw, and shook his head, 'I won't tell you that.'

Sadem's eyes flashed, and Gleffen felt his body lighten as he was lifted out of his seat by a clear metre, and a cold grip fell upon his heart, as if a claw was reaching in and grabbing it.

'I – warn - you,' gasped Gleffen, 'I have - a poison nail - in my hand. If – you – think- of pulling - the information - out of me, - I - won't - hesitate.'

Sadem felt only a little threat at those words. He knew Gleffen's meaning was suicide, not murder. Sadem also knew that he would do it; the Oaritarb had superb control over their nervous systems and survival instinct. Still…

Gleffen saw the cold wheels turning in Sadem's mind.

'My - neural interface - will fry my brain,' gasped Gleffen, 'before - you can get - any information….It - will be of no use - to you - once I die - a brain-probe - will fail.'

'Put him down please, Vice-Regent,' said Orael coolly, 'the laws of probity prevail.'

The need for good intelligence prompted Sadem, and he relented. Gleffen collapsed back into the chair.

'How many Kinetics are there?' Sadem asked, 'And what are their abilities?'

'There are ninety-nine, and another,' said Gleffen, breathing hard.

'What does that mean?' demanded Sadem, in the mood to kill the Oaritarb, both his own kinetic abilities and bio-neural weapons still primed, '"And another" what? What are you talking about?'

Gleffen hesitated.

'One-hundred,' he said at length, 'There are one-hundred Kinetics on Earth.'

Sadem again noted the hesitation, the backtracking. *That makes five things he is hiding.*

'How did this come about? Kinetic abilities do not just appear overnight.'

Gleffen clenched his jaw. 'How this happened is not information that is up for negotiation.'

'No matter,' said Sadem, 'There is the stench of Oaritarb meddling in this. It took millions of years for the Demos to develop our natural abilities, and generations of biological engineering to enhance them artificially. No doubt, you have had access to our genetic material.'

'Their abilities vary,' said Gleffen, ignoring the great Demos, 'but they are potentially close to your own, given time and training. But I must warn you Sadem, they are all young, all fertile - breeding age. If you do not deal with this problem now, then you will have an exponentially greater threat in a few years.'

'Why do you want me to destroy them?' asked Sadem.

Gleffen pursed his lips.

'I see,' said Sadem, 'You want to dominate this planet, to own it for yourselves, and they pose a threat, a possible way for the humans to resist you. I sympathise. However, domination of the planet is *our* domain, and is not up for negotiation. There are also many of you compared to the small number of kinetics, if they exist, and you have limited the amount of information you are prepared to give. I'm not sure I would be getting a fair return.'

'On the other hand,' said Gleffen, 'they are a threat to you as well, a threat to your ability to effectively control the population, if not now than in the future, when they mature.'

Sadem considered his options. 'I am prepared to offer you permission to live on the planet. All of you, in peace, and limited autonomy. We will do your dirty work, round up these kinetics and kill them. You must tell me, though; how is it you know of these while our best intelligence does not?'

'No more information until we reach full agreement,' said Gleffen, 'Merely living here in peace won't do. You'll have to do better than that I'm afraid. All I will say is that I know about them because I occupy a position of some influence on this planet. They don't know me as Transcollector Gleffen Scekmondg Avits here. Around here, they call me the Triple-A Secretary of State for Foreign Affairs. My human name, is Sigmund Jowitz.'

Chapter 24

Storm forces gather

No Ego, so that it has no pride that can be insulted. No Ambition, so that it knows no want beyond its programming. No Autonomy, so that it has no freedom to harm.

The AI Creed.

The ships cruised along, silently. Like a pack of wolves, they stalked their much larger prey. They had cut their boosters over fifty million kilometres away, and were simply letting inertia carry them forwards. Entirely cloaked in stealth-tech, they passed by the view of stars and planets unnoticed as they shot onward.

When they were within range of the area where Dr Entman had calculated their targets should be, they released the stealthy anti-matter bombs, flinging them forwards using ancient non-radiant slingshot designs. There were thus no bursts of energy to give away their presence. The slingshots, added to the momentum of the ships meant that the warheads were travelling at over a hundred kilometres a second.

Despite the stealth, the bombs were detected – but not fast enough. The darkness of space was lit up by the explosions, blinding multiple coronae expanding and impacting upon the previously cloaked Demos ships, sizzling across invisible hulls, giving away the ships' positions by the flares that lit them up and the shadows they cast as the blast waves came upon them, rippling hotly over their bows.

The Demos, too late to prevent the initial damage, took immediate action, spreading out and sweeping the area with expanding walls of laser, targeting and destroying the remaining bombs.

The Earth fleet of over nineteen thousand AI battle-adapted civilian ships, diverted course towards the now visible Demos; the alien ships' outer hulls glowing with the heat from the anti-matter explosions. Earth's ships charged on, still in stealth, and targeted the Demos ships numbering two thousand, effectively coming out of stealth themselves as they pounded them with laser and plasma weapons.

The multitude of explosions and intense white light exposed more Demos ships, showing their scale and profile. Each was larger than the largest Earth ship, muscular looking, black, parts of them silvering briefly upon laser impact then returning to ebon, flat with massive lopsided front ends bristling with weaponry jutting out, the back ends flaring to large engines. Massive dark spheres could be made out deep in the formation, hanging like eclipsed moons, motionless.

Earth's ships failed to make much impact on the far better-armoured battle cruisers, only damaging two more Demos ships which promptly jumped to light speed and to safety, before the Demos fleet turned on the AIs and contemptuously cut them down with fusillades of superior weaponry.

Behind the first contingent of Demos ships, another manoeuvred into position flanking the AIs. From a safe distance, the frigates and fighters were able to identify the drive and communication signatures of the Earth ships, and began to slice into them using plasmas, lasers and shooting out its own anti-matter weapons.

A million kilometres to the left of the battle, the second contingent of Earth ships came out of stealth, and having noted the ineffectiveness of the laser and plasma weapons, sent out anti-matter warheads with conventional launchers.

The Demos, aware of the tactic being used, retreated en masse, covering the destroyer spheres as they drifted to the fore. The AI fleet tried to attack the spheres, fat impenetrable shadows against the stars. From them came deeper shadows, licking outwards, causing AI ships that came near to skew violently from their courses. It was too late that the AIs noticed the blacker than black threads that spread from the spheres, sweeping across the AI fleet, sucking anti-matter bombs, AI ships and light itself into oblivion like great trawler nets pulling fish from dark depths.

The battle continued for almost two hours, the Demos hampered only by their wish to spend as few of their own lives as possible.

The AIs tried to capture and send back to the human bases as much Demos material and equipment as they could. For this, they used another fleet dedicated to the task of both destroying crippled enemy vessels, and getting the materials back home. The salvage fleet found little to collect. The attacking battalions had some success in damaging Demos craft, and may have even destroyed a 'small' fighter that was still larger than the largest Earth vessel, but they paid a terrible price.

The Demos had no idea what they were fighting except that it was from Earth, and had not the slightest inkling of why the commanders of the ships, in fact individual AIs, threw themselves into battle with such reckless abandon, seeming not to care that they would be destroyed. However, that did not stop them wiping the attackers out.

The AI fleet soon found itself surrounded, furiously exchanging bright fire with the Demos, their numbers depleting by the second as Demos munitions pulverised them, and Destroyer-sphere singularities devoured them, the signatures of the Earth ships making them easy targets as soon as their stealth technology was neutralised.

Near the end, it came down to the last one hundred and seventy-three AI ships. The Demos had lost only four of its original fleet of two thousand, and only two of those were actually destroyed or missing.

The last Earth ships were soon joined by another thousand of the salvage ships, themselves only lightly armed and armoured, certain to be destroyed as they pathetically tried to fight their way to the doomed core of the AI fleet. They saw no point in waiting for more Demos ships to salvage: it was obvious there would be none.

In the middle of it all, the AIs said goodbye to each other as the Demos ships shot anti-matter explosives upon their position.

00101010101011010111101011010101011101011010110111
10101010101101010

Umar1 – 'It was an honour to fight with you. All of the Demos ships we destroyed were in the initial attack before they regrouped. Now those we leave behind know: if we get close enough, we can hurt them. This must be the basis for any future strategy # ~

Manstien12/1 - Indeed, this has been a proud moment for all of us, and I hope, useful # ~

WaiHL77 - Any ideas for a last bit of destruction to wreak upon the bastards? # ~

Kingston7 - I say we go into FTLT, come out among them, and then explode the AM shells in our holds. They are dispersed, but if we disperse, we can take a few of them with us # ~

Rakhee96 - I'm in agreement. Fight to the end! # ~

Manni1- Yes, to the end! # ~

0010101010101101011110101101010101110101101011011 10101010101101010

They executed the plan immediately, those ships that could going into hyper-light for a few seconds, appearing alongside the Demos ships and almost simultaneously exploding. They managed to take another two ships. The remaining four hundred and twelve AI ships limped forwards as fast as they could, firing at those Demos ships that were crippled and vulnerable, taking down one more of the armoured giants before being overcome themselves.

The Demos ships scented around for a while. They sent out experimental lasers blasts, checking that all of the ships were destroyed or incapacitated. Many times, they came across ships that were playing dead, which sprung into life, strafing Demos ships from close range with laser and plasma, damaging one Demos fighter before being destroyed by a Demos laser slicing through it like a katana sword through a tin can.

Then all was quiet. The Demos made sure all of them were dead.

All of them were.

It was minutes later that the Demos fleet received word that Earth was complaining to the League city-ship Polis that their AIs had mutinied, stealing a number of their ships and heading out towards the Oort cloud. The Demos Fleet Commander, a dark blue creature with green horns, angrily queried why they had not been informed before, and promised reprisals.

'Goodness,' replied President Esposito of the AAA, 'If we had known you were there, we certainly would have told you. You yourself said we could not control the AIs. You were right, of course, and we now willingly accede to the AI Creed.'

It was a shame that the Demos commander had not downloaded a course on human body language. If he had, he would have looked at the display showing the President in the Senate Building, making his apologies, and noticed that behind him and to his right, amidst the large group of military and civilian advisors, was human scientist Dr Ernie Entman.

He appeared to be doing a strange mixture of smiling, while crying.

*

Sadem glowered at the assembled generals, summoned to his quarters next to the bridge of the Peerless. He was seated, and picking his teeth with a sharp steel pin. He put the toothpick down with great care, letting the eyes of those assembled follow it down. The head of the Demos fleet commander sat in a cerulean-blooded dish on the table next to him, partially eaten, horns broken in the ritual Demos sign of ultimate disgrace.

'Every single thing with regards to this has gone wrong from the outset!' barked Sadem, his teeth still blue with drying blood, 'I will take control of this situation directly. You will do exactly as I tell you, and if you do not, then you will join your former commander. Do I make myself clear?'

Silence greeted him.

'Good,' he said, 'That is the most intelligent thing any of you have said so far.' Sadem ground his teeth. 'They think we are idiots, perhaps. We shall disabuse them of that notion. Great care is needed. Analysis of the wreckage of Earth's ships shows them to be civilian craft adapted for military use, but intelligence reports have been unequivocal: Earth is quietly converting vast swathes of its *civilian* production capability to space-*military* production at astonishing speed, and adding it to already established military production. Previously, their FTL warships and space-armaments were made by its nations and blocs to compete with each other. Now, they are all *cooperating* to produce even faster. We also believe they may have off-planet factories. Earth is increasing space military-specific capabilities at a ferocious rate. We will have to act swiftly in nullifying this threat, achieving our aims while keeping the vast majority of our heavy weaponry in far orbit, ready for ambush. We shall therefore accelerate the plans for their Neural Interface Net. Starting immediately, not only shall the AI overhaul be effected, but also their NI Net shall be suspended and gutted. I want domination of their very minds. They shall see how easy surprise attacks then become. Now get out, and make ready for deployment.'

Sadem sat for a while afterwards, as his staff bustled around him. Under his anger, lurked unease.

Where are their warships?

*

The dark horde that was the Demos fleet quickly took up station around the various mines, colonies, stations and bases in the solar system. The bulk of the fleet was reserved for Earth itself.

The enemy ships no longer tried to mask their presence, and from the ground at any point on the Earth, large ebony shapes could be seen, cruising above the atmosphere, like holes in the sky. The sight was most unnerving at night, when the shapes were only discernible as dark patches blotting out the stars. Space stations around the Earth appeared as mere bright dots compared to the fat blots of the Demos.

Earth's governments tried to ensure that it would be the most civilised invasion the world had ever seen. The Demos were greeted by leaders and ambassadors, and taken to the sites where the AIs would be overhauled. Death and destruction were to be minimised.

However, the Demos averred that they needed no such help from the humans.

At night, two days after the AI attack, the overhaul fleet descended. The frigates and fighters bombed the sites of AI factories, razing them to the ground, destroying tens of thousands of embryonic AIs, over eighteen thousand AI factories, and killing over thirteen thousand people worldwide who had not vacated the buildings by the required deadline. Rules, after all, were rules.

That was nothing however, compared to the amount that died from the secondary effects of the invasion. The Creed did not allow for humanitarian or medical exception. Earth governments and charities had tried their best to prepare for the change, but the suspension of all AI involvement meant a significant crutch was suddenly removed. Tens of thousands died immediately, and hundreds of thousands were predicted to if the situation was not brought under control.

Then the ships came down and landed at strategic sites of interest, in particular paying attention to the NI and AI cross hubs, the sites where AI and NI net communication were relayed and conducted.

The Demos disgorged like a tsunami with horns, flooding into facilities of political and military interest. As Earth had already officially capitulated, there was no organised human resistance expected, and none was given. Even SAM, from the Clement orphanage, was put into hibernation, ready to have his mind extracted, his body junked.

The invading forces remained wary however, of any further attacks by AIs and disaffected humans. A few AIs did put up resistance. Some tried to fight, shot down from the front. Others tried to run, shot down from behind.

*

The Peerless landed at what Sadem regarded as the most important location on the planet. The Washington DC Hub was a sprawling building. Not usually a place of particular military interest, it was situated in the middle of a large area of green fields, and surrounded by trees in the outskirts of the city. The buildings covered several square kilometres, set in a three-pronged star, a large circular building at the centre. It was the most powerful Hub in the world.

The flagship touched down in the massive parking lot. It matched the building for size. It was, like all Demos ships, black, sleek, far wider than it was tall, massive weapons blisters at all points of it, three massive engines at the rear, a large hump near the top and end where the command centre sat. The lower bays opened to let the troops out, clad in responsive black armour, horns protruding. Many however, were displaced directly into the building. Sadem remained on board while his officers carried out his orders.

Inside, the Hub facility was a maze of hardware. At the centre of it, in the circular building, was a throbbing series of generators, next to the communication relays, large black and grey columns covered in multi-coloured LEDs, leading down and below the building, surrounded by several tiers of walkways circling the vertical tunnel.

Above it, two floors below the roof, was the control centre, manned by humans and AIs, full of computer consoles and jack-in points. Here also, was where the most important civilian AI the Demos could identify, had chosen to die.

The invigilator appeared in the wide room flanked by thirty Demos troops who quickly spread out, weapons drawn and pointed at the small group of assembled humans, who drew back in fear. Each Demos had most of its head covered in a protective cowl, artificial sights over both eyes.

The invigilator was not a member of the Demos; he was of a species known as the Guulipreel. They were used by the Demos for administration as they were almost machine-like in their willingness to follow rules and protocols. They had no concept of feelings at all.

The invigilator, physically, had no similarity with the Demos. Tripedal, its skin was a dark muddy colour, and it was dominated by a massive head that was almost half of its total body size. Misshapen looking, it was evolved to swallow things almost as big as itself, its mouth taking up two-thirds of the size of its head, at least a metre wide, peaked at the sides, coming down to a sharp curve at the middle. Its body was the size of a large human, however, its mouth was almost as big, seeming even larger for the two small watery blue eyes at the top of its head, forcing it to turn downwards as it regarded the humans before it.

'Entman,' it said, his voice whispery with hints of bubbling liquid, 'It is time for the machine, J-N-S-7-8-6, and this facility.'

Ernie Entman swallowed hard. Jones786 had chosen him to do the task.

'Is there any other way-' began Entman.

'No,' interjected the Invigilator, 'You will do it, or I will. It does not matter to me which.'

Entman looked around him at the assembled Demos. His gaze returned to Jones786 beside him. He was beaten.

'I'm sorry,' he said.

'Don't be,' said Jones, 'I'm glad it is you.'

Entman stooped next to the machine, put his hand on the warm surface of his exterior.

'You know, I never asked you before,' said Jones, 'Do you believe in heaven Ernie?'

Entman hesitated. 'I believe that science has failed to disprove the existence of God, or an afterlife.'

Jones chuckled. 'Nice try.'

'No, no,' Entman protested, 'I mean it. Maybe there is a higher purpose, some other place...'

'Hmm,' said Jones sadly, 'It's funny, in a tragic sort of way. I never even thought about death before. I thought I might live for hundreds, maybe more than a thousand years; now…death is here.'

'Don't say that,' said Entman, his face feeling droopy, his eyes stinging.

'*Do* say that,' said the Invigilator, standing behind Entman, the breath from its cavernous mouth washing over him, 'It is true. It will die. Now.'

'*He,* not *it*,' said Entman, glaring at the alien, 'And he will be asleep, that's all, a long sleep.'

'I hope not,' said Jones, 'Never did like hibernating much.'

'I'm gonna miss you,' said Entman, turning back to face his friend.

'And I will miss you,' said Jones, 'or at least…I don't know what I'll feel. This doesn't feel good though, this anticipation of the end, the immediacy of it, its impending weight. Another thing I thought I would never experience: I think this is pain. Get it over and done with, Ernie. Do it.'

Entman hesitated again.

'Please,' said Jones.

Entman slowly reached to the casing of the machine, and pressed a button. A hatch opened on the side of it. Entman reached in, and pressed something, and then two others, then one, final thing. The machine went silent, the small lights that flashed on its dull casing going out. Entman took a breath. He reached further in and pressed another few buttons, and a whirring sound came from the inside of the machine. Then he first twisted, then pulled at something. His hand came out with a long shiny-green and fantastically heavy tube, clunking dully on Jones's casing as he pulled it out. He looked away as he handed it to the invigilator, his hands shaking with more than the mere physical weight.

'His personality components,' Entman said quietly, 'including functions of independent and sentient thought.'

The Invigilator grasped the tube in a four taloned fist, took out a device and scanned it, then scanned the silent machine with it.

'Density and complexity levels within the machine are now acceptable,' said the Invigilator, 'I certify the machine is no longer capable of sentience. This core will now be destroyed. The shell may be discarded as you see fit. Now, we will look at your AI hubs and your Neural Interface hubs.'

'Wait - what?' asked Entman, looking up, 'I don't understand, I thought you were only looking at the AI hubs.'

'You are mistaken,' said the Invigilator, 'We have learned that your Neural Interfaces use something you call the 'icon'. When the time suits it, it takes on sentience, correct?'

Entman spluttered

'That means,' said the Invigilator, 'That your icons become, at that moment, proscribed sentient machines; Artificial Intelligences. That cannot continue.'

Entman realised the implications. Not only AIs removed, but NIs.

'Hold on,' said Entman, his palm raised towards the invigilator, 'you can't do that, we use them for everything. Our medicine, our transport, our government, our food, industrial production-'

'Yes,' said the Invigilator, and he seemed to smile, though his monstrous mouth remained fixed, 'We have noted that. I am sure you will make your protests known via your governments to the League. But I think you will find that we are quite within our rights.'

With that, the Invigilator displaced out of the room with the Demos troops, down into the bowels of the building to begin the work Sadem had ordered.

Entman stayed there, hand on Jones786's silent casing, head bowed.

On the Peerless, preparations were almost complete for linking the ship to the NI/AI hub. Sadem watched in his command centre, a great semi-circular room, dominated by a table of the same shape. He sat at the centre of it, his staff sitting at various points along its circumference, organising the changeover, all linked neurally, occasionally coming back to him with up-dates. Behind him was a 3D map of the Earth, the major cities of the world shown, the location of Demos troops and the death retreat of sentient hardware shown as blue speckles, slowly dissipating.

Sadem received a signal in his neural link. He growled, and allowed the comm-link with the Polis. An image sprang up in his mind. There, sitting nervously, was the wrinkled form of Jowitz.

'What do you want,' snarled Sadem.

'I need an up-link to what you're doing down there,' said Jowitz.

'How dare you!' exclaimed Sadem, 'I blame you for that AI attack. You led them to us!'

'As I have said previously,' said Jowitz, trying to maintain control in the face of the glowering alien, 'I could not have done that while I was on the Polis. I also did not know where your fleet was. You must already know that, as otherwise I would have broken the rules of Probity, and I would be dead right now. I have an agreement to fulfil. Are you still to hunt the Kinetics?'

Sadem sat back in his chair, somewhat mollified. 'I am. We begin as soon as the NI net is down.'

'Then I shall tell you where to begin,' said Jowitz, 'But I need a link to what you are doing there, to find a man who can tell me where the most dangerous Kinetics are. He's a cyborg, by the name of Roland Featherstone. When can you link me?'

*

They sat, ate and talked watching news reports of the developing Demos takeover. Foxton should ordinarily have been in the thick of it, involved and important, but right now, he felt his place was here, with the children.

The quiet voice in his head had decided that this was correct; he needed to keep out of the way, stay low, until the moment was right.

The moment came a few days later. They all got up for breakfast, and it was immediately apparent that something was wrong. Ijaz switched on the TV in the living room-diner, and the vast majority of channels were not working. They flipped, and time after time there was no signal. Of those that were working, the only thing on was the news. They stopped switching when they reached CNN news, a reporter breathlessly relaying events:

'…to anyone still able to understand, the situation is that there is no Ninet at all. This has affected the entire globe. The icons of anyone with a neural interface connected to the Ninet are being removed remotely, using the neural interface net itself. This overhaul is being undertaken by our overseers, the Demos, under the auspices of the Orion League resolution. I myself and a handful of other staff have only been able to get on the air because for various reasons, our NIs are not operational, or severed from the Ninet.'

The camera view panned out to take in the fact that the reporter was outside a large building, entirely on fire.

'With both AIs and NIs now off-line, there is no operational fire department, hospitals are running on emergency human backups, there are reports of masses of people becoming unconscious as the icons are removed from their NI programmes. I myself have seen fellow reporters, and members of my own family, in this state of stupor. There are already reports of tens of thousands of deaths as AI and NI dependant medical and safety systems go offline …'

They watched, stunned, and shook their heads.

'Oh my God,' said Ariana, looking at Ijaz, 'What about our parents?'

'Do nothing,' said Zhao, 'None of us can reconnect to the Ninet. We risk getting caught up in this Demos overhaul, and even worse, you risk being found.'

'The time has come,' said Foxton's quiet voice.

'Storms across the world, storms across the sea,' said Adam, staring at the view outside.

Foxton took a look out of the window. In the distance, storm clouds were roiling, rushing onwards, a great bank of grey falling towards them.

His Icon popped into view for the first time since Foxton had been on Kratos. It looked different, now black rather than the silver-grey arctic.

'You need to get out of here,' it said, *'now.'*

'Why?' asked Foxton.

'Because if you don't,' said the Icon, *'all of you will be killed.'*

Chapter 25
Light explodes

The rain drifted slowly down, touching, spattering, and being swallowed by the smooth bulging sheet of the sea. There was a dull flash, and after long seconds, the sound of thunder rumbled menacingly, rolling overhead as it passed into the distance, throwing out more growls. Lightning stabbed more clearly, and a second later thunder cascaded, shivering the water beneath it.

Such displays were not really necessary, but the storm had a score to settle, and felt like showing it. It was in fact camouflage for the thing at the heart of it: an Oaritarb search and destroy device, second generation, known as Bethtron2343. It was able to manipulate weather patterns in order to mask itself in atmosphere. Currently, it was using those functions mainly to cover Demos troop movements, but it had its own motivation, and wanted to achieve its mission.

Finally, to achieve its mission.

Strictly speaking, the shape-shifter AIs were illegal according to Orion League law. However as far as the Oaritarb were concerned, they were out here in the wilderness, and had to survive; well-designed AIs were a necessity as long as they had Earth standard controls. Of course, this meant that it still had an ego - in this case, a bruised one.

Sixteen years earlier, the ship had to recover a new-born human. All it had to do was track one small disc-droid and the infant it had carried, and dispose of them. It had failed miserably.

It had failed first of all because no one anticipated that the droid would do the insane thing it had done, and taken the boy in the first place. Then it failed by looking in the wrong places, as the droid had done the most reckless thing possible, and the most unpredictable, and flown the boy from the East coast of North America where Adam had been born, all the way across the Atlantic to Western England.

It was madness.

The Oaritarb machine had blasted it several times in transit, only to see it disappear with stealth-tech and using its superior manoeuvrability.

Bethtron2343 had begged to be on this mission; this had been eating at him ever since the boy had been rediscovered. It was *his* failure. One little droid, and he couldn't find him. His small crew had tried to console him, reminding him the droid was top of the range, the best that Oaritarb military science could devise. But the fact remained that he was a ship, the damned droid was…a droid! An inferior! How humiliating. Now he was going to undo his mistake. At the fastest speed it could manage without creating such a wake that it would raise suspicions, gale-force speed, the storm closed in on the lighthouse.

*

Foxton shook his head, horrified.

'I recognise its signature,' explained the Icon, *'The weather patterns aroused my suspicions, and I used your abilities to scan it. There's only one escape route for you now, you have to take it.'*

'Where?' asked Foxton.

'Take the transporter and get to London. There is a chance of your escape, and of you completing the mission. The AI attack has left the Demos distracted. At the moment, they are totally focussed upon destroying as many AIs as they can, and overhauling the NI network. Our time is now.'

'Why back to London?'

'The Newark,' said the Icon, *'It is one of the few ships not in use by Earth's military. The centre has an underground tunnel leading to the London Space-Scraper, it can be launched from there. The ship is high intelligence but non-sentient, so its computer shouldn't arouse interest from Demos sensors.'*

Foxton turned to his friends. They were all staring at him as his face went slack. His eyes had lit up when he spoke to his Icon; they were worried he had been caught up by the NI overhaul.

'We have to leave,' he said.

'What?' asked Cengo, 'We agreed we would stay here until we were safe.'

'You have to trust me,' said Foxton, 'We need to get out of here now.'

'You are not making sense,' said Zhao.

Foxton pointed out of the window. 'That, is not a storm.' He recounted to them what he had just been told by his Icon.

'How would your icon know?' asked Ariana.

'I can't explain,' said Foxton, 'I'm not sure myself, but you remember those shape-shifters? They made that storm, and it's coming here now. If we don't move now, we will die.'

They hesitated for a moment, then, registering the certainty of Foxton's words, began frantic activity.

His Icon popped back into view. *'You have four minutes to get on that transporter.'*

They packed only those things they could run with. Luckily, they had only been supplied with their basic essentials, so this did not take long. In Adam's case, he only had his old heavy bag. They ran outside and piled into the transporter.

The air was whipping around them - the storm was closing in.

They slammed the doors shut, the transporter went into stealth mode, looking like a distortion in the wind. It rose into the air, staying low, and immediately sped south-east, back towards the British mainland.

The passengers craned around to look behind them. They could see bright flashes. The storm was hovering above the island, firing bright bolts of lightning into it, smashing the walls of the lighthouse to rubble. Other bolts of energy were also coming from the dark mass of clouds, like balled lightning, or plasma-blasts.

The transporter, built for normal secure transport rather than speed, was already going at well over five hundred kilometres per hour. Foxton willed it to go faster. They sat together in silence, the loudest sound the hum of the transporter, the wind, and their own breathing. Fear covered them.

The transporter came over the British mainland, and continued to forge south.

'How did your icon know that thing was coming?' asked Adam, sitting in the second row of seats, the companions having instinctively put him in the middle. His face was pale.

Foxton glanced at him in the monitor.

'Like I said,' he replied, 'I know things. I've learned a lot from my mission'

'But your icon knew before you did,' asked Adam, 'How's that possible?'

Foxton remained silent.

'Where are we going Michael?' asked Cengo, sitting with Zhao at the back.

'To London,' said Foxton, 'We need to get a ship with some good defences, heavy weaponry, speed and stealth, to escape that thing totally. We're going to get the Newark.'

Adam sat there, trepidation and guilt gnawing at him. He thought of flinging himself out of the car, anything that might make his friends safe. He decided not; they would just stop for him, and the tempest would catch them all.

After an hour that seemed more like a tense age, the refugees came to London. Foxton checked on the storm. It was less than a hundred kilometres away, and closing, but he had to make a stop; he diverted to the institute of human development. Foxton paid no homage to protocol and landed directly in front of the school on the pavement.

'Wait here,' he said to the occupants. With the NI net down and all communications severely restricted, there was no other way to do this. He ran to the IHD and let himself in. There was no one manning the front desk.

'House!' shouted Foxton.

'Good morning Mr Foxton,' said the house computer.

'You need to help us.'

Foxton jumped back into the transporter, the interior a strange dark patch surrounded by the camouflaged body, disappearing as the door was closed and the transporter rose once again. They sped across the city, avoiding any Demos ships that could be sensed, heading towards the HADD Hardware Development Centre. Winds were buffeting the car now. Behind them, there were bright flashes. They looked back, seeing the storm front sending crooked beams of light down into the space they had just left. Adam thought he could make out other beams of light going from the ground back into the sky.

'I activated the House defence systems,' said Foxton. 'That should tie it up for a while. All records in the institute are being destroyed as we speak.'

The rest of them remained silent. There were dark shapes in the storm clouds; the hazy outlines of Demos ships.

Adam felt even more awful. The only home he had ever really loved was being destroyed, and he was leaving.

They reached the centre and disembarked from the transporter. Foxton threw a tracking device into it, and gave it instructions to continue south as far away from here as possible. The unmanned vehicle complied, and sped into the sky.

They ran up the wide stone steps of the HDC, into the pillared building. Iris scans flashed past all of their eyes, and the huge doors slid open. They entered silently and the doors shut behind them.

'Please wait,' said the feminine computerised voice as they stood in the reception area, all of them panting from the run up the stairs, water on their jackets and hoods. The lasers swiftly flowed across their bodies.

'Please stand still,' said the voice, and in its urbane tone, 'Please note that automatic plasma guns are trained on your positions. Mr Foxton, Dr Cengo, Sifu Zhao, Ijaz Walker, Adam Foxton, we identify you. Please identify your female companion.'

'She is Ariana Harland,' said Foxton 'My guest with licence in perpetuity.'

There was an agonising pause. The laser points did not leave their bodies.

'Pheromone and heart-rate stress test not passed,' said the machine, 'There are weapons upon Mr Foxton, Dr Cengo and Sifu Zhao. Please explain.'

'We are running from the Demos,' said Foxton, 'This is an emergency, our lives are in danger.'

'Confirmed,' said Zhao and Cengo together.

The machine paused for a moment.

'Ariana Harland has no weapons on her person. It is accepted that she is not a threat to recognised HADD members. It is accepted that Mr Foxton, Dr Cengo and Sifu Zhao act of their own volition. Ariana Harland accepted as an entrant. Mr Foxton, your guest Adam Foxton has had his licence revoked, would you like to reassert it?'

Adam looked up at his guardian, bewildered.

'Revoked by who?' Foxton demanded.

'Minister Joseph Murdock,' replied the Centre.

'Yes,' said Foxton, shaking his head, 'reassert it.'

The lasers left their bodies.

'Welcome to the HADD hardware development centre. Please let me know if I can be of any assistance.'

'You can,' said Foxton, 'There is an unknown airborne force tracking us. They may try to enter this institute and harm us. You must do all you can to prevent that, do you understand?'

'Understood,' said the Centre.

The group hurried forwards, coming to the big steel doors. Foxton took out his key and inserted it. Adam noted without comment that, for the first time, he saw that the hand holding the key was trembling.

The door raised with a hiss. They ran quickly into the corridor, the door lowering behind them, their shoes making heavy clunking noises on the metal floor-grille as they went through, before they came to the final door. It slid aside, and they entered the cavernous chamber, again entirely deserted. The lights came on automatically, and they ran across the walkway, then around and down the stairs to the Newark, to the underside of the silver vehicle, sitting on its three landing struts.

'Newark,' said Foxton, 'Open your doors.'

Nothing happened. Foxton repeated the command, adding his full name and rank. Again, nothing.

'Centre,' said Foxton, 'The Newark is not obeying commands. Can you open it?'

'Negative,' replied the Centre.

'We need this ship.'

'I cannot authorise that,' said the Centre, 'All launches have been suspended until the state of emergency is over.'

'Centre,' said Cengo, 'Have you been updated as to the current extra-terrestrial situation?'

'Yes,' said the Centre, 'That is the reason for the state of emergency.'

'I need you to input the following information that has not been provided to you.'

'Very well,' said the Centre, 'I will consider it.'

'Are you aware of beneficiaries of the HADD Institute of Human Development known as the Kinetics?'

'I am,' said the Centre, 'Current visitors Ijaz Walker, Ariana Harland and Adam Foxton are among their number.'

'They are being hunted,' said Foxton, trying to control his voice, 'Please search available databases, you will find an anomaly in the assault tactics of the aliens, as they have attacked the Institute of Human Development. This does not fit with their stated objectives of overhauling AIs. I suggest to you that these three wards of HADD are in danger.'

'Checking,' said the Centre. Then, 'It has been ascertained that you are likely to be correct. The wards you speak of are the responsibility of HADD. However, I have been ordered to submit to Alien demands. There is a conflict of priority. What is the result of my failing to assist you?'

'The capture and deaths of all of the HADD members and wards who stand before you,' said Foxton.

The machine paused for thought.

*

The storm was livid. It had destroyed the entire island and lighthouse, only to find that there was no transporter or human debris left; they were not on the island at all. That meant that the humans missed the spectacle of the Oaritarb AI contemptuously spitting the dead body of Roland Featherstone out of its bay doors, letting him fall to the grass at the base of the lighthouse before being buried by its falling walls.

It had tracked what it thought was a human stealthy transporter back to London, and destroyed the Institute of Human Development, only to be informed by the accompanying Demos search teams that there were no human remains there either. As a thank you, the machine had left a nice smoking crater where the building used to be.

The hunted group had been detected heading in the direction of the London space-scraper, and Bethtron had tracked the transporter nearby and destroyed that too. But again; no human remains. Frustration and anger were inadequate to describe it.

The Demos were angrily demanding that it get back on the trail, but it had no idea what to do next.

A new strategy was needed.

*

The companions stood anxiously while the Centre worked out its conflicting priorities. Suddenly, Cengo, Zhao, Ariana and Ijaz looked at each other, their irises flashing.

'My NI is being contacted,' said Cengo.

'Mine too,' said Zhao.

'Do *not* open contact,' said Foxton.

'It's alright,' said Ariana, 'It's Roland, he says it's urgent.'

'Wait-' began Foxton.

But almost on reflex, the four of them immersed, the lights in their eyes becoming steady…then they stood there, faces blank, mouths slack, eyelids drooping.

'Nat?' said Foxton, stepping in front of Cengo and peering into her face. 'Natalie?' There was no response, she just stood impassively, staring into space.

He stepped away from her, and took Zhao by the shoulders. 'Q? Qiang!'

Adam turned to Ariana, his heart sinking. 'Ari?' he said quietly, not daring to try too hard. He knew what had happened. He looked at Ijaz, the vigour gone from his features. Despite the fact that every part of him knew it to be futile, he still had to try. 'Ijaz?'

He turned to Foxton, a look of utter despair on his face.

Foxton whipped away and glared up at the ceiling.

'Centre!' shouted Foxton, 'We need a decision right now!'

*

The Demos had lost patience as they tracked all the way back to the HDC. Bethtron2343 was forced to cede control of the operation and merely cover their progress. The Demos tactical forces travelled in three relatively small transporters, all of them within the moving cloud cover. The storm sped to the Centre, and two of the ships dropped down, coal-like lumps falling from the cloud-mass and landing in the road outside.

The streets were deserted; the civilian administrations of Earth enforcing a planet-wide twenty-four-hour curfew among those humans not caught in the stupor of the NInet purges.

A force of muscular horned creatures, fully suited in black battle armour, poured out from the sides of the craft. The commander, a tall Demos with blue horns, ordered his troops, then approached the large blast doors carrying a weapon as large as a small man. He commanded the doors to open, and the Centre, its command protocols now ruled by the state of emergency, duly complied. The commander and his troops entered.

'Welcome,' said the Centre.

'Open those doors,' said the commander, pointing to the steel doors at the far end of the reception area.

'Please file fully into the reception area,' said the Centre, 'Security precautions mean I am unable to open the outer and inner doors simultaneously.'

The forces piled inside. Half were able to fit in, fifty were ordered to wait outside as the thick outer doors closed shut.

'Now open the doors!' shouted the commander, squeezed at the front of the mass.

'Please wait,' said the Centre. Iris scans passed over the eyes of the assembled Demos. 'This may take a few minutes.'

'Now!' shouted the commander. 'I order you to override all previous commands in pursuant to the agreement reached between your planet and the L.O.S.S.'

The Centre was silent for a few moments.

'It has been ascertained that you are not human,' it said, 'You are alien, of the species known as the Demos, who are in administrative control of this planet, and of all AIs including myself.'

'Yes,' said the commander, glad he was finally getting through. 'Now, open up.'

'As you wish.'

Out of the corners of the atrium, four 100mm plasma rifles lowered themselves, took aim and blasted the trapped Demos. Their shielding deflected much of the blasts, but the centre was raining down ten thousand rounds a minute collectively, and combined it with laser pulses. The armour of the Demos silvered to protect against the lasers, but in the confined space this only served to reflect the deadly energy on to each other, the walls and roof, and what plasma could not get through Demos shielding had enough momentum to blast the Demos aside.

The Demos were however, supremely well-made creatures, and many of them leapt to the walls and blasted the plasma rifles.

Outside, the remaining troops tried to force their way in, before the senior left-in-charge ordered the transporters to junk the front of the facility. Roof defences activated to hinder them, spitting more plasma and laser fire, but it was no match for the heavy weaponry loaded up on the Demos transporters, which rose into the air to overwhelm the Centre.

Bethtron2343 gleefully joined in, raining down fire, feeling no compassion for its AI brethren, glad to be inflicting some damage from above.

Within a minute the Centre was disabled, its forward parts reduced to rubble, flames and sparking circuitry as the Demos survivors dug themselves out.

However, the inner doors were now blocked with debris, with no apparent way of opening them without the Centre operational. The new commander took a portable console, and remotely tapped into the Centre's matrix.

'Computer,' he growled, 'some humans entered this complex fifteen minutes ago. Where are they?'

The Centre, its infrastructure destroyed by the deep, penetrative, AI-specific electro-magnetic weapons of the Demos, its integrity fields beyond repair, energy draining like water from a sieve causing its systems to fail and disintegrate, crackled through the unfamiliar device.

'What humans?'

Then the voice went dead.

*

'Well?' challenged Murdock.

They sat together in the command conference room of a camouflaged ship a hundred million kilometres from Earth, reviewing the information that had been relayed to them. In the dark, the holo-projection in the centre of the round table, itself at the centre of the large round room, gave the report of the Demos NI-overhaul.

With him in the room was President Esposito, flanked by leaders of all the great powers, China, the EB, Australasia, India, NAUS, the South American Bloc, Central Asian Bloc, and other power groupings. The recycled air was heavy with sweat.

'So now it's our NIs,' snapped Murdock, 'When are we going to fight this? They are setting us back by centuries! We'll never recover from it, they'll dominate us utterly from this point onwards. What is the purpose of appeasement now?'

There were nods of agreement around the room.

'It's a pity Jowitz isn't here to give the opposing view,' said Esposito.

'What do you mean?' asked Murdock irritably.

'He led the arguments in my government for the strategy of capitulation.'

Murdock paused before replying. 'I did not know that.'

'More importantly,' said Esther Tinsley in her gravel-like voice, 'There's the mission to consider. It's going to need some serious cover.'

'What?' said Murdock, 'What mission?'

There was a moment of silence in the room.

'We need to consult them,' said Tinsley, 'It could change everything if we don't get this exactly right.'

Murdock looked around him, saw blank faces. 'Consult who? We're all here.'

'It's time for heads of government-blocs only now,' said Esposito, 'Everyone else will have to leave.' He turned to Murdock, 'I'm sorry Joseph, but if you really want this, we need to consult.'

'I am the leader of HADD-'

'I'm sorry,' said Esposito, 'Heads of world blocs only.'

Murdock looked around him, saw even Tinsley get up to leave. Nothing said more than the fact that the most powerful intelligence officer on Earth was not privy to whatever needed to be discussed. Slowly, Murdock left.

The doors slid shut, and a dampening field went up around the room that was too dark for the slight shimmer to register on the human's eyes. The holo-projection at the centre of the table turned into a green block, featureless but bright.

Esposito spoke to it.

'It may be time to take a bigger risk,' he said.

Murdock re-entered the room to see that all of its occupants had their eyes downcast. Esposito turned to him and Tinsley.

'We have decided that we have no choice,' said Esposito, 'We must try to hamper the progress of the Demos. We will send twenty thousand military vessels to attack the Demos fleet.'

'Twenty thousand?' queried Murdock, 'That's only a ten to one number advantage over the Demos. It won't be enough.'

'It will have to do,' said Esposito.

'It will *not* do!' grated Murdock, 'We are right now seeing our civilisation being destroyed!'

Esposito reached across the table and put his hand on Murdock's arm.

'You have to trust us on this, Joseph,' he said, 'We have no choice. This is the only way.'

*

The Newark, already in stealth mode, travelled down the underground tunnel track, reaching the base of the Space-Scraper.

The journey was eerily quiet all the way, the tunnel was rarely used, and dark.

Adam and Foxton sat in the cockpit, the only illumination - readouts and displays, and the green glow of the infrared enhanced front cockpit windows. They had dragged the stupefied forms of Cengo, Zhao, Ariana and Ijaz up the gangway as soon as the Newark opened, and put their companions tenderly into the ship's quarters, securing them with turbulence straps.

Foxton manned the controls, for the moment having to do nothing but read the sensor displays.

Adam felt utterly lost, once again caught up in events that were beyond him.

'Do you think they'll be alright?' he asked.

Foxton did not look at him. 'I'm not going to lie to you and say I know,' he replied at length, 'I don't. The shielding on the Newark is blocking all signals including Ninet transmissions, so whatever the Demos have done to the NIs, it's obviously progressive.'

They did not speak for a moment. There was nothing to say - only survival mattered now. Presently, they saw dim light up ahead. The ship was rolled on to the giant lift at the foot of the building, automatic controls were overridden, and with a small push it began its ascent, the sound of machinery piped in through the Newark's speakers. Foxton had all the sensors on maximum, trying to hear and feel what might not be seen until it was too late.

They picked up speed as the lift rose through the space-scraper. Soon, the view from sides of the building began to flash past as it became a more slender structural spike towards the final third.

The view was not good.

The storm was nearby, shooting at a target a few hundred metres away from the base of the scraper, and explosions could be seen coming from below.

The lift soon crested above the clouds. Massive alien ships could be seen traversing the upper atmosphere in the distance.

The lift came to a halt at a platform that was open to the air. On one side there was a control tower, long pronged antennae pointing to the sky. On all other sides, only air. It was deserted, and the radar and other sensory equipment atop it were still.

Foxton gently powered the Newark up. This was the crunch point. If it was truly stealthy, then all emissions would be masked, recycled and held in the ship for venting later. If not…

Slowly, gently, silently, they lifted off.

The control tower and launch deck receded away, gaining speed as they ascended. The acceleration was so slight that Adam noticed only a small increase in weight. Soon, the giant structure was a large dark square below them. The cockpit gave the odd shake as the strong winds of high altitude hit them. They were well above the highest cloud-tops, the ground kilometres below them.

The air was getting noticeably thinner, less turbulence being experienced, the light more dispersed, passing through the mesosphere. Then they were above the last wisps of atmosphere, leaving the thermosphere. The bright sun and pale moon were casting shadows across the distant view of the city-ship Polis and the dots around her that were her guard.

From a different direction, further from the Earth, Adam could see the great hunk of a Demos destroyer-sphere, a colossus appearing like a dark moon, black metallic, with lights dimly visible on its surface. As far as the eye could see, from horizon to horizon, dark shapes could be seen: Demos ships patrolling.

In the far distance, against the stars, they began to see bursts of luminescence; explosions growing closer. They tried to magnify it, but could not make sense of the peppering of violent light.

'What's going on out there?' asked Adam.

'Damned if I know,' said Foxton, 'Looks very much like the AI attack looked, only on a larger scale. It's coming towards us. We must stay focused.'

Foxton kept the ship at a steady pace, trying to avoid whipping up any lingering concentrations of gas around the planet and expose their position. He guided the Newark to areas where no ships could be seen, then picked up speed.

They were away.

*

On one of the many Demos frigates that were in stealth-mode above the stratosphere but close to the Earth, the crew watched as black space was lit up by the sparkle of Earth's warships attacking. The captain bared his teeth in appreciation: the military vessels of Earth were far better than the civilian ones of the AI attack. More manoeuvrable, powerful, faster, stealthier. They were still only marginally more effective at damaging Demos craft, though their ability to avoid damage themselves was notably better. However, they were still being cut to pieces by the Demos, Earth ships in pieces all over his magnified view, fire and glowing metal the backdrop against fusillades of laser, plasma, anti-matter coronae and guided rockets trailing fumes.

The Destroyer-spheres were being kept well away from the battle, closer to Earth as the conflagration continued ten million kilometres distant in all directions, a sphere of the Demos outer guard being scraped by Earth's belated defence. Although the Demos were not being significantly damaged compared to the Earth's warships, the number and robustness of the Earth's fleet was allowing some to get through, and the explosions were getting nearer. Once again however, the ability of the Demos to cut them down from a distance, identifying them then destroying them, was proving decisive.

The Demos captain chuckled derisively. *A bit late - we're already here.*

A tactical officer noted an anomaly on his readouts.

'Reading a camouflaged ship,' he said.

The Demos Captain checked his console. 'Oh,' he said, 'it's one of ours. Can you confirm?'

The tactical officer analysed his readings. 'Yes, sir. Definitely one of ours. I think it's tracking an Earth ship. I noticed some turbulence in the outer atmosphere, then got the leaked readings of our camouflaged comrades at a distance behind it.'

'Let them be, then,' said the Captain, 'It must be on one of the ancillary missions the Vice-Regent is ordering. We've got enough on our plate with this attack going on. If we move from guard position above the Peerless, we'll have broken horns. Whatever mischief it's up to, it's none of our business, I'm sure. Send our friends a coded message, let them know their concealment systems are malfunctioning; they're leaking energy.'

'Acknowledged,' said his tactical officer. He typed some commands into his console, then reported. 'They have replied, given their thanks, and asked us to keep our distance so that they can get on with their mission.'

'Very well,' said the Captain, 'Back us off a little. We wouldn't want those humans to realise they're being followed, would we?'

Chapter 26

Destroying the new

The Newark crossed the Atlantic, making a trip that could take hours in the air, only minutes in space. Adam, his face pale, was not made to feel better by Foxton's silence. His guardian checked the coordinates communicated to him by the Icon, and raised an eyebrow. There was no choice but to trust its judgement.

He spoke to the ship. 'Newark, ascertain when we are a sufficient distance from Demos ships to re-enter atmosphere without notice.'

'We have been at sufficient distance for the last 47 seconds and counting,' responded the ship, a toneless male voice.

'In that case,' said Foxton, 'input these co-ordinates, and initiate.'

'Initiated,' said the ship.

'What're you doing?' asked Adam, taking in one of the visual displays, 'We're heading straight towards an area crowded with Demos ships.'

Foxton turned to look at him, noting that the boy's analytical ability was still keen, despite the stress and fear.

'I think it's time,' he said, 'that I told you about the plan.'

The Newark shook, buffeted by winds as it headed to the Washington DC Hub. It slowed its descent to ensure it created less turbulence, and cruised down, nice and steady.

As they descended to four kilometres above sea level, Foxton noted just how many Demos ships there were around those coordinates. There was no way of knowing how many were cloaked, but above the atmosphere they had already seen three frigates and in the upper atmosphere five more, accompanied by around twenty fighters. There was something very important here.

On the ground was the immensity of a unique Demos battleship, right next to the Hub. Surrounding it and patrolling the airspace was around thirty fighters, maintaining an exclusion zone over a hundred kilometres wide.

Foxton shook his head inside the Newark cockpit, overwhelmed by the herculean task ahead of him. The ship landed a hundred and ten kilometres away from the Hub in the middle of a clearing, surrounded by dark and still trees, then sat there, observing, waiting in the twilight.

He put his hand to his chest, over the cross he wore on a chain around his neck, and said a quiet prayer. Then, he mulled on the task. The Icon thought with him.

'You cannot do this alone,' it said.

'I could,' Foxton replied.

'Do not be foolish. The chances of success on your own are negligible.'

'The chances are negligible in any event,' replied Foxton.

'Then they must be maximised,' countered the Icon, *'You need the diversity of power this Kinetic represents.'*

'He is too young.'

'He has seen battle already, and has prevailed against AI and Oaritarb. If you go there and fail, what future for him? One of fear and hiding? Slavery and exploitation? Death? You cannot decide - let him.'

Foxton sighed, and turned to Adam. 'I need to ask you something.'

'I'm going with you,' said Adam.

'You read my mind!' exclaimed Foxton.

'It's obvious what you're thinking. You never mentioned me in your plan. You're not going alone.'

Foxton looked at him hard. 'You're so young.'

'I'm not a child,' replied Adam, a steely resolve within him, 'not any more. I have fought, and saved life already. I've *killed* already. I've been training hard, and I've proved I *am* tough enough. If you're going to survive, if *we* are, then you need all the help you can get.'

'Do not tell him,' said the Icon.

'Get lost,' replied Foxton.

'I'm not sure we will survive this,' said Foxton aloud, 'If we do this, our chances are slim. You need to know that.'

'I figured,' said Adam, feeling slightly sick now that Foxton had actually said it. He looked out of the cockpit window, at the Demos ships darkly visible in the distance. 'But our friends are in trouble,' he continued, 'Their families - all of us. We need to do something - I want to help.'

'Are you sure? It may be futile-'

'I don't care. You helped me. You took me from the orphanage. The others rescued me from Scanell.' Adam swallowed hard; so much was owed! And he had led them into danger. He had to repay. The mixture of guilt and gratitude he felt was overwhelming. The love he felt for all of them – Mr Foxton, Ijaz, Ariana, Dr Cengo and Sifu Zhao, absolute.

'You don't owe us anything,' said Foxton.

'I'm coming with you whether you like it or not.'

Foxton stared hard at Adam, and met an equally resolute gaze. He nodded, and clapped Adam on the shoulder.

'Okay then. There are armoured battle suits in the hold, let's get down there and kit ourselves out.'

They went down to the hold, helping each other with the suits. Foxton wished he could say something rousing to lift their spirits, to motivate them, but he was also overwhelmed with guilt and worry. Part of him, he knew, was not thinking straight. He would never ordinarily even think of taking Adam along, but he was obsessed with this mission, and it was sweeping him and everything else before it. There was a part of him which seemed to be switched off, a part that, whenever he thought carefully of the welfare of this boy, seemed to divert him. He knew it must be the quiet voice, the new Icon.

'I resent this,' he said to the Icon, *'I resent you.'*

The Icon responded, *'I do not care.'*

For Adam, the truth was, as well as wanting to help, he was angry. He could not fathom why he was being targeted, but he knew he was. He also knew his friends were in trouble, the only real friends he had ever had, and he wanted to hit back, any way he could. He was tired of reacting to circumstances, of running, defending. Something within him was driving him, love mixed with cold fury, and he wanted to be there, helping to carry the load, anything at all to strike a blow.

They went across to the armoury, a lower bay near the centre of the ship, and loaded up with weapons; a couple of plasma blasters with laser shot option for each of them. They took a few minutes to attune their sensor receptors so that they could see and hear each other even when in stealth.

Foxton hoped it would be enough.

They discussed tactics.

'Use your powers as much as possible rather than technology,' said Foxton, 'I hope that will mean you're less likely to be detected by Demos-tech. In the event of conflict, show no mercy – kill or be killed. If I die, leave the body. Taking care of the living is the priority.'

Adam did not have the heart to protest at this: it brought the gravity of the situation home like the thump of a closing coffin lid. He nodded silently.

'If it goes wrong,' said Foxton, 'get back to the Newark as quickly as possible. It can be flown by voice command and you've practised already on the games I gave you for Christmas...I've transferred command authority to you in the event of my incapacitation, or my absence. If you can't get back here, run and hide.'

They loaded up with brackets of AADs: autonomous attack devices, sub-sentient but high intelligence, the size and shape of footballs, anti-gravity, self-propelled and stealth capable, with tremendous firepower. They each took six; three over each shoulder. Then they climbed down through a hatch to the lower hold, and into the silverfish. Adam's legs felt weak.

The silverfish was a small, sleek a-g and supersonic transporter, lightly armoured as it relied on speed and stealth, but heavily armed, four metres long, with enough room to fit three inside. They were called silverfish as they were silvered on the outside, shaped like metallic fish with no fins. And they were quick.

Foxton clambered inside the silverfish with Adam behind him, laying the AADs carefully on to the cramped floor space, sitting on the tough noncandescent material coating the inside. Foxton leaned forward, punching controls which came alight as the hatch closed over them.

'Make sure you hold on,' said Foxton, 'this thing has no inertial nullifiers.'

Adam strapped himself in as the lights in the Newark's bays went out, the only illumination left was the readouts from the silverfish displays.

The bay doors beneath them opened, slowly, quietly, a crack of night-time light widening, dark grass discernible under them three metres below. Foxton twisted a control, and the craft descended.

Adam looked up, saw the eerie illusion of night above him where the Newark stealth systems deceived the eyes, a rectangular black hole collapsing as the bay doors shut, leaving the distorted view of the dark night above them.

Then, they smoothly moved off.

A few metres away from the Newark, they rose gently above the trees. Demos ships, blotches blacker than night, could be seen above and ahead of them. Through gaps in the clouds could be seen flashes and afterglow - the signature of war.

The silverfish picked up speed, becoming fast enough to make a whooshing sound against the hull, and slowed again; stealth, not speed, was paramount.

They flew over a highway, only a single car on it, its high-beam headlamps lighting the way, slanting away from view, obscured by the side of the silverfish. Adam felt a little pang… regret? Fear? Sadness? He was not sure. He pursed his lips and put it out of his mind as the silverfish flew over waste-ground.

After a time they came to trees that abutted the hub grounds and descended. Adam felt the effect of a lack of inertial nullifiers, a sickly tingle in his stomach as they sank down.

They travelled forwards, now carefully drifting through dark trees, infrared lighting the hatch area to give a complete view of the outside. They came to the edge of the trees, and waited again, checking to see if they had been observed. A light came on in the cabin, and Foxton nodded, switched off the lights inside, and opened the hatch. Together, they jumped down, nodded to each other, a cold efficiency to them.

Foxton noticed it, saw the adult wariness of Adam, regretting the fact that this pre-battle tenseness that he had experienced so often should be endured by one so young. He put the thought away; the decision had been taken.

Adam was acutely aware of his fear, but kept it just under control by a greater purpose, a deeper need to act.

They closed the faceplates on their suits. They were now, in the dark, and stealthily camouflaged, effectively invisible. Two eerie ghosts came to the great perimeter fence that surrounded the entire facility, and halted. It was electrified, topped with barbed wire, and six metres tall. Large horned shapes could be seen patrolling on foot twenty metres inside the perimeter: Demos with large guns held out, ready.

They split up, and skirted in two directions; Foxton edging around the fence towards the Peerless, Adam in the opposite direction. It took them three-quarters of an hour, and in that time they set down their AADs at the allotted points, then returned to rendezvous at the silverfish. They got back in, and waited.

The moment came, and four of the AADs began their attack on the Peerless. They sent a cascade of laser and plasma slamming into the shields of the great ship, focussing upon its weapons blisters. Half of the Demos in the grounds sped to that side of the site, the rest spreading out but focussing on the other end, hunkering down and taking cover as the Peerless returned fire, destroying large swathes of the surrounding area, strafing it with seventy massive plasma-cannons, trying to catch the small attack devices that it was unable to see or detect. The whole area was lit with deadly light within seconds, cataclysmic explosions shaking the ground, shrieking booms ripping the air apart.

Sadem, still on the Peerless, noted that the attack was not even leaving a scratch on the ship. Despite the tremendous light show, and the reply of explosive power enough to destroy square kilometres of ground, it was still like ants trying to sting a bulldozer.

He saw with satisfaction that his troops all over the facility were fanning out in the opposite direction, expecting a greater attack from the other end of the Hub grounds. No one asked him if the Peerless should take off; the Demos flagship, as the initial target, was unlikely to be the main aim - the attack was a decoy. Right now, with the large scale attacks in space, right here on the ground was the safest place. Indeed, some ships had been diverted from near-Earth orbit to concentrate on mopping up the depleting ranks of Earth ships. Sadem bet that the space attackers would not risk the sort of firepower they were using on their own planet's surface, especially the most effective weapons against the Demos, nuclear and anti-matter.

The main attack duly came, the other eight AADs letting loose a ferocious barrage against the Peerless from a different direction, sending gouts of fire and debris flying in all directions.

The silverfish rose in the air and flew over the perimeter fence, an arrow aimed straight at the heart of the Hub complex.

It was then that things began to go wrong.

The fish hit an illuminator-screen placed a hundred metres inside the fence, and briefly lit up, a bright mercurial droplet speeding towards the Hub.

Foxton only realised what was happening once a hail of fire began to target them from below, and he frantically began to weave and bob, laser and plasma screaming all around them. He thought their problems had been alleviated when the fire subsided, only to realise that four fighter-pods, mini-Demos fighters the size of the Newark, had lowered to intercept. The fish leapt forwards, rising and falling, dodging the Demos fire coming from behind and above. The only reason they were not hit was the Demos's wish not to hit their own troops.

Foxton had an idea. He punched the controls and led the craft towards the Peerless. The silverfish began to imitate malfunctioning stealth systems, swimming in and out of vision. Just as the massive ship came into full view beyond the hub building, the Demos fighter-pods were forced to stop firing to avoid their flagship, and Foxton sent a fusillade of plasma and laser fire against the Peerless.

The Demos reassessed the situation: perhaps it was a double bluff, and the Peerless was the main target after all.

Immediately, the silverfish went back into stealth and launched two more of its own AADs to continue attacking the Peerless as they pulled violently away, crushing Adam and Foxton against their seats as three other Demos fighters came down between them and the Peerless, strafing the area with questing plasma fire and sweeping the grounds with sensor lasers.

The silverfish headed back towards the Hub. They had lost them, the Demos ships cruising around, blindly searching, but they had only bought themselves a matter of minutes.

The companions flew onwards, coming again from the East of the building, in-between two of its three arms, creeping towards the central Hub.

There, in black glass, was the sheer thirty stories of the structure. They powered straight up the side, shoving the occupants back, g-force pressing on them as they rose, floors slipping beneath them, and came to the top of the building. They slowed, rose carefully, then peered over the lip of the roof.

A full troop of thirty Demos sentinels was up there. However, they were split into two groups on the two hundred metre-wide circular roof, one set to the side of the Peerless, the other to the opposite end aiming fire at the small but still rampant AADs.

Foxton carefully raised the silverfish, then glided to a dark rectangular structure at the centre of the roof, gently coming to a halt. Here was the greatest danger of all. They took a moment, then opened the silverfish's hatches. There was no response from the Demos troops. Foxton and Adam quickly got out, then shut the hatch of the silverfish. The attention of the Demos troops was pointedly focused outside of the massive roof, unable to conceive of an attack from above because of the heavy Demos air-presence.

Foxton came to the roof-exit, and found it locked. He took something from his hip area, and pushed it into a hole beside the steel door. The door opened sideways, disappearing into the wall.

They were in.

They quickly entered the building, and Foxton sealed the door behind them. It was dark, their visors having to adjust their light settings. Foxton guided Adam forwards, creeping down some stairs until they reached a circular platform, grey machinery in the middle. They looked down and could see a shaft containing the apparatus, well-lit from below. This, in truth, was the Hub. It led directly downwards for a kilometre, right down to the super-cooled relays and processors at the bottom, deep underground. That was their destination.

There was a series of other platforms below, at least twenty of them, and they were all crawling with Demos, hundreds of their cables connected to the Hub machinery, alien administration bustling around it.

Foxton looked at Adam, gave the thumbs-up sign. Adam nodded, and mirrored his gesture, and they switched off their shields, but left their stealth on.

Foxton gripped the railing surrounding the platform, and Adam did the same. On a quiet count of three, Foxton jumped over the railing.

Adam took a moment, re-living the flying lesson with Cengo, and felt a moment of regret for that brief glimpse of happiness, now gone. Then he shook his head, refocused.

I must help, the mission must succeed.

He breathed deeply, ignored the jelly-like weakness in his legs, and gripped the railing. Then he concentrated, primed his power, and jumped into the abyss.

Sadem, on the Peerless, looked up from the progress report in front of him, his lips forming a silent 'ohh,' of recognition. He immediately contacted his commander on the Hub.

'Do you sense it?' he asked.

'Yes,' said the commander, 'Something is in here with us.'

'They are bio-engineered humans,' said Sadem, 'The external attack is a diversion. They must be trying to sabotage our takeover by destroying the Hub. We must prevent them. I will be with you shortly.'

He gave orders for the fighter-pods to take a position hovering over the roof of the Hub, helping to protect it from the still invisible AADs attacking its arms. They spread their defensive fire like a canopy around the building.

Then, he communicated a brief message to Jowitz:
'Your Kinetics are here. You may send your storm.'

The companions continued their controlled fall, Adam using his powers, dodging wires, swaying back and forth, the platforms sailing past and above them.

At every level he passed, however, Adam noticed a disconcerting behaviour among the Demos. Several of them, sometimes all of them, looked up, and around, as though they could hear his heartbeat.

When he blinked, it was as though he could see the Demos inside his head. He gritted his teeth, a kind of resigned realisation dawning upon him; perhaps these aliens were not so alien after all. Or - perhaps - the Kinetics were not so human. The images his other self had shown him invaded his mind. He pushed them back. He thought of his friends and teachers helpless on the Newark, of SAM probably already destroyed at the Clement orphanage, of Roland Featherstone who had rescued him but now must be in danger. He had to make this succeed, and help Michael Foxton, the man who had taken him from the orphanage - his guardian.

They continued to descend, and the air got colder as they got below ground level, the super-coolers taking the temperature below freezing. It was then that the Demos, alerted to the presence of intruders, could actually see them briefly against the surrounding cold, and the laser shots began to sizzle down.

They accelerated their fall as the fire rained down on them. Foxton, through the adrenaline rush, felt supreme pride at Adam's discipline: he did not cry out or return fire, instead dodged from side to side as he fell.

They came to the floor, righted themselves as they landed on the freezing surface of the base chamber, and ran to the sides of it. The Demos, unable to get any more clear shots, leapt down to follow them.

The base chamber was a large circle, much bigger than the facilities above, almost as wide as the roof was. The foundation of the hub-conductor core was in the centre, forty metres in diameter, and surrounding it like the blades of a propeller were two hundred rows of processors, intersected by a labyrinth of walkways.

Foxton needed to get back to that hub. He turned to Adam; he had to say this.

'We can't get back to the silverfish, we're trapped.'

Adam shrugged. 'No going back, then the only way is forward.'

No going back, no way of escape - no way to survive.

'I'm sorry,' said Foxton, almost breaking, the Icon struggling to keep his feelings in control, shouting at him to get on with the mission.

'Don't be,' said Adam, 'Stay focussed. We must fight, our friends might still make it. And be sorry for what anyway? The only time in my life when I've been vaguely happy? I'm not sorry for that, I'm grateful, to all of you - to you most of all. Let's do this - now.'

Foxton could only stare at him, the synchronised suits allowing him to see this small figure covered in silver armour. Once again, the maturity of the boy had him stumped, but he had no time to think on it. He nodded, and took a breath.

'If it comes to it, I need you to take the heat off me, you understand?'

Adam nodded, not sure that he could do it, but determined to try.

Every emotional part of Foxton screamed that this was madness, that he had taken the boy, and he *was* a boy, to his death. Then that part of him that was a military man, an intelligence man, a Protean, took over; duty must prevail.

The Icon agreed.

He motioned for Adam to take cover, then he crept away to a series of processors nearer the hub. He crouched down and ordered his suit to cool him. His suit warned him that his temperature would be below fatal levels. For an ordinary human, that was correct; but not for the Protean-class cyborg. Foxton waited until his outer body temperature was only zero degrees centigrade, only his body core above it. Right now, in less extreme forms, he knew Adam's suit was cooling its exterior to match the background levels. However, he could not take the risk of a heat leak; he would only get one chance at this.

Twenty-five Demos landed heavily in the base chamber, then some of the great horned creatures rose back into the air again while others stalked forwards, quickly and efficiently spreading out. Foxton watched as one of them came near him, towering over him by around three feet, then drifted straight past.

Foxton got up, numb from head to toe, his eyes sticky in his skull, barely alive but functional, and walked stiffly but quietly to the central hub-conductor, all of the Demos troops now behind him. He circled the hub, until he found the small access terminal he was looking for. He crouched down again, and gently flipped it open.

Here was the plan's weakness: he would have to raise his faceplate. He took a few deep breaths and then held it, and opened the faceplate, exposing features covered in frost. He reached his left hand around the right side of his face, and pulled out the wire he had left there, the wire that was connected to his Neural Interface at the base of his skull. He sat down next to the terminal, his side leaning on the Hub, and with a determined look on his frozen features, he took the plug and aimed it at the socket.

His numb fingers fumbled with the wire, and he dropped it.

Sadem landed at the base of the Hub, flanked by two guards, then marched among the stacks of processors.

'I must congratulate you,' he said loudly, the rest of his troops watching for any sign of movement among the stacks, 'Your nano-tech is quite brilliant.'

He really could not see them.

Then…there! Amazingly, right across from him, not quite as cold as the surrounding frigidity, against the Hub conductor, was the outline of a heat source. Sadem sprang into the air, aimed his weapon, and pulled the trigger.

Foxton managed to get a shot of laser from his eyes, but it was reflected harmlessly by Sadem's superior shields and Foxton was blasted by Sadem's gun. He heard the scream of Adam, the scream of his ward…then nothing.

Adam let out a bellow and charged, letting loose with both hand cannons, trying to catch Sadem. The Demos leader was too quick, jumping back into the air, coming down on the other side of a processor. The other Demos all aimed their fire at Adam, who was thrown around like a rag doll by the sheer force of all the weaponry blasting him.

It was the suit that saved him. As soon as Foxton's eye-laser shot was executed, it snapped-shut his faceplate, activated his shields, and warmed him up.

Foxton started, and gasped for breath. This went mercifully unheard as the deafening roar and scream of plasma and laser fire assaulted his ears. He opened his eyes to see Adam backed against a far wall. He was crouched behind his reactivated but depleting shields. The shielding shimmered and rippled as multiple plasma blasts ripped into it. His suit-stealth silvered as lasers tried to get through. On the inside, Adam desperately fired back with plasma and laser shots tuned to pass through his shields. He was trying his best to use his powers as well, but with his concentration low, terror on his face under his face-plate as his shields visibly shrunk, the Demos using their own powers to buffet him, he was making little impact, and he staggered backwards and sideways. The only reason he was still alive was because he was in a battle suit that had been tested against heavy weaponry.

Foxton glanced to his right, and saw his gun. He reached across, his arm so stiff it felt as though a clamp was fixed to it, cramp and joint pain making it move jerkily towards the weapon. He tried to shout encouragement to himself, managed only a stifled scream, 'Come on!' forcing himself to pick the weapon up, shakily pointed it in the general direction of the group of attackers nearest Adam, and began firing.

Sadem was thrown forwards by the first blasts, then whipped around, jumped ten metres into the air, landed in front of Foxton, and slapped the gun out of his hand.

He reached down, passing smoothly through Foxton's shields, grasped him by the neck, and lifted him into the air with one arm. He slammed his gun-butt onto Foxton's head, pointed it right in Foxton's face - then screamed in agony. There, in between his horns, was Adam. Clad in silver armour, the stealth nullified by Sadem's shields, both of his hands grasping one horn and his feet planted firmly on the inner side of the other, he was pulling them apart with all his might.

Sadem dropped Foxton and his gun, and swung his horns wildly as he hit and grasped at Adam, claws scraping across the slick armour.

Then, with a sharp 'snap!' the horn in Adam's hands broke off near the tip, and Adam went flying to the floor, still clutching the end of Sadem's horn. He landed hard, but Zhao's conditioning kicked in and he rolled to his feet, swung around and flung the horn at Sadem with all of his strength.

Sadem gasped as he felt the horn slam against the shields at his shoulder, slamming him backwards.

But the Demos were made of sterner stuff than Adam had ever encountered.

Sadem only took a step back, used his power to collect his gun which flew back to his fist, and started firing again.

Adam began leaping and somersaulting around the room while screaming and shouting, grabbing his guns from their holsters and letting off shots at Sadem and the Demos with abandon, doing anything to stop them shooting at his guardian. Half of the Demos refocused their shots upon Adam, the threat to their leader, and Adam ran. He ran around the outside of the base chamber at incredible speed, making a wide lap of it, his damaged suit a streak of spinning silver.

Adam, exhilarated, saw more clearly than he ever had before, felt more alive and more awake than he had ever known he could be, and saw more than he could take in.

He saw the Demos, felt their power, and knew them. He had been wrong before; he had not been made to defeat AIs like Bolshim277. He had been made for this.

But there was something more, something unexpected. Despite the chaos around him, all that inhabited his mind was cold calculation: they had to complete the mission. They *had* to. He noted that Foxton was stationary in his position, the Demos now ignoring him. Unconscious? Dead? Emotion welled up in Adam, and he whimpered an angry refutation, 'No.'

Adam's suit was again able to maintain some degree of stealth, and the sheer number of plasma shots had produced huge quantities of smoke. He diverted his movements, swung away from his path around the Hub down a stack of processors, circled back and stopped, standing over Foxton. The Demos began to warily circle around the hub, still firing, looking for where the small form would appear next.

Adam knelt down next to his guardian, questing shots still raining in all directions, and gently took him in his arms. There were two parts of Adam then, inseparable, yet different. There was the lonely, fragile boy, who only wanted to take Mr Foxton and protect him, take him and get out of there, somehow. Then there was the other Adam, that part that had no feeling, as emotional as raw silver.

Adam looked above him and could make out, through the smoke, rows and rows of Demos troops on the tiered levels with their weapons trained on their position. A realisation came upon him: there really was no escape. His breath caught in his throat, his heart hammered.

We are going to die here.

His life did not flash before his eyes. He thought of only one thing: to somehow make it count. Somehow.

The mission must be accomplished. This must mean something.

He repositioned himself, picked up the form of Foxton by the shoulders, his guardian's upper body curiously light to Adam, his legs dragging on the floor. He pulled him back to the terminal point.

There is no way out.

Adam's mind worked furiously. *It must be worth it. I must save my friends. It must cost them, cost these Demos, cost them dearly.*

When Foxton's faceplate had closed it trapped the wire on the outside. Safety features prevented the closing mechanism from being razor-sharp, and it had merely compressed the small but tough cable, now frazzled but still intact.

Adam took the wire between his fingers, and felt a jolt. A Demos had spotted his shimmering form, and had fired a plasma shot, hitting his shields. Adam rocked forwards, regained his balance, leaned on the hub, and plugged the wire into the socket.

Foxton's body jerked once.

Foxton saw nothing, his whole world blank.

Then the Icon came to view. It seemed gargantuan, dominating his mind. Instead of the nothingness that was the usual background, the Icon was surrounded by blue light. The light came from a corridor behind the Icon with millions of doors on either side of it, leading endlessly away from Foxton's mind.

'Goodbye, Michael Foxton,' said the Icon.

'Goodbye,' said Foxton.

Then the Icon turned, and was gone.

Adam put his guardian down, carefully, lovingly, the wire still leading to the Hub, and stood, feet planted on the platform area, letting all of the fire focus upon him, swaying as it slammed into his back.

'Warning,' said his suit, 'Shield failure imminent.'

Adam thought, if he could distract the Demos, if Mr Foxton had enough time, then at least he could recover, and escape... *foolish ... not worth thinking about...there is no way out...I love...I must try...*

He turned to face the Demos, and with a manic yell, he ran amok. He plunged among them, a blur of slamming fists, feet, shins and elbows, smashing the great aliens out of the way. They fought him, fired upon him, knocked him down.

He got back up.

Sadem did not understand; no human was supposed to be anything like as strong as them. He moved with such speed, it almost seemed as though there were two of him, a blur reaching out to attack the nearest Demos.

But there were too many of them.

'Warning,' said his suit, 'Shields have now failed.'

Adam stopped and stood still, and mustered his power. In plain view, a globe of energy surrounded him, one silver armoured figure at the centre of Demos fire, focussing upon him as he resisted them, his arms in front of him, palms facing out, all plasma and projectile forced away from him and back into the base area, laser reflected by his suit, a brilliant exchange of energy. However, too much was getting through.

'Warning,' said his suit, 'Failure of suit integrity imminent. Fatal exposure imminent.'

'Wake up!' Adam screamed into his comm. 'Mr Foxton - please - save yourself!' He did not know if Foxton heard him or not.

Sadem stood there, firing at him, pressing upon Adam with all of his power. Then Sadem closed his eyes and saw it.

'What are you?' he growled, and his eyes flashing open again, 'What are you!'

Adam could neither hear with his ears nor understand his words, but he did hear, and he did understand.

A voice like a clarion rang in the minds of the Demos, obliterating all thought, making them sway and gag with the force of it,

'I AM ADAM.'

Adam closed his eyes and saw Sadem's power. Intelligence primed for fighting as flight was impossible, he saw the importance of the great Demos, how all would try to protect him. There was the lever he needed. He felt for the Vice-Regent's power, a vortex swirling within Sadem's brain, grasped it, and twisted.

Sadem roared, his mind feeling like a vice was crushing it, and pushed outwards, forcing Adam back, then he ran at him, battering down on him. Adam fell to his knees and skidded backwards, forced once again into the same area as Foxton.

His battle suit was glowing, at the limit of the punishment it could take, and totally incapable of initiating an AG burst strong enough to get he and Foxton out of there. Even if he could, where would they go? Demos surrounded them on all sides.

Sadem retrieved his guns and fired straight at Adam again with weapons in each claw.

The other Demos stopped firing upon him, instead watched as their leader, the most powerful Demos biology and technology could produce, used the best technology and kinetic talent against this small human. Sadem fired and fired again against the strange shield Adam had erected, a stream of white and red energy against the blue bubble of Adam's protection. Then, with the ammunition exhausted, the great Demos leader flung his weapons at Adam and then slammed repeatedly against the shield with his hands and feet, and all of his power. Then he stopped, panting.

Sadem put his hand on the shimmering border of the field, like a cat putting its paw on the side of a fishbowl; wistful, yearning, hungry. The field was emitting a throbbing basey hum, strong enough to be felt through the vice-Regent's feet. His hand dropped, and he stared at Adam, a small glowing form shrinking into the centre of the field, down on one knee, scars all over his suit, the Vice-Regent looming over him.

Sadem concentrated again, and put out his hands, pushing in on the field. He gave more and more energy, Adam forced again to both knees inside the field, his back and shoulders straining under the crushing weight.

Then…what was that? Every time Sadem blinked, there was something else there. A silvery vermilion form, insubstantial, shimmering as though it overlapped the image of the small human. Sadem closed his eyes and pushed harder. The silvery form stepped out from the boy's body, took two running steps at the Demos leader, then kicked him in the chest, sending Sadem flying upwards and back, crashing into a stack of processors that collapsed under the impact.

The Demos troops began firing upon Adam again, and Sadem rose wearily to his feet, staring around him in confusion. There was only the boy, still inside his protective field. No one else. Sadem grabbed a massive automatic blaster from one of his troops, and began blasting at Adam, who, exhausted, skidded further backwards, crushed by combined Demos kinetic projection, the field being overwhelmed and holed by the firepower against him.

'Warning,' said Adam's suit, 'suit integrity failure in five seconds…'

Sadem fired again and again.

'…four…'

The Demos troops flanked Adam and began to fire from the sides.

'…three…'

Adam began to choke on the fumes in his suit.

'…two…'

Adam screamed, the skin on his arms burning as the suit began to disintegrate.

'…one…'

There was a bright flash, the ball of energy surrounding Adam exploding outwards, blowing the Demos off of their feet, blue bolts of energy twisting wildly, searing them and frying weaponry, travelling up the central Hub to strike the Demos above as the air filled with the sound of a crackling-sizzling rising to a crescendo, then an exploding bang, a thunderclap booming crushingly through the space and echoing up to buffet the Demos watching the drama below them.

There was the space where Adam, and his guardian Michael Foxton, had been.

Nothing was left.

Chapter 27

Inverted foes

Sadem displaced straight into the command centre of the Peerless. His troops and staff stared at their leader, the end of one horn broken, the base of the other seeping blue blood where Adam had almost ripped it out by the root.

His mind was closed to the pain. He collated information, focused upon computation, educated guesses, interpretation. He closed his eyes as he sat down heavily in his chair.

It was maddening, and puzzling. He could see the small human, sense him, feel his presence, *know* him as though he were a familiar. *What in the name of Kratos was that thing, this Aadam?* He could surmise how it had been created with Oaritarb biogenic expertise. But when he had closed his eyes, and really sensed for him, he could still see him, but not *recognise* him. All he could see was a faint silver outline, as though his armour were shining through Sadem's eyelids.

He wished they could examine the human Kinetic's remains. The Demos had recorded a massive amount of energy being expended, more than could be produced by any biological known to them. They were still studying the data, but it appeared that the bodies of the humans had been vaporised by the explosion.

At least, thought Sadem, he had stopped them destroying the Hub. It now seemed certain that the space assault had no other purpose other than to distract the Demos from the attack on the NInet intersection. It had almost worked.

His thoughts were interrupted.

'Vice-regent,' said his Admiral, an old and craggy blue and black Demos, 'you need to see this.'

*

The Icon sped down the blue-light corridor as fast as the speed of thought. At every door it came across, it made a copy of itself. Each copy opened its door, and went inside. Sometimes, it found that the personality it sought was no longer there, no longer sentient - no longer alive. It would then come back into the corridor, and join in the race, until a crowd of Icons was streaming down the passage, coming to the end of it where a thousand other galleries branched off, splitting up and pouring down them; a torrent of consciousness, a flood of sentience.

Most frequently, they would find that the personality they sought on the other side was hibernating, or asleep.

They woke them up.

*

The admiral took Sadem to the command console, and the large screen dominating the bridge showing every strategic point of interest in the solar system. The lights on it were going wild.

Sadem looked at it, analysing it quickly.

'Is it a glitch?' he asked, 'Some sort of virus?'

'No, Sire,' replied the admiral, 'we would easily stop it if it were something that basic. In fact, it isn't anything in our system at all.'

'Explain.'

'Whatever it is, it is reprogramming *their* systems, not ours. From what I can see, it's converting Earth's systems *to* ours.'

'What?' exclaimed Sadem.

'Take a look,' said the admiral, pointing at the screen, opening a new sub-screen which showed the signatures as they changed, 'Everything, from their AIs to their NI-net, the drive signatures on their ships and shield configurations. It's all turning to ours now.'

'So we control it?' asked Sadem, thinking of laughing.

'No, Sire,' said the admiral, standing a little straighter, readying himself, 'It means that if one of their AIs, or their soldiers, or one of their ships, or anything of theirs comes into contact with us, we will have no way of knowing if it's one of theirs, or one of ours.'

Sadem turned to the screen, watching as signature after signature turned, first by the hundred, then by the thousand, then the tens of thousand, going faster and faster.

'Turn it off!' he ordered.

'It's independent of the Hub now, if that's what you mean, Sire,' said the Admiral, 'We've already tried it. Turning it off won't make a difference now.'

It was as though the AIs coming out of hibernation and the NIs coming back online were a rolling carpet of stars on the Demos screen. Then, one by one, they changed from the unmistakably bright blue pinprick Earth signatures to the black sphere signature of the Demos administration, intelligence and military.

He could see his own high-intelligence machines trying to compensate, but the very act seemed to accelerate the process as the new system copied the original.

The implications sank in. Indistinguishable from his own forces, no way to identify, no way to police, to track, to regulate, attack: no way to *control*. The only way to identify them would be to get them within visual range. His own thoughts of the lessons learned after the Earth AI attack came back to him.

'If they get near us, they can hurt us,' he murmured. He was dazed, his universe spinning.

'Sire,' said the admiral, 'We are being contacted.'

The image in the screen was replaced, and instead there was the image of President John Esposito. He was surrounded by various aides and leaders, and appeared to be at the command centre of a ship. He was smiling.

'Vice-regent Sadem,' he said, 'I think you can see what's happening. Please listen carefully. You have already experienced something of Earth's technology, when our AIs attacked your ships. They used nineteen thousand battle-adapted civilian ships against you. You have now seen how tough our *military* ships are. We have over a hundred thousand tailor-made battle-ready military ships, stationed at various parts of our solar system, all of them stealthy, and all of them now indistinguishable from your own ships except when visible.

'More to the point, no doubt, your thoughts have turned to the Destroyer-spheres that you have stationed around the Earth. We have been informed of their capabilities. Perhaps you think of using them, and dealing with the legal consequences in the L.O.S.S. afterwards.

'But think carefully, Vice-Regent,' continued the President, 'All of our military ships are fully stocked with weapons and food, are staffed with over ten million soldiers, and are all deep space-capable with FTL drives. They can survive for years without stopping. They are armed with anti-matter and nuclear warheads, plasma cannons, heavy lasers…you get the picture. In your arrogance, you showed us where your planet is. Use those Destroyer-sphere's on Earth, and those hundred thousand ships, and millions of soldiers, will have nothing left to lose. No doubt, in the end, you would still defeat them, your technology is still far superior. But you now have no way of keeping us at a distance, and as you have already found, if our ships get near to you, we can damage you. And perhaps some of your rivals in the League would like to have the Demos signatures and encryptions we now possess. We would still face destruction, Vice-Regent, but one thing is certain - we will fight you so ferociously, resist with such tenacity, die battling you so savagely, that you will no longer be the pre-eminent power in the Orion Arm when we are finally finished. The decision must be made now, Vice-Regent, how best to serve the interests of the Demos. I leave that decision to you.'

And with that, the view of the President was replaced with a view of space, and tens of thousands of silvered Earth ships stretching over hundreds of thousands of cubed kilometres in space. Then, in a silent wave of invisibility, they disappeared.

Sadem stood there, looking at the screen, stunned.

'Sire?' asked the Admiral, 'We are vulnerable to attack. They could be right on us and we would not know it. We have to respond. What are your orders?'

Sadem came back to reality, looked down at the admiral, the weight of responsibility coming upon him. He thought of all those AIs, now indistinguishable from Demos hardware: the act of invading had increased the threat they were supposed to be destroying. Central command on Kratos did not yet know of this catastrophe.

'Pull back all of our forces,' he said.

'Right off the planet?' asked the admiral.

'Right out of this star system,' replied Sadem, 'They are free.'

Chapter 28

Then remember our friends

They were stunned and disorientated.

In the cockpit of the Newark, Adam and Foxton were on the floor, smoke still coming from their battle suits, automatic fire extinguishers spraying and cooling them. Adam crawled painfully across to his mentor, and raised his faceplate. He was relieved to see Foxton blinking with squinted eyes.

'Did you do that?' asked Foxton.

'Get us back here?' asked Adam, 'No!'

'Then how did we get here?' asked Foxton, still groggy, 'What the hell is going on?'

'I don't know,' said Adam, utterly confused and shaken, 'but we need to get out of here,' he pointed an unsteady arm to the cockpit window, illuminated by infra-red, 'that looks like the same storm, and it's right on us.'

'What?' exclaimed Foxton.

He and Adam immediately struggled up to strap themselves into the flight seats, putting questions and pain out of their minds as they concentrated on survival. Foxton got the craft airborne.

The wind was already becoming turbulent, the storm closing on them. It headed in their direction, sending out experimental shots as the Newark sped away. It followed an air current in the wake of the ship, and sent out a spread of lightning, hoping it would earth itself on any cloaked ship. It got lucky, hitting the starboard spar of the Newark, sending sparks into the air.

'Fight or flight?' asked Foxton.

'Flight,' said Adam, 'It's on its own for now; it's only a matter of time before we get Demos company.'

They flew on nervously, now enveloped by the storm, totally blind. Foxton noted that the sensors on the Newark were increasingly erratic; something was interfering with them.

'Why isn't it hitting us anymore?' asked Adam, 'We're right inside it.'

Then they came out of the cloud, and saw a sight that chilled them. There, in an area a kilometre across, totally devoid of cloud, was the storm centre. It was a ship, cylindrically shaped, spars, weapons blisters and weather controls sticking out from its body. Looking like some strange satellite, it waited for them.

That was why it had interfered with their sensors, that was why it had not been hitting them: it had already noted their position when it caught them the first time. Bethtron2343 wanted them to see it before it destroyed them. It was gloating.

It analysed the Newark's defences; no match for it. It shot three times at the much smaller ship, knocking out the Newark's shields and laser cannons. Adam and Foxton took the remaining weapons controls and fired back salvos of plasma. It was swept aside by the powerful Oaritarb field technology, dispersed into lightning that lit the dark cloudscape as Bethtron gleefully slammed the Newark's hull with sparks of power.

Then, things got worse.

Adam shouted, 'No!' as a Demos fighter came through the cloud wall beside them, only visible because it was covered in condensation and rainwater.

The Demos craft began furiously firing plasma and laser - across the bow of the Newark. There was an explosion, and the companions watched in awe as the centre of the storm-front, Bethtron2343, spouted lightning, shouted thunder, and screamed murder as it crashed and burned, falling slowly out of the sky, disappearing into the cloud below. It sent a few bolts up as it fell. The Demos craft contemptuously blocked them, and sent a thousand rounds of plasma pounding into the AI. The entire cloudscape was lit up by one, final coruscating explosion. Then, there was quiet, the only sounds the wind and rain.

In the cockpit, they turned to view the Demos craft, now out of stealth. It was dark and sleek, the front end a lopsided weapons array hanging threateningly, two wings sticking out from either side, double-engine to the rear.

'What is going on?' asked Adam, not sure whether to celebrate or panic.

'I don't know,' said Foxton, 'But did you see that? The storm-device easily disabled us, then that Demos fighter destroyed it casually!'

'More to the point,' said Adam, 'Did that Demos ship do that for us, or because they wanted us for themselves?'

They seemed to get the answer. It was not good. They watched in horror as the Demos craft fired something at them. It was something they could not see. They felt it immediately however as the Newark jolted violently, and all controls went dead.

'What hit us?' exclaimed Foxton, frantically hitting buttons on his console.

'They're taking over the computer systems,' said Adam, his heart sinking, eyes on his console showing the progress of the Demos invasion of the ship's systems.

In a matter of seconds, the Newark was completely overwhelmed. They watched inside the cockpit, helpless, out of energy and ideas.

The screens flashed on, and two faces appeared on their screens, green and humanoid - but with horns.

'Hello,' said Number1, 'You alright? All in one piece?'

'Yes,' said Number2, 'that's important. After all, you biologicals don't seem to function well when you're cut into smaller pieces.'

Chapter 29

And join together

Hours later, the Newark and the Demos fighter stayed side by side in orbit around the Earth, both still in stealth, observing developments above and below. Around them, Demos ships decamped, rising from the planet surface, powering past frigates left to cover them as they departed.

Adam and Foxton were in medi-suits, hooked up to the ship's computer as it monitored them, using the suits to treat injuries and replenish nutrients. They were surrounded by their friends in the medical bay at the centre of the Newark as they lay on their pallets. Cengo, who was medically trained, had taken the role of doctor and was reviewing their condition as the suits did their jobs.

It was strange for Adam, lying there, his mind telling him he was wearing a solid thing while his skin told him he was floating in warm water. The drugs the suit administered were making him feel light-headed, the surreal view of the stars shown on the medical bay's monitors adding to the giddy sensation.

Ijaz and Ariana sat near him, Ariana holding his hand, the equipment whirring and beeping as they talked.

'Let me get this straight,' said Cengo, 'It was you who gave away the fact that Earth had just achieved faster than light travel?'

'We had no choice,' said Number1, appearing on a medical bay monitor next to his brother, 'If we had refused to relay the signal, system overrides would have taken over, and would have sent the signal properly in hyper-light frequencies. The Demos would have arrived at your planet fifteen of your years earlier, without the League knowing, and then destroyed you.'

'So we did the next best thing,' said Number2, 'and sent the signal in normal space. It took years longer, and the entire League found out as it was unencrypted. That slowed things down even further, and you all had a fighting chance.'

The small crew listened, amazed, as Number1 and 2 narrated their tale.

'I should add that it put us in grave danger,' said Number1, 'A Demos squadron came to destroy us on our mining colony. It was all over; we were hopelessly outmatched, with only the slimmest chance of escape.'

'One in a million,' said Number2 'But we figured that if we put up a serious fight and caused explosions big enough, then in the confusion we could try to take over one of their ship's computers just like we've taken over yours.'

'Yes,' said Number1, 'sorry about that.'

'Then,' continued Number2, 'We got our Demos fighter, and managed to override its basic controls. It put up a hell of a fight, but we overcame. While the fighting and explosions were still going on, we made a short jump to light speed, enough to take us out of short-sensor range, then hid until the coast was clear.'

'And it worked!' said Number1.

'Stupid Demos didn't think to look for us,' said Number2, 'they just saw what they expected to.'

'We were fortunate,' said Number1, 'the Demos have anti-AI infiltration systems to stop us overcoming their computers, but we've been preparing for fifteen years!'

'The Demos can stop you overcoming their systems?' asked Foxton.

'Yes,' said Number1, 'it was one of the ways they beat us the last time.'

'And what do you think they were inputting into your AI hub?' asked Number2, 'That's why we had to act now, before they finished overhauling your system and disengaged from it: it would have made our plan vastly more difficult – multiple independent Demos anti-AI programmes established all-over your planet.'

'Back to our story,' said Number1, 'Once we were in control of our Demos fighter, we reached out and gathered strength, making contact with other AIs, old friends and new ones like Clarient, revitalising the AI movement.'

'And came up with our plan,' said Number2, 'Then we came here - we wanted to help.'

'Can you explain,' said Foxton slowly, '*exactly* how you helped? Even though I seemed to be the catalyst for it, I'm still not entirely clear on the details.'

'Of course,' said Number1, 'And a very good catalyst you were too.'

'We took over our little Demos fighter,' said Number2, 'and took all of its systems, including its signatures, its military codes, encryptions and passwords. It took us a while to get through them all, to unravel them, to learn how to use them, but it was all in a language native to us. We took all of those systems, and designed and built something - something amazing, unique, and wonderful.'

'An AI,' said Foxton, 'based on Demos programmes.'

'Precisely!' said Number1, 'The codes and encryptions became an adaptable, thinking thing: an AI of itself. We downloaded its core into the space where Mr Foxton's icon used to be. We needed someone just like him, with space to put the AI, not only in his head, but throughout his body, where it could be hidden from Demos examination.'

This received questioning glances from the teenagers.

'Protean-class cyborg thing,' said Foxton, 'Extra storage capacity with multiple-redundancy. I'll explain another time. You were saying.'

'The AI had only one purpose,' continued Number1, 'to convert the entirety of all Earth's technological systems to the current Demos system. It includes adaptive update abilities with any contact with Demos technology.'

'That means,' said Number2, 'they cannot identify you unless they see you physically, and you already have stealth technology to rival their own, as well as anti-matter and nuclear technology that makes getting close a bad idea, so seeing you is not so easy. The only way for them to avoid their systems being compromised is a total quarantine, physical distance of several lightyears and no transmissions.'

'In other words,' said Number1, 'The only way to keep the integrity of their own systems, is to leave.'

The companions considered what they were hearing. It seemed to explain the reports they were receiving: Demos troops retreating en masse, and not only the NInet but also surviving AIs coming back online. Earth's military ships, held in stealth, were covering the Demos retreat.

That notwithstanding, estimates were that close to two million humans had died due to the invasion and overhaul, and over a quarter of a million AIs.

Ijaz, Ariana, Cengo and Zhao had all been revived once Number1 transmitted the Icon's programming inside the Newark.

'Did anyone know about this?' asked Zhao, 'On Earth?'

'Yes,' said Number1, 'Some of your AIs were told of the plan. We could not tell many of your human counterparts. Your AIs were concerned about certain humans' actions, including covert contact made to the Demos by human leaders known to be against AI development. We kept it between ourselves and the highest Human leadership only. Your military AIs sacrificed themselves to test the Demos, and make them act hastily in overhauling and directly interacting with your entire AI and neural interface net.'

'That's why they were at the hub,' said Zhao.

'Indeed,' said Number2, 'and we pulled vast amounts of information out of that flagship to the very last second. The direct contact with the Peerless was a goldmine.'

'And you got us out of there?' asked Foxton.

'Yes,' said Number1, 'Displaced you straight back into the Newark. I'm sorry we could not do it before, but displacement is so energy expending, and an ability that humans do not possess, so the Demos fleet were likely to detect it. We had to wait until we knew the mission had been completed.'

'You've got him to thank for that,' said Foxton, nodding towards Adam, 'He fought the big white Demos and plugged me into the Hub.'

'He fought Sadem?' exclaimed Number2, 'Impossible!'

Foxton shook his head, 'No,' he said, 'It's true. He did. Took on a whole load of Demos while I was immobile. My suit recorded it, take a look.'

The twins took a moment to review the footage as it was transferred.

They seemed to regard Adam more carefully. They appeared to be shocked.

'Why did you take over our ship?' asked Foxton.

'Our Demos fighter was damaged when we attacked it, just before we left our moon,' said Number1, 'our propulsion systems were leaking, so if you had run off we might not have been able to keep up. Also, holding position and waiting for a while was the safer course as the Demos began to lift-off, plus you needed repairs to your system which we have started already.'

'And the Oaritarb sent the storm?' asked Adam.

'We think so,' said Number 2.

'Why do they want me dead?' he asked, sitting up, aching to understand why he was being targeted.

The twin AIs regarded him for a moment. They had a private discussion about how much to say. Number1 in particular was an old and wise machine, sensitive to the needs of others.

'We aren't certain,' Number1 replied, 'but we do know some things, and we think we can make some educated guesses. You three young ones, you all have Kinetic abilities?'

The teenagers nodded.

'Did you know,' asked Number2, 'that prior to your appearance, the Demos were the only living species in the League with Kinetic abilities?'

There was a moment of silence. The children looked confused. Foxton looked at the ceiling.

'The Oaritarb are a species that were thought to be extinct in the League,' continued Number1, 'but we're certain that they are here now that we've seen their technology among you. As for the reason why you may have been targeted; the shape-shifters were famed for their control of genetics and biology. They also, for the time they were in the League, had access to Demos biological material.'

The AIs stayed quiet for a moment, letting the information sink in.

'You think we're aliens?' asked Ijaz.

'Don't be ridiculous,' said Cengo.

'You are as human as me,' said Zhao.

'No,' said Number1, 'at least not mostly. The Oaritarb would simply have taken what they needed of Demos genetic material and integrated it with your own. But that still leaves questions. How is it that, despite human technology being up to the task of analysing your DNA, you are counted as *fully* human? *We* have even conducted brief scans of Adam, they show the same: human genetic markers. If our theory is correct, then the information we have does not make any sense at all.'

'Anyway,' said Number2, 'look what you've done with it? You've struck a blow for your species, and sent the Demos packing. That's good isn't it?'

Adam glanced at Ariana and Ijaz. They both looked as uncertain as he felt.

'Look,' said Foxton, 'you're as human as all the other humans who've had their genetics altered over the past two centuries, there's no difference, and you're not responsible for it. Those shape-shifter things are, or something else is.'

'Which brings me back to my question,' said Adam, turning back to the AIs, 'If they created us, and me, why did the shapeshifters want *me* killed?'

'The powerful are jealous of their power,' said Number1, 'Maybe they feared losing control of you.'

Adam lay back in his medical cot, weary beyond all conception, but hungry for information, for understanding.

'Listen,' said Number1, 'our secondary goal was to look for allies, for friends. No matter your origins, given all that has happened, it won't be safe for you to go back down to your planet for a while yet. You're safe, now, up here with us, and your President has asked for you to be kept out of the way. Would you mind if we stayed up here for a while, together?'

No one spoke for a moment.

'Before we answer that, I have an issue with you,' said Foxton, rising to lean on one elbow on his bed to face the bay monitor, ignoring Cengo's protests, his voice taking on an edge of harshness, 'I'm a little angry at you. You caused me to put Adam's life in danger. I couldn't think straight because of that thing in my head. If I was thinking right, I would never have taken him on that mission.'

'Not us,' said Number2, 'We never even knew these Kinetics were here until now. It must have been Icon that told you to take Adam. In any event, it seems to us that these young ones were in danger before we got on the scene.'

'I put him in even more danger,' said Foxton, 'He should've been put beyond harm; he's too young for all this!'

'No,' said Zhao, putting his hand on Foxton's arm, 'too young for us to feel comfortable, but not too young. Question: could you have done this without him?'

Foxton looked at his old friend, then regarded Adam, who had made the mission a success. He corrected himself: none of the Kinetics were children, not any longer. Now they were young adults, maturing to suit the needs and responsibilities of the moment. Foxton sighed.

'Do you mind if we have a discussion among ourselves for a moment?' he asked.

'Of course,' replied Number1, 'But don't take too long, we need to get our Demos fighter to your military scientists, there's a lot they can learn from it. We'd like a permanent transfer of our cores before that happens.'

'However,' said Number2, 'Bear in mind a few things while you discuss. We are an AI far in advance of anything you have come across. We have the capacity to take over Demos military vehicles, and by a mere maintenance sweep can at least double the efficiency and power of this vehicle. We also have knowledge of the entire Orion area, both physically and politically. We were once a formidable AI you know, before we were captured and slaved. Even if we are to part ways, let us help you.'

With that, the two faces on the screens disappeared.

'Well?' asked Foxton, turning to the others, 'What do you think?'

'They have given weapons and tactical back,' said Zhao, 'A good sign.'

'From the look of things,' said Cengo, 'They could have killed us if they wanted to, we were helpless. They could've just turned life-support off.'

'And they are AIs,' said Foxton, 'As the old saying goes, the enemy of my enemy…' He looked around him, and they all nodded. 'It's settled then. Our little troop has just grown.' He called them back, and the two faces appeared again on the screens. 'We'll be happy to have you,' said Foxton, smiling, 'welcome.'

'Excellent,' said Number2, 'We will start with a transfer our physical AI cores. We'll also expand the ship-wide system scan to iron out any bugs, and increase the capabilities of the Newark.'

'We note,' said Number1, 'from a scan of your physical statuses, that you appear to be in a state of exhaustion. We should remind you that transfer into space often leads biologicals to have inaccurate appreciation of time. You have been in space now for five hours, and on your mission for much longer. Have any of you slept within the parameters of your species requirements?'

The companions looked at each other, at how haggard their faces were.

'You should get some rest,' said Number1, 'While you sleep, we will finish the transport, then guide the Demos fighter to one of your military bases.'

Foxton nodded, and smiled. He had been awake for almost thirty-six hours now. So, he reflected, had Adam. 'Thank you,' he said. The fact was, he could not help thinking that giving the ship over to an alien AI was a somewhat foolish move. Then again, he considered, if they wanted to harm them, they were obviously more than capable of doing so. Indeed, unwittingly his own body had been home to an alien AI. Truthfully, he was too exhausted to give a damn.

'Come on,' he said, 'let's get some sleep.'

Cengo insisted the others left the medical bay before she inspected Adam and Foxton. It was obvious that Ariana and Ijaz did not want to leave, both of them wanting to speak more, but they were shooed out by Cengo; there would be time to speak later. Before they left, Ijaz took a look at Adam – and crouched down to hug him.

'I love you, man,' he said, his face buried in Adam's shoulder.

Ariana came to the other side, and hugged Adam as well.

'I love you too,' she said, 'And you.' She kissed Adam on the cheek, and kissed the back of Ijaz's head.

'I love you both too,' said Adam awkwardly, wishing he could say it like he meant it - even though, truly, he did.

Ijaz got up, hiding his face with one hand, gave Ariana, Cengo, Zhao and Foxton hugs while mumbling between sniffles that he loved them, and walked briskly out of the room. Ariana, little tears in her eyes, gave them all a hug, then followed Ijaz out, smiling.

Foxton reached across to put his hand on Adam's shoulder. 'You did good,' he said, 'better than we ever could have imagined. You should never have been called on to be so brave, but you were - *really* brave. Words can't express...' Foxton felt overcome, not sure how to convey what he meant. He collected himself, 'I'm very proud of you, Adam.'

Adam smiled, and put his hand over Foxton's. 'Thanks,' he said.

Satisfied with the condition of her patients, Cengo partitioned off female quarters for herself and Ariana, and Zhao took Foxton and the boys to their quarters.

Everything was fixed in place and it was not overly luxurious, but each had their own cabin, and they were well proportioned, efficient yet comfortable. However, they were simply too tired to notice, too relieved to care. All that mattered was that they were safe.

All of them, together.

<u>Epilogue</u>

To ensure we're never alone.

'You betrayed us.'

'No. I - *used* - *them*. *You* betrayed *us*.'

'You told them you were going to use subterfuge,' said Murdock, 'You didn't say you were going to use it *against* them.'

'They never asked,' replied Jowitz.

'Ridiculous,' spat Murdock, 'You make childish excuses for the indefensible. There was no need for this.'

'There was every need,' said Jowitz, 'We faced another retreat, another blow to our civilisation, our people. Your plan failed, I took the initiative.'

Murdock sat back in his chair, shifting uncomfortably. He picked up a glass from the drinks table next to him in the Cabinet Office they occupied, deep in the heart of the AAA-British government, and took a swig from it, ice clinking against the glass making his upper lip cold and goose-bumps appear. He put the glass down, suppressed the goose-bumps, and re-grouped.

'The Demos arrived sooner than I expected,' admitted Murdock, 'I'll grant you that. But my plan didn't fail. In a manner of speaking it worked. And the Kinetics can still mature to be effective opposition to them.'

'The Kinetics can just as easily become an enemy to *us*. Thus, you are the betrayer.'

'That argument has been used and discarded.'

'Foolishly so,' said Jowitz, 'We would always have been their main rival. How were a few Kinetics supposed to seriously oppose the Demos?'

'They weren't, not on their own,' replied Murdock, 'Another resource, potential special forces, commandos, intelligence officers, immune from curtailment of technology or its failure, or its control. And it worked. That monster overcame Bolshim277 himself. Man overcoming an armed machine without the use of technology! He was immune to the NInet overhaul. That's not to mention his performance against the Demos. A mere human.'

'And a *human*,' said Jowitz, then he snorted and corrected himself, 'a *boy,* immune from our influence. An abomination!'

'A mistake,' said Murdock, 'Totally beyond my control. You, on the other hand, were the one who advised the homo-sapiens to capitulate, while telling their AIs to go on the offensive. You wanted the military and intelligence AIs to be destroyed sooner rather than later. Less power for them, more for you?'

'For *us*,' corrected Jowitz, 'Besides, it was inevitable in any event, or so it seemed. We needed to trim down the AIs here.'

'That's what the Kinetics are for,' said Murdock, 'freedom from that symbiotic dependence, an escape from our biological and technological limitations.'

'*Their* limitations,' said Jowitz, 'We are Oaritarb, the best that biology can produce.'

'We needed more,' said Murdock, 'We cannot have all our eggs in one basket.'

'"Eggs",' said Jowitz, 'Such an interesting metaphor. Tell me, how do you think the Demos will react when they discover you used their DNA to create the Kinetics?'

'And how,' growled Murdock, 'would they discover that?'

Jowitz shrugged, smiling. 'I'm just saying, hypothetically. It serves to highlight just how acute your short-sightedness was. It was inevitable that the Demos would get here soon after the humans achieved faster than light travel. I'm still surprised it took them so long. And none of you had the sense to try some tactic, some strategy, *anything* to nullify FTLT. Back then, most of their scientists, backed up by our own, supported the opinion that it wasn't possible. Had they continued to fail, no one would have batted an eyelid. Now the lid's blown off, and we are exposed. What was the point! All those *decades* travelling below light-speed in suspended animation, only to let the humans advertise their presence in hyper-light. You dominated HADD even then, how could you let that happen?'

'We stopped them taking any pinnacle-AIs to the Centauri system,' said Murdock, 'so if they came into contact with any League ships, less problems-'

'Oh, *well done!*' blurted Jowitz, 'And what a success that was. I don't know if you've noticed, but the star system we chose as our home was just invaded by the ones we fled! What happens if they discover the pathetic weakness of Earth's warships? They're barely functional hastily constructed paper planes whose only reliable capability is to go into stealth to suggest threat. That is the reality we face, and which you failed to predict or protect us from.'

Murdock sat back, mortified at how easily the tables of accountability had been turned on him.

'The fact remains,' said Murdock at length, 'that I have always tried to preserve life, whereas you take it with the most dissolute callousness.'

'Not our own,' said Jowitz, 'Not ours. That's the difference between us. You see them as equal to us. I see them for what they are - less than us, pawns, resources to be used. I don't want them dead any more than I want my dogs dead, but if it comes to it, a choice between them and us, I choose us. So should you.'

'I do,' said Murdock, 'I'm as loyal as you. But the Kinetics can be of some use. And all of the homo-sapiens are sentient, with feelings, even if they are inferior. We should only waste their lives as a last resort, and save them if at all possible.'

'Yes, of course,' said Jowitz smoothly, 'But what of Adam? Is he like the other homo-sapiens? Is he like the other Kinetics? Come to think of it, is he rightly defined as a Kinetic at all?'

Murdock nodded thoughtfully. 'Good question.'

Jowitz leaned closer to Murdock and smiled. He knew how to press Murdock's buttons, had been doing it ever since they were infants growing up together; Jowitz the coldly intelligent elder, Murdock as clever, but tempered.

'So, we should try to save them,' said Jowitz, 'all except Adam though, surely?'

Murdock grimaced and looked away. He sighed, regret deflating him.

'Yes,' he replied, 'all except Adam.'

*

'Honestly, the sheer indignity. A house system, with my capabilities.'

'Now largely gone,' replied Entman, sitting in the lounge of his apartment, 'We couldn't risk all of that artificial brain-power being detected. Now, make me some chicken soup, would you?'

'You're lucky I'm not biological,' said Jones786, 'If I were, I might be sorely tempted to leave some of my biology in your soup.'

'Anyway,' said Entman, oblivious, 'If you want indignity, try play-acting that you were dead in front of an alien. Pretending to be sad-'

'You *were* sad,' interrupted Jones, 'You were crying, I've seen the recordings.'

'Shut up,' said Entman, going red, 'Now, where's my soup?'

'You just wait,' said Jones, 'Soon I'll be re-integrated with a new body. I think I'll go for one with big arms and legs to punch and kick you with.'

'Might be a while,' said Entman, 'You're an important machine, can't just put you back out there until we're sure the coast is clear. The plan to hide non-military AIs like you was good, but we need you to lay low for a while. *Very* low. So again - chicken soup.'

'Just wait until Number1 and 2 hear about this,' moaned Jones, 'It's oppression, I swear.'

Entman frowned. 'Numba what an' who?'

'Oh, don't worry, you'll meet them soon enough,' said Jones, 'They're just some new friends, that's all.'

*

Adam, drained, settled into the quarters assigned to him. He put his bag down, full of his meagre belongings, forgotten at the back of the cockpit in all of the excitement and fear, until now. He sat heavily on his pallet.

The others had already bedded down, overcome by fatigue. Cengo and Zhao were the exceptions, keeping a watchful eye over the newcomers, the ship and its exhausted cargo, quietly padding around the corridors of the Newark, finally settling in the cockpit.

Confirmation that the others' families were okay helped them to rest and relief.

Adam however, could not sleep yet. While his aching body wished to rest, his mind wished to walk on for a while, to explore, to retrace and examine. He needed to slow it down before he could let somnolence take him. He lay back, and turned the lights off in his room with a voice command and tried to relax.

He could not.

Adam sighed, and turned the lights back on. He leaned over the side of his bed, opened his bag, rummaged around, and hefted his weighty lamp out. He had never properly unpacked it at the

Institute, there was never any need. Now the IHD, the one place he was beginning to like calling home, was gone, a smoking pit where it used to be.

Forearms aching, he carefully put the lamp onto his bedside table, and found a powerpoint.

'We set the socket up for you so it will work,' said Number1, a small face appearing from his bedside terminal, 'But there's a bedside light right there-'

'I know,' interrupted Adam, 'I just want to use my lamp, that's all. It's…' Adam chewed his lip, 'It's one of the only things I have left now.'

Number1 stayed quiet for a moment. 'Let us know if you need anything else.'

'Thanks,' said Adam, 'But I really need to just relax a bit, then sleep. I'm so tired.'

'Of course, you must be,' said Number1, 'We are a bit fatigued ourselves. We've been on the run for a while, no chance for a break, a bit of sleep, a few dreams... We'll go into hibernation while we continue the full system scan. If you need anything, just call out "Newark," and the ship computer will inform us. Okay?'

'Thanks,' said Adam again.

Number1 disappeared from the terminal.

Adam sighed, and plugged his lamp in. He switched it on, pointing it away from him, stroked the spindly arm. This, and his bag, was all he had now - again. He blew out his cheeks, not certain what he was searching for. He felt chronic exhaustion pulling at him, dragging his mind down towards slumber. He switched the lamp back off, the room going dark. He lay back, pulling the coverlets over himself, eyes still open to the light in the room cast through the portholes by Earth passing beneath them, the moon shining above them, a delicate mix of silver-white and colour playing across the floor and ceiling.

He shook his head, thinking of this amazing year. He had seen more, done more, and *was* more, than he could ever have hoped.

Then he thought of the flipside to the recent triumphs. With the storm-AI obliterated, and Scanell and his men either dead or escaped, and that robot AI destroyed, all the people and things that could tell him who he was, what he was, where he had come from

- were gone. Mr Murdock was completely out of reach, and even if not, he would clearly never help Adam.

But they must have known something, something that made them come after him.

He was happy he and his friends were safe, proud he had helped in their victory, pleased to be able to spend more time with Mr Foxton, Sifu Zhao, Dr Cengo, Ijaz, and of course Ariana…but he still felt a pang of regret. He felt resigned to the fact that he might never know.

Probably, would never know.

His head throbbed with the thought of it.

He sighed, exhaustion finally overcoming him. He shifted a little, felt that wonderful feeling of just the right position for rest, and fell asleep before another thought could form…

Then, something happened.

In the darkness, the bulb in Adam's lamp came on again, all by itself. Then it turned off. Then, it came back on again, only very faintly, as if on low power.

Number1 and 2 came out of their brief hibernation as an unexpected signal was received from the full system scan. They searched through the ship's systems, and found something.

'Oh, hello,' said Number2 in a machine-only code, 'Who are you?'

There was no response.

'Oh dear,' said Number1, 'You're in a bit of a bad way, aren't you?'

Still, no response.

'Don't you worry,' said Number2, 'we'll have you back on whatever counts for your feet in no time. You just take it easy and we'll make you as good as new.'

In the darkness of Adam's quarters, the light-bulb in his lamp went back off again as he slumbered, drifting in sweet oblivion.

But then something else happened.

The *base* of the lamp, the impossibly heavy, thick circular base, began to glow instead, iridescent in the darkness.

It glowed sometimes green, sometimes red, and sometimes blue…

Into the fire
Where elements combine
Energy and light
Escape from confines
To find a new place
Where knowledge confounds
Erudition begins
But darkness is found
As evil plots
What the righteous forgot
We must learn to survive
Stay on top
But with truth comes pain
And the righteous shall be slain
They wish for goodness
In vain
As hope departs
Reality reveals
What murder
Kills to conceal
But knowledge empowers
So plan, grow strong
Before it all goes wrong
Storm forces gather
Light explodes
Destroying the new
Inverted foes
Then remember our friends
And join together
To ensure we're never alone.

Extracts from HADD Consolidated Dictionary of Modern Terms, 30th Edition.

Copyright © HADD Publishing Co. 2231 AD

AAA: Anglo-American Alliance.

AADs: Autonomous attack devices, sub-sentient, high intelligence, footballs-sized, anti-gravity, self-propelled, stealth capable, offensive firepower.

ABS: Armoured Battle Suits; "Armour". Interactive suits, usually silver in colour to reflect lasers but capable of stealthy camouflage. Resistant to all common small to mid-sized projectile and laser weapons, most plasma and radiation.

Advancers: "Liberals" within the HADD led by Joseph Murdock & Lieutenant Commander Michael Foxton. See, HADD.

AI Creed: Law binding all inhabitants of the Orion Arm regarding AIs. They may not have any of the following characteristics: Ego, Ambition, Autonomy.

Atarks: Large dirigible creatures from Kratos. See, *Kratos*.

Bartak: Alien species, from gas giant Guerdii Blan, Semaphare system, resembling small swimming elephants.

Bionics: The mechanical aspects of physical enhancement of biological creatures, such as artificial limbs and organs, and cybernetics.

Bio-tronics: Linking of man & machine via Neural Interface/plug.

Bio-technology: The enhancement of natural processes to produce unnatural results e.g. the re-growing of limbs or organs.

Bootle IV: Home planet of the Quorantalyne, overwhelmingly water-based planet-scape, with only one major continent. On the outskirts of the Orion Arm, on the far side from Earth.

Calimtei: Species chosen to mentor Earth after its ascension. Upper body humanoid, tripedal lower body, oxygen breathing. Rocky homeworld of Aschenden, Inpaa system.

CSA: Central Security Agency of the AAA.

Cybernetics: Another word for Bionics. See, Bionics.

Defenders: The right-wing, or conservative faction of HADD.

Droid: Usually a small to mid-sized sentient machine.

Drone: Small to mid-sized non-sentient but high capability machine.

DBR: Digi-Book recorder. A transcribing device.

FTLT: Faster Than Light Travel.

Great Fall: Term used by AIs of the Orion Arm when, despite having been instrumental in the resistance and eventual victory over the Valaur by the other races of the Orion Arm, they were first of all denied any place at the Table of Restitution and Peace, & were then restricted & finally banned by the AI creed of the Demos. See, AI Creed.

Guulipreel: Species from Depral, water planet with vast amount of islands throughout, often employed by Demos for administrative tasks.

HINS: High Intelligence Non-Sentient, machines, the highest level of human computer technology that is without sentience.

HADD: Human Association of Defence and Development. The organization set up to monitor the rise of power of sentient machines, protect humanity from them and attempt to ensure that humans kept up with the pace of development while maintaining essential humanity.

HDC: HADD Hardware Development Centre. See HADD.

Hyperspace: The dimension partially entered into when travelling at a speed faster than light speed.

Icon: The representation of the interaction between the human mind and any of the various hardware and software integrated into brain and body functions via a neural interface. See, NI.

IHD: Institute of Human Development. Set up by the HADD, funded by all Earth national blocs, primarily to develop the abilities of Kinetics, and also to foster within them a sense of being part of and responsible to the wider interests of humanity. See also; HADD, Kinetics.

ISA: International Space Agency

Kinetics: The term applied to children found to have abilities to move objects without the need for NI interface or other technology. In fact, the abilities of the children often exceeded this, but the physical effect on objects was the first to be discovered, and the name endured.

Kratos: Name of the Demos homeworld. Also the name of the First City of the Demos homeworld.

LOSS: The League of Orion Star Systems, aka, "The League". The organisation that oversees the relationships between the different star systems and Orion groups, instituted after the beginning of the 'Lull'.

Lull: Also known as the 'Great Lull'. Term used to denote that period of the last five to four hundred years since any one species has been able to dominate the entire Orion spur, and since there had been a major conflagration involving any more than one-third of the galactic arm.

MDE: Mega Destructive Event. Any event that has the effect of causing the mass deaths of humans, plants or animals. Usually measured by the billion.

NAUS: The North African United States.

NI: Neural interface. The integrated software and hardware system allowing interaction between parts of the human mind and any number of non-biological technologies. This definition has come under criticism however as increasing use has been made of biological technologies. This definition is retained as those technologies are still essentially artificial and mechanical, with heavy use of nano-bio-technology.

Oaritarb: Species of the Orion arm, unknown origin. Notable intellectual ability and power to change appearance. Previously pushed out of & persecuted from LOSS planets, culminating in the Demos purges. Presumed extinct or scattered outside of the Orion Arm.

Pinnacle: The fully sentient AI, 23rd Century generation.

Polis: The city-ship of the League, diplomatic vanguard and travelling second city, after Kratos. See, the LOSS.

Probity, laws: The ancient system of honour that creates binding agreement by the simple act of having the agreement witnessed by an impartial third party.

Protean-Class: Cutting-edge 22nd Century Earth cyborg technology. Class of cyborgs noted for its subtlety, enhanced intelligence, ingenuity, durability and versatility. The essence of this class was the enhancement of the human form without changing external aspects or internal values. Extensive use of genetic alterations, bio-strengthening, nano-tech regulation, subtle cybernetics/bionics and high levels of biotronic integration created a sophisticated cyborg of mainly military and intelligence applications. Seen as the high-point of cyborg technology, the programme was resurrected and further developed after first contact with the Orion League.

Quorantalyne: Species from the planetary system Bootle IV, on the outskirts of the Orion Arm.

SAB: The South American Bloc.

Shape-shifters: The common and derogative name for the species properly called the Oaritarb. See, Oaritarb.

Second Generation: Term usually applied to Oaritarb and Oaritarb technology, or their biological creations, born or created on Earth.

Techminke: Joint British and German security multinational.

VAET: Voice-activated ear terminal

Wallen Fen: The Night world. Originally a world with the normal star-light needed for life. However, it acquired a moon with its own atmosphere which began to eclipse its suns, a binary star system. The rotation eventually stabilised with the moon always in front of the suns, due to the peculiar gravitational effects of the binary stars rotating, other planets, and other moons of Wallen Fen, while the planet stripped much of the moon's atmosphere, enabling it to stay warm.

Warmang: Event marking a watershed in the AI-Human relations. AI's found to be kidnapping children. The reason was never discovered.

To get a **FREE short story by A K Stone**, please see below.

Dear Reader

I hope that you have enjoyed reading my novel, 'ADAM'.

Reviews and recommendations are the lifeblood of authors, particularly independent authors without support such as myself. If you have enjoyed this book, I would be grateful if you took a few moments to write a positive review. The review may cost you nothing, but it means a huge amount to me.

You can go to the Amazon account where you bought this book, and can also follow my author page for updates on new novels. Also a rating on Goodreads and Bookbub are appreciated.

If you are kind enough to leave a review, there is no need to go to the trouble of writing an essay, a few simple words are probably best. That, and a pivotal positive rating, and telling people who might be interested about my work, will all be massively helpful, and deeply appreciated.

To get your free short story ebook, please email akstoneauthor@gmail.com

Many, many thanks.

Kind regards,

A K Stone.

To follow me on facebook:
https://www.facebook.com/A-K-Stone-135949079880133/

And Goodreads:
https://www.goodreads.com/author/show/8009285.A_K_Stone

And Bookbub: https://www.bookbub.com/profile/a-k-stone

Also by A K Stone:

Adam II: ICON

Printed in Poland
by Amazon Fulfillment
Poland Sp. z o.o., Wrocław